About the

USA Today bestselling author **Anna DePalo** is a Harvard graduate and former intellectual property attorney who lives with her husband, son and daughter in her native New York. She writes sexy, humorous books that have been published in more than twenty countries. Her novels have won the *RT Book Reviews* Reviewers' Choice Award, the Golden Leaf, the Book Buyer's Best and the New England Readers' Choice. You can sign up for her newsletter at: annadepalo.com

Rebecca Winters lives in Salt Lake City, Utah. With canyons and high alpine meadows full of wildflowers, she never runs out of places to explore. They, plus her favourite holiday spots in Europe, often end up as backgrounds for her romance novels because writing is her passion, along with her family and church. Rebecca loves to hear from readers. If you wish to e-mail her, please visit her website at: rebeccawinters.net

Andrea Laurence is an award-winning contemporary author who has been a lover of books and writing stories since she learned to read. A dedicated West Coast girl transplanted into the Deep South, she's constantly trying to develop a taste for sweet tea and grits while caring for her husband and two spoiled golden retrievers. You can contact Andrea at her website: andrealaurence.com

Fake Dating

Fake Dating:
Scandal in the Spotlight

ANNA DePALO

REBECCA WINTERS

ANDREA LAURENCE

MILLS & BOON

First Published in Great Britain 2024
by Mills & Boon, an imprint of HarperCollins*Publishers* Ltd,
1 London Bridge Street, London, SE1 9GF

www.harpercollins.co.uk

HarperCollins*Publishers*
Macken House, 39/40 Mayor Street Upper,
Dublin 1, D01 C9W8, Ireland

Special thanks and acknowledgement are given to Rebecca Winters for her contribution to T*he Vineyards of Calanetti* series.
Special thanks and acknowledgement to Andrea Laurence for her contribution to the *Daughters of Power: The Capital* series.

ISBN: 978-0-263-32309-2

HOLLYWOOD BABY AFFAIR

ANNA DePALO

For DeLilah & Bob,

thanks for the support & encouragement

One

Actress and Stuntman Lovefest! More Than Movie Pyrotechnics on Display.

The gossip website headline ran through Chiara Feran's head when it shouldn't have.

She clung to Stunt Stud's well-muscled shoulders, four stories up, wind blowing and helicopter blades whipping in the background—trying to act as if her life depended on it when the truth was that only her career did. After all, a gossip site had just written that she and Mr. Stunt Double were an item, and right now she needed the press distracted from her estranged father, a Vegas-loving card-sharp threatening to cause a controversy of his own.

She tossed her head to keep the hair out of her face. She'd learned Stunt Stud's first name was Rick when they'd rehearsed, but she thought *insufferable* was a better word for him. He had remarkable green eyes...and he looked at her as if she were a spoiled diva who needed the kid-glove treatment.

I don't want you to ruin your manicure.

Thanks for your concern, but there's a manicurist on set.

They'd had a few brief exchanges over the course of filming that had made her blood boil. If the world only knew... True, his magnetism was enough to rival that of the biggest movie stars, so she wondered why he was content with stunt work, but then again, his ego didn't need any further boosting. And the rumors were that he wasn't who he seemed to be and that he had a shadowy, secretive past.

There was even a hint that he was fabulously wealthy. Given his ego, she wouldn't be surprised if he'd put out the rumors himself. He was a macho stuntman ready to save a damsel in distress, but Chiara could save herself, thank you. She'd learned long ago not to depend on any man.

She opened her mouth, but instead of an existential scream, her next line came out. "Zain, we're going to die!"

"I'm not dropping you," he growled in reply.

Chiara knew his voice would be substituted later with her costar's by the studio's editing department. She took perverse satisfaction in calling him by her costar's character name. And since Rick was pretending to be her costar, and her costar himself was just acting, she was two steps removed from reality.

And one long fall away from sudden death.

Even though both she and Rick had invisible harnesses, accidents could and did happen on movie sets. As if on cue, more explosions sounded around them.

As soon as this scene was over, she was heading to her trailer for coffee and maybe even a talk with Odele—

"Cut!" the director yelled through a bullhorn.

Chiara sagged with relief.

Rick barely loosened his grip as they were lowered to the ground.

She was bone-tired in the middle of a twelve-hour day on set. She didn't dwell on the other type of tired right now—an existential weariness that made it hard to care about anything in her life. Fortunately filming on this movie was due to wrap soon.

Action flicks bored her, but they paid the mortgage and more. And Odele, her manager, never stopped reminding her that they also kept her in the public eye. Her Q score would stay high, and it would keep those lucrative endorsement deals flowing. This film was no exception on both counts. *Pegasus Pride* was about a mission to stop the bad guys from blowing up the United Nations and other key government buildings.

As soon as her feet hit the ground, she ignored a frisson of awareness and stepped away from Rick.

His dark hair was mussed, and his jeans clung low on his hips, a dirty vest concealing his tee. Still, he managed to project the authority of a master of the universe, calm and implacable but ready for action.

She didn't like her reaction to him. He made her self-conscious about being a woman. Yes, he was all hard-packed muscle and latent strength. Yes, he was undoubtedly in top physical shape with washboard abs. But he was arrogant and annoying and, like most men, not to be trusted.

She refused to be intimidated. It was laughable really—after all, *her* bank account must dwarf his.

"Okay?" Rick asked.

His voice was as deep and rich as the hot chocolate she wished she had right now—damn him. It was a surprisingly damp and cold early April day on Novatus Studio's lot in Los Angeles. "Of course. Why wouldn't I be?" Dozens of people milled around them on the movie set. "All in a day's work, right?"

His jaw firmed. "This one is asking for more than usual."

"Excuse me?"

He looked at her quizzically. "Have you spoken to your manager recently? Odele?"

"No, why?"

His gaze moved to her trailer. "You may want to give it a go."

Uh-oh.

He fished his cell phone out of his pocket and showed her the screen.

It took a moment to focus on the newspaper website's headline, but once she did, her eyes widened. Chiara Feran and Her Stuntman Get Cozy. Is It More Than High Altitudes That Have Their Hearts Racing?

Oh...crap. Another online tabloid had apparently picked up the original gossip site's story, and worse, now Rick was aware of it, too. Heat rushed to her cheeks. He wasn't *her* stuntman. He wasn't her anything. Suddenly she wondered whether she should have sent that first story into internet oblivion when she'd had the chance by denying it. But she'd been too relieved they were focusing on a made-up relationship rather than the real pesky issue—her father.

At Rick's amused look, she said abruptly, "I'll talk to Odele."

He lifted her chin and stroked her jaw with his thumb—as if he had all the right in the world. "If you want me, there's no need for extreme measures like planting stories in the press. Why not try the direct approach?"

She swatted his hand away and held on to her temper. "I'm sure there's been a mistake. Is that direct enough for you?"

He laughed at her with his eyes, and said with lazy self-assurance, "Get back to me."

As if. In addition to her deadbeat father making news, she had to contend with burgeoning rumors of a relationship with the last stuntman on earth she'd ever walk the red carpet with.

She turned her back on Rick and marched off. The man sent a red mist into the edges of her vision, and it had nothing to do with lust. She clenched her hands, heart pounding. Her jeans and torn tee were skintight—requisite attire for an action movie damsel in distress—and she was aware she was giving Rick a good view as she stomped away.

At her trailer, she banged through the door. She immediately spotted Odele sitting at a small table. The older woman lifted her head and gave Chiara a mild look from behind red glasses, her gray bob catching the light. If Chiara had learned anything during her years with her manager, it was that Odele was unflappable.

Stopping, Chiara touched her forehead. "I took pain medication for my headache an hour ago, and he's still here."

"Man problems have defied pharmacology for decades, honey," Odele replied in her throaty, raspy voice.

Chiara blurted out the gossip about her and Rick, and the stuntman's reaction. "He thinks he's God's gift to actresses!"

"You need a boyfriend," Odele responded cryptically.

For a moment, Chiara had trouble processing the

words. Her mind, going sixty miles an hour, hit the brakes. "What?"

She was one of those actresses who got paid to be photographed sporting a certain brand of handbag or shoes. She glanced around her trailer at the gleaming wood and marble countertops. She had more than she could possibly want. She didn't desire anything, especially a boyfriend.

True, she hadn't had a date in a long time. It didn't mean she couldn't get one. She just didn't want the hassle. Boyfriends were work…and men were trouble.

"We need to retain a boyfriend for you," Odele rephrased.

Chiara gave a dismissive laugh. "I can think of many things I need, but a boyfriend isn't one of them. I need a new stylist now that Emery has gone off to start her own accessories line. I need a new tube of toothpaste for my bathroom. And I really need a vacation once this film wraps." She shook her head. "But a boyfriend? No."

"You're America's sweetheart. Everyone wants to see you happy," her manager pointed out.

"You mean they want to see me making steady progress toward marriage and children."

Odele nodded.

"Life is rarely that neat." She should know.

Odele gave a big sigh. "Well, we don't deal in reality, do we, honey? Our currency in Hollywood is the stardust of dreams."

Chiara resisted rolling her eyes. She *really* needed a vacation.

"That's why a little relationship is just what you need to get your name back out there in a positive way."

"And how am I supposed to get said relationship?"

Odele snapped her fingers. "Easy. I have just the man."

"Who?"

"A stuntman, and you've already met him."

A horrifying thought entered Chiara's head, and she narrowed her eyes. "You put out the rumor that Rick and I are getting cozy."

OMG. She'd gone to Odele with the rumor because she expected her manager to stamp out a budding media firestorm. Instead, she'd discovered Odele was an arsonist…with poor taste in men.

Odele nodded. "Damn straight I did. We need a distraction from stories about your father."

Chiara stepped forward. "Odele, how could you? And with—" she stabbed her finger in the direction of the door "—him of all people."

Odele remained placid.

Chiara narrowed her eyes again. "Has he said anything about your little scheme?"

"He hasn't objected."

No wonder Rick had seemed almost…intimate a few minutes ago. He'd been approached by Odele to be her supposed love interest. Chiara took a deep breath to steady herself and temper her reaction. "He's not my type."

"He's any woman's type, honey. Arm candy."

"There's nothing sweet about him, believe me." He was obnoxious, irritating and objectionable in every way.

"He might not be sugar, but he'll look edible to many of your female fans."

Chiara threw up her hands. It was one thing not to contradict a specious story online, it was another to start pretending it was *true.* And now she'd discovered that said story had been concocted by none other than her own manager. "Oh, c'mon, Odele. You really expect me to stage a relationship for the press?"

Odele arched a brow. "Why not? Your competition is making sex tapes for the media."

"I'm aiming for the Academy Awards, not the Razzies."

"It's no different from being set up on a date or two by a friend."

"Except you're my manager and we both know there's an ulterior motive."

"There's always an ulterior motive. Money. Sex. You name it."

"Is this necessary? My competition has survived extramarital affairs, DUIs and nasty custody disputes with their halos intact."

"Only because of quick thinking and fancy footwork on the part of their manager or publicist. And believe me, honey, my doctor keeps advising me to keep my stress level to a minimum. It's not good for the blood pressure."

"You need to get out of Hollywood."

"And you need a man. A stuntman."

"Never." And especially not *him*. Somehow he'd gotten his own trailer even though he wasn't one of the leads on this film. He also visited the exercise trailer, complete with built-in gym and weightlifting equipment. Not that she'd used it herself, but his access to it hadn't escaped her notice.

Odele pulled out her cell phone and read from the screen: "Chiara Feran's Father in Illegal Betting Scandal: 'My Daughter Has Cut Me Off.'"

Oh…double damn. Chiara was familiar with yesterday's headline. It was like a bad dream that she kept waking up to. It was also why she'd been temporarily—in a moment of insanity—grateful for the ridiculous story about her budding romance. "The only reason I've kept him out of my life for the past two decades is because he's a lying, cheating snake! Now I'm responsible not only for my own image, but for what a sperm donor does?"

As far as she was concerned, the donation of sperm was Michael Feran's principal contribution to the person she was today. Even the surname that they shared wasn't authentic. It had been changed at Ellis Island three generations back from the Italian *Ferano* to the Anglicized *Feran*.

"We need to promote a wholesome image," Odele intoned solemnly.

"I could throttle him!"

Rick Serenghetti made it his business to be all business. But he couldn't take his gaze off Chiara Feran. Her limpid brown eyes, smooth skin contrasting with dark brows and raven hair made her a dead ringer for Snow White.

A guy could easily be turned into a blithering fool in the presence of such physical perfection. Her face was faultlessly symmetrical. Her topaz eyes called to a man to lose himself in their depths, and her pink bow mouth begged to be kissed. And then came the part of her appearance where the threshold was crossed from fairy tale to his fantasy: she had a fabulous body that marked her as red-hot.

They were in the middle of filming on the Novatus Studio set. Today was sunny and mild, more typical weather for LA than they'd had yesterday, when he'd last spoken to Chiara. With any luck, current conditions were a bellwether for how filming on the movie would end—quickly and painlessly. Then he could relax, because on a film set he was always pumped up for his next action scene. In a lucky break for everyone involved, scenes were again being shot on Novatus Studio's lot in downtown LA, instead of in nearby Griffith Park.

Still, filming wasn't over until the last scene was done.

He stood off to the side, watching Chiara and the action on camera. The film crew surrounded him, along with everyone else who made a movie happen: assistants, extras, costume designers, special effects people and, of course, the stunts department—*him*.

He knew more about Chiara Feran than she'd ever guess—or that she'd like him to know. No Oscar yet, but the press loved to talk about her. Surprisingly scandal-free for Hollywood...except for the cardsharp father.

Too bad Rick and Chiara rubbed each other like two sheets of sandpaper—because she had guts. He had to respect that about her. She wasn't like her male costar who—if the tabloids were to be believed—was fond of getting four-hundred-dollar haircuts.

At the same time, Chiara was all woman. He remembered the feel of her curves during the helicopter stunt they'd done yesterday. She'd been soft and stimulating. And now the media had tagged him and Chiara as a couple.

"I want to talk to you."

Rick turned to see Chiara's manager. In the first days of filming, he'd spotted the older woman on set. She was hard to overlook. Her raspy, no-nonsense voice and distinctive ruby-framed glasses made her ripe for caricature. One of the crew had confirmed for him that she was Odele Wittnauer, Chiara's manager.

Odele looked to be in her early sixties and not fighting it—which made her stand out in Hollywood. Her helmet hair was salt-and-pepper with an ironclad curve under the chin.

Rick adopted a pleasant smile. He and Odele had exchanged a word or two, but this was the first time she'd had a request. "What can I do for you?"

"I've got a proposal."

He checked his surprise, and joked, "Odele, I didn't think you had it in you."

He had been propositioned by plenty of women, but he'd never had the word *proposal* issue from the mouth of a Madeleine Albright look-alike before.

"Not that type of proposition. I want you to be in a relationship with Chiara Feran."

Rick rubbed his jaw. He hadn't seen that one coming. And then he put two and two together, and a light went off. "You were the one who planted that story about me and Chiara."

"Yup," Odele responded without a trace of guilt or remorse. "The press beast had to be fed. And more important, we needed a distraction from another story about Chiara's father."

"The gambler."

"The deadbeat."

"You're ruthless." He said it with reluctant admiration.

"There's chemistry between you," Odele responded, switching gears.

"Fireworks are more like it."

Chiara's manager brightened. "The press will eat it up. The stuntman and the beauty pageant winner."

So Chiara had won a contest or two—he shouldn't have been surprised. She had the looks to make men weak, including *him*, somewhat to his chagrin. Still, Odele made them sound like a couple on a C-rated reality show: *Blind Date Engagements*. "I've seen the media chew up and spit out people right and left. No, thanks."

"It'll raise your profile in this town."

"I like my privacy."

"I'll pay you well."

"I don't need the money."

"Well," Odele drawled, lowering her eyes, "maybe I can appeal to your sense of stuntman chivalry then."

"What do you mean?"

Odele looked up. "You see, Chiara has this teeny-weeny problem of an overly enthusiastic fan."

"A stalker?"

"Too early to tell, but the guy did try to scale the fence at her house once."

"He knows where she lives?" Rick asked in disbelief.

"We live in the internet age, dear. Privacy is dead."

He had some shred left but he wasn't going to go into details. Even Superman's alter ego, Clark Kent, was entitled to a few secrets.

"Don't mention the too-eager fan to her, though. She doesn't like to talk about it."

Rick narrowed his eyes. "Does Chiara Feran know you approached me?"

"She thinks I already have."

All right then.

He surmised that Odele and Chiara had had their talk. And apparently Chiara had changed tactics and decided to turn the situation to her advantage. She was willing to tolerate him…for the sake of her career at least. He shouldn't have been surprised. He'd already had one bad experience with a publicity-hungry actress, and then he'd been one of the casualties.

Still, they were in the middle of the second act, and he'd missed the opening. But suddenly things had gotten a lot more interesting.

Odele's eyes gleamed as if she sensed victory—or at least a chink in his armor. Turning away, she said, "Let me know when you're ready to talk."

As Rick watched Chiara's manager leave, he knew there was a brooding expression on his face. Odele had presented him with a quandary. As a rule, he didn't get involved with actresses—ever since his one bad episode—but he had his gallant side. On top of it, Chiara was the talent on his latest film—one in which he had a big stake.

As if on cue, his cell phone vibrated. Fishing it out of his pocket, Rick recognized the number on-screen as that of his business partner—one of the guys who fronted the company, per Rick's preference to be behind the scenes.

"Hey, Pete, what's going on?"

Rick listened to Pete's summary of the meeting that morning with an indie director looking for funding. He liked what he heard, but he needed to know more. "Email me their proposal. I'm inclined to fund up to five million, but I want more details."

Five million dollars was pocket change in his world.

"You're the boss," Pete responded cheerfully.

Yup, he was…though no one on set knew he was the producer of *Pegasus Pride*. He liked his privacy and kept his communications mostly to a need-to-know basis.

Right. Rick spotted Chiara in the distance. No doubt she was heading to film her next scene. *There* was someone who treated him more like the hired help than the boss.

Complications and delays on a film were common, and Rick had a feeling Chiara was about to become his biggest complication to date…

Two

"Hey."

It was exactly the sort of greeting she expected from a sweaty and earthy he-man—or rather, stuntman.

Chiara's pulse picked up. *Ugh.* She hadn't expected to have this reaction around him. She was a professional—a classically trained actress before she'd been diverted by Hollywood.

Sure, she'd been Miss Rhode Island, and a runner-up in the Miss America pageant. But then the Yale School of Drama had beckoned. And she'd never been a Hollywood blonde. The media most often compared her to Camilla Belle because they shared a raven-haired, chestnut-eyed look.

Anyway, with her ebony hair, she'd need to have her roots touched up every other day if she tried to become a blonde. As far as she was concerned, she spent enough time in the primping chair.

She figured He-Stuntman had gotten his education in the School of Hard Knocks. Maybe a broken bone or two. Certainly plenty of bumps and bruises.

Rick stopped in front of her. No one was around. They were near the actors' trailers, far away from the main action. Luckily she hadn't run into him after her talk with Odele two days ago. Instead, she'd managed to avoid him until now.

Dusk was gathering, but she still had a clear view of him.

He was in a ripped tee, jeans and body paint meant to seem like grease and dirt, while she was wearing a damsel-in-distress/sidekick look—basically a feminine version of Rick's attire but her clothes were extratight and torn to show cleavage. And from the quick perusal he gave her, she could tell the bare skin hadn't escaped his notice.

"So you need a boyfriend," he said without preamble.

She itched to rub the smug smile off his face. "I don't need anything. This would be a completely optional but mutually advantageous arrangement."

And right after this conversation, she was going to have another serious talk with her manager. What had Odele signed her up for?

"You need me."

She burned. He'd made it sound like *you want me*.

"I've been asked to play many roles, but never a stud."

"Don't get too excited."

He grinned. "Don't worry, I won't. I have a thing for the doe-eyed, dark-haired look, but since Camilla Belle isn't available, you'll do."

The flames of temper licked her, not least because he was clued in as to her Hollywood doppelgänger. "So you'll settle?"

"I don't know. Let's kiss and find out."

"If the cameras were rolling, it would be time for a slap right now," she muttered.

He caught her wrist and tugged her closer.

"This isn't a movie, and you're no actor!" she objected.

"Great, because I intend to kiss you for real. Let's see if we can be convincing for when the paparazzi and public are watching." He raised his free hand to thread his fingers through her hair and move it away from her face. "Your long dark hair is driving me crazy."

"It's the Brazilian-Italian heritage," she snapped back, "and I bet you say the same thing to all your leading ladies."

"No," he answered bemusedly, "some of them are blondes."

And then his mouth was on hers. If he'd been forceful, she'd have had a chance, but his lips settled on hers with soft, tantalizing pressure. He smelled of smoke from the special effects, and when his tongue slipped inside her mouth, she discovered the taste of mint, too.

She'd been kissed many times—on-screen and off—but she found herself tumbling into this one with shocking speed. The kiss was smooth, leisurely…masterful but understated. Rick could double for any A-list actor in a love scene. He touched his tongue to hers, and the shock and unexpectedness of it had her opening to him. As an unwritten rule, actors on-screen did not French kiss, so she was already in uncharted territory. The hard plane of his chest brushed against her, and her nipples tightened.

Think, Chiara. Remember why you don't like him.

She allowed herself one more second, and then she tore her mouth away and stepped back. For a fleeting moment she felt a puff of steam over his audacity. "All right, the screen test is over."

Rick curved his lips. "How did I do?"

"I don't even know your last name," she responded, sidestepping the question.

"I'll answer to anything. 'Honey,' 'baby,' 'sugar.'" He shrugged. "I'm easy."

"Clearly." This guy could charm his way into any woman's bed. "Still, I'd prefer your real one for when the police ask me to describe the suspect."

He grinned. "It's Rick Serenghetti. But 'darling' would add the appropriate air of mystery for the paparazzi."

Serenghetti. She knew an Italian surname when she heard one. "My last name was originally Ferano. You know, Italian."

His smile widened. "I'd never have guessed, Snow White."

"They used to call me Snow White, but I drifted," she quipped. "Not suitable for the role."

"No problem. I'm not Prince Charming. I'm just his body double."

She wanted to scream. "This is never going to work."

"That's why you're an actress." He looked curious. "And, Odele mentioned, a beauty contestant. Win any titles?"

She made a sour face. "Yes. Miss Congeniality."

He burst out laughing. "I won't ask what your talent was."

"Ventriloquism. I made my dummy sing."

"'Some Day My Prince Will Come'?"

"Nothing from *Snow White*! I was also Miss Rhode Island, but obviously that was on the state level." She'd gone on to be a finalist in Miss America, which was where she'd earned her title of Miss Congeniality.

"Rhode Island is the smallest state. Still, the competition must have been fierce."

"Are you mocking me?" She searched his face, but he looked solemn.

"Who, me? I never mock women I'm trying to score with."

"Wow, you're direct. You don't even like me."

"What's *like* got to do with it?"

"You have no shame." When it came to sex, she was used to men wanting to bed anyone in sight. This was Hollywood, after all.

"Is it working?"

"Nothing will work, except Odele convincing me this is a good idea."

Rick frowned. "You mean she hasn't already?"

It took Chiara a moment to realize he wasn't joking. "Please. She may have persuaded you to go along with her crazy scheme, but not me."

"I only went along with it because I thought you'd said yes."

Chiara watched Rick's dawning expression, which mimicked her own. "I believed you'd agreed."

"Stuntmen are made of sterner stuff." He threw her attitude right back at her.

Chiara realized they'd both been tricked by Odele into believing the other had agreed to her plan. Rick had dared to kiss her because he thought she'd already signed up for her manager's plot. "What are we going to do?"

Rick shrugged. "About the gathering media frenzy? We're already bickering like an old married couple. We're perfect."

Chiara's eyes widened. "You can't tell me you're se- riously considering this? Anyway, we're supposed to act like new lovebirds, not a cantankerous old married couple."

"If we're already arguing, it'll make our relationship seem deeper than it is."

"Skip the honeymoon phase?" she asked rhetorically. "What's in this for you?"

He shrugged. "Have some fun." He looked at her lingeringly. "Satisfy my fetish for Snow White."

Chiara tingled, her breasts feeling heavy. "Oh, yeah, right…"

"So what's your take?"

"This is the worst storyline to come out of Hollywood."

For the second time in recent days, Chiara banged open the door of her trailer and marched in. "I can't pretend to be in a relationship with Rick Serenghetti. End of story."

Odele looked up from her magazine. She sat on a cushioned built-in bench along one wall. "What's wrong with him?"

He was too big, too macho, too everything—most of all, *annoying*. She still sizzled from their kiss minutes ago, and she didn't do vulnerability where men were concerned. But she sidestepped the issue. "It's the pretending part that I have trouble with."

"You're an actress."

"Context is everything. I like to confine my acting to the screen." Otherwise, she'd be in danger of losing herself. If she was always pretending, who was she? "You know I value integrity."

"It's overrated. Besides, this is Tinseltown."

Chiara placed her hands on her hips. "You misled me and Rick into thinking the other one had already agreed to this crazy scheme."

Odele shrugged. "You were already open to the idea.

That's the only reason it even mattered to you whether he was already on board with the plan."

Chiara felt heat rise to her face, and schooled her expression. "I'm not signing up for anything!"

Her conversation with Rick had had no satisfactory ending. It had sent her scuttling, somewhat humiliatingly, back to her manager. Chiara eyed the shower stall visible through the open bathroom door at the end of the trailer. If only she could rinse off the tabloid headlines just as easily.

"Fine," Odele responded with sudden and suspicious docility, putting aside her magazine. "We'll have to come up with another strategy to distract the press from your father and amp up your career."

"Sounds like a plan to me."

"Great, it's settled. Now…can you gain twenty pounds?" Odele asked.

Chiara sighed. Out of the frying pan and into the fire. "I'd rather not. Why?"

She'd gained fifteen for a film role two years ago in *Alibis & Lies*—in which she'd played a convicted white-collar criminal who witnesses a murder once she's released from jail and thinks her husband is framing her. To gain the weight, she'd indulged her love for pasta, creamy sauces and pastries—but she'd had to work for months with a trainer to shed the pounds afterward. In the meantime, she'd worn sunglasses and baggy clothes and had lain low in order to avoid an unflattering shot by the paparazzi. And she'd been disappointed not to get a Golden Globe nomination.

She wondered what movie project Odele had in mind these days… Usually her talent agent at Creative Artists sent projects her way, but Odele kept her ear to the ground, too.

"Last time I was heavier on-screen, I got a lot of backlash." Some fans thought she'd gained too much weight, some too little. She could never please everyone.

"It's not a film," Odele said. "It's a weight-loss commercial."

Chiara's jaw dropped. "But I'm not overweight!"

Odele's eyes gleamed. "You could be."

Chiara threw her hands up. "Odele, you're ruthless."

"It's what makes me good at what I do. Slender You is looking for a new celebrity weight-loss spokesperson. The goodwill with fans alone is worth the pounds, but Slender You is willing to pay millions to the right person. If you land this contract, your DBI score will go up, and you'll be more likely to land other endorsement deals."

"No." Her manager was all about Q scores and DBIs and any other rating that claimed to measure a celebrity's appeal to the public. "Next you'll be suggesting a reality show."

Odele shook her head. "No, I only recommend it to clients who haven't had a big acting job in at least five years. That's not you, sweetie."

For which Chiara would be forever grateful. She was having a hard enough time being the star of her own life without adding the artifice of a reality show to it.

"How about writing a book?" Odele asked, tilting her head.

"On what?"

"Anything! We'll let your ghostwriter decide."

"No, thanks. If I have a ghost, I won't really be writing, will I?" Chiara responded tartly.

"You're too honest for your own good, you know." Odele sighed, and then suddenly brightened. "What about a fragrance?"

"I thought Dior just picked a new face for the brand."

"They did. I'm talking about developing your own scent. Very lucrative these days."

"You mean like Elizabeth Taylor's White Diamonds?"

"Right, right." Odele warmed up. "We could call it Chiara. Or, wait, wait, Chiara Lucida! The name suggests a bright star."

"How much is an Oscar worth?" Chiara joked, because her idea of becoming a big star involved winning a golden statuette.

"Of course, an Academy Award has value, but we want to monetize all income streams, sweetie. We want to grow and protect your brand."

Chiara sighed, leaning against the walnut-paneled built-in cabinet behind her. There'd been a time when movie stars were just, well, movie stars. Now everyone was *a brand*. "There's nothing wrong with my brand."

"Yes, of course." Odele paused for a beat. "Well, except for the teeny-weeny problem of your father popping up in the headlines from time to time."

"Right." How could she forget? How could anyone fail to remember when the tabloids followed the story breathlessly?

"How about a lifestyle brand like Gwyneth Paltrow or Jessica Alba has?" Odele offered.

"Maybe when I win an Academy Award or I have kids." Both Alba and Paltrow had had children when they'd started their companies.

At the thought of kids, Chiara had an uncomfortable feeling in the pit of her stomach. She was thirty-two. She had an expiration date in Hollywood *and* a ticking clock for getting pregnant without spending thousands of dollars for chancy medical intervention. Unfortunately the two trains were on a collision course. If she was going to avert disaster, she needed to have a well-established career—er, Oscar—before she caved in to the public clamor for her to get a happily-ever-after with marriage and children.

Of course, she wanted kids. It was the husband or boyfriend part that she had a problem with. Michael Feran hadn't set a sterling example for his only child. At least she thought she was his only child.

Ugh. Her family—or what remained of it—was so complicated. It wouldn't even qualify as a Lifetime movie because there was no happy ending.

Still, the thought of a child of her own brought a pang. She'd have someone to love unconditionally, and who would love and need her in return. She'd avoid the mistakes that her parents had made. And she'd have something real—pure love—to hold on to in the maelstrom of celebrity.

"So," Odele said pleasantly, "your other options aren't too appealing. Let me know when you're ready to consider dating Rick Serenghetti."

Chiara stared at her manager. She had the sneaking suspicion that Odele had known all along where their conversation was heading. In all probability, her manager had been set on showing her the error of her ways and her earlier agreeableness had just been a feint. "You're a shark, Odele."

Odele chuckled. "I know. It's why I'm good at what I do."

Chiara resisted throwing up her hands. Some actresses confided in their personal assistants or stylists. She had Odele.

"So what's got you down?"

Rick figured he needed to work on his acting skills

if even Jordan was asking that question. "I don't know what you're talking about."

They were sitting in his kitchen, and he'd just handed his brother a cold beer from the fridge. He grabbed opportunities with his family whenever he could since he spent much of his time on the opposite coast from everyone else. Fortunately, since his current movie was being filmed on a Novatus Studio lot and nearby locations around LA, he was able to get to his place at least on weekends—even if home these days was a one-bedroom rental in West Hollywood.

"Mom asked me to check on you." Jordan shifted his weight on the kitchen barstool.

"She always asks you to check on me whenever we're in the same city. But don't assume the reconnaissance runs one way. She wants me to keep an eye on you, too."

"My life hasn't been that interesting lately."

Jordan was in town because his team, the New England Razors, was playing the Los Angeles Kings at the Staples Center. He was the star center player for the team. The youngest Serenghetti brother also had movie star looks, and hardly ever let an opportunity pass without remarking that their parents had attained perfection the third time around.

Rick followed hockey—family loyalty and all—but he wasn't passionate about it like Jordan and their older brother, Cole, who'd also had a career with the Razors until it had ended in injury. Rick had been a wrestler in high school, not a hockey team captain like his brothers.

The result was that he had a reputation as the family maverick. And hey, who was he to argue? Still, he wasn't intentionally contrary—though Chiara might want to argue the point.

An image of Chiara Feran sprung to mind. He'd been

willing to tease her about playing a couple, especially when he'd thought Chiara was going along with the idea. After all, it was nice, safe, *pretend*—not like really getting involved with an actress. And it was fun to ruffle Chiara's feathers.

If he was being a little more serious, he'd also acknowledge that as a producer, he had a vested interest in the star of his latest film maintaining a positive public image despite her problematic family members—not to mention staying *safe* if she really had a would-be stalker.

Still, being a *pretend boyfriend* and *secret bodyguard*, if Odele had her way, was asking a lot. Did he have enough to overcome his scruples about getting involved with a celebrity? Hell, even he wasn't sure. He'd been burned once by an aspiring starlet, and he'd learned his lesson—never stand between an actress and a camera.

For a long time, he'd counted actors, directors and other movie people among his friends. Hal Moldado, a lighting technician, had been one of those buddies. Then one day, Rick had run into Isabel Lanier, Hal's latest girlfriend. She'd followed him out of a cafe and surprised him with a kiss—captured in a selfie that she'd managed to take with her cell phone and promptly posted to her social media accounts. Unsurprisingly it had spelled the end of his friendship with Hal. Later he'd conclude that Isabel had just been trying to make Hal jealous and stay in the news herself as an actress.

The saving grace had been that the media had never found out—or cared—about the name of Isabel's mystery man in those photos. It had been enough that Isabel looked as if she were cheating on Hal, so Rick had been able to dodge the media frenzy.

Ever since, though, as far as he was concerned, starlets were only interested in tending their public image.

And up to now Chiara had fit the bill well—even if she hadn't yet agreed to her manager's latest scheme. After all, there was a reason that Chiara had partnered with someone like Odele. She knew her celebrity was important, and she needed someone to curate it.

But Odele had increased the stakes by referring to a possible stalker… It complicated his calculations about whether to get involved. He should just convince Chiara to get additional security—like any sane person would. Not that *sanity* ranked high on the list of characteristics he associated with fame-hungry actresses.

Jordan tilted his head. "Woman in your thoughts?"

Rick brought his attention back to the present. "Anyone ever tell you that you have a sixth sense where the other sex is concerned?"

His younger brother smiled enigmatically. "Sera would agree with you. Marisa's cousin is driving me crazy."

Their brother Cole had recently married the love of his life, Marisa Danieli. The two had had a falling-out in high school but had reconnected. Marisa's relatives were now an extension by marriage of the Serenghetti clan—including Marisa's younger cousin Sera.

Apparently that didn't sit well with Jordan.

"I'm surprised," Rick remarked. "You can usually charm any woman if you set your mind to it."

"She won't even serve me at the Puck & Shoot."

"Is she still moonlighting as a waitress there?" Rick had had his share of drinks at Welsdale's local sports bar.

"Off and on."

He clasped his brother's shoulder. "So your legendary prowess with women has fallen short. Cheer up, it was bound to happen sometime."

"Your support is overwhelming," Jordan replied drily.

Rick laughed. "I just wish Cole were here to appreciate this."

"For the record, I haven't been trying to score with Sera. She's practically family. But she actively dislikes me, and I can't figure out why."

"Why does it matter? It won't be the first time a family member has had it in for you." Jordan had come in for his share of ribbing and roughing up by his two older siblings. "What's to get worked up about?"

"I'm not worked up," Jordan grumbled. "Anyway, let's get back to you and the woman problems."

Rick cracked a careless smile. "Unlike you, I don't have any."

"Women or problems?"

"Both together."

Jordan eyed him. "The press is suggesting you have the former, and you look as if you've got the latter."

"Oh, yeah?"

"Who's the starlet on your latest film?"

"Chiara Feran."

His brother nodded. "She's hot."

"She's off-limits."

Jordan raised his eyebrows. "To me?"

"To anyone."

"Proprietary already?"

"Where did you get this ridiculous story?"

"Hey, I read."

"Much to Mom's belated joy."

Jordan flashed the famous pearly whites. His good looks had gotten him many modeling gigs, including more than one underwear ad. "*Gossipmonger* reported you two have been getting cozy, and the story has been picked up by other websites."

"You know better than to believe everything you

read." If the gossip had reached Jordan, then it was spreading wider and faster than Rick had thought. Still, he figured he shouldn't have been surprised, considering Chiara's celebrity.

"Yup. But is it true?"

Frankly, Rick was starting not to know what was true anymore, and it was troubling. "Nothing's happened."

Except one kiss. She'd tasted of peaches—fruity and heady and delicious. He'd gotten an immediate image of the two of them heating up the sheets, his trailer or hers. She challenged him, and something told him she'd be far from boring in bed, too. Chiara was full of fire, and he warmed up immediately around her. The trouble was he might also get burned.

Jordan studied him. "So nothing's happened yet…"

Rick adopted a bland expression. "Unlike you, I don't see women as an opportunity."

"Only your female stars."

"I'm done with that." Isabel had been the star of Rick's movie when they'd been snapped together. The fact that they'd both been working on the film—he as a stuntman and secretly as a producer, and she as an actress—had lent an air of truth to the rumors.

Jordan looked thoughtful. "Right."

Rick checked his watch because he was through trying to convince his brother—or himself. In a quarter of an hour, they needed to head to dinner at Ink, one of the neighborhood's trendy restaurants. "Just finish your damn beer."

"Whatever you say, movie star," Jordan responded, seemingly content to back off.

They both took a swill of their beers.

"So, the new digs treating you well?" his brother asked after a moment.

The apartment had come furnished, so there wasn't a hint of his personality here, but it served its purpose. "The house is nearly done. I'll be moving in a few weeks."

Jordan saluted him with his beer bottle. "Here's to moving up in the world in a big way." His brother grinned. "Invite me to visit when the new manse is done."

"Don't worry. I'll tell the majordomo not to throw you out," Rick replied drily.

Jordan laughed. "I'm a babe magnet. You'll want me around."

Privately, Rick acknowledged his brother might have a point. These days, the only woman he was linked to was Chiara Feran, and it wasn't even real.

Three

For two days, Rick didn't encounter Chiara. She and Adrian Collins, the male lead, were busy filming, so today Rick was hitting the gym trailer and working off restless energy.

So far, there'd been no denial or affirmation in the press that he and Chiara were a couple. As a news story, they were stuck in limbo—a holding pattern that kept him antsy and out of sorts. He wondered what Chiara's camp was up to, and then shrugged. He wasn't going to call attention to himself by issuing a denial—not that the press cared about his opinion because for all they knew, he was just a stuntman. They were after Chiara.

After exiting the gym trailer, Rick made his way across the film set. He automatically tensed as he neared Chiara's trailer. Snow White was a tart-tongued irritant these days—

He rounded a corner and spotted a man struggling with the knob on Chiara's door.

The balding guy with a paunch was muttering to himself and jiggling the door hard.

Frowning, Rick moved toward him. This section of the set was otherwise deserted.

"Hey," he called, "what are you doing?"

The guy looked up nervously.

All Rick's instincts told him this wasn't a good situation. "What are you doing?"

"I'm a friend of Chiara's."

"Does she know you're here?"

"I've been trying to see her." This time there was a note of whininess.

"This is a closed set. Do you have ID?" Rick didn't recall seeing this guy before. He was within a few feet of the other man now. The guy stood on the top step leading to the door of the trailer. Rick could see perspiration had formed on the man's brow. Was this the creepy fan Odele had referred to?

Rick went with his gut. "I'm her new boyfriend."

The other guy frowned. "That's impossible."

Now that he was closer, Rick could see the other man was definitely not the glamorous or debonair celebrity type that he would expect an actress like Chiara to date.

In the next second, the guy barreled down the trailer's steps and shoved past him.

Rick staggered but grasped the trailer's flimsy metal bannister to keep himself upright.

As Chiara's alleged friend made a run for it, Rick instinctively took off after him.

The man plowed past a crew member, who careened back against a piece of lighting equipment. Then two extras jumped aside, creating a path for the chase.

The guy headed toward the front gate of the studio lot, where Rick knew security would stop him. Rick could only guess how the intruder had gotten onto the lot. Had he hidden in the back of a catering truck, as paparazzi had been known to do?

Gaining on Chiara's admirer, Rick put on a final burst of speed and tackled the guy. As they both went down, Rick saw in his peripheral vision that they'd attracted the security guards' attention at the front gate.

The man struggled in his grasp, jabbing Rick with his elbow. "Get off me! I'll sue you for assault."

Rick twisted the man's arm behind his back, holding him down. "Not before you get written up for trespassing. Where's your pass?"

"I'm Chiara's fiancé," the guy howled.

Rick glanced up to see that two security guards had caught up to them. "I found this guy trying to break into Chiara Feran's trailer."

"Call Chiara," her alleged fiancé puffed. "She'll know."

"Chiara Feran doesn't have a fiancé," Rick bit back.

Someone nearby had started filming with his cell phone. *Great.*

"We're together. We're meant to be together!"

Nut job. Rick was in great physical shape due to his stunt work, so he wasn't out of breath, but Mr. Fiancé was no teddy bear, either; he continued to put up a struggle.

Suddenly the trespasser wheezed. "I can't br-breathe! Get off me. I have asthma."

Great. Rick eased back and let one of the security guards take over while the other spoke into his radio.

Things happened slowly but methodically after that. Police were summoned by the studio's security, and Chiara's special fan—who'd given his name as Todd Jeffers—was led away. Eventually Rick was questioned by a police officer. Chiara materialized soon after and was similarly prodded for details by the officer's partner.

Before the police left, Rick gleaned that Chiara's overly enthusiastic fan would be charged with criminal trespass, disorderly conduct and harassment. *Well, that's something.* But by the time Rick had finished talking about the incident to Dan, the director, Chiara had holed up in her trailer.

Rick eyed Chiara's door, twisted his mouth in a grim line and made his way to the trailer for some answers.

He didn't bother knocking—chances were better for a snowstorm in LA right now than for her rolling out the red carpet for him—and simply marched inside.

He came up short when he found Chiara sitting at a cozy little table, a script in front of her.

She was memorizing her lines? He expected her to be rattled, upset...

He looked around. The trailer was a double-decker, and with walnut paneling, it was swankier than his own digs, which were done in a gray monochrome and had no upper level.

When his gaze came back to rest on Chiara, she tilted her head, and said, "People weren't sure when you tackled him whether it was a stunt, or if you were rehearsing a scene from the movie."

"You're welcome." Leaning against a counter, he folded his arms, like a cop getting ready for an interrogation. He wanted answers only she could provide, and after getting into a fight with her admirer, he was going to get them. "Luckily you weren't in your trailer when he got here."

"I was rehearsing. We're shooting a difficult scene."

Rick figured that helped explain why she was sitting with a script in front of her, though he imagined her concentration was shot.

"I can only imagine the press coverage that today will

get." A horrified look crossed her face, and she closed her eyes on a shudder.

So she wasn't as unaffected as she seemed. In fact, Rick had already dealt with suppressing the video of him tackling Jeffers. The person who'd been taping had turned out to be a visiting relative of one of the film crew. But even if those images didn't become public or weren't sold to the tabloids, the media would get wind of what happened from the police report and show up for Jeffers's court hearing. Then, of course, Jeffers himself might choose to make a public statement...

"Hey, at least it'll take attention away from your father's latest losses at the gambling tables." He wondered if Chiara appreciated just how close she'd come to danger. It had been dumb luck that her overly enthusiastic fan hadn't found her earlier.

She opened her eyes and raised her head. "Yes, how can I forget about my father? How can anyone?"

"So you have a stalker." He kept his tone mild, belying the emotions coursing through him. *Damn it*. Chiara was slender and a lightweight despite her mouth and bravado. His blood boiled just thinking of some jerk threatening her.

"Many celebrities have overly enthusiastic fans." She waved her hand, and Rick could practically see her walls going up. "But my property has a security gate and cameras."

Rick narrowed his eyes. "Have you dealt with this Todd Jeffers guy before? What kind of unstoppable fan is he? The sort who writes you pretty letters or the type who pens twisted ones?"

She shrugged. "He tried to scale my property fence once, but he was spotted by a landscaper and shooed away even before he got within view of the security cameras. I haven't heard from him in the months since."

So today's guy was the same person who'd shown up at Chiara's house once, and yeah, she wasn't understanding the risk... Still, Rick strove for patience. "How do you know it was Jeffers at your house that day?"

She hesitated. "He wrote to me afterward to say he'd tried to see me."

"He wrote to you about an attempted criminal trespass?" Rick let his tone drip disbelief. "Have you gotten a temporary restraining order?"

Chiara sighed. "No. He's never been a physical threat, just a pest."

"Just because he *only* tried to jump the fence doesn't mean that's what he'll settle for doing in the future. There's often an escalation with these nut jobs once they figure out that plan A isn't working."

Chiara raised her chin. "He's probably a lonely, starstruck guy. Plenty of fans are."

"Probably? I don't deal in probabilities. Your run-of-the-mill serial killer often starts out torturing animals before moving to the big time. As I said, escalation."

"Like A-list stars starting out in B movies?" she asked snippily.

"Right," he said, his voice tight even as he ignored her flippant attitude. "Listen, Snow White, there are villains out there aside from the Evil Queen."

Rick raked his fingers through his hair. He could understand why this guy was besotted with Chiara. Unfortunately Chiara herself wasn't appreciating the gravity of the problem. They were like two trains on parallel tracks. "You've got a stalker. It's time you acquired a boyfriend. Me."

He'd been mulling things over, his mind in overdrive

ever since he'd tackled Jeffers. If he pretended to be Chiara's boyfriend, he could stick close and keep an eye on her. Maybe once this guy realized Chiara had a supposedly real boyfriend, he'd back off. Odele may have been onto a good idea.

Chiara opened and closed her mouth. "You're not in the protection business."

"I'm appointing myself right now. Besides, I've got the right background. I used to do security." He'd worked as a guard at an office building during his college days and beyond in order to earn extra cash. He'd been a good bouncer, too. His parents had instilled the value of hard work in their children even though they'd been well-off.

Chiara slid off her seat and stood. In the confined space, she was within touching distance. "You can't unilaterally decide to be my protector." She spluttered as if searching for words. "I won't agree to it."

"You could solve two problems at once. The bad press from your father, and the issue of your stalker and needing security. Don't quibble."

"I'll get a restraining order."

He took a step forward. "Damn straight, you will."

"So I don't need you."

"You need physical protection, too, unless you have seven dwarves hanging around, because a court order is just a piece of paper." He didn't want to think about how many news stories there'd been concerning an order of protection being violated—and someone getting hurt or killed.

She looked mutinous. "I'll hire professional security."

"It still won't solve the problem of your father and distracting the press."

Chiara threw up her hands.

"Don't worry. I'll always be a step behind you, like a good prince consort—I mean, bodyguard."

"Hilarious."

"I'll make sure to hold an umbrella open for you in the rain," he added solemnly.

"What's in this for you?"

"Let's just say I have a vested interest in the star of my next blockbuster staying safe until the end of filming. Everyone working on this movie wants to see it finished so they can get paid."

"I thought so. Well, my answer is still no."

He'd given her the wrong answer, and she'd responded in kind. "Do you just act contrary, or is this your best side?"

"How can you say that about the damsel in distress you helped save from a helicopter?" she asked sweetly.

"Exactly."

They were practically nose-to-nose, except because she stood several inches shorter than his six-foot frame, it was more like nose-to-chin. But then she raised her face to a stubborn angle, and he abandoned his good intentions about keeping himself in check during this conversation.

Hell, here goes nothing.

He tugged her forward and captured her mouth. It was just as good as before, damn it. There was a little zap of electricity because they were differently charged, and then he was kissing her in earnest, opening that luscious mouth and deepening the kiss.

She smelled faintly of honeysuckle, just like Snow White ought to. He caressed her cheek with the back of his hand. She was petal-soft, and he was getting hard.

After what felt like an eternity, she pushed him away.

Her chest rose and fell, and he was breathing deeply with arousal.

She touched her fingers to her lips and then shot fire at him with her eyes. "That's twice."

"Are we getting better? We've got to be convincing if we're going to pull this off."

"We're not practicing scenes, but if we were, try this response on for size." She stretched out her arm and pointed to the door of the trailer, giving him his marching orders.

It was a proverbial slap in the face, but Chiara was wrong if she thought he was backing down. "Let me know when our next scene is scheduled for filming. It might be time to throw a plate or break something. For real, not pretend."

After this parting shot, he turned and headed to the door, almost laughing as he heard her bang something behind him.

"She doesn't want to get extra security." Rick ran his hand through his hair. "She's stubborn."

"Hmm." Odele nodded. "And I'm her manager, so I don't know this?"

"And reckless, too." They were sitting in Novatus Studio's commissary having coffee before lunchtime. Rick had asked to meet and had told Odele not to mention it to Chiara. "How long has this guy Todd been hanging around thinking he's her special friend?" *Or fiancé.*

Odele shrugged. "Several months. I had staff look at Chiara's fan mail after he showed up at her house. He'd sent an email or two, and my assistant says he's cropped up on social media, too. Then he started a fan club and wanted autographed photos."

"And now he's moved on to believing he's her fiancé."

Odele sighed. "Some people buy into the Hollywood celebrity stuff a little too much."

Right. Rick leaned back in his chair. "Besides trying

to scale the fence at Chiara's house, has he made any other moves?"

"Not until yesterday. At least not that I know of." Odele took a sip from her cup. "I've already instructed Chiara's attorney to go for a restraining order."

"You and I both know it's only a piece of paper, but she doesn't want to consider additional physical security. Not even if I appoint myself." Rick didn't hide the frustration in his voice. Damn it. Who was he kidding? Chiara would resist, especially if it was him.

"So you're considering my idea of being a pretend boyfriend? You need to move in."

Rick shook his head in exasperation because Odele was a bulldozer. "If she doesn't want a fake relationship and won't tolerate a bodyguard, she definitely won't have someone living in her house."

If he and Chiara lived under one roof, they'd drive each other crazy. He'd alternate between wanting to shake some sense into her and take her to bed. And she'd… Well, she'd just rage at him and deny any sparks of a simmering attraction.

It was a recipe for disaster…or a Hollywood movie.

Odele gave him a mild look. "It's all a matter of how it's presented to her. If you're going to distract the press as her new boyfriend, the story will play even bigger in the media if you move in. There'll be more opportunities for the two of you to be photographed together."

"*Pretend* boyfriend." Everyone needed to be clear on the fake part, including and particularly *him*, if he was going to get involved with another actress.

Odele inclined her head. "Leave convincing her to me. I won't say anything more about having you function as a bodyguard. But believe me, the press attention surrounding her father is really upsetting her."

In Rick's opinion, Chiara should be spending more time worrying about her stalker than about her estranged father. Still… "Tell me about Michael Feran."

Odele set aside her coffee cup. "There's not much to say. Chiara's parents divorced when she was young. Chiara and her mother were in Rhode Island until Hollywood beckoned. Her mother died a few years ago. She developed sepsis after an illness. It was a shock for everyone."

"But her father continues to make waves."

"Last year, he accepted money from a third-rate weekly to dish about Chiara."

Rick cursed.

Odele shot him a perceptive look from behind her red glasses. "Yes, Chiara felt betrayed."

So Chiara's was far from a fairy-tale upbringing. No wonder she was prickly around him, and no doubt distrustful of men.

"Take it from me. Be the good boyfriend that she needs and keep an eye on her. Just don't bring up the bodyguard part to her."

"A pretend boyfriend." *Pretend* being the operative word there. He wasn't sure if he was reminding himself or Odele, though.

"Right."

Right.

Chiara took Ruby out of her box and perched her on her knee. The dummy wore a sequined gown, and her hair and face were worthy of a Vegas showgirl.

Chiara sat at the writing desk occupying one corner of her master bedroom. There'd been a break in filming for the weekend, and she was happy to retreat to her sanctuary. She needed time away. First her father, then Rick and finally a stalker had frayed her nerves.

Still, even though it was a beautiful and sunny Saturday afternoon, and she should have been in a great mood, she...*wasn't*. She was irritable and restless and anxious. She'd been having trouble memorizing her lines ever since the attempted break-in at her trailer. *Pegasus Pride* was an action flick, so the script wasn't heavy, but there was still dialogue that she had to be able to say without prompting.

Frustrated, she'd finally resorted to using Ruby to help her relax. She hadn't taken the dummy out in months, but ventriloquism kept her in touch with her former life—and at moments like these, let her deal with her present concerns.

Chiara searched the dummy's face. "What am I going to do?"

Ruby tilted her head.

"I must be out of my mind to be talking to a dummy by myself."

"You're not alone if you're having a chat with someone," Ruby responded in her singsong voice. "I just help you figure things out, sugar."

"I thought that's what Odele is for."

Ruby waved her hand. "You already know where Odele stands. She's on the hunk's side, and frankly, I don't know why you aren't, too." Ruby tossed her hair—because rolling her eyes was out of the question. "He's delicious."

"Annoying. You're reading too much gossip."

"I have to, it's about you," the dummy chirped. "Anyway, it's time you let someone under your skin, and back into your bed. And Rick...that body, that face, that kiss. Need I say more?"

"You are saucy and naughty, Ruby."

"And you wish you could be. Let your hair down, sugar."

Chiara's gaze fell to the laptop at her elbow. "I have too many responsibilities...and plenty of problems."

The headline on the computer screen spoke for itself: Chiara Feran's Father Thrown Out of Casino.

Maybe now that he couldn't gamble because he'd been caught counting cards, Michael Feran would stay out of trouble. But Chiara knew that was wishful thinking.

The public thought she had an enviable life—helped by Odele's relentless image craftsmanship. But the truth...

She'd never thought of herself as a beauty queen, for one. Oh, sure, she'd been blessed with good genes—a nice face and a fast metabolism that meant it wasn't impossible to adhere to Hollywood standards of beauty. But she also considered herself an outsider. She'd been raised by an immigrant mother, grown up enduring cold New England winters and would have still been doing theater but for a quirk of fate and Odele risking taking her on as a client.

She liked her privacy, her best friend was a smart-mouthed talent manager ripe for caricature and her sidekick was a doll made of wood. Obviously Todd Jeffers was crazier than she gave him credit for if he couldn't pick a better-credentialed starlet to stalk. And now she had a rumored *boyfriend*—a muscle-bound stuntman who looked as if he could enter a triathlon.

She'd already ignored a text from Odele about the latest headline, but Chiara knew her manager was right—they needed a distraction *fast*...

Her lawyers were due in court in the coming days to get a temporary restraining order—so there'd be more unwanted press attention because of her unpleasant fan.

Still, Rick Serenghetti? *Argh.*

Her cell phone buzzed again, a telltale ringtone, and this time Chiara knew she couldn't ignore it. With an apologetic look, she propped Ruby on a chair and took the call. "Hello, Odele."

"Enjoying your time off?"

"Define *enjoy*. I'm memorizing my lines." Among other things. She cast Ruby a hush-hush look.

"Rick needs to move in if we're going to make this fake relationship work. It'll help believability."

"No." The refusal fell from her lips without thought. Rick in her house? They'd throttle each other…if they weren't jumping into bed. And the contradiction of trying to make a *fake* relationship *work* was apparently lost on her manager.

Odele sighed. "We need to move quickly. I'm going to tell my assistant to break the story on social media accounts so we can control the initial message. I took an amateur shot with my cell phone of you and Rick seemingly engaged in an intimate conversation on the Novatus Studio lot."

"Of course you did."

"It looks great. Really like the two of you having a tête-à-tête," Odele added, warming to her subject and ignoring the sarcasm.

"Did it also look as if I was going to kick him in the shins?"

"And I've already set up a print interview for the two of you with a trusted reporter," Odele went on as if she hadn't heard.

"I'm not looking for a protector. And have you even done a background check on Rick Serenghetti? Maybe he's the one I need safeguarding from!"

Rick was dangerous to her tranquility, but she didn't care to delve into the reasons why. He had a way of looking at her with a lazy, sultry gleam that she found…annoying—yes, definitely annoying.

She'd done a quick search online for him—*only* for the purpose of satisfying herself that he didn't have a criminal record, she told herself—and had come up with nothing. She supposed no news was good news.

"Who said anything about a bodyguard?" Odele said innocently. "This is to help everyone believe you two are an item."

So Rick had backed off the part about offering personal protection? Somehow she had her doubts. "He doesn't need to move in to do that. What ever happened to dating? We're going from zero to sixty."

"It's Hollywood. Pregnancies last five months, and babies arrive right after the wedding. Everything is fast here."

Chiara couldn't argue. Celebrities were well-known for trying to hide their pregnancies from the press until the second trimester or beyond.

"Do I need to resend you the latest headline about Michael Feran?" Odele asked.

"I've already read it. I should have taken a different surname when I started my career."

"Too late now, sweetie. Besides, the media would have found him anyway, and he'd still be giving you trouble."

"Yes, but it would have made the connection between us seem less close."

"Well, time to distance yourself by cozying up to a hot stuntman."

"I know I'm going to regret this," Chiara muttered.

"I'll arrange for him to move in at the end of the week," Odele responded brightly.

"The guest bedroom, Odele!"

Four

Rick roared up on his motorcycle.

Since he was in temporary digs, and most of his stuff was in storage, he didn't have much to bring to Chiara's house in the affluent Brentwood neighborhood. Instead, he'd had a taxi deposit his suitcases and duffel bags at the foot of Chiara's front steps shortly before his arrival midafternoon.

Looking up, he eyed the house. It was a modest size by Tinseltown standards. Three bedrooms and three baths, according to the write-up on a celebrity gossip site. Reminiscent of an English cottage, it had white stucco walls, an arched doorway and a pitched roof with cross-gables and a prominent chimney. Lush gardening added to the atmosphere of a place that might be featured in *Architectural Digest*.

He'd taken Odele's advice and planned to say nothing about being a bodyguard. As far as Chiara was concerned, he was here only as a pretend live-in boyfriend. He had no idea, however, how Odele had convinced Chiara to let him move in.

By the time he'd taken off his helmet, Chiara was standing on the front steps.

"Of course you'd ride a motorcycle," she commented.

He gave an insouciant smile.

"I thought it was an earthquake."

"I rock your world, huh?"

"Please."

He looked at her house. "Nice digs. I should have guessed a typical English-style cottage for you, Snow. But where's the thatched roof?"

"Wrong century," she responded. "Where do you call home?"

He gave a lopsided grin. "Technically a small apartment in West Hollywood, but my heart is always where there's a beautiful woman."

"I thought so."

He couldn't tell what she meant by her response. Still, he couldn't resist provoking her further. "Shouldn't we kiss for the benefit of the paparazzi and their long-range lenses?"

"There are no photographers," she scoffed.

"How do you know? One could be hiding in the bushes."

She eyed his suitcases. "I'll put you in the guest bedroom."

"Relegated to the couch already," he joked. "Are you going to do a media interview about our first lovers' spat?"

The temperature between them rose ten degrees, and even the planted geraniums perked up—they apparently liked a good show as much as anybody.

"Hilarious," Chiara shot back, "but it's a perfectly fine bed, not a couch."

"And you won't be in it."

She cast him a sweeping look. "Use your imagination. A make-believe relationship means pretend sex. But something tells me you have no problem with letting your dreams run wild."

"Will you still awaken me with a kiss, Snow White?"

She huffed. "You're hopeless. I don't do fairy tales, modern or otherwise."

"That's obvious."

"Don't act as if you're disappointed. Your forte is action flicks, not romantic comedies."

"Then why do I feel as if I'm trapped in a romance?" he murmured.

"Go blow something up and make yourself feel better."

"It's not that type of itch that I need to scratch."

She huffed and then turned toward her front door. "I'll have you checked for fleas then."

Rick stifled a grin. This was going to be one interesting stay.

After he got settled in the guest bedroom, he found Chiara in the large country-style kitchen. Warm beige cabinets and butcher-block countertops added to the warm atmosphere. Sniffing the air, he said, "Something smells delicious."

She glanced up from a saucepan on the range, edible enough herself to be a food advertiser's dream. "Surprised?"

"That you cook? Gratified."

"Dinner is beef Stroganoff."

"Now I'm surprised. You're an actress who eats."

"Portion control is everything."

"Can cook. I'll check that little detail off my list."

She cast him a sidelong look, her cloud of dark hair falling in tantalizing waves over one shoulder. "What list?"

"The one that Odele gave me. A little quiz for the both of us...so we can get acquainted. Be believable as a couple."

Chiara frowned, and then muttered, "Odele leaves nothing to chance. Next thing, she'll have us convincing the immigration service that we're not in a sham marriage for a residency card."

"Because you need one...being from the Land of Fairy Tales?" He almost got a smile out of her with that.

"What do you—I mean, Odele—want to know?"

Rick consulted his cell phone. "What first attracted you to me?"

Chiara spluttered and then set down her stirring spoon with a *clack*. "This is never going to work."

"Come on, there must be something that you can tell the reporters."

She looked flustered. "Does she ask you the same question about me?"

He lowered his eyelids. "What do you think?"

As the question hung there, Rick's mind skipped back to their stunts...the rehearsals...every single moment, in fact, that he'd become aware of her close by. The air had vibrated with sexual energy.

Chiara wet her lips. "I'll take that as a 'Yes, she did ask.'"

Rick gave her a seductive smile. "When you showed up for the rehearsal of our first stunt, I knew I was in trouble. You were beautiful and smart and had guts." He shrugged. "My fantasy woman. The perfect match."

Chiara blinked.

After a pause, he asked, "Sound good enough for an interview answer?"

She seemed to give herself a mental shake, and then pursed her lips. "Perfect."

He focused on her mouth. *Kissable, definitely.* "Great."

She slapped the lid on the saucepan and made for the kitchen door. "Things are simmering. Dinner will be ready in thirty minutes."

"It'll give you time to think of your own answer to Odele's question," he called after her, and could swear she muttered something under her breath.

But when she was gone, Rick acknowledged that much as he enjoyed teasing Chiara, the joke was on him. Because she was his dream woman. If only she wasn't also a publicity-hungry actress...

Through dinner, he and Chiara trod lightly around each other. The beef Stroganoff was delicious, and he helped clean up—a little surprised she didn't keep a full-time housekeeper even if she traveled a lot. Afterward, she excused herself and retreated to her room, announcing that she had to memorize her lines.

Left to his own devices, he took a quick tour of the house and grounds, familiarizing himself with its security...and possible vulnerability to intruders. Then, with nothing more to do, he headed to bed.

Passing Chiara's door, he could see a light beneath, and shook off thoughts of what she wore to bed and how her hair would look around her bare shoulders above a counterpane... Still, in the guest bedroom, he found himself punching his pillow multiple times before he drifted off to sleep.

"Rick?"

He opened his eyes and saw Chiara's shadowy silhouette in his bedroom doorway. His lips curved. Apparently she'd had a hard time sleeping, too.

She walked toward him, and he made no attempt to disguise his arousal—he'd been thinking about her. Her short slip with spaghetti straps hid little, her nipples jutting against the fabric. She had a fantastic figure. High breasts and an indented waist…softly curved hips. His fingers itched to touch her.

Instead, he propped himself on the pillows behind him.

She sat down on the side of the bed, and her hand brushed his erection.

He saw no prickliness—just need…for him.

"What can I do for you?" His voice came out as a rasp.

Chiara's eyes glowed in the dim light afforded by the moon. "I think you know."

She leaned closer. Her lips brushed his and her pretty breasts tantalized his bare chest.

He cupped the back of her head and brought her closer so he could deepen the kiss. His tongue swept inside her mouth, tangling and dueling with hers.

She moaned and sank against him, breaking the kiss just long enough to say, "Love me."

He needed no further invitation. He pulled her down onto the mattress next to him and covered her body with his.

She responded with the lack of inhibition that he'd hoped for, arching toward him and opening in invitation, her arms encircling his neck as she met the ardor of his kiss.

His only thought was to get even closer…to sink into her welcoming warmth and find oblivion.

It would be sweet release from the restless need that had been consuming him…

Rick awoke with a start. He couldn't tell what had jerked him from his fantasy, but the room was empty, and he was alone in his bed.

He was also frustrated and aroused.

He groaned. *Yup.* It was going to be torture acting as if he were Chiara's boyfriend and hiding the fact that he was her protector.

The next morning, Chiara was up early for the drive to Novatus Studio. She donned jeans and a knit top. No use prettying up since she'd be sitting in a makeup chair at work soon enough. In fact, it was so early, she figured she might be able to get in a few minutes to study today's lines of dialogue before the drive to the lot.

Concentrate, that's what she had to do. But she hadn't slept well. In bed last night, she'd stared up at the ceiling, very aware of Rick's presence in her house.

What attracted her to him?

He was the epitome of rough manliness—cool, tough and exuding sex appeal. His green eyes were fascinatingly multihued, and even the hard, sculpted plains of his face invited detailed study by touch and, yes, taste.

A woman could feel safe and sheltered in his arms.

And there was the problem. She'd learned a long time ago not to rely on any man. Starting with her father, who'd disappeared from her life at a young age, and had become a gambling addict and reprobate.

She didn't hear a sound from Rick's room, so she tiptoed downstairs with script in hand.

When she reached the kitchen, she was taken aback to spot him sitting outside on the veranda, gazing at the sunrise, dressed in black denim jeans and a maroon tee. He looked peaceful and relaxed, so far from the constant motion and barely leashed energy that she was used to from him.

As if sensing her presence, he turned and met her gaze.

Rising, he gave a jaunty salute with the mug in his hand and said, "Good morning."

"I didn't hear you," she blurted as he entered through the French doors.

"We stuntmen can be stealthy."

She lowered her lashes and swept him with a surreptitious look. His jeans hugged lean hips and outlined muscular legs. The tee covered a flat chest and biceps that were defined but not brawny. He had the physique and face for a movie screen, except there was nothing manicured about him. Rick had a rough male aura instead of polish.

She looked at the cup in his hands. "I didn't even smell the brew."

"It's not coffee. It's a vitamin power drink."

Ugh. "For your superhero strength."

"Of course." He gave her a wicked smile. "Helps with the stamina. Sleep well?"

"For sure. And you?" She refused to give an inch, treating him with cool civility, even if that smile made her body tighten.

"Naturally."

The truth was she'd lain awake and tossed around for close to two hours. She wondered how she was going to maintain this charade...especially since Rick was adept at provoking her. And she refused...*refused*...to dwell on his kiss.

"Nice story about your father in the news. I had time to catch up on the headlines while I waited for you to come down, Sleeping Beauty."

Damn it. She should have gotten up even earlier. "My father?"

"Yeah, you know, the guy who shares a last name with you."

"That's all we have in common," she muttered.

"Nice story about the card counting recently."

"Maybe he'll stay out of trouble now that he's been barred from his favorite haunts." Casinos were Michael Feran's drug of choice.

"Is that what you're hoping?"

"Why are we discussing this?"

He shrugged. "I figured we should talk about the reason we're together." A smile teased his lips. "It seems logical."

So he wanted an extension of yesterday's get-to-know-you? *No, thanks.* Not that last night's question had haunted her sleep or anything. "We're not together."

"It's what the tabloids think that matters."

Argh.

"So Michael Feran is a sensitive topic."

Chiara walked to the kitchen cabinets. "Only in as much as he's a liar, gambler and cheat."

"Hmm…must be hard to share the same surname."

She got a glass and poured herself some water from the fridge's water filter.

"Eight glasses a day?"

She glanced at him. "What do you think? It's good for the complexion."

"You're very disciplined."

She took a sip. "I have to be."

"Because your father isn't?"

"I don't define myself relative to him."

Rick's lips twitched. "Okay, so you're not your father."

"Of course."

"How old were you when he walked out?"

She put down the glass. "Nearly five. But even when he was there, he wasn't really. He disappeared for stretches. Some of it was spent touring as a sax player with a band. Then he moved out for good a few days before my fifth birthday."

"Must have been rough."

"Not really. The party went on without him." She remembered the pink heart piñata. Her first major role was putting on a smile for the photos when it was just her and her mother.

"Did he ever try coming back?"

"There were a few flyovers until I became a teenager."

"Brief?"

"Very." Either her parents would argue, or Michael Feran would quickly move on to his next big thing.

"Right." Rick looked as if he'd drawn his own conclusions.

"Why are we talking about this?" she asked again, her voice sharp.

"I need to get the story straight so I'm not contradicting you when I speak."

"Well, there's nothing to tell."

"That's not what the press thinks."

Yup, he had her there. Which was the crux of her problem. Straightening her shoulders, she grabbed her car keys from the kitchen counter. On second thought, she could have breakfast at the studio—there was always food around. "Well, I'm off. See you on set."

"I'm coming with you," Rick responded casually. "Or rather, you're coming with me."

She stopped and faced him. "Excuse me?"

"My car or yours?"

"Do you have an endless supply of pickup lines?"

"Do you want to find out?"

"No!"

"That's what I thought you'd say." He took a sip from

his mug. "How can we be two lovebirds if we don't arrive together?"

"We're trying to be discreet at work."

"But not for the press."

"Anyway, you own a motorcycle."

"Look outside. I had my car deposited here early this morning by a concierge service."

Rats. He'd been up even earlier than she'd thought. She tossed him a suspicious look and then walked over to peer out the French doors. She spotted a Range Rover in the drive. "Lovely."

"I think so."

She glanced back at Rick with suspicion, but he just returned a bland look. Another of his sexual innuendoes? Because it was impossible to tell what he'd been referring to—her or the car.

Then she sighed. She had to pick her battles, and it was clear the drive to the office was not one worth fighting over.

Rick walked toward her, pausing to glance at a script that she'd left on the counter yesterday. "It's early. Want me to quiz you on your lines?"

"No!" Not least because there was a scene were the leads got flirty.

Rick raised an eyebrow and then shrugged. "Suit yourself but the offer stands. Anytime."

Yup, he was an anytime, anywhere kind of guy.

"What else are we supposed to do while we're shacked up together?" he asked, his eyes laughing at her.

She raised an eyebrow. "Go to work?"

Within the hour, she and Rick pulled up to the gate to Novatus Studio in his car.

Rick rolled down his window in order to give his identification to security, and with a sixth sense, Chiara turned her head and spotted a hovering figure nearby. The flash of a paparazzi camera was familiar.

"Odele," she muttered, facing forward again.

There was a good chance that her manager had tipped off a photographer so someone could snap her and Rick arriving *together* at the studio. Odele was determined to give this story her personal spin.

Rick gave an amused look. "She thinks of everything."

Rick tried to be on his best behavior, but having some fun was oh-so-tempting...

The Living Room on the first floor of The Peninsula Beverly Hills was nothing if not a den for power brokers, so he supposed it was perfect for a print interview over afternoon tea with *WE Magazine*—which wanted the dishy scoop on Chiara's new relationship.

Rick eyed the sumptuous repast set out on the coffee table before them: finger sandwiches, scones and an assortment of petite pastries. Arranged by Odele, of course, the afternoon tea in The Living Room was worthy of a queen. Of course, all of it went untouched.

This wasn't about food, but business. *Showtime in Hollywood.*

When he and Chiara had arrived at Novatus Studio that morning, Odele had surprised them with the news that she'd arranged a friendly press interview for them later the same day. Chiara was already scheduled to have the cover of the next issue of *WE Magazine* in order to promote the upcoming release of *Pegasus Pride*, but Odele had deftly arranged for it to become a joint interview about her new relationship. He and Chiara had left work early, because Odele had already spoken to Dan, the director, about their appointment. Dan had been happy to oblige if it meant more positive ink ahead of the release of the film—everyone was banking on it opening big at the box office.

Rick had to hand it to Chiara's manager—she wasted no time. But he knew what Odele was thinking—better to get ahead of the gossip by getting your own version of the story out there before anyone else's. So he'd gone along with the whole deal.

Too bad Chiara herself didn't want him here. But Odele had insisted, arguing his presence would make the relationship more believable. As Odele had put it, *Readers inhale romance. Touch each other a lot.* To which Chiara had responded, *Odele, I'm not making out in public for the benefit of gawkers.*

Now, at his sudden grin at the recollection, Chiara shot him a repressive look. She'd already told him she saw his role here as a yes-man supporting player. He figured he could bridge the gap between stuntman and Prince Charming easily enough, but if Chiara thought he'd toady to a gossip columnist, she had another think coming. He stretched and then settled one arm on the back of the sofa—because he knew it would drive Chiara crazy.

The couch was in a cozy and semiprivate corner. The interviewer, Melody Banyon—who looked to be in her late forties and was a dead ringer for Mindy Kaling—leaned forward in her armchair. "So was it love at first sight?"

From the corner of his eye, Rick noticed Chiara's elbow inching toward him, ready to jab in case he made a flippant comment. But then Chiara just smiled at him before purring, "Well, I don't usually notice the stuntmen on my movie sets…"

Rick glanced at the interviewer and a corner of his mouth lifted. "You could say Chiara's manager played matchmaker. She thought we'd be perfect for each other."

Chiara's eyes widened, but then she tossed him a grateful look. "Yes, Odele is always looking out for my best interests…"

Melody gave a satisfied smile. "Great, just great." Repositioning the voice recorder on the table before them, she looked back and forth between her interview subjects. "And I understand you two just moved in together?"

"Yup," Rick spoke up, unable to resist. "Like yesterday." It was also roughly when their whole "relationship" had started.

Chiara shot him a quelling look, and he tossed back an innocent one. He moved his arm off the sofa, gave her shoulder a squeeze, and then leaned in and nuzzled her temple for a quick kiss.

"Mmm," Melody said, as if tasting a delicious story, "you two move fast."

Rick relaxed against the sofa again, and responded sardonically, "You don't know the half of it."

He knew he risked Chiara's wrath, and he was surprised to find himself relishing the challenge of sparring with her again. No doubt about it—they set sparks off in each other. And it would probably carry over to the bedroom.

He glanced at Chiara's profile. She was a beautiful woman. Winged brows, pink bow lips, thick, rich chocolate hair and a figure that was hourglass without being voluptuous. She was also talented and tough enough to play a kick-ass action movie heroine and do her own stunts. He had to respect that—all the while being attracted as hell—even though he knew celebrity actresses like her couldn't be trusted.

They were duplicitous—they had to be for the press. *Like right now.*

Chiara seemed chummy with Melody—as if they

were friends, or at least acquaintances from way back. Melody asked a few questions about *Pegasus Pride*, and Chiara answered, while Rick threw in a few sentences at the end.

He wasn't the star attraction here, and there was no use pretending otherwise. Sure, he had a lot riding on this film—money and otherwise—but he wouldn't be why this movie succeeded, or not, at the box office. Chiara was the public face of *Pegasus Pride*.

After a few minutes, Melody changed the subject, mentioning the upcoming Ring of Hope Gala to Benefit Children's Charities, for which half of Hollywood turned out. "So give me the scoop, Chiara." Her voice dipped conspiratorially. "What will you be wearing?"

"I haven't decided yet. There are two dresses…"

"Give me the details on both!" Melody said, her face avid with anticipation.

Rick suppressed a grunt. As far as he was concerned, a dress was a dress. He didn't care what it was made out of—whether a pride of lions had to be sacrificed for the embellishment, or the designer used recycled garbage bags. His youngest sibling might be an up-and-comer in the fashion business, but it was all the same to Rick— or as his sister liked to say, *Bless your style-deaf soul.*

"There's a one-shoulder pale blue column dress from Elie Saab. The other gown is a red chiffon—"

"Oh, I love both! Don't you, Rick?"

If it wasn't for Chiara's significant look, Rick would have answered that *naked* was his first preference. Chiara had a body that invited fantasies even, or especially, if she was aiming verbal barbs at him.

He settled back. "I don't know…isn't pale blue the color for Cinderella?"

Chiara turned to him and smiled, even as her eyes shot a warning. "Wrong fairy tale."

When Melody just appeared confused, Chiara cleared her throat. "Well, keep your eyes open on the night of the gala to find out which dress I go with."

The reporter pressed Stop on her recorder. "So when am I going to see you again, Chiara? Girls' night sometime at Marmont? Paparazzi snapped Leo there just last week."

Rick raised his eyebrows. From the lack of a ring, Rick deduced Melody was divorced, widowed or had never married. "You ladies do go for the chills and thrills."

Chateau Marmont was a trendy celebrity haunt. Some booked one of the hotel rooms for privacy, and others just went to party and be seen. But he preferred his thrills a little more real than a Leonardo DiCaprio sighting.

"I'd love to, Melody," Chiara said, "but can I take a rain check? This movie is wearing me out—" she looked down demurely "—when Rick isn't."

Yup, strong acting chops.

Melody laughed. "Of course. I understand."

When Melody excused herself a moment later in order to freshen up, Rick regarded the woman who'd been driving him crazy. "So…I wear you out?"

Chiara flushed. "Don't look at me that way."

"Mmm. The image of us and a bed is sort of stuck in my mind."

Chiara shifted, and her skirt rode up her leg.

He focused on her calves. She had spectacular legs. He'd seen them encased in skintight denim on set, and in a barely there miniskirt in a photo that had circulated online. He imagined those legs wrapped around him as he lost himself inside her…

On a whim, he reached out and took her hand, and caressed the back of it with his thumb.

"What are you doing?"

Was it his imagination or did her voice sound a little uneven?

"Move closer," he murmured. "There's a photographer watching us from across the room."

Her eyes held his. "What? Where?"

"Don't look." Then he leaned in, his gaze lowering.

Chiara parted her lips on an indrawn breath.

Rick touched his mouth to hers.

When Chiara made a sound at the back of her throat, he deepened the kiss. He stroked and teased, wanting more from her, craving more and not caring where they were. When she opened for him, he fanned the flames of their passion, cupping her face with his hand as she leaned closer.

When her breast brushed his arm, he tensed and stopped himself from bringing his hand up to cup the soft mound in public. He wanted to crash through her barriers, making his head spin with the speed of it.

As if sensing someone approaching, Chiara pulled back and muttered, "We have to stop."

Rick spotted Melody walking back from across the room, a big grin on her face. Obviously the reporter had seen the kiss. Odele would be pleased. "Not if we're going to pretend to be a couple."

When the reporter drew near, she teased, "Did I say you two are fast? Now, that moment would have provided some photo op for the magazine!"

Rick settled back and forced a grin for the reporter's benefit. "We'd be happy to give a repeat performance."

"No, we wouldn't," Chiara interjected, but then she smiled for Melody's benefit. "I'll make sure you get plenty of good pictures for the cover story at the photo shoot tomorrow."

"Of course," Melody said politely, maintaining her perkiness as she sat down to gather her things.

Rick hadn't gotten an invitation to the photo shoot—which was just as well. They were boring and went on for hours. Apparently, though, even Odele had drawn the line at a cozy tableau of him and Chiara with their arms around each other.

"Do you have a cover line yet for this article, Melody?" Chiara asked, her face suddenly turning droll. "Or has Odele already suggested one?"

Rick knew from his experience with movie promotions that the cover line was the front cover text that accompanied a magazine article: *From Tears to Triumph*, *I'm Lucky to Be Alive*, or even the vague but trustworthy standby, *My Turn to Talk*.

"No," Melody said, "Odele hasn't offered anything."

"How about 'Chiara Feran—True Love at Last'?" he offered drily.

Melody brightened. "I love it. What about you, Chiara?"

Chiara looked as if she was ready to kick him out of this interview, and Rick suppressed a laugh.

Oh, yeah, this was going to be a roller coaster of a relationship. *Make-believe* relationship.

Five

Soon after she and Rick arrived at her house—a place that she used to consider her haven and sanctuary until Rick moved in—she decided to escape to the exercise room to let off steam. Every once in a while, the urge to do the right thing and work out for the sake of her career kicked in, so she changed into a sports bra and stretchy pedal pusher exercise pants.

It had been a long day, and she'd risen early only to find Rick in her kitchen. At the studio, she'd gotten prepped in her makeup chair and then shot a few scenes. Afterward, she'd still had to be *on*, public persona in place, for the interview with Melody. It hadn't helped that the whole time she'd been aware of Rick lounging beside her—his big, hard body making the sofa seem tiny and crowded.

He'd enjoyed toying with her, too, during the interview. She'd been on pins and needles the whole time, wondering whether he'd say the wrong thing and Melody would see through their charade.

Except the kiss at the end had been all too real. She'd tasted his need and his slow-burn desire underneath the playfulness, and she'd responded to it.

I have to be more careful.

And on that thought, she entered the exercise room and came to a dead halt.

Apparently Rick had had the same idea about burning off steam. And in a sleeveless cutoff tee, it was clear he was in phenomenal shape.

She'd seen her share of beautiful people in Hollywood. But Rick was…impressive. He had washboard abs, a sprinkling of hair on his chest and muscles so defined they looked as if they could have been sculpted by a Renaissance master.

She shouldn't be once-overing him. She was still annoyed with his behavior in front of Melody that afternoon.

Rick looked up and gave her a careless lopsided smile. "Enjoying the view?"

A wave of embarrassment heated her face. "Nothing I haven't seen before."

"Yeah, but I'm not airbrushed."

And there was the problem in a nutshell.

"Need an exercise buddy?"

Oh, no. They were so not going to do this together. "I don't need you to act as my workout instructor. I've been doing fine on my own."

"Yeah," he drawled, "I can tell."

She gave him a quelling look and walked toward the weight bench.

He followed her and then scanned the weights. He

lifted one of the lighter ones as if it were a feather and placed it on the bar.

She put her hands on her hips. "What do you think you're doing?"

"Helping you out, but not as much as I'd like."

"You're already doing more than I want, so let's call it a draw and say we're splitting the difference."

He quirked his lips. "Just trying to get you to release that pent-up energy and frustration."

She narrowed her eyes and then lay back on the bench as he fixed the weight on the other side. Unfortunately she hadn't anticipated how much he seemed to be looming over her from this angle.

She flexed and then grasped the barbell. Before she could do more, however, Rick adjusted her grip.

"I started with sixty pounds," he said, stepping back. "That's about right for a woman your size."

Chiara wondered how much he lifted. He'd hoisted her with amazing agility and ease during their stunts…

Then she turned her attention back to the weights, took a breath and began lifting. Once, twice… Rick faded into the background as she brought the same attention to the task as she did to acting.

"Slow and smooth," he said after a few minutes. "Slow and smooth… That's right."

Damn it. Chiara's rhythm hitched as she brought the weight back up again and then down. She refused to look at Rick. He was either a master at sexual innuendo or set on unintentionally making her lose her mind.

She gritted her teeth and lifted the weight a few more times. After what seemed like an eternity, during which she refused to show any weakness, Rick caught the barbell and placed it on the nearby rack.

Chiara concentrated on slowing her breathing, but her chest still rose and fell from the exertion.

Rick leaned over her, bracing himself with one hand on the metal leg of the weight bench. "Nice work."

They weren't touching but he was a hair's breadth away—so close that she could get lost in the gold-shot green of his eyes. Her mind wandered back to their last kiss…

He quirked his lips as if he knew what she was thinking. "Want to indulge again?"

She pretended not to understand his meaning. "No, thanks. I'm dieting. You know Hollywood actresses. We're always trying to shed a few pounds."

Rick's eyes crinkled. "Seems more like fasting to me."

Damn him. As a celebrity, it wasn't as if she could just get online, or even on an app, and hook up with someone. There was her public image to consider, as Odele never stopped reminding her, and she didn't want to be exploited for someone else's gain. As a result, she'd had far fewer romantic partners than the press liked to imagine. These days, a lot of men were intimidated by her status. But not Rick. He was just a lone stuntman, but he had enough ego for an entire football team.

Still, need hummed within her, and her skin shivered with awareness. What was it with this man? He had a talent for getting under her defenses, and together they were combustible.

"Have I been doing it right?" His eyes laughed at her.

"What?"

"The kissing."

If the response he stirred in her was any indication, then…yeah. She tingled right now—wanting him closer against her better judgment. "All wrong."

"Then we need to practice." His lips curved in a sultry smile. "For the photographers and their cameras."

She'd walked into that one. "There isn't one here right now."

"Then we'll need to make this real instead of make-believe," he muttered as he focused on her mouth. "You have the fullest, most kissable lips."

Chiara inhaled a quick little breath. It was heady being the focus of Rick's attention. He brought the same intensity to kissing as he did to his stunts.

But instead of immediately touching his mouth to hers this time, he surprised her by smoothing a hand down her side.

She shivered, and her nipples puckered, pushing against her sports bra. She itched to explore him the way he was doing to her. She raised her hand to push him away, but instead it settled on his chest, where she felt the strong, steady beat of his heart.

"That's right," he encouraged. "Touch me. Make me feel."

She parted her lips, and this time he did settle his mouth on hers. She felt a little zing, and was surrounded by his unique male scent.

His chest pressed down on the pillow of her breasts, but he didn't give her all his weight, which was still braced on his arms.

Wrapped in his intoxicating closeness, she felt him everywhere, even on the parts of her body that weren't touching his.

His hand cupped her between her thighs, where her tight spandex shorts were the only barrier between her heat and his. He stroked her with his thumb, again and again, until she tore her mouth from his and gasped with need.

She grasped his wrist, but it was too late. Her body splintered, spasming with completion and yet unfulfilled desire.

When she looked up, she was caught by his glittering gaze. She was vulnerable and exposed, more so even than when they'd been hanging from a helicopter and his embrace had been a haven.

She could tell he wanted her, but he was holding himself in check, his breathing heavy.

Sanity slowly returned. This was so wrong.

"Let me up," she said huskily.

He straightened, and then tugged on her hand to help her up.

"I don't want this," she said, standing and knowing the last thing she needed was to feel this way—especially when wrong felt…right.

"Sometimes what we think we should want is beside the point."

She wanted to argue, but for once, she didn't know what to say.

"I'm going to take a cold shower," he said with a rueful smile, and then turned.

She half expected a teasing addition—*Want to join me?*

But he said nothing further, and somehow she found his seriousness more troubling than his playfulness.

Bed & Breakfast in Brentwood. Chiara Feran and Her Stuntman Seen Moving in Together.

Chiara stalked back to her trailer along a dirt path, her scene complete. Filming had moved for today from the Novatus Studio lot to nearby Griffith Park.

The blog *Celebrity Dish* had scooped *WE Magazine* and run a relationship story about her and Rick. Melody should still be happy about her exclusive interview, but it hadn't taken long for the gossip to start making the rounds...

Chiara attributed her bad mood to lack of coffee... and a certain stuntman.

Yesterday afternoon, they'd had a near tryst on her weight bench. There was no telling what he was capable of if he stayed in her house much longer.

She'd shown up at work at six in the morning intent on avoiding Rick, and had sat in the makeup chair. It was now ten, and there was still no sign of him. After their encounter in the exercise room, she'd heard him shower and leave her house. He still hadn't returned when she'd gone to bed hours later.

Perhaps he'd met and hooked up with a woman. Not that it was her business. Even if it meant he'd gone straight from her arms to those of another... *Damn it.*

At least *Pegasus Pride* would wrap soon. They were in the last days of filming. The scenes that she'd been in with Rick acting as a body double for her costar Adrian had been thankfully few.

Head down, she turned a corner...and collided with a solid male chest.

The air rushed out of her, and then she gasped.

But before she could wonder whether her favorite fan had made a surprise appearance again, strong arms steadied her, and she looked up into Rick's green eyes.

"You."

"For two people who are roommates, we hardly ever run into each other," he said in an ironic tone.

Chiara blinked. His hands were still cupping her upper arms, the wall of his chest a mere hair's breadth away. The heat emanated from him like a palpable thing.

"It's a big house and an even larger movie location."

She sounded breathless and chalked it up to having the air nearly knocked out of her.

He was irritating but also impossible to ignore—and she'd been throwing her best acting skills at the problem.

"Miss me?" he teased drily. "I thought we were supposed to be joined at the hip these days."

How could she answer that one? After he'd left last night, she'd succumbed to a restless night's sleep. He'd left her satisfied and bereft at the same time. Sure, she'd gotten release, but they'd missed out on the ultimate joining, and hours later, her body had craved it. At least he wasn't openly chastising her for her artful dodge that morning.

He stepped closer and eased her chin up, his gaze focused on her lips. "I missed you."

"The mouth that can't stop telling you off?"

He gave her a crooked smile. "We'd be good in bed. There's too much combustible energy between us. Admit it."

"Can't you tell good acting when you see it?"

"That was no act. If that wasn't an orgasm last night, I'll stand naked under the Hollywood sign over there." With a nod of his head, he indicated the iconic landmark in the distance.

"We are acting. This is fake. We're on a movie set!"

"Yup," he drawled and glanced around, "and I don't see any cameras rolling right now. Just because we're playing to the media doesn't mean we can't have fun along the way."

She didn't do *fun*. She left that to her dice-rolling father, who'd run away from responsibility—a wife, a child, a home...

"Oh, I like it!"

Chiara turned and spotted Odele.

"Did I interrupt something? Or let me rephrase that one—I hope I was interrupting something!"

"He needs to go," Chiara retorted.

Odele looked from her to Rick and back. "What went wrong? It's only been—" she checked her watch "—two days."

"A lover's spat," Rick joked. "We can't keep our hands off each other."

Odele's eyes gleamed behind her red glasses. "You can't quit now. The press is reporting Chiara's father was tossed out of a Vegas casino."

Rick quirked a brow at Chiara.

"On top of it," Odele went on, "there's a big fundraiser tomorrow night, and I managed to secure a ticket for Chiara's date."

"And let's not forget *WE* just got the exclusive interview that *we* are an item," Rick continued drolly.

Chiara faced her nemesis. "You are impossible."

"Just acting the part."

"You're giving an Oscar-worthy performance in a B movie."

"I believe in doing my best," Rick intoned solemnly. "My mother raised me right."

She wanted to claim his *best* wasn't good enough, but the truth was he'd been…impressive so far. "This isn't working."

"You don't want me?" He adopted a wounded expression, but his eyes laughed at her.

Grr. "I'm stuck with you!"

"Then why don't you make the most of it?" His voice was smooth as massage lotion. "Who knows? We might even have fun together."

The last thing she needed was his hands on her again.

"*Fun* is not the word that comes to mind. This is crazy. Are we nuts?"

"You know the answer to that question. I hang from helicopters for a living—"

"Clearly the altitude has addled your mind."

"—and you are an actress and celebrity."

"*Fame* is a dirty word in your book?"

Rick shrugged. "I'm camera-shy. Call it middle-child syndrome. I leave the high-profile celebrity stuff to my older and younger brothers."

She frowned. "You're an agoraphobic stuntman?"

He bit back a laugh. "Not quite, but putting on the glitz isn't my thing."

"Odele just mentioned we have a big fund-raiser to attend tomorrow night," she countered. "And since you signed up for the boyfriend gig, you'll need to put on a tux."

"Trust me, you'll like me better naked."

Chiara felt her cheeks heat, and on top of that, her manager was tracking everything like a talent agent on the scent of a movie deal.

She narrowed her eyes at Rick. "Oh? Is that the usual attire for reclusive stuntmen?"

He gave a lazy smile. "If we live together much longer, you'll find out."

She hated his casual self-assurance. And what was worse, he was probably right...

Chiara gave her manager a what-have-you-gotten-me-into look, but Odele returned it with a beatific one of her own.

"I came to tell you that you're needed. Dan wants to reshoot a scene," Odele said.

Chiara wasn't normally enthusiastic about retakes, but right now she thought of it as a lucky break...

ANNA DePALO   79

* * *

Hours later, during some downtime in his schedule, Rick sat in a chair outside the gym trailer, his legs
propped on a nearby bench. He consulted his cell phone
to make sure he was caught up on work.

Often his emails were mundane matters sent by a business partner, but today, lucky him, he had something
more salacious to chew over. All courtesy of *Celebrity
Dish*—and a specific actress who'd occupied way more
of his thoughts than he cared to admit.

After his encounter with Chiara in her exercise room
yesterday afternoon, he'd done the only thing that he
could do in the face of frustration and lack of consum-
mation: he'd taken a cold shower and then sat alone at a
nearby sports bar to have dinner.

Still, now that the story had progressed in the media to
him and Chiara shacking up, Rick knew he'd better tackle
his family. In the next moment, his cell phone buzzed,
and Rick noted it was Jordan before answering the call.

"Wow, you move fast," his brother said without preamble. "One day you're denying there's anything going
on, the next you're moving in together."

"Hilarious."

"Mom asked. Has she rung you yet?"

"Nope." Camilla Serenghetti was probably vacillat-
ing between worry and being ecstatic that her middle son
might have gotten into a serious relationship—preferably
one heading toward marriage and children.

"She's concerned some temptress has worked her
wiles on you, and not just on the big screen, either. I
told her that you're not innocent and naive enough to resist a beautiful woman."

"Finger-pointing never got you anywhere, Jordan."

"Except for some scratches and bruises from you and Cole in retribution. But don't worry, I bounced back."

"Clearly," Rick responded drily.

"Mom is talking about coming to the West Coast to tape an episode of her cooking show. You know, do something different and expand the audience, and if I'm not mistaken—" his brother's voice dripped dry humor "—she wants to check up on you."

No, no and no. The last thing he needed was for his mother to add a sideshow to the ongoing drama with Chiara—though Camilla Serenghetti would no doubt easily become best buds with Odele. Two peas in a pod. Or as the Italians liked to say, *due gocce d'acqua*—like two drops of water. *In a pot of boiling pasta water.* Still, the thought gave him an idea...

"Mom can't come here."

"She's worried about the show. The station is under new management and she wants to make a good impression."

"Fine. I'll go to her."

The idea was brilliant. If he delivered Chiara Feran to his mother's show, he'd drive up ratings for a program that was only in local syndication. And it would add steam in the press to his and Chiara's supposed relationship. All while getting Chiara out of her house in LA and away from her crazy fan.

It was fantastic...clever...an idea worthy of Odele.

Rick suppressed a smile. Chiara's manager would love it.

"You're serious?" his brother asked.

"Yup." If he was going to engage in this charade, he was going to be all in.

With that in mind, he ended his call with Jordan and went looking for his favorite actress.

Things had slowed down on set because Adrian Collins didn't like some of his lines and had holed up in his trailer with a red pen. Rick would have gotten involved and gone to read the riot act to the male lead, but he didn't like to blow his cover. Not even Dan knew how much he had invested in this movie.

Besides, Adrian's antics were mild in comparison to other off-camera drama he'd witnessed on movie sets—stars kicking each other, hurling curses and insults, and throwing tantrums worthy of a two-year-old while breaking props. Yet another reason he hadn't gotten involved with mercurial actresses...until now.

As luck would have it, he soon caught up with Chiara some distance from the parked movie trailers. She was walking back alone, picking her way along a dusty path, apparently having finished filming another scene.

Maybe it was unfulfilled sexual desire, maybe it was the picture she presented, but his senses got overloaded seeing her again. Since this morning, she'd changed into business attire because her scenes called for her to have escaped from a federal office building. She was wearing a pencil skirt paired with sky-high black pumps and a white shirt open to show a bit a cleavage. The effect was sexy in an understated way.

He liked the way the light caught in her dark halo of hair—which was just the right length for him to run his fingers through in the throes of passion. His body tightened.

He wasn't one to be overcome by lust—particularly where actresses were concerned—but Chiara was just the package to press his buttons. He hadn't been kidding when he'd said she was his type. His brothers would say he was attracted to women who were a study in contrasts: dark hair against a palate of smooth skin; humor and passion; light and hidden depths... On top of it all, Chiara was blessed with a great figure, which was emphasized at the moment by a come-hither outfit made for the big screen...and male fantasies.

He, on the other hand, was in his usual stunt clothes for this movie: a ripped tee, makeup meant to resemble dirt smeared on his abs, an ammo belt across his chest and another one slug low on his hips with an unloaded gun. He felt...uncivilized.

And the setting was appropriate. They were at the bottom of a canyon, surrounded by mountain roads and not far from actual caves. Only the presence of the Hollywood sign spoiled the effect of unspoiled nature.

Still, he tried for some semblance of polite conversation when they came abreast of each other. Thanks to Jordan, he had a brilliant idea—one that should deal with multiple problems at once. "I have a favor to ask."

She looked at him warily. "Which is?"

He cleared his throat. "I'd like you to appear on my mother's cooking show."

Her jaw went slack. "What?"

He shrugged. "If you appear on her show, it'll feed the rumors that we're involved. Isn't that what you want?"

"Your mother has a cooking show?"

He nodded. "It's on local TV in Boston and a few other markets, and it films not far from my hometown of Welsdale in western Massachusetts. *Flavors of Italy with Camilla Serenghetti.*"

Chiara's lips twitched. "So you're not the Serenghetti closest to fame? I'm shocked."

"Not by a long shot," he returned sardonically. "Not only is Mom ahead of me, but my brothers and sister are, too."

Chiara looked curious. "Really?"

He nodded. "You don't watch hockey."

"Should I?"

"My kid brother plays for the New England Razors, and my older brother used to."

She seemed as if she was trying to pull up a recollection.

"Jordan and Cole Serenghetti," he supplied.

"And your sister is...?"

"The youngest, but determined not to be left behind." He cracked a grin. "She's a big feminist."

"Naturally. With three older brothers, I imagine she had to be."

"She had a badass left kick in karate, but these days she's rechanneled the anger into a fashion design business."

Chiara's eyes widened. "Ooh, I like it already it."

So did he... Why hadn't he dreamed it up before? He had an opening with Chiara that he'd been too blind to see till now. "Mia would love it if you wore one of her creations."

"I thought I was helping your mother."

"Both." He toasted his brilliance. "You can wear Mia's designs on the cooking show."

Chiara threw up her hands. "You've thought of everything!"

Rick narrowed his eyes. "Not everything. I still need to figure out what to do about your overenthusiastic fan and your Vegas-loving father. Give me time."

Number three on his list was getting her into bed, but he wasn't going to mention that. He didn't examine his motives closely, except he was nursing one sad case of sexual frustration since their truncated tryst on her weight bench late yesterday. He tucked his fingers into his pockets to resist the urge to touch her...

He cleared his throat. "It would mean a lot to her if you made an appearance as a guest. The show is doing well. The name recently changed from *Flavors of Italy* to *Flavors of Italy with Camilla Serenghetti*. But the station is under new management, and Mom wants to make a good impression."

"Of course," Chiara deadpanned. "It's a slow climb up the ladder of fame. I can relate."

"Mom's is more of a short stepladder."

"What happens when your mother and I land on the cover of *WE Magazine* together?" Chiara quipped. "Will you be able to deal with being caught between two famous women?"

"I'll cross that bridge when I come to it," Rick replied drolly. "And knowing Mom, she'll want to be on the magazine with the both of us, like a hovering fairy godmother."

"She sounds like a character."

"You don't know the half of it."

"This is serious," she remarked drily. "You're bringing me home to meet Mama."

"In a sense," he said noncommittally—because what he wanted to do was bring her home to bed. "She'd be even more impressed if you'd starred in an Italian telenovela."

"A soap opera?" Chiara responded. "Actually I was a guest on a couple of episodes of *Sotto Il Sole*."

Rick's eyebrows rose.

"It was before I became known in the States," she added. "My character wound up in a coma and was taken off life support."

"They didn't like your acting?"

"No, they just needed more melodrama. My character was an American so it didn't matter if I spoke Italian well."

"Still, my mother will eat it up." He flashed a grin. "No pun intended."

In fact, Rick suspected his mother would love everything about Chiara Feran. Their relationship "breakup," which inevitably loomed on the horizon, would disappoint his mother more than a recipe that didn't work out. He'd have to fake bodily injury and blame the rupture with Chiara on the distance created by their two careers...

"What about filming?" Chiara asked with a frown.

"We're in the last few days. Then Dan will move to editing. I can arrange with Odele for us to fly to Boston once you're done with your scenes. Mom's taping can wait till then." He didn't add he still had to broach the subject with his mother, but she'd no doubt be thrilled to move heaven and earth with her producers in order to fit a star of Chiara's caliber into the schedule.

"Where will we stay?" Chiara pressed.

Rick could tell she was debating her options, but the wavering was a good sign. He shrugged, deciding to seem nonchalant in order to soothe any doubts she had.

"I've got an apartment in Welsdale."

"Oh?"

"It has a guest bedroom." Still, he hoped to entice her into making their relationship in the bedroom more real—purely for the sake of their romantic believability in front of the press, of course.

"Naturally."

"Don't worry, though," he said, making his tone gently mocking. "There'll be enough luxuries for an A-list celeb."

Chiara narrowed her eyes. "You think I can't rough it?"

He let his silence speak for him.

"As a matter of fact, I was born and raised in Rhode Island. I'm used to New England winters."

"Of course, Miss Rhode Island should visit her old stomping grounds."

"I was an undergraduate at Brown."

"Rubbing shoulders with other celebrity kids?"

"Financial aid. Where did you get your stunt degree?"

He quirked his lips. "Boston College. It's a family tradition."

"Now you've surprised me. I expected the school of hard knocks… So, what have you told your family about us?"

He shrugged. "They read *WE Magazine*." He flashed a smile. "They know I have the goods."

Chiara rolled her eyes. "In other words, they think we really are an item?"

"My ego wouldn't have it any other way."

"I'm not surprised."

Rick heard a noise, and then felt a telltale little jolt, followed by a gentle rocking.

Chiara's eyes widened.

"Did you feel that?"

She nodded.

Earthquakes were common in Southern California, but only a few were strong enough to be felt. "We may have sensed it because we're at the bottom of a canyon." Rick looked around, and then back at her with a wry smile. "I'm surprised you didn't fling yourself into my arms."

"We actresses are made of sterner stuff," she said, tossing his words from days ago back at him.

He stifled a laugh. "We made the ground move."

"It was a truck rumbling by!"

"My motorcycle sounds like an earthquake, but an earthquake is just…a truck rumbling by?" he teased.

"Well, it's not us making the ground move, much as you have faith in your superpowers!"

Rick laughed and then glanced around again. "This earthquake didn't seem like a strong one, but you might want to rethink your position on my rocking your world."

"Your ego wouldn't have it any other way?" she asked archly.

"Exactly. Good follow-up, you're learning." He glanced down at her impractical footwear. "Need a hand…or a lift?"

She raised her chin. "No, thanks."

He doubted she'd thank him if he said she looked adorable. "You know, if you left one of those shoes behind…"

"A frog would find it?"

"Some of us are princes in disguise—isn't that how the story goes?"

"Well, this princess is saving herself," she said as she walked past him, head held high, "and not kissing any more frogs!"

Six

The Armani suit was fine, but Rick drew the line at a manicure. He did his own nails, thanks.

In his opinion, premieres and award ceremonies were an evil to be endured, which was another reason he liked his low-profile, low-key existence. Tonight at least was for a good cause—the Ring of Hope Gala to Benefit Children's Charities.

The fund-raiser also explained why Chiara's spacious den was a hub of activity on a Saturday afternoon. The room was usually a quiet oasis, with long windows, beige upholstery and dark wood furniture. Not now, however.

Chiara sat in the makeup chair. Someone was doing her hair, and another person was applying polish to her nails, and all the while Chiara was chatting with Odele. A fashion designer's intern had dropped off two gowns earlier, and at some point, Chiara would slip into one of them, assisted by plenty of double-sided tape and other tricks of the Hollywood magic trade.

Rick figured this amounted to multitasking. Something women were renowned for, and men like him apparently were terrible at—when the reality was probably that men just preferred to do their own nails.

Suddenly Odele frowned at Chiara. "Have you gone through your normal skincare regimen?"

"Yes."

Rick almost laughed. For him, a regimen meant a grueling workout at the gym to get ready for stunts on his next film. It didn't apply to fluffy skincare pampering.

Odele rolled her eyes. "I imagine you raided the kitchen cabinets for sugar and coconut oil, and threw in some yogurt for one of your crazy DIY beauty treatments."

From her chair, Chiara arched her eyebrows, which had been newly plucked. "Of course."

Rick studied those finely arched brows. He hadn't known there was such a thing as threading, and especially not applied to eyebrows. He was a Martian on planet Venus here. Still, he could understand that for an actress like Chiara, whose face was part of her trade, the right look was everything. Subtle changes or enhancements could impact her ability to express emotional nuances.

His gaze moved to Chiara's mouth. Their interlude in the exercise room still weighed on him. She'd been so damn responsive. If she hadn't put a stop to things, he would have taken her right there on the weight bench. In fact, it had been all he could do to keep a cool head the past few days. If it hadn't been for work on the movie set and coming back exhausted after a fourteen-hour day...

Odele sighed. "You're the bane of my existence,

Chiara. You could be the face of a cosmetics and skin-care line. You're throwing away millions."

"My homemade concoctions work fine," Chiara responded.

"You make your own products?" Rick asked bemusedly.

Chiara shrugged. "I started when I was a teenager and didn't have a dime to my name, and I saw no reason to give it up. I use natural items like avocado."

"Me, too," Rick joked. "But I eat them as part of my strength-training routine."

Chiara peered at him. "I could test the green stuff on your face. You might benefit."

Rick made a mock gesture warding her off. "No, thanks. I'm best friends with my soap."

"Not everyone is blessed with your creamy complexion, Chiara," Odele put in. "Have a little sympathy for the rest of us who could use expensive professional help."

The hairstylist and manicurist stepped away, and Chiara stood, still wrapped in her white terry robe. "Well, time to get dressed."

Rick smiled. "Don't let me stop you."

Odele steamed toward him like a little tugboat pulling Chiara's ship to safe harbor. "We'll call you when we need you."

He shrugged. "More or less explains my role."

Without waiting for further encouragement, he stepped out of the room. For the next half hour, he made somewhat good use of his time by checking his cell phone and catching up on business. Finally, Odele opened the door and motioned him into the den again.

Rick stepped back into the room...and froze, swallowing hard.

Chiara was wearing a one-shoulder gown with a short

train. The slit went all the way up one thigh, and the deep red fabric complemented her complexion. She had the ethereal quality of, well, a fairy-tale princess naturally.

"I can't decide which gown," she said.

"The one you're wearing looks good to me."

He knew what the big minefields were, of course. *Do I look fat in this dress?* The automatic answer was *no*. Maybe even *hell, no*. Still, he was ill-equipped for the bombshell that was Chiara Feran—sex poured into a gown.

"You look spectacular," he managed.

She beamed. "I'm wearing a Brazilian designer. I have a platform, and I want to use it."

He knew what *he* wanted.

He'd like nothing better than to swing Chiara into his arms and head for the bedroom. He wasn't particular about *where* frankly, but he didn't want to scandalize her entourage. And if Odele was tipped off, she would be on the phone with Melody Banyon of *WE Magazine* in no time to report his and Chiara's relationship had become serious—never mind that it was make-believe.

Still, the evening was young, and Chiara's manager wouldn't be here at its close...

Flashbulbs went off around them in dizzying bursts of light. The paparazzi were out in full force for this red-carpet event. Chiara gave her practiced smile, crossed one leg in front of the other and tilted her head, giving the photographers her best side.

Her one-shoulder silk organza gown had a deep slit revealing her leg to the upper thigh. It was a beautiful but safe choice for an awards show. Invisible tape ensured everything stayed in place and she didn't have a wardrobe malfunction. Her hair was loose, and her jewelry was limited to chandelier earrings and a diamond bracelet.

The Ring of Hope Gala to Benefit Children's Charities was being held at The Beverly Hilton Hotel. The hotel's sixteen-thousand-foot International Ballroom could seat hundreds—and did for the Golden Globe Awards and other big Hollywood events. Soon she and Rick would be inside, along with dozens of other actors and celebrities.

Rick's hand was at the small of her back—a warm, possessive imprint. It was for the benefit of the cameras, of course, but the reason didn't matter. He made her aware of her femininity. She'd never been so attuned to a man before.

Despite the presence of plenty of well-known actors tonight, Chiara saw women casting Rick lingering looks full of curiosity and interest. He had a blatant sex appeal that was all unpolished male...

Chiara put a break on her wayward thoughts—aware there were dozens of eyes upon them. Not only were bulbs constantly flashing, but the press kept calling out to them.

"Chiara, look this way!"

"Who's the new guy, Chiara?"

"Can you tell us about your gown?"

"Who's the mystery man?"

Chiara curved her lips and called back, "We met on the set of *Pegasus Pride*."

"Is it true he's a stuntman?"

She cast Rick a sidelong look, and he returned it with a lingering one of his own. She could almost believe he was enraptured for real...

"I don't know," she murmured, searching Rick's face. "Do you know some stunts, honey?"

"Not for the red carpet," he said, smiling back. "Maybe I should practice."

Ha. In her opinion, he was doing just fine with his *publicity stunt* for the red carpet. He was *too* believable in the role of boyfriend.

She knew what the headlines would say, of course. *Chiara Feran Makes Debut with New Man.* She and Rick had given their interview to *WE Magazine*, but every media outlet wanted their own story.

Chiara smiled for another few moments. Then she linked hands with Rick and moved out of the spotlight so the next prey—uh, *celebrity*—could take her place. She knew how these things worked.

She and Rick walked into the Hilton, where sanity prevailed in contrast to the paparazzi and fans outside. They followed the crowd toward the International Ballroom. Fortunately she didn't cross paths with anyone she knew well. She wasn't sure if she was up for further discussion of her ultimate accessory—namely, Rick.

When they reached their table, she sighed with relief. *So far, so good.*

"Rick, sugar!"

Chiara turned and spotted an actress she wasn't well-acquainted with but whose name she'd come across more than a few times. *Isabel Lanier.*

She'd never heard Rick's name said in the same breath as *sugar* before. In her opinion, *spice* was more appropriate.

"Wow, I haven't seen you in ages!" Isabel said—and though she addressed Rick, she directed her crystalline blue gaze to Chiara. "And you're one half of an item, too, I hear."

"Isabel, this is—"

"Chiara Feran," Chiara finished for him.

She assessed the other woman. Isabel Lanier had a reputation in Hollywood, and there wasn't enough Botox in LA to make it pretty. She'd slept with directors to land supporting roles. She'd broken up a costar's marriage by having an affair with him during filming. And she'd been named in a lawsuit involving back rent on a house in the Hollywood Hills.

Isabel looked her over in turn, and then, directing her gaze to Rick, murmured, "I'm so glad you've moved on, sugar, and to another actress, too. No bad feelings, hmm?"

Rick seemed to tense, but then Chiara wondered whether she was imagining it.

Isabel fluttered her mascara-heavy eyelashes. "I'd love to talk to you about—"

"Isabel, it was a surprise running into you. Glad you're well."

The dismissal on Rick's part was polite but unmistakable.

Chiara wondered about his past tie to Isabel. It gave her a bad feeling—though, of course, not jealousy. What had Rick been thinking? Isabel? *Really?* The woman's reputation followed her like a trail of discarded clothing in a tacky Vegas hotel room.

Isabel gave them a searching look, and then nodded as if reaching a conclusion. "It's time I got back to my date."

"Hal?" Rick inquired sardonically.

Isabel tossed her head, her smile too bright. "Oh, sugar, you know better." She flashed her hand and a ring caught the light. "But this time, I did find one who is for keeps."

"Congratulations."

The smile stayed on Isabel's lips but her eyes were sharp. "Thank you."

When the other woman moved off, Chiara turned to Rick. "Should I ask?"

"Will you be able to stop yourself?"

"Do you date all your leading ladies?"

"In Isabel's case, it was more her trying to hook up with me. Misguidedly, as it turned out."

Chiara raised her eyebrows.

"Isabel is the reason that I don't get involved with starlets. They're trouble."

"Men are trouble."

"Finally, a topic that we agree on," he quipped. "The opposite sex is trouble."

Chiara shrugged. "Isabel Lanier seems an odd choice for you."

Chiara definitely wasn't jealous. The irony wasn't lost on her, though. Usually her dates were the ones having to contend with overeager male admirers. Now the shoe was on the other foot—sort of.

"Possessive?" Rick asked, lips quirking, as if he'd read her mind.

"Don't be silly," Chiara retorted.

"It's not like you to get territorial, but I like it."

"So what is the connection between you and Isabel Lanier?" she tried again.

Rick regarded her for a moment. "Isabel made a play for me in front of some photographers. Unfortunately her boyfriend at the time was also a good friend of mine. End of friendship."

"Why would she do that?"

Rick gave her a penetrating look. "Fame, public image, to make Hal jealous. You know, all the likely ulterior motives."

She didn't want to dwell on their own ulterior motives right now.

"Shall we sit down?" Rick asked.

She felt compelled to go on. "If you were more high profile, the organizers here would have made sure your path didn't cross Isabel's, and that you were seated on opposite sides of the ballroom."

"Fortunately I'm not. High profile, that is."

"But I am." Chiara made a mental note to put the word out that she and Isabel should be kept apart—at least until her "relationship" with Rick came to an end.

Rick pulled out a chair for her, and she sat down. As Rick turned to acknowledge a waiter, Isabel fished the cell phone out of her clutch and typed a quick text to Odele. No time like the present to make sure a viper stayed in her tank, she thought, her mind traveling back to Isabel.

After that, the evening passed quickly and painlessly. The master of ceremonies was a well-known comedian, and he drew regular laughs from the crowd, who dined on butterfly salmon pâté with caviar and peppered chateaubriand with port wine glacé.

Before long, Chiara found herself heading home with Rick. She'd never had a live-in significant other, and in the past, it had been easy enough to say goodbye at the end of a date. Not this time, however. *Awkward.*

When they entered the hushed silence of her foyer, she faced Rick. She reminded herself that she held the cards here. She was the celebrity. This was *her* house. And he, for all intents and purposes, was *her* employee, thanks to Odele.

Still, it was of little help when faced with Rick's overwhelming masculinity.

He was tall and broad, and all evening she'd been ignoring how he filled out his tux. Should she be surprised he even owned one?

Rick quirked his lips. "I guess this is the part where I kiss you good-night—" he glanced past her to the stairs "—except I'm staying here." His gaze came back to hers, and he looked at her with a slow deliberateness.

All of a sudden, she was searching for air. They hadn't been this close since their encounter in the exercise room, and she'd vowed it was an experience that would never, ever be repeated.

But the memory of how easily he'd aroused her—her body tightening and then finding blessed release—played havoc with her senses and scruples right now.

He bent his head, and said in a low voice, "It would aid in believability."

There was no need for him to elaborate. If he kissed her…if he excited her…if they became lovers…

Yes…no. She mentally shook her head.

He looked down at her gown, and she felt his gaze everywhere—on her breasts, her hips and lower…

"Do you need help with that dress?" he muttered, his eyes half-lidded. "There's no Odele here, no designer's assistant or fashion stylist."

Didn't she know it. They were alone, and the quiet of the night and the empty house surrounded them. The only illumination was the dim light that she'd left on in the foyer.

Chiara cleared her throat. "You did well tonight for an agoraphobic stuntman."

"Isn't this the time in the movie for a love scene?" he teased.

She tried gamely for her typical maneuver. She did *outrage* really well. "This isn't a movie and we're not—"

"Actors," he finished for her. "I know."

He took her hand and drew her near. Another smile

teased his lips. "That's what's going to make this so great. No pretending."

She swallowed. "I don't know how not to pretend."

The brutal honesty escaped her before she could help herself.

"Just feel. Go with your instincts."

"Like method acting?"

"Like real life." He settled his hands and massaged her shoulders. "Relax. We stuntmen are not so bad."

"Are you the baddest of the bunch?" she asked, her voice husky.

His smile widened. "Want to find out if I'm the Big Bad Wolf?"

"Sorry, wrong fairy tale again."

She could feel the heat and energy coming off him even though only his hands touched her. She was attuned to *everything* about him. As an actress, she was trained to observe the slightest facial sign, the subtlest inflection of voice, the intention behind a touch. But with Rick, she quivered with sensation approaching a sixth sense.

Slowly he raised her chin, and her gaze met his.

They'd been working up to this moment ever since the exercise room, and she saw in his eyes that he knew it, too.

He searched her face and then, focusing on her mouth, he brushed her lips with his.

She parted for him on an indrawn sigh, touched her tongue to his and twined her arms around his neck. She needed this, too, she admitted, and for tonight at least she couldn't think of a reason to deny herself.

He settled his hands on her waist, and she felt the press of his arousal. He deepened the kiss, and she met him, not holding back. Her evening clutch slipped from her limp hand and hit the ground with a small *thump.*

He broke the kiss, only to trail his mouth, whisper-soft, across her jaw and to her temple.

"Rick…"

"Chiara."

"I…"

"This isn't the time to start one of your arguments."

"About what?"

"About anything."

He nuzzled the side of her neck, and she angled her head to afford him better access. She fastened her hands on his biceps in order to anchor herself, and the hard muscle under her fingers reminded her that he was built… and right now primed to mate with her.

Chiara felt that last realization to her core, even as Rick's lips sent delicious shivers down her spine.

One of his hands shifted lower and settled on her exposed thigh. She felt the caress of his slightly callused fingers.

He kissed the shell of her ear, and then whispered, "Your dress has been giving me a thrill all evening."

"Oh?" she managed.

"The slit is so high…playing peekaboo all the way up…making me wonder whether this time I'll get a glimpse…"

She gave a throaty laugh. "I'm not commando. I don't take those kinds of risks."

His hand moved lower, slid under the slit and covered her. "Oh, yeah? But I want you to go on all kinds of adventures with me. Let me show you, baby…"

Chiara's eyes closed and her head fell back as Rick's finger slipped inside her and the pad of his thumb brushed her in a wicked dance. Her lips parted. *Oh, my.* They hadn't even made it past the inside of her front door and all she wanted to do was strip for him and let him take her against the hard wall of the foyer, pounding into her until she wept with the pure ecstasy of it, her legs wrapped around him and holding him close.

"Ah, Chiara." His voice sounded rough with arousal as he nipped and nibbled along her jaw. "So hot. There's nothing cold about you."

His words wrapped around her like a warm caress. She'd worked all her life to get her walls up and, most of all, be independent and succeed. But with Rick, her defenses came crashing down, and in their place rushed in powerful need.

Rick snaked his free hand beneath the one-shoulder bodice of her gown and cupped her breast. He kneaded her soft flesh and she peaked for him.

A moan escaped her.

"I should have stuck around earlier tonight so I'd know how you got into this gown, and how to get you out," he muttered.

A laugh caught in her throat, but then the buzz of a cell phone interrupted the mood like the beam of car headlights slicing through the night.

It took a few moments for Chiara to clear her head and get oriented. And then she flushed. She and Rick had gone from zero to sixty in minutes, and any longer…

As her phone continued to buzz from the inside of her clutch on the floor, she pulled away from Rick, and he dropped his hands and stepped back.

"You don't have to answer it," he said roughly.

"It's Odele. I can tell from the ringtone." She started to bend down, but Rick was faster and retrieved the clutch for her.

"You don't have to answer it," Rick commented, his voice edged with frustration.

Flustered and still aroused, Chiara gathered her scattered thoughts. "She's used to having her calls answered. I—I've got to take this. I've…got to go."

"Of course." His expression was sardonic, knowing, and he raked his hand through his hair. "I'm guessing it's time for another cold shower."

Turning away from Rick to regain her composure, she hit the answer button. "Odele, hello?"

"Hello, sweetie. How are you? Did you have a fine evening?"

"Yes, of course," she answered as she hurried up the stairs. "What can I do for you, Odele?"

"I'm responding to your request, hon."

For a moment, Chiara was confused, but then she remembered her text to Odele earlier in the evening.

"From what I could see on TV, you and Mr. Stuntman were doing an excellent job at your first public appearance together. But then I got your message about keeping you and Isabel Lanier separated at future social events. Did something happen that I'm not aware of?"

Chiara didn't know whether to be relieved or frustrated. If not for Odele's untimely—or rather, timely—call, she'd have been moments away from inviting Rick to follow her to the bedroom. A mistake that she would have regretted.

"Not that I don't have sympathy," Odele went on in her trademark raspy voice. "Isabel Lanier reeks of tacky perfume, and her manager is worse."

Chiara smiled weakly. Leave it to Odele to be competitive with even Isabel's snarky manager.

"So, honey, are you going to tell me what the story is, or make me guess? I have my sources, you know."

Chiara lowered her voice even as she reached the privacy of her bedroom and flipped on the light. "Rick and Isabel were involved at one point."

"Really?" The word was a long, drawn-out drawl.

"Well, not really." Chiara dropped her clutch on the vanity table. "She sort of threw herself at him in a publicity stunt and that was the end of his friendship with her then boyfriend."

"Damn it, I knew her manager was cunning."

"It takes one to know one, Odele."

"Okay, all right," her manager responded grumpily. "Now that I've got the details, I'll put the word out about Isabel and file away the information for any future events that I book you for."

"You're a doll, Odele."

"Oh, stop," her manager rasped. "I'm a barracuda in a town infested with sharks."

When she ended the call with Odele, Chiara sighed. The conversation had let sanity back in. She couldn't get involved with Rick. Sweet heaven, she didn't even like him. She *couldn't* like him.

Too bad she was having an increasingly hard time remembering why.

Seven

Welsdale was a quaint New England town with brick buildings dotting the main streets and colorful homes lining the back roads.

Chiara could hardly believe she was here except that Odele had, of course, loved Rick's idea for an appearance on his mother's cooking show. Before Chiara had caught her breath, she and Rick had been on an early flight from Los Angeles to Boston.

She supposed it was just as well. Ever since the Ring of Hope Gala last weekend, she'd done her best to keep Rick at arm's length. Only a long couple of days on set had saved her. She'd collapsed into bed, exhausted, late at night.

From the airport, where Rick had a car in long-term parking, they drove to Welsdale and then, after no more than twenty minutes on oak-lined roads, to a stunning home on the outskirts of town. Rick had mentioned that his parents were hosting a small party at their house.

The elder Serenghettis lived in a Mediterranean-style mansion with a red-tile roof and white walls. Set amidst beautiful landscaping, the house greeted visitors with a stone fountain at the center of a circular drive.

Chiara didn't know what she had expected, except perhaps a humbler abode. Clearly she'd been wrong in her assumptions. Rick came from an established family and a comfortable background, unlike her.

When they stepped inside, Rick stretched out his arms and joked, "Welcome to the Serenghetti family reunion."

Chiara blinked. "They're all here?"

"We like to support Mom."

Oh, sweet heaven. She wasn't prepared for this. The gathering was larger than she'd expected, and it seemed that assorted Serenghettis were sprinkled among the crowd.

There'd be no Feran family reunion, of course. Or if there were, it would be at a Las Vegas gaming table, where she'd be settling her father's debts.

People were standing around chatting in the family room and adjacent living room, and she noticed in particular how two of the men were as attractive as Rick. It appeared the Serenghetti men came in one variety only: drop-dead gorgeous.

"Come on," Rick said, cupping her elbow. "I'll introduce you."

As they approached, one of the two men glanced at them and then came forward. "Ah, the prodigal son returning to the fold..."

"Stuff it, Jordan." Rick's tone was good-natured—as if he was used to being ribbed.

Jordan appeared unabashed and gave Chiara an openly curious look. "Well, this time you've outdone yourself. Mom will be pleased. But how you managed to convince a beautiful actress that you've got the goods, I'll never know." He held out his hand. "Hi, I'm Jordan Serenghetti, Rick's better-looking brother."

"Which one of us was a body double for *People*'s Sexiest Man Alive?" Rick retorted mildly.

"Which one is featured in an underwear ad on a billboard in Times Square?" Jordan returned.

"Nice to meet you," Chiara jumped in with a light laugh. "I've been putting up with his humor—" she indicated Rick "—for days. Now I see it's a family trait."

"Yes, but I'm younger than Rick and our older brother, Cole, so I like to say our parents achieved perfection only the third time around."

When Rick raised his eyebrows, Chiara laughed again. It was good to see Rick getting back some of his own.

Rick's gaze went to the arched entrance to the family room, and Chiara spotted an attractive woman with honey-blond hair caught in a ponytail, a nice figure showcased in tights and a short-sleeved athletic shirt. Unlike many women in Hollywood, she seemed unaware of her beauty, sporting a fresh-faced natural look with little makeup.

"Your nemesis is here," Rick murmured.

Jordan followed his brother's gaze. "Heaven help us."

At Chiara's inquiring look, Rick elaborated. "Serafina is related to us by marriage. She's Cole's wife's cousin. She also happens to be the one woman under the sun Jordan can't charm."

Jordan wore an unguarded look that said he was attracted like a bee to nectar—and befuddled by the feeling. Chiara hid a smile. She suspected that like her, Jordan lived in a world with plenty of artifice—big-time sports likely resembled Hollywood that way—and Serafina was a breath of fresh air.

Serafina was something different, and Jordan appeared at a loss as to how to deal with her. Relative? Friend? Lover? Maybe he couldn't make up his mind—and it wasn't only his choice to make, either.

"Excuse me," Jordan announced. "Fun just walked in."

"Jordan," Rick said warningly.

"What?" his brother responded as he stepped away.

"Just make sure that while you're getting a rise out of our newest in-law, you don't come in for a pounding yourself."

Jordan flashed a quick grin. "I'm counting on it."

Chiara watched Serafina's eyes narrow as she noticed Jordan step toward her. It seemed as if Jordan wasn't the only one who was aware of someone else's every move...

Then Chiara quashed a sudden self-deprecatory grimace. She couldn't judge Serafina. She herself was attuned to Rick's every gesture.

At that moment, the other attractive man Chiara had spotted earlier approached.

"Hi, I'm Cole Serenghetti," he said, holding out his hand.

"Chiara Feran," she responded, shaking hands.

She could tell on a moment's acquaintance that Cole was the serious brother.

Unlike Jordan and Rick, Cole's eyes were more hazel than green. Still, the family resemblance was strong. But Chiara noticed that Cole sported a scar on his cheek.

A beautiful woman walked up to them, and Cole put his arm around her. She had the most translucent brown eyes that Chiara had ever seen, and masses of brown hair that fell in waves and curls past her shoulders.

"This is my wife, Marisa," Cole said, looking affectionately at the woman beside him. "Sweet pea, I'm sure you've heard of Chiara Feran."

"I loved your movie *Three Nights in Paris*," Marisa gushed, "and I follow you online."

Chiara smiled. "It's good to meet you. So you like romantic comedies?"

"I adore them." Marisa threw a teasing look at her husband. "Though it's hard to get Cole here to watch them with me."

"Ouch." Cole adopted a mock-wounded expression. "Hey, I'm just showing family loyalty to Rick for his adventure flicks."

"A great excuse," Marisa parried before turning back to Chiara. "You aren't filming a romantic comedy now, are you?"

Chiara sighed. "Unfortunately no." Unless she counted the banter that she had going on with Rick offscreen. "Blame Hollywood. Action movies bring in the big bucks at the box office."

Marisa made a sympathetic sound.

"You're a woman after my own heart," Chiara said.

"I've had my tenth grade students watch you in the film adaptation of *Another Song at Dawn*," Marisa added enthusiastically. "I've taught here in Welsdale."

Chiara warmed to the other woman. "I'm so glad. That's the nicest compliment—"

"Anyone's ever paid you?" Rick finished for her.

Cole cast Rick a droll look. "Quite the romantic boyfriend, aren't you?"

Chiara flushed. "I meant the best professional praise."

Cole and his wife just laughed.

"Cole's gotten better with sharing warm thoughts since we've gotten married," Marisa added, throwing a playful look at her husband, "but I'm still not finding little heart drawings in my lunchbox."

Chiara envied Cole and Marisa's obvious connection.

In contrast, she and Rick pushed each other's buttons. Then she reminded herself there was no *her and Rick*. They had a fake relationship for the benefit of the press.

When Cole and Marisa excused themselves, another woman approached, and Chiara again saw a resemblance to Rick.

"Chiara, this is my younger sister, Mia," Rick said.

Mia was slender and lovely, with arresting almond-shaped green eyes. She could have qualified as a model or actress herself.

"I wish I could say Rick has told me a lot about you," Mia quipped, "but I'd be lying."

"Family," Rick muttered. "Who needs enemies?"

Mia tossed her brother a droll look that made Chiara smile.

"Rick mentioned you're a designer," Chiara said.

"He did?"

"I'd love to see some of your creations."

"I'm based in New York."

"Do you have something that Chiara could toss on for an appearance on Mom's cooking show?" Rick prompted.

When Mia rolled her eyes, Chiara held back a grin.

"Leave it to my brother to give me the professional opportunity of a lifetime, and no fair warning."

"Hey," Rick said, holding up his hands, "I did tell you to bring a trunk of stuff to show a friend of mine."

"Yeah, but you didn't say who!"

"Don't you read any of the celebrity glossies or supermarket tabloids?" Rick countered. "I'm dating one of the hottest actresses around."

Chiara felt a wave of heat at the word *hottest*.

"How am I supposed to know what's true and what isn't?" Mia responded. "It's a good thing I know my way around a needle and thread for a little nip and tuck if necessary."

"I'm not that thin," Chiara chimed in.

"Yeah, she has the appetite of a lumberjack," Rick agreed jokingly. "I should know. I've carried her out of exploding buildings and onto a helicopter with one hand."

"Hilarious, Rick," Mia said. "Next you'll be telling us that you have real superpowers."

Rick arched an eyebrow. "Ask Chiara."

Chiara flushed again. The last thing she wanted to do was discuss Rick's prowess—sexual or otherwise— with his siblings.

When Chiara didn't immediately reply, Mia laughed. "I guess you got your answer, Rick."

An older woman came bustling over, clapping her hands. "*Cari, scusatemi.* I'm sorry, I was speaking on the phone with my producers."

Rick's face lightened. "Don't worry, Mom. We're all good here. Just introducing Chiara to everybody."

Rick's mother clasped her hands together. "I'm Camilla. *Benvenuti.*"

"Thank you for the welcome, Mrs. Serenghetti," Chiara said.

"Camilla, please. You are doing me a huge *favore.*"

"She mixes Italian and English like they're flour and water," Rick said in a low voice. "Interrupt at your own risk."

"Now, Chiara—what a lovely name! You are Italian and Brazilian, no?"

She nodded her head.

"You are a celebrity, yes? And beautiful, too, no?"

"Um…"

"*Basta, così.*" Camilla nodded her head approvingly.

"It is enough. You are doing me a huge *favore*. Anything else will be extra filling in the cannoli, no?"

"Mrs. Serenghetti—"

"Camilla, please. Do you want me to demonstrate a recipe to you on the show, or—" Camilla brightened hopefully "—you have one to share?"

"Actually I do." Chiara had been thinking about the show on the plane ride. She didn't want to disappoint. It had nothing to do with Rick, but rather her own high standards and integrity, she told herself. "I used to visit relatives in Brazil when I was growing up. Italian food is very popular there."

Camilla beamed.

"Brazilian barbecue—" Chiara began.

"Churrascaria, sì."

"—is well-known, but we also have *galeteria*. It's chicken and usually an all-you-can-eat pasta and salad. So I would like to make a pasta dish that sounds Italian, but was really popularized by the Italian immigrant community in Brazil. *Cappelletti alla romanesca.*"

"Perfetto." Camilla nodded approvingly.

Mia linked arms with her mother. "Excuse us while I get Mom's opinion on how to finish the tagliatelle salad."

When his female relatives had departed, Rick turned to Chiara with a bemused expression. "I'm impressed. Have you actually made this dish before?"

"Please." Chiara gave him a long-suffering look. "Do I look Brazilian and Italian to you?"

"Yes, but—"

"Trust me." The words were out of her mouth before she could stop them.

"Isn't that my line?" he mocked.

She felt the heat rise in her cheeks and turned away. "Rick!"

Chiara spotted an older version of Rick coming toward them.

"Brace yourself," Rick murmured. "You have yet to meet the most colorful member of the family. Serg Serenghetti."

Oh, dear.

"So the prodigal son has returned."

"Wrong script, Dad," Rick quipped. "This is *The Son Also Rises.*"

Serg Serenghetti fastened his eyes on Chiara. "What do you see in this guy?"

Chiara gave a weak smile.

"How do you know about us?" Rick retorted, addressing his father.

"I read *WE Magazine*," Serg grumbled. "Same as everyone else. Your mother leaves copies lying around." Serg lowered his brows. "And with my recovery, I have plenty of time to surf the internet for news about my wayward children."

Rick looked at Chiara and jerked a finger in his father's direction. "Do you believe he knows about surfing? He's keeping up with those teenagers that make action flicks such blockbusters at the box office."

As Rick poked fun at his father, his tone was laced with affection.

Serg grumbled again. "I've known a lot about a lot for a lot longer than you've been around, but all I get is guff from the young pups."

Rick pulled out a chair, and Serg sank into it.

"He's still recovering from a stroke," Rick murmured for her benefit.

Oh. Chiara felt a tug at her heartstrings. Beneath the bluster, the affection between father and son sounded loud and clear. In contrast, her relationship with her father was a distant echo.

Chiara realized that with the Serenghettis, she was in for something new and different from her own experience. And as she settled into a conversation with Serg, she realized that might not be such a bad thing—except for the fact that meeting his family made Rick even more likable and attractive, and she was already in danger of succumbing to him…

Rick couldn't believe his eyes, but then he should have known Chiara would be a natural in front of the cameras—even on Camilla Serenghetti's cooking show.

He was also tense. He wanted this episode to boost ratings for his mother, but he had little idea about Chiara's cooking skills, let alone how they'd play out on television. And he also wanted Chiara and his mother to get along.

So far so good.

"The reason I'm not wearing an apron," Chiara said brightly into the camera, "is because this outfit is too scrumptious to cover up." She gestured at her V-neck berry-colored top with clever draping, the cream trousers underneath barely visible above the kitchen counter. "It's courtesy of Camilla's daughter, Mia Serenghetti, whose clothes are mouth-watering."

Camilla laughed, and because she sat next to him in the audience, Rick could tell his sister looked amused.

"I guess Camilla is not the only talented one in the family."

"*Grazie tanto*, Chiara *bellissima*," his mother said.

"*Prego.*" Chiara acknowledged the thanks and then dumped prosciutto in a blender before smiling at the studio audience. "I sometimes prefer an electronic device to hand-chopping. Goes faster, too."

As she scanned the buttons on the blender, Rick realized something was wrong and started to rise from his front-row seat.

Chiara pressed a button, and prosciutto pieces started flying everywhere.

Chiara yelped, and Camilla covered her mouth with her hands. The audience exploded in shocked laughter.

Rick stared, and then sank back into his seat.

Chiara quickly pressed another button to turn off the blender, and then she and Camilla stared at each other... before dissolving into peals of laughter.

"Oops." Chiara looked into the camera and shrugged, a teasing smile on her face. "Next time I'll remember to put the top on the blender first. But first let's get this cleaned up."

Moments later, after help from behind-the-scenes staff, Chiara raised a wineglass, and she and Camilla toasted each other.

Rick watched, fascinated by the interplay between the two women. Looking around him, he realized everyone else was entertained, as well.

After that, Chiara proceeded to prepare the cappelletti recipe without another hitch. She chopped more prosciutto, by hand this time, and added it to a shallow pan containing peas, mushrooms and a light cream sauce. With a saucy look, she added a touch of *vino* from the open wine bottle, and said with a wink, "Do try this at home, but not too much."

His mother laughed, and then both she and Chiara took more sips from their wineglasses.

Rick couldn't imagine what they were both thinking, but when Chiara motioned for his father, Serg, to join them from the audience, Rick knew things were only going to get more interesting. His father was a character, but this was the first time Serg had been so public since his stroke.

Rick made to help his father out of his seat, but Serg just batted his hand away.

"Bah!" Serg said, doing a comical rendition of a grumpy old man even though he had the grin of an eager fan.

"I hear Camilla's husband, Serg, knows his way around wine," Chiara announced. "Perhaps he can suggest a vintage to pair with my dish."

"I'd be happy to," Serg replied as he climbed the two steps to the stage. "It's not every day that my son brings home a beautiful actress."

Rick suppressed an embarrassed groan. His and Chiara's pretend relationship had just gotten a major advertising boost from his father. Odele would be overjoyed.

When Serg reached the stage, he sampled the cappelletti dish from a plate Camilla handed to him. After taking a moment to savor, he declared, "Bianco di Custoza, Verdicchio or Pinot Bianco."

Chiara beamed. "Thank you so much for the wine suggestions, Serg."

Serg winked at the audience. "You know I'm Italian, so I suggest Italian wines. I like them on the dry side, but you can pair this dish with a lighter Chardonnay if you like."

Getting the signal from a producer offscreen, Camilla addressed the camera in order to wrap up the show. "*All prossima volta*. Till next time, *buon appetito*."

As the show's support staff approached to remove Camilla's and Chiara's mics, Serg returned to his seat.

"Good job, Dad," Rick remarked with a smile. "I didn't know you had it in you."

He was still trying to process Chiara's interaction with

his parents on camera. It was like she'd known them forever, it had been so natural.

"Bah!" Serg said, though his expression again belied his grumpiness. "Don't be jealous I was the one called on stage by a beautiful woman. You've got to work it, Rick."

"And a star is born," Rick replied with dry humor to his sister, who gave a knowing smile.

"Do you want my autograph?" Serg chortled, picking up his sweater from his seat as Mia moved to help him.

Rick stepped off to the side, and when Chiara approached, minutes later, he remarked, "That was quite a scene-stealing performance."

"It's why I'm an in-demand actress."

She looked sexy in Mia's designs, and he liked her even more for lending her celebrity to help his family.

"So it was all planned?"

"Planned? Like reading lines?" She shook her head. "No. More like improv and stand-up comedy."

"It worked."

"I hope the show's ratings reflect it." She shrugged. "Viewers want drama and action. Or maybe I just think that because I've been doing too many adventure movies."

"Hey—" he chucked her under the chin "—that's how you met a hunky stuntman who's given you a new lease on life in the press."

"Oh, yes, the media." She made a disgruntled sound that he didn't expect. "Of course, I have to attend to my public persona."

He tucked his hands in his denim pockets—because the urge to comfort and, even more, get closer to her, was overwhelming. "So who is the real Chiara Feran? Odele mentioned a few details about your childhood and parents."

She sighed, and there was a flash of pain. "My mother was in some ways a typical stage mother, but in other ways, she wasn't. She had thwarted dreams of being a star, so she was ambitious for me."

"Things didn't work out for her?"

"Well, she had some modest success in Brazil, so she went to Hollywood. But the Portuguese accent didn't help when it came to acting roles. Who knows what would have happened if she'd stayed in South America."

Curious, Rick asked, "Your mother didn't want more kids?"

Chiara sobered. "No. Her marriage broke up, and I was enough for her to handle as a single parent living far from her family in Brazil. Plus, I was her spitting image in many ways, so she already had a Mini-Me. She died a few years ago, and I still miss her a lot. I have mixed feelings about my childhood, but I loved her with my whole heart. She did the best she could in raising me."

Rick was starting to understand—a lot. Chiara's upbringing couldn't have been more different from his own. While he'd been tossing around a football in the backyard with his siblings, she was probably being prepped and groomed for a chance to appear in a national commercial or catalog.

"Your mother should think of doing a food blog," Chiara commented, changing the subject. "She needs to think of branching out and building the Camilla Serenghetti food empire."

"Empire?" he repeated in a sardonic tone. Because while it was one thing for his mother to have a local cooking show, it was another for her to be an empress in the making. Still… "She'll like the way you think, and appreciate the pointers on building a brand."

"Of course. That's what we're about in Hollywood.

Building a brand." Chiara looked around. "You, on the other hand, are about wholesomeness, surprisingly enough. Or at least your family is. You come from a nice little town in Massachusetts that's ages away from the Sunset Strip."

"You grew up in Rhode Island, not far from here. You're not so different."

Chiara shook her head. "I'm all about performing these days. The show must go on."

"Whatever the cost?" Rick probed.

Chiara nodded. "Even if the show is a sham."

"And yet, I think of you as real and vital," Rick replied, stepping closer. "And my physical reaction to you definitely is."

She gave a nervous laugh and shook her head. "You must be mistaken. I'm Snow White, remember? A make-believe character."

Rick's lips twitched. He wasn't sure when they had gotten so mixed up. Suddenly *she* was insisting she was a make-believe character, and *he* was arguing the opposite.

One thing was for sure: he was more determined than ever to finish exploring their very real attraction. He'd kept his distance since they'd left Los Angeles, but he wanted her with a need that was getting hard to ignore.

In the now nearly empty television studio, Chiara stood to one side, waiting for assorted Serenghettis to depart. Rick was speaking to his mother and one of her producers, no doubt making sure everything was in order with respect to today's guest appearance.

Chiara was glad for the respite. Minutes ago, her conversation with Rick had devolved into a far more intimate and personal exchange than she'd been prepared for. What had she been thinking?

She'd revealed more about her background and her mother than she'd intended. And then she hadn't been able to keep out the wistfulness when contrasting her circumstances with Rick's own family. *Wholesome. Warm. Loving.* She felt relaxed here, in the embrace of the Serenghettis and away from her problems—the limelight, her father, her would-be stalker...

Still, she'd dodged the very real emotional and sexual currents between her and Rick by making light of the matter. *The show must go on.* She doubted Rick would be satisfied with that response, however. Awareness skated over her skin as she remembered the gleam in his eyes followed by his words: *I think of you as real and vital. And my physical reaction to you definitely is.*

Her resolve to keep him at a distance was weakening, aided by her very real yearning for what he'd had—still had—in comparison: a tight-knit family who cared about each other.

As if on cue, Rick's sister appeared, her face wreathed in a wide smile. "Thank you for the on-air plug, Chiara. You are the perfect model to bring out the best in my designs."

Chiara smiled back and then touched the other woman's arm. "Don't mention it."

"I've never dressed someone so high profile before. You have a great sense of style."

"I owe a lot to my former stylist Emery. But she went off to start her own accessories line, so I'm open to new ideas." Chiara's eyes widened, as an idea struck. "I should connect the both of you. Emery would be a natural complement to your clothing line."

Mia gave a look of wry amusement. "I can see it now—'ME by Mia Emery... Not Your Mom's Everyday.'"

"Perfect." So this was what it might be like to have a sister. Chiara let the wistful feeling wash over her again.

Mia tilted her head. "Rick isn't the only maverick in the family, though he likes to think so. I've abandoned the family construction business and run off to New York to follow the bright lights of fashion."

"You make *maverick* sound like a bad thing. It's not so terrible."

"Not so wicked, you mean?" Mia gave a sly grin. "So Rick's worked his charm on you then?"

Chiara's face warmed. Was it *charm*—or something more? Just a short time ago, she'd have called Rick the least charming man she knew, but somehow her feelings had been changing. Now with his family, she was even more...charmed.

Mia leaned in conspiratorially. "You're beautiful, smart and famous. How did you and Rick wind up together?"

"We...um..." Somehow she couldn't bring herself to lie to Rick's sister, so she finished lamely, "Don't believe everything you read in the press."

What could she say? *We're not really a couple. It's a big fat lie.* Even if she was having increasing trouble remembering that, especially surrounded by the Serenghettis.

"I see," Mia responded, and then nodded as if satisfied. "Well, you two bounce off each other in a charming way. It's as if Rick has met his match."

Even if that were true, it meant one of them was going down for the count...

"You're someone who can't be impressed by his money," Mia added.

What? Chiara mentally shrugged, and said carefully, "I'm not sure how much money Rick has."

Mia laughed. "Neither am I, but after making a killing with his hedge fund, he's got enough to play with."

Hedge fund? Chiara felt her head swim. Rick was a gritty rolling stone of a stuntman as far as she knew. If he had millions, what was he doing...?

"He's a stuntman," she blurted. "He jumps off buildings, leaps from moving cars..." *And embraces actresses while hanging from a helicopter.*

"And takes big risks with money by betting things are going up or down in value." Mia shrugged. "Same thing."

Chiara froze. Mia made it seem as if Rick was a risk taker—which wasn't far from her gambling father. She'd never seen the similarity, and now she was in a very public relationship with Rick. She needed therapy...and not the kind provided by pretending to talk with a wooden dummy, either. *Sorry, Ruby.*

But even more shockingly, Rick wasn't merely a stuntman, he was—

"*Pegasus Pride* is his baby right now," his sister said.

Chiara blew out a breath and tried to keep her voice steady. "He's got money invested in the film?"

Mia nodded. "You didn't know?"

Nope. Otherwise she'd never have spent her time insulting the boss—the producer of her current film—who could have had her fired any day.

Mia gave a choked laugh. "That's just like Rick. He always wants to keep a low profile." Her eyes suddenly danced. "We're still talking about his favorite childhood Halloween costume. You know, he just tossed a brown paper bag over his head and made cutouts for eyes."

"And the school play?" Chiara nearly squeaked.

"Stage crew, or he'd play the tree, of course."

"Well, he's graduated to leaping from speeding motorcycles and hanging from airplanes," Chiara replied drily. *And tricking unwary actresses.*

She glanced over at Rick. Why hadn't he told her? She'd thought...they'd... Chiara nearly closed her eyes on a groan.

She *really* needed to talk to him. But not around his family. No, she'd have to wait for the right moment...

Eight

Chiara somehow managed to keep her silence until they were at Rick's place.

At least now she understood why he might be checking his phone all the time. He was a behind-the-scenes Hollywood power player who liked to keep his name out of the press. And perhaps he needed to keep track of his substantial financial investments, too.

When they arrived at his condo, she was impressed all over again. But at least now she was prepared for what she found, unlike when they'd first arrived in Welsdale. The airy space had the stamp of muted luxury: exposed brick, rich leathers, recessed lighting and electronics hidden behind sliding panels of artwork. Nearly floor-to-ceiling windows made the most of the apartment's perch on the top floor of a block of high-priced condos, and Welsdale's evening lights twinkled outside.

How was it possible she'd been in the dark? She'd researched Rick again online after her conversation with Mia, and nothing had come up. He was good at covering his tracks. Except she was on his trail, thanks to his sister.

She sauntered into the muted light of the living room ahead of Rick. He was dressed in slacks and an open-collar navy shirt. A five o'clock shadow made him look even sexier.

Chiara smoothed her hands down the front of her pants. Then, taking a deep breath, she pinned Rick with a steady gaze. "You didn't tell me you're the producer of *Pegasus Pride* as well as doing its stunt work."

When he didn't react, she didn't know whether to stamp her foot or applaud his acting skills.

"Surprise."

"Now is not the time for humor, Serenghetti."

"When is?" He continued to look relaxed.

She placed her hands on her hips. "You misled me."

"You didn't ask. Anyway, does it matter?"

"I never date the boss," she huffed. "I don't want the reputation of being the actress who slept her way to the top."

On the long list of what he'd done wrong, it was one of the lesser of his transgressions, but she was nearly speechless and didn't even know where to begin.

Rick, though, had the poor grace to smile. "Does it help to know I'm only the behind-the-scenes guy? I'm an investor in Blooming Star Productions."

"Why don't you get your mother a cameo in a movie then? She could play herself. A cook with a local television show trying to make it big."

"God help us."

Chiara narrowed her eyes. "And where did you get the money to be the financial backer for a film production company?"

She'd heard it from Mia—and hadn't quite believed it—so she wanted confirmation from the source himself.

He shrugged. "I worked on Wall Street after Boston College and created a hedge fund."

She felt light-headed when he told her this, just as she had at the television studio. How much money were they talking about? Millions? Billions?

As if reading her mind, he said, "I've made a few best-of lists, but I left New York before joining the billionaires' club."

She figured he had serious bank dwarfing that of a run-of-the-mill actress. "It's unheard of to be both a producer and a stuntman!"

"They're not as different as you think. Both involve calculated risks. One with money, the other physically."

His words echoed Mia's earlier. What was this, a Serenghetti press release? Or did Rick and his siblings just think alike?

She should have been able to read the signs and put them together. They were all there. The expensive car. The apartments on two coasts.

He shrugged again. "I'm a maverick."

"You said you lived in a rental in West Hollywood!"

"Until the house is finished. It's under construction."

"And where is this house?" she asked suspiciously.

"Beverly Hills."

But of course. "Brentwood must seem…quaint to you."

There were plenty of celebrities in her section of LA but it was a little more low-key than the brand-name neighborhoods where tourists flocked—Beverly Hills, Bel Air…

Rick's lips twitched. "Brentwood has its charms, particularly if there's a thatched English cottage…and fairy-tale princess involved."

"She's the kick-ass modern variety," she sniffed—because she should be verbally demolishing him right now for letting her believe he was just an *aw-shucks* stuntman living for the next thrill and its accompanying paycheck.

"Don't I know it." His eyes laughed at her.

"Why would you give up New York, the financial industry and your own hedge fund to go out West to Hollywood?"

He smiled a little, still unflappable. "New challenges. Hollywood is not that different from Wall Street. The studios take major gambles with movies. Different rules, but the same game. And it's still about trusting your instincts and making money—or not."

"Well, it all makes sense now—" sarcasm crept into her tone "—except for the part where you led me to believe you were a regular Joe."

"Is this our first argument?"

She nearly snorted. "Or our hundredth."

He sauntered closer. "Would it have made a difference if you'd known?"

"You could have hired a stable of bodyguards for me with your bank!"

"Ah," he drawled, "but then I wouldn't have had the pleasure of...your company."

"The joy of sparring with me, you mean? And living in a humble cottage instead of a castle in Beverly Hills?"

He burst out laughing. "I'm paying you enough to live in more than a humble cottage."

"But are you paying me enough to put up with you?"

He gave a sultry smile and reached for her. "I don't know. Let's find out."

She should be mad at him. She *was* angry with him. Still, it didn't matter. The truth was she'd been lured in by the seductive cozy family life of the Serenghettis. She yearned for it. They were miles removed from her existence in Southern California, and the distance wasn't just a matter of geography.

When Rick's lips met hers, Chiara was transported, winging through the clouds as if they were performing another one of their stunts. Exhilaration ran through her, the feeling humming alongside one of safety, family... and coming home.

He molded her to him with his hand on her back, making her feel his need—his desire. She rested her hands on his shoulders, and then, caving, slid her arms around his neck, bringing his head closer.

Rick lifted his head slightly, and muttered against her mouth, "We need props."

She gave a choked laugh. "This is not a film scene."

Rick raised his eyebrows. "You're an actress who's not into role-playing?"

"I like to keep it real. Well, except for this pretending about being a couple that Odele has me doing!"

"Believe me, this is as real and raw as it's going to get."

Awareness shivered through her. "Okay, what if I'm a chilly A-list actress and you're...the help who is intent on seducing me?"

"There's nothing cold about you, Snow," he said, tilting up her chin. "Well, except for maybe your nickname."

"But you're here to melt me?"

He flashed his teeth. "I'm trying."

It had been safer to pretend he was the help. Just the movie stuntman. Or the make-believe boyfriend. Not a man whose wealth dwarfed hers. One who had no use for her money or her fame and celebrity. One who'd put himself on the line to protect her—just because.

She didn't know what to do with a man like that. She'd

spent years living as if she didn't need any man. Because she could provide for herself, thanks. But with Rick, she was at a disadvantage. He'd come to her defense against a stalker, and now it turned out he was her boss. She didn't have the upper hand. He didn't need her for anything, either.

Well, except for sex. He clearly wanted her *badly*.

And what was wrong with making herself feel feminine and powerful for an interlude? After all, it wasn't as if she was giving up something. Except she risked falling for him.

The pent-up desire that she'd been feeling these weeks and refusing to acknowledge slipped from its shackles. Rick drove her crazy, and it was a thin line between being irritated and jumping his bones. Giving in meant easing some of the frustration, and suddenly nothing else mattered.

Seeming to read the assent in her eyes, Rick slowly took off her clothes, tossing the pieces aside one by one onto nearby furniture and peeling away her defenses to find what was in no way artifice. Then he shed some of his own clothes until they were both down to underwear.

She shivered as the cool air hit her.

"Let me warm you up," he muttered.

She wanted to say he already had, and that that was the problem. She was melting, her defenses flowing away like so much ice under a hot sun.

Chiara stepped out of the clothes pooled at her feet. Clad in just a lacy black bra and the barest slip of underwear, she had no mask. But if she felt nervous, the naked appreciation stamped on Rick's face put an end to it. She straightened her shoulders, and the resulting movement thrust her breasts forward, their peaks jutting against their thin covering.

Rick's face glowed with appreciation, and then he muttered what he wanted to do with her, his prominent arousal testimony to his words. Waves of heat washed over her, and she sucked in a breath.

He stepped forward, and when the backs of her legs hit the sofa, she let herself fall backward, bracing herself with one hand on a pillow. Rick followed, bent and took one of her nipples in his mouth through her bra, fabric and all, suckling her gently.

Chiara gasped, a strangled sound caught in her throat, and need shuddered through her. Her head fell back when he pushed aside her bra and transferred his attention to her other breast. She was awash in sensation, the universe popping with a kaleidoscope of color.

Rick knelt, pulled her to the end of the sofa arm so that her legs straddled it, and then pushed aside her underwear to use his mouth to love her some more. Cries of pleasure were ripped from her throat...and she felt herself splintering—until she bucked against him with her release.

Afterward, Rick straightened and shed his underwear like a man possessed. Watching him, Chiara stood up and did the same, her remaining garments melting away.

Rick suddenly cursed. "Damn it. Protection is still packed in my suitcase."

"I'm on contraception," she said throatily, dizzy with want.

His gaze caught with hers. "I want you to know I've gotten a clean bill from my doctor. I would never put you at risk."

She licked her lips. "Same goes for me."

They looked at each other for a moment, neither moving, savoring this moment.

And then Chiara held her hand out to him. "We're not going to make it to the bed, are we?"

He gave her a lopsided smile. "Stuntmen can do it everywhere."

Chiara followed his gaze to the nearby long leather ottoman, which doubled as a coffee table. *Oh.* As she bent to sit on it, Rick followed her down, giving her a long, sweet, lingering kiss.

When she embraced him, he entered her in one fluid movement, rocking her to her core. Joined to him, Chiara gave herself up to sensation, following the pace that Rick set.

When she felt Rick tighten, nearing his climax, she ran her hands over his ripped arms and bit back a moan.

"Let me hear you," Rick said as the air grew thick with their deep breathing.

"Rick, oh…now."

And just like that, as he thrust deep, Chiara felt herself coming apart again, dazed with her release.

Rick gave a hoarse shout and buried himself in her, collapsing into her embrace.

Chiara had never felt so at one with someone…exposed and yet secure.

As she walked by, Chiara glanced in her hallway mirror and resisted the urge to pinch herself. She looked happy…relaxed…and yes, sexually satisfied. Filming was over, so the main item on her agenda today was reading a script for a role that she was considering.

Ever since she and Rick had returned to LA from Welsdale two days ago, she'd been in a lovely cocoon. She flushed just thinking about what they'd done yesterday. Foreplay on the weight bench, but the exercise mat and even the jump rope had come in handy…

Walking into the den, she plopped herself on the couch, feet dangling off one end. She began reading the script on her tablet. Moments later, Rick walked in.

After an extraordinary bout of sex this morning, he'd gone out to run errands and she hadn't seen him in the two hours since. He looked just as yummy as earlier, however. They were both dressed in sweats, but somehow, he managed to make his look sexy rather than casual. He hadn't bothered shaving this morning, and she'd come to like the shadow darkening his jaw. Contrasting with his wonderful multihued eyes, it lent him an air of quiet magnetism...

Rick nodded toward the device in her hand. "Have you checked the news yet?"

"No, should I? I just sat down." She belatedly realized he looked more serious than usual.

Rick folded his arms and leaned against the entryway. "Well, the good news is your temporary restraining order came through, so your bad fan can be arrested for getting too close."

"Great." She hadn't given much thought to Todd Jeffers in the past several days, though now that she was back home and he knew her address, she supposed she did feel an undercurrent of more stress. She asked cautiously, "What's the bad news?"

"Your father has gotten himself arrested."

Chiara leaned her head back against the pillows and closed her eyes briefly. "In Sin City? What could he have possibly done? The police turn a blind eye to practically every vice imaginable there. Even prostitution is legal in parts of Nevada, for heaven's sake."

"Apparently he argued about a parking ticket."

"Sounds just like him. Responsibility has never been his strong suit."

"You have to deal with the daddy problem."

"I've never called him *Daddy*," she scoffed, straightening. "Sperm donor, maybe. Daddy, no."

"Whatever the name, you'll keep having the same pesky PR problems if you don't address the issue. And your next big movie might not come with a stuntman willing to double as the star's boyfriend."

"Hilarious." Still, she felt a pull on her heartstrings at the reminder that their arrangement was temporary and fake.

Rick dropped his arms and sauntered into the room. "We may have had some success in distracting the press from your father recently, but you need to turn around and face the issue."

"I don't run from anything," she scoffed again.

"Right. You're a daredevil. Guess who gave you the risk-taking gene?"

She shrugged off a sudden bad feeling as she got up. "I don't know what you're talking about."

Rick's gaze was penetrating. "What do you think gambling is? It's a high from taking risks. There's a rush from the brain's rewards system. You like risks, your father likes risks. Different species of risk, but same family."

She had *nothing* in common with her father. How dare Rick make that connection? Even worse, it was one she hadn't seen coming. So she was in a profession with big highs and lows... So she did some of her own stunts...

Rick folded his arms again. "The funny thing is the only situation where you won't take a chance is arranging a meeting with Michael Feran."

"I don't have anything to say to him."

Rick tossed her a disbelieving look. "Of course you do. You have a lifetime's worth of questions to grill and cross-examine him with," he said pleasantly, "but let's just stick with the issue at hand, which is getting him to stop attracting bad press."

She jutted her chin forward. "And how do you propose I do that?"

"I've got some ideas...ones that might appeal to his own self-interest."

"Oh? And since when have you turned into a psychologist?"

Rick braced his hands on his hips. "People management is part of the job description for a Hollywood producer. And stunt work is about getting your mind ready to conquer fear about what could happen to your body. Mind over body."

"Thanks for the tip."

"I also found your Las Vegas showgirl ventriloquist's dummy on the chair where you left her. She had plenty of insights about you," he joked, "but mostly she was content to just sit there and listen."

"She's trashy."

Rick choked on a laugh. "Great. She'll be popular."

"You like them that way," she accused.

"I like you. The dummy is just the repository for the part of your personality that you're afraid you might have inherited from your father."

"Oh, joy."

Rick suddenly sobered. "Your father has a gambling problem, and I understand addiction. Hal went back to drinking too much after Isabel's antics sent him into a spiral."

"You never mentioned there were consequences from Isabel's media stunt." She caught herself at Rick's droll look at the mention of the word *stunt*. "Sorry, bad choice of words. I meant her diva moment for the press."

Rick dropped his hands and shrugged. "Hal is sober

these days after a stint in rehab. Or so I hear through the grapevine…since we don't socialize anymore."

Chiara was starting to understand more and more about Rick's wariness regarding the limelight, actresses and fame in general. An aspiring actress had not only cost him a friendship but had crushed someone he knew.

"I'll even offer my house for a meeting with your father," Rick went on. "Odele can contact Michael Feran and figure out the details, including flying him to Los Angeles. I'll pick up the tab."

She sighed before asking wryly, "So all I have to do is show up?"

"Affirmative."

"Your house isn't even finished!"

"There's landscaping and stuff still to be done, but it's habitable. And more important, it's neutral territory for a private meeting with your father." He raised his eyebrows.

"Is there anything you haven't thought of?" she demanded.

He gave her a lingering look. "There are still a few fantasies that I'm playing with…"

"You know, it's astonishing you come from such a nice family considering—"

"I'm an ego-driven macho stuntman who doesn't respect the rights of actresses to do their own daredevil acts and knows nothing about the uses of double-sided tape?"

"No, considering your dirty mind."

One side of his mouth lifted in a smile. "Well, that, too. I know plenty of uses for tape and blindfolds and silk ties."

Oh…wow.

Rick's eyes crinkled. "Stunts call for diverse props."

"I go propless."

Rick stepped closer and murmured, "Interesting. No need of any assistance?"

She tossed her hair back as sexual energy emanated off him in luscious waves that wrapped themselves around her. "Yes, I go it alone."

He reached out and took a strand of her hair in his fingers. "Might be more fun if it's two."

"Or three or more?" she queried. "What's your limit? A menagerie?"

He gave a soft laugh. "A couple is good. The number of times, on the other hand…limitless, I'd say."

Her breath started coming quick and shallow. *Oh.*

She swallowed and focused on the faint lines fanning out from the corners of his eyes, and the ones bracketing his mouth.

He lowered his head and then touched his lips to hers, and she sighed. He nudged her—once, twice, coaxing a response. *Open. Open.*

Chiara shivered and felt her breasts peak even though only their lips were touching. She leaned in, falling into something that she knew was bottomless…still relatively unknown…and exciting.

Rick deepened the kiss and raked his fingers through her hair, his hand anchoring at the back of her head. They moved restlessly, unable to get enough of each other.

Then Chiara followed Rick's lead as they stripped off their clothes hurriedly, desperate for skin-on-skin contact. When they were down to underwear, he stopped her.

She drank him in from beneath lowered lashes. He was hot and male and vital. There was the ripped midriff, muscular arms, taut legs…the erection pushing against his boxers. Suddenly she needed to catch her breath.

He lowered the straps of her lacy bra and peeled the garment away from her, and then swallowed. "Chiara."

"Make love to me, Rick."

It was all the invitation that he needed. He kissed her with unrestrained passion, pulling her close as her arms wrapped around his neck. And she responded with a hunger of her own, the feel of his arousal against her fueling her passion.

When she broke away, she pushed down her panties and he did the same with his boxers. And then they were tumbling onto the sofa, reaching for each other in a tangle of limbs and desperate passion.

She grasped Rick's erection and began a pumping motion designed to stoke his passion and hers. He was warm, pulsating male—rigid with his need for her.

He tore her mouth from hers and expelled a breath. "Chiara, we've got to slow down or this is going to be over—"

"Before the director yells cut?" she purred. "There is no director, Stunt Stud."

He gave a strangled laugh. "Stunt Stud?"

"It's the name I came up with when I was objectifying you."

"I was going to say to slow down or this will be finished before you're satisfied."

"Worried I won't be able to keep up with you?" In response, she led his hand to her moist heat, already ready for him.

He stilled, and in the next moment, he was pushing her back against the pillows. Then he sheathed himself in one long stroke that had them both groaning.

As Rick hit her core, she arched her back, taking him in.

She followed his lead and the rhythm he set…building and building until she hit her climax in one husky cry.

"Chiara." In the moment after Rick called her name, he groaned, stiffened and then spilled inside her.

He slumped against her, and she cradled him.

Contentment rolled through her—a feeling that had been too elusive in her life until now...

Nine

When they pulled up in Rick's Range Rover to the nearly completed house, Chiara sucked in a breath. *Wow.*

Nervousness about the upcoming meeting with her father, who was scheduled to arrive within the hour, was replaced by happy surprise.

Rick's home wasn't a house but a castle. It was all gray stone and stunning turrets. She loved it.

She was so entranced that Rick had already come around and opened the car door for her before she thought to get out. She could see there was plenty of landscaping yet to be done, but still the effect from the outside was stunning.

"Want to take a look?" Rick teased as she got out. "I'm sure you've seen plenty of impressive homes belonging to famous people."

None shaped like a castle. She looked at the mansion, and then glanced at Rick. "I'm impressed. You have the castle…were you looking for your fairy-tale princess?"

Rick's lips curved. "Only you can answer that, Snow."

He put his hand at her elbow. "Come on, let's look inside. It's done except for minor details, and is sparsely furnished."

Rick's house—*castle*—made her home look like a small and cute cottage.

Chiara gasped when they entered the foyer. She'd seen this house in her mind's eye.

The double-height entry was airy and sunny but also warm and inviting. Done in light colors, it belied the imposing exterior. A curving staircase led to the upper levels, and various open doorways offered glimpses of other parts of the house.

She followed Rick in a circuit of the ground floor. A warm, country-style kitchen with beige cabinetry and a large island connected to a spacious dining room. An immense living room was bifurcated by a two-way fireplace and was made cozy by coffered ceilings in a warm mahogany wood. A library, den, two bathrooms and a couple of storage rooms for staff rounded out most of the lower level. The only thing missing was furnishings for a family...

When they came full circle back to the entry, Chiara's gaze went to the staircase leading to the upper floors.

Rick adopted a teasing expression. "In case you are wondering, a home office with a built-in desk sits at the top of the principal turret. I haven't stashed a fairy-tale princess there."

"Rapunzel?" She tapped her chest. "Wrong fairy tale. I'm Snow, remember?"

Despite her joking, she felt comfortable here—too at home. It was almost enough to make her forget she was about to have one of the most significant meetings of her life.

She was an actress, she reminded herself sternly. She needed to adopt a persona—a shield—and get what she wanted out of this meeting.

As if reading her thoughts, Rick said, "You and your father can meet in the library. It has two club chairs and a coffee table at the moment."

"Okay." Why had she let Rick talk her into this? She knew he had a good point—dragons must be faced—but she wasn't relishing the chance to slay one of hers. She almost gave a nervous laugh at the thought of Rick cast as her knight in shining armor...

Except of course, she didn't believe in such knights or in Prince Charming—or in fairy tales, for that matter. Though she was having a hard time remembering that these days.

At the sound of a car pulling up, Rick said, "That must be him. I had a driver pick him up from the hotel where he stayed last night after his flight from Vegas."

"Oh, good," she managed, and then cleared her throat.

Rick looked at her searchingly, and then cupped her shoulders. "Are you okay?"

She gave him a blinding smile—one she usually reserved for the cameras. "Never better."

"Remember, you're in charge here. You hold the cards."

"Playing cards are what I intend to take out of his hands."

Rick lifted one side of his mouth. "Sorry, bad choice of words. I'll meet him outside and show him into the library."

"Of course." She'd dressed in a navy shirt dress—something she'd pulled out of the closet herself. Because even if Emery hadn't headed off to start her own fashion line, Chiara couldn't imagine asking a stylist about what to wear to a meeting with her estranged father. For some occasions in life, there was *no* fashion rule book.

Rick shoved his hands into his front pockets and nodded, the hair on his forearms revealed by rolled-up shirtsleeves. "Back soon."

When Rick turned away, Chiara walked into the library. And then, because she couldn't think of what else to do, she faced the partially open doorway...and waited.

The sound of quiet voices reached her. Greetings were exchanged...and then moments later, she heard footsteps.

Someone stepped into the library, and she immediately recognized Michael Feran—*her father*.

Her heart beat a thick, steady rhythm. She hadn't expected to feel this nervous. She hated that she did. *He* was the one who should be tense. After all, he'd walked out on her.

She hadn't seen him in person in years, but the media had made sure she hadn't forgotten what he looked like. She wished she could dismiss him as a gaunt and lonely gambling addict wallowing in his misery, but he looked... good.

She silently cursed the Feran genes. They'd graced her with the looks and figure that had propelled her to the top in Hollywood, but they also hadn't skipped a generation with Michael Feran. His salt-and-pepper hair made him look distinguished—a candidate for the father role in any big studio blockbuster.

"Chiara." He smiled. "It's wonderful to see you."

She wished she could say the same. Under the circumstances, it was a forced meeting.

At her continued silence, he went on, "I'm glad you wanted to meet with me."

"Rick convinced me that I needed to have this face-to-face meeting."

Michael Feran smiled. "Yes, how is the stuntman?" So her father read the press about her. *Of course.*

"I met him when I came in. Is he a candidate for future son-in-law?"

Chiara was hit with a sudden realization that left her breathless. She was falling for Rick. She had fallen for him. But they'd never discussed making their fake relationship permanent... She pushed aside the thought that had come with staggering clarity because if she dealt with any more emotion right now, she'd overload.

Instead, she forced herself to focus on Michael Feran. "You're creating unwanted publicity."

"I see."

"Why did you talk to that tabloid about me last year?" It was an unforgivable transgression to add to his list of sins.

"Money would be the easy answer."

She waited.

He heaved a sigh. "The hard one is that I wanted your attention."

"Well, you got it." She folded her arms.

She wasn't going to offer him a seat, and she sure wasn't going to sit down herself, despite the fact that Rick had pointed out this room had comfortable chairs. Michael Feran had to understand this was a halfhearted welcome and not an olive branch.

His gray brows drew together. "I probably didn't go about it in the best way. Believe it or not, it was the only time I took money from a reporter."

"Because you needed to pay off your gambling debts," she guessed.

He looked aggrieved. "It was a mistake. One I don't intend to make again."

She was definitely going to see to it that he didn't spill the beans again.

"Usually I'm winning at the card tables. Enough to pay my bills."

"Naturally. It's what matters in life." She couldn't help the tone of heavy sarcasm in her voice. "But you're generating bad press."

"Chiara—"

"Do you have any idea what it meant for a little girl to wake up wondering if her father had bolted again?" she interrupted, even while she didn't know why she was being so forthright. Maybe it was because, without even realizing it, she'd waited years for this opportunity to confront him about his misdeeds. Just as Rick had suggested.

"Chiara, I know I hurt you." Her father paused. "That's why I stopped showing up after you turned five. I thought that not making a sudden appearance was better than hurting you by coming and going."

He made it seem as if he'd done her a favor. She remembered the betting games they'd played when she was young. *I bet I can throw this pebble farther. Race you to the tree, loser is a rotten egg.* Even then Michael Feran hadn't been able to resist a bet. "You left a wife, a child, a home…"

"You don't know what it's like to walk away from a family—"

"I never would."

"—but you get to reinvent yourself with every film role."

"It's acting." First Rick, now her father. Was there no man in her life who could understand she was just pretending? She *liked* acting.

"You can become someone different, follow your dreams…"

Of course, but… She was so *not* going to feel sorry for him.

Michael sobered. "I can't turn back the clock."

She took a deep breath and addressed the elephant in the room. "Why did you leave that first time?"

She'd never asked because posing the question might be interpreted to mean she cared what the answer was. And she'd spent years making sure she didn't care—ignoring Michael Feran, leading her glamorous life and making sure her image stayed polished. Except he kept putting a dent in it.

Her father looked at her for a long moment, and then heaved another sigh. "I was an ambitious musician and I had dreams to follow, or so I thought."

She could relate to the career and the ambition part. Wasn't that what she'd spent her life pursuing? She loved acting…getting to know a character…and, yes, even getting immersed in a role. Except had she ever gotten to know herself—before Rick convinced her to stop and deal with her problems?

"I had some moderate success. We were the opening act for top singers. But I never broke through in the way you have." There was a note of pride in Michael Feran's voice, before he went on, "You're more successful than I was. Maybe…you always wanted to prove you could be more successful."

Again, she was floored by his observation. Had her drive to succeed been motivated by her need to outperform him—the absentee father? She'd never looked at it that way, but in any case she wasn't about to admit anything, so she said aloud, "You don't know me."

Michael Feran's face turned grave. "I don't. I don't know you, but I'd like to."

"As you said, we can't do a rewind."

"No, no, we can't." His face was grave, sad.

"You'd have to clean up your act if we're going to be any sort of family."

Where had that offer come from? But the minute the words were out of her mouth, her father perked up. *Her father.* Looking at his face, the resemblance was undeniable. She saw herself in the texture of his dark hair sprinkled with gray, in the shape of his face...in the slant of his aquiline nose.

Okay, she did feel sorry for him. He'd done very little for her since she was born, but he'd done even less for himself. Maybe it was for the best he hadn't been in her life. She'd been protected from the gambling...drifting... *Ugh.* It sounded just like life in Tinseltown, except she was committed to clean living even if she was based in Hollywood.

"I'd like to try," he said.

"Well, you're going to do more than try this time, you're going to succeed. You're checking into rehab for your gambling addiction." She felt...powerful...in control...*relieved.* She'd been the helpless kid who'd watched him walk away, not knowing when her father would be back, if ever. But this time, she was calling the shots.

She set down her terms. "I'm prepared to offer you a deal. You get into a facility to help with your problem and agree to stop making headlines. In return, I'll cover your living expenses. The deal will be in writing, and you'll sign."

She had Rick to thank for that bit of inspiration. After their last sexual encounter, they'd sat in her garden and watched the sun set. He'd revealed himself to be more than a lover. He'd shown himself to be a partner and skilled negotiator who'd helped her come up with a plan for this meeting.

"And if I relapse?" There was a hint of vulnerability in her father's eyes that she hadn't expected.

"Then back to rehab you go...for as long as it takes."

He relaxed into a smile. "That's a gamble I'm willing to take."

"Because you have no choice."

"Because I want to improve if that means having a relationship with you, Chiara." As if he sensed she might argue, he continued in a rush, "It's too late for me to help raise you, but I hope we...can be family."

Family. Wasn't that what she'd yearned for when she'd been around the Serenghettis? And now here was her *father* offering the ties that bind. Choked up by emotion, she cleared her throat. "Fine, it's a role I'm willing to take on, but I'm putting you on notice, I expect an Oscar-worthy performance from you as a family member getting a second chance."

An unguarded look of hope crossed her father's face before he responded gruffly, "I have faith that the acting gene runs in the family."

Trouble for Chiara Feran and Her New Man? Sources Close to the Couple Admit That Blending Two Careers Is Causing Stress.

Chiara looked up from her cell phone screen and at Odele's expectant gaze. Her manager was clearly waiting to hear what Chiara thought about the web site that she'd told her to pull up.

They were sitting sipping coffee in the Novatus Studio commissary. Chiara had met Rick here earlier, where postproduction work had begun on *Pegasus Pride*. As an actress, she wasn't involved in picture and sound editing, but since Rick was a producer on this film, she'd tagged along when he'd said he was interested in checking in with Dan to see how things were going. Afterward, she'd made her way to the commissary to wait for Odele, so they could discuss business.

"Well, what do you think?" Odele asked in her raspy voice, nodding to the cell phone still clutched in Chiara's hand.

"You fed this story to *Gossipmonger*?"

Odele nodded. "I needed a way to hint at a possible end to your dalliance with Rick now that your father is going to rehab, while still keeping you in the public eye."

"I'm still wrapping my head around the fact that you didn't know Rick was a wealthy producer!"

Her manager shrugged. "He's a wily one, I'll admit. I thought I knew everyone in this town, but I guess I can be forgiven for not being acquainted with every silent investor in a film production company. Once you told me about the pile that he built in Beverly Hills, I realized I should have had him on my radar, though, I'll give you that."

"We don't need to rush to bring the ax down on the Chiara-Rick story, do we?" Chiara set down her phone, her heart heavy.

Odele was right. She no longer had to worry about her father making bad headlines, and she had Rick to thank for helping to engineer the resolution to that situation. It also meant she no longer *needed* Rick. Wasn't the entire purpose of their fake relationship to divert attention from her father's negative publicity?

Odele gave her a keen look. "No rush…but planning ahead wouldn't hurt, sweetie. Drop a few suggestions in the press that all might not be happily-ever-after. So when the story does end, it won't seem abrupt and it'll be a soft blow."

For whom? Chiara stifled the question even though she couldn't tell if Odele was referring to the hit to her or to her public image. Did it matter? The two were intertwined. She and Rick weren't a *relationship*, after all, but a *story*.

Chiara worried her bottom lip with her teeth. "Has Rick seen this headline?"

Odele adjusted her glasses. "Of course. I ran into him earlier when you'd momentarily left his side. He knows the script. He's known it from the beginning."

Chiara blanched and glanced down at her coffee cup. So he had seen it, and judging from Odele's expression, it hadn't ruffled him. He knew the bargain they'd struck.

Chiara squared her shoulders, seeing with clarity the road ahead—the path that had been there from the beginning. If she made the first move for a clean break, it didn't even have to damage Rick's reputation. She was familiar with how these things worked. A face-saving explanation would be issued. She could even see the headline: *Snow White and Prince Charming Go Their Separate Ways.*

She was doing Rick a favor. He'd never wanted to be tied to an actress…a *celebrity*. He could take his bow and retreat behind the curtain to his nice quiet life—on his large estate in LA. She was being fair.

But the two of them definitely needed to talk. *Soon. Right now.* Before she fell apart…or at least deeper into the warm cocoon of their relationship, where it was *her love* and his…*what*? He'd never come close to saying he loved her. Her heart squeezed and she blinked against a sudden swell of emotion.

She was a highly rated actress—she could do this.

She had sudden flashes from interludes in his arms.

They'd been wonderful…but there'd been no promise of forever, and tomorrow started today. The next chapter.

Chiara looked at her watch. Rick was supposed to meet her here when he was done. And now she had more than enough to say to him…

She forced herself to continue her conversation with Odele, but twenty minutes later when her manager left to make her next meeting, Chiara was relieved…and then nervous as she waited for Rick to show up.

After a quarter of an hour, he walked in, looking casual…relaxed…happy. And as attractive as ever in gray pants and a white shirt.

Chiara swallowed when he gave her a quick peck on the lips.

He sat down across from her at the small table and then lounged back in his chair.

"How did your meeting with Dan end?" she asked brightly.

"Fine. The editor showed up and we discussed plans for the rough cut." He cracked a grin. "Dan's grateful to you for not needing many retakes and keeping us on schedule. Everything's looking great, and with any luck, the box office receipts will reflect it."

They talked about the postproduction work for a few more minutes. Then when the conversation reached a lull, she jumped in and said, "So you must be relieved." He looked at her quizzically, and she shrugged. "Odele's latest planted story in the press."

"I don't give a damn about Odele's PR moves."

His words surprised her, but then hadn't he always been anti-publicity?

"Okay, but we need to talk—" she wet her lips "—because the reason we got together as a couple no longer exists."

She willed him to…what? Get down on bended knee and pledge his eternal love? She'd said all along that she didn't believe in fairy tales.

She smiled tentatively. "Thank you for helping me resolve the impasse with my father. He loves your idea of the two of us partnering to combat his gambling addiction." Her expression turned wry. "Odele likes it, too, of course. She thinks it would be a good way to turn a negative story into a positive one. I could even take it on as a charitable cause."

Rick inclined his head but looked guarded. "Okay, yeah."

"But now that the problem with my father is gone," she said, taking a deep breath, "we no longer have to continue this farce."

Had she really said *farce*? She'd meant to say…

Rick's expression hardened. "Right."

"You disagree?"

He leaned in. "You're still that little girl who is afraid of being abandoned—of someone walking out on her again."

"Please, I know where you're going with this is, and it's not true." It wasn't abandonment she was scared of. She was a grown woman who feared she'd have her heart broken. *Her heart was broken*—because she was in love with Rick and he steered clear of actresses.

Still, wasn't his keen perception what she liked about him? Loved? Yes, *loved*—in addition to his humor, intelligence and daring. They were qualities that appealed to different sides of her personality, even if they made her uncomfortable and yes, infuriated her sometimes.

"What about your overeager admirer?" Rick demanded.

"That's my problem to deal with."

"And mine."

She furrowed her brow. "What do you mean?"

"I mean my role here wasn't solely to play boyfriend but to make sure you stayed safe."

Her eyes narrowed. "Odele hired you?"

"She didn't need to hire me. Do you know how much money I have invested in *Pegasus Pride*? Keeping the main talent safe was inducement enough."

She felt his words like a blow to the chest. All those lingering touches, kisses, and his motivation had been... "You lied to me."

"Not really. You knew I was primarily a fake boy-friend."

"And secondarily a rat."

He raised his eyebrows. "You're offended because I may have had ulterior motives, too, in this game of ours?"

Yes, it had been a game. She was the fool for forgetting that. "I'm annoyed for not being told the whole truth. At least I was clear about my motivations."

"Yes, and you're determined not to rely on any man, aren't you?"

"Was Odele in on this?" she countered.

He shrugged. "We might have had a conversation about how it was in everyone's interest for me to keep an eye on you."

"Everyone's interest but mine," she said bitterly.

Rick set his jaw. "It was in your best interest, too, though you're too pigheaded to admit it."

Her heart constricted. Had he meant those things he'd whispered in the heat of passion—or had she run into the biggest actor of all? Even now, the urge to touch him was almost irresistible.

How had this conversation gotten very serious and very bad so fast? She'd wanted to talk about their charade and give him an out that she hoped he *wouldn't* take. Instead, she was left deflated and wondering whether she'd ever understood him.

Still, she rallied and lifted her chin. "You should be glad I'm setting you free. We never talked about forever, and you don't like fame. You don't want to be dating an actress, even if it's pretend." Two could play at this game. If he was going to cast her as another high-maintenance starlet, albeit one with an aversion to vulnerability where men were concerned, then she could portray him as camera-shy and hung up on celebrity.

He firmed his jaw but took a while to answer. "You're right. Fame isn't my thing." He raked a hand through his hair. "I should have learned that lesson with Isabel."

Chiara held back a wince. In some ways, she understood. The last thing some stars' egos could handle was to be cast in someone else's shade. There were A-list celebrities who refused to date other A-list celebrities for that very reason. Still, it rankled. She was not some random fame-seeker. If she couldn't fall in love with a celebrity, and an anonymous civilian would be put off her fame, who was left? Did she have to settle for a brief interlude with a stuntman with hidden layers? Was that all there was for her?

She lifted her chin, willing it to hold firm. "It's probably best if you moved out at this point. We could do with some space." Then she decided to echo Odele. "It'll plant the seeds for when our breakup is announced."

Rick's expression tightened. "Can't forget to spin it for the press, right?"

Ten

Chiara looked in her bathroom mirror. It had been a month since her breakup with Rick. A sad, depressing but uneventful month...*until now.*

She looked down at the stick in her hand. There was no mistaking the two telltale lines. Two lines that were about to change her life. She was pregnant.

The irony wasn't lost on her. She'd been wrestling with how to combine a career with her desire to start a family. Now the decision had been made for her.

As she disposed of the stick in the bathroom's wastepaper basket, she thought back to the last time she and Rick had been intimate—and her mind whirled.

She'd recently discovered that she'd expelled her contraceptive ring. It had probably gotten dislodged during rigorous sex, and then gone down the toilet afterward without her knowing it. Preoccupied with her breakup with Rick, she hadn't dwelled too much on it. But now...

Chiara looked at herself in the bathroom mirror as she washed her hands. She didn't look any different—*yet*.

She'd spent years trying not to be pregnant. She had a career to tend.

But while it wasn't the best of circumstances, it wasn't the worst, either. *A baby.* She was in her early thirties, financially independent, and had an established career. She'd always wanted a child, and in fact had started worrying that she couldn't see how it was going to happen. It had finally come to pass, but in a way she hadn't planned or foreseen. She'd been drawn to the Serenghettis, and now she was pregnant with an addition to the family. If things had been different—if Rick had loved her—she'd have been overjoyed right now instead of shadowed with worry. Still, she let giddiness seep through her. *A baby.*

She walked into her bedroom and sat on the bed, taking a calming breath. Then she picked up the phone receiver, toyed with it and replaced it. She had to tell Rick, of course…but she just needed time to process the information herself first. This wasn't avoidance or procrastination. At least that's what she kept telling herself…

She got up, paced, went downstairs to poke around in her fridge and then came upstairs again to stare at her phone.

When she couldn't stand it any longer, she called Odele and spilled all to her manager.

Odele was surprisingly equanimous at the news.

"Don't you know this means I'll be too pregnant to take on another action movie?" Chiara demanded, because she knew career suicide was at the top of Odele's list of sins.

"You wanted to stop doing them anyway."

Chiara lowered her shoulders. "Yes, you're right."

"What was Rick's reaction?"

"I haven't told him yet. I've been working up to that part."

There was a long pause on the line as Odele processed this information. "Well, good luck, honey. And remember, it's best to eat the frog."

"We fairy-tale types are supposed to kiss them, not eat them," Chiara joked weakly. "But okay, I get your point about doing the hard stuff first and getting it over with."

"Exactly."

"I just…" She took a deep breath. "I'm not sure I'm prepared to make that call to Rick." *Just yet.*

"I'm always here to help."

"Thanks, Odele."

The next day, Chiara wasn't feeling calm exactly, but she'd come down from her crazy tumult of emotions. She ventured out to her doctor's office for a consultation, having gotten herself an early appointment after there was a cancellation.

She didn't go into detail with the staff on the phone. She knew how juicy a piece of gossip a pregnant actress was, and medical staff had been known for leaks despite confidentiality laws. Out of an abundance of caution, she wore sunglasses and a scarf when she showed up for her appointment—because the paparazzi also knew that staking out the offices of doctors to the stars was a great way to get a scoop, or at least a tantalizing photo.

Dr. Phyllia Tribbling confirmed she was pregnant and assured her that everything was fine. She told her to come back when she was a few weeks further along.

Chiara found she was calmer after the doctor's visit, no doubt due to the obstetrician's soothing manner.

She spent the rest of the day researching pregnancy

online. She didn't dare visit a bookstore—and certainly not a baby store—because of the risk of being spotted by the press. Instead, she stayed home and took a nap. She should have read the signs in her unusual weariness lately, but pregnancy had been the last thing on her mind.

When she woke late in the day, she checked herself for any sign of morning sickness, but didn't feel a twinge. With the all-clear, she fixed herself a salad and a glass of water. Walking into the den, she sat on the sofa and placed the food on a coffee table.

After a few bites, she scrolled through the day's news on her phone.

When she came across a headline about herself, it took her a moment to process it, but then she nearly collapsed against the cushions.

Chiara Feran Is Pregnant!

She scanned the article and reread it, and then with shaking fingers, called her manager.

"Odele," she gasped. "How did *Gossipmonger* get this info?"

"They probably saw you exiting the doctor's office, sweetie," Odele said calmly. "You know, paparazzi like to stalk the offices of celebrity gynecologists and obstetricians."

"I just got back! Not even the gossip sites operate that fast." Chiara shook her head, even though her manager wasn't there to see it. "I should have worn a wig."

"I don't think that would have done the trick," Odele said drily. "Now, not getting knocked up to begin with, that would have done it."

Chiara's eyes narrowed. "You didn't feed them this story, did you?"

"No."

"But did you slip someone a tip to watch the doctor's office?" Chiara pressed.

"You have a suspicious mind."

"Did you?"

"I might have mentioned Dr. Tribbling has seen a lot of business lately."

"Odele, how could you!"

"Why don't you call Mr. Stuntman and let him know he isn't shooting blanks?" Odele answered sweetly.

"Why?" Chiara was close to wailing. She'd done it enough times on-screen to know when she was nearing the top of the emotional roller coaster.

"Better to squelch the rumor fast that you've broken up with Rick. Otherwise we'll be putting out fires for months. The press loves a story about a spurned pregnant woman going it alone."

Chiara took a breath. "Rick and I are broken up. Period."

"Not as far as the press is concerned. They're going to love stringing your two names together in real and virtual ink."

"And that's the only thing that matters, right?"

"No…it isn't." Odele sighed, softening. "Why don't you talk to him? Then reality and public perception can be aligned."

Chiara steeled herself and took a deep gulping breath. "Odele, you're fired."

They were words she'd never thought she'd say, but she'd had enough of manipulation…of public scrutiny… of Hollywood…and yes, of one stuntman in particular.

"Sweetie, you're overwrought, and it can't be good for the baby. Take time to think about it."

"Goodbye, Odele."

Yes, she'd calm down…right after she burst into tears.

* * *

Rick spit out his morning coffee. The hot liquid hit the oatmeal bowl like so many chocolate chips dotting cookie batter.

He prided himself on being unflappable. A cool head and calm nerves were a must in stunt work, particularly when something unexpected happened. But as with everything concerning Chiara, levelheadedness walked out the door with his better judgment.

He looked around his West Hollywood rental, still his home since Chiara had canceled his roommate privileges and his Beverly Hills place wasn't finished. The rain hitting the windows suited his mood. Or rather, it fit the rest of his life, which stretched out in a dull gray line in front of him. He got the same adrenaline rush from being with Chiara as he did from stunts, which probably explained the colorlessness of his days since their breakup.

Except now… *Chiara was pregnant.*

Rick was seized by turns with elation and shock. A baby. His and Chiara's. He was going to be a father.

Of course he wanted kids. He'd just never given much thought to how it would happen. He was thirty-three and at some point he'd be too old for stunt work. Sometime between now and then, his life would transition to something different. He figured he'd meet a woman, get married and have kids. Except along the way, he'd never foreseen a fake relationship with a maddening starlet who would then turn up pregnant.

Suddenly someday was now…and it wasn't supposed to happen this way—knocking up an actress tethered to fame when they weren't even married, living together or talking about forever.

Chiara infuriated and amused him by turns, the combustible passion between them feeding on itself. They were good together. Hell, he'd thought things had been heading to…something. But never mind. She'd made it clear he'd served his purpose and now there was no role for him in her life.

Now, though, whether she liked it or not, he had a place. She was pregnant.

He wondered whether this announcement was a public relations ploy, and then dismissed the idea. Chiara had too much integrity. He knew that much even though they were no longer a couple.

Still, she hadn't had the decency to tell him, and his family would be reading the news online and in print, just like everyone else. Her handlers hadn't yet sent out a second volley in this juicy story, but already he was looking like a jerk. *He just broke up with her, and now his ex-girlfriend has announced she's pregnant.* That's what everyone would think. *Maybe he left her because there was a surprise baby.*

There was one thing to do—and he wasn't waiting for an invitation. He still had the passcode to Chiara's front gate, unless she'd changed it.

Rick got his wallet, keys and phone, and then made a line for the door. He'd woken up this morning moody and out of sorts—more or less par for the course for him since his breakup with Chiara, but that was even before realizing he'd been served up as delicious gossipy dish for his neighbors to consume along with their morning coffee.

He cursed. "Moody" had just given way to "flaming-hot pissed off."

He made record time on the way to Chiara's house, adrenaline pumping in his veins. He knew from experience working on stunts that he was operating on a full head of steam. He needed to force himself to take a breath, slow down, collect his thoughts… *Hell.*

A baby. And she hadn't told him.

When he got to Chiara's front gate, rationality returned enough for him to pause a moment and call her from his cell. The last thing he needed was for Chiara to assume her surprise visitor was her stalker.

"It's Rick, and I'm coming in," he announced when she picked up, and then hit the end button without waiting for a response.

When he got to the house, the front door was unlocked and he let himself in.

He found Chiara in the kitchen, dressed in an oversize sweater and leggings, a mug in one hand.

His gaze went to her midriff, before traveling back to her face. Not that she would be showing yet—but she did look weary, as if she hadn't slept well. He resisted the urge to stride over and wrap her in his arms.

"I assume you unlocked the door for me when I called from the gate and that you don't have a standing invitation for your overeager fan to walk in." It was a mild reproach, much less than he wanted to say.

She set the mug down. "What do you think?"

"You're *pregnant.*" The last word reverberated through the room like the sound of a brass bell.

Chiara blanched.

"I found out the news with the rest of the world."

"I didn't have time to call you first." She wrung her hands. "The story broke so fast."

"You could have called me when the pregnancy test came back positive."

She hugged her midriff with her arms. "I wanted to be sure. I only went to the doctor yesterday."

"How did this happen?" he asked bluntly.

She raised her eyebrows. "I think you know."

"Right." *Mind-blowing sex.*

"My contraceptive ring accidentally fell out, and I didn't notice. I didn't give it much thought when I realized what happened." She shrugged. "I've always wanted kids. I guess it's happening sooner than I anticipated."

A very real sense of relief washed over him at her words. She wanted this baby, but birth control failure had led to very real consequences for the both of them. "You're going to announce we're still together."

She blinked. "Why?"

"Why? Because I don't want to look like a first-class jerk in front of the world, that's why."

"That your reason?" She appeared bewildered and a flash of hurt crossed her face.

"Aren't you the one who has been all about public image until now?" he tossed back. "Maybe this pregnancy is another PR stunt."

She dropped her arms, her expression turning shocked and offended. *"What?"*

"Are you saying Odele didn't plant the story in *Gossip-monger*?"

"I didn't know anything about it!"

He let another wave of satisfaction wash over him before he turned all-business. "Anyway, it doesn't matter. We're going to start acting and pretending like we never have before—the happy couple expecting a bundle of joy."

She lifted her chin. "I don't need your help."

He knew Chiara had the resources, but that was beside the point. "Sweetheart," he drawled, making the endearment sound ironic, "whether you want it or not, you've got it."

"Or?"

"Odele will be needing medication to deal with the ugly media firestorm."

"And will a wedding in Vegas follow?" she asked sarcastically. "I'll need to put Odele on retainer again."

"Whatever works."

She threw up her hands. "It's ridiculous. How long do you plan for this to go on?"

Until he figured out his next steps. He was buying himself time. "Until I don't look like a loser who abandoned his girlfriend the minute she turned up pregnant."

Rick paced in the nearly empty library of his multi-million-dollar new home. Raking his fingers through his hair, he stared out the French doors at the blazing sunshine bathing his new property in light. He'd just met with a landscaper and walked over the grounds. This morning, his appointment had been uppermost in his mind...until he'd checked the news.

Still, what was it all for? He'd bought and renovated this house as a keen investor...but now it felt insignificant. Because what really mattered in his life was half a city away. *Pregnant. With his baby.*

His gaze settled on the two upholstered armchairs. He'd brokered a cease-fire and even a rapprochement between Chiara and her father, but he couldn't figure out how to dig himself out of a hole—except by muscling in on Chiara earlier and ordering her to get back together until he figured things out. But then what?

His cell phone buzzed, and he fished it out of his pocket.

"Rick." Camilla Serenghetti's voice sounded loud and clear.

Rick hadn't even bothered to look at who was calling. He hadn't had a chance to figure out what to say to his family, but it was showtime.

"I read I'm going to be a grandma, but I know it can't be true. My son would have told me such happy news."

Of course.

"I told Paula at the hairdresser, 'No, no, don't listen to *Gossipmonger*. I know the truth.'" Pause. "Right?"

Rick raked a hand through his hair. "I just found out myself, Mom."

His mother muttered something in Italian. "So it is true? *Congratulazioni*. I can't believe it. First Cole has a surprise wedding. Now you have a surprise baby."

"You still have Jordan and Mia to count on." His remaining siblings might go a more traditional route.

"No, no. I'm happy…*happy* about the baby." His mother sounded emotional. "But no more surprises. *Basta*—enough, okay?"

"I'd like nothing better," he muttered, because he'd gotten the shock of his life today.

When he got off the phone, he texted his siblings.

The gossip is true, hang tight.

He knew he had to deal with stamping out questions—or at least holding them off—until he figured things out. Before he could put away his cell, though, his phone rang again.

"Rick."

"What can I do for you?" Rick recognized the voice, and under the circumstances, Chiara's father was the last person he wanted to have a conversation with. Michael Feran had his number from when he'd helped broker the meeting with Chiara, but he'd never expected the older man to use it.

"This is an odd request."

"Spit it out." The words came out more harshly than Rick intended, but it had already been a hell of a day.

Michael Feran cleared his throat. "I can't get in touch with Chiara."

Great. "What did you do, Michael?"

"Nothing. I called her at eleven, when we'd agreed to talk."

Rick knew Chiara had opted to periodically touch base with her father now that she was paying his bills.

"No one answered."

"I was heading out, and I'm not far from her house. I'll swing by." He didn't examine his motives. Michael Feran had given him another excuse to see Chiara, and maybe this time they could have a more satisfactory meeting— one that didn't end with her turning away and him walking out.

Besides, she was pregnant. His gut tightened. She could really be in trouble.

"Good." An edge of relief sounded in the older man's voice. "And I understand congratulations are in order."

"To you, too."

"Thank you. I just got an invite to be a father again. I didn't expect being a *grandfather* to be part of the bargain. At least not so soon."

"I'm sure," Rick replied curtly. "But one thing at a time. I'll go check on the mother-to-be now."

After ending the call, Rick made for the front door. For the second time that day, he found himself racing to Chiara's house, adrenaline thrumming through his veins.

She was fine. She had to be fine. She was probably dealing with pregnancy symptoms and in no mood to talk to her father. In the meantime, he might have another opportunity to set things to rights between them.

Marry me. The words popped into his head without thought, but of course they were the right ones. Right, natural…logical.

Exiting his house, he got behind the wheel of his Range Rover for the drive to Brentwood. Fortunately, traffic was light, and he reached Chiara's house faster than he expected.

When he reached her front gate, he tried calling her again. And when she didn't answer, he stabbed in the security code, jaw tightening.

Moments later, he pulled up in front of Chiara's house and saw her car parked there. His gut clenched. *Why isn't she answering her phone?*

Noticing the patio door open at the side of the house, he strode toward it…and then froze for a second when he realized there was broken glass on the ground.

Stepping inside the house, he could sense someone was there. Then he saw a man reflected in a mirror down the hall. The intruder crouched and ducked into the next room.

Rick's blood pumped as he raced forward. Damn it, he'd be lucky if this was an ordinary street burglar. But the brief glimpse he'd caught said this guy resembled Chiara's stalker.

Chiara came out of the marble bath in her bedroom suite and then walked into the dressing room. She pulled underwear and exercise clothes from a dresser and slipped into them.

In order to help her relax, she'd just taken a shower— and intended to take another after her workout. Her doctor had cleared her for moderate exercise in her first trimester.

After her argument with Rick earlier, she'd been torn

between wanting to cry and to wail in frustration. Her life had been a series of detours and blind turns lately...

She went downstairs to her home gym, and then glanced out the window at the overcast day. It suited her mood. Even the weather seemed ready to shed some tears...

Suddenly she spotted a hunched figure darting across the lawn. Frowning, she moved closer to the window. She wasn't expecting anyone. She had a regular cleaning service, and a landscaper who came once a week, but she didn't employ a live-in caretaker. There was no reason to, since she was often away on a movie set herself. Still, thanks to her fame, and now a sometime stalker, she had high fences, video cameras, an alarm system and a front gate with a security code. Even if she no longer had a bodyguard...

How had he gotten in?

As Chiara watched, the intruder slipped around the side of the house and out of view. Moments later, she heard a crash and froze. She ran over to the exercise room door and locked it.

Spinning around, she realized how vulnerable she was. Her workout clothes didn't have pockets, and she'd left her cell phone upstairs. She'd also never put a landline extension in this room, because there'd seemingly been no need to. The gym was on the first floor and faced a steep embankment outside. While it would be hard for someone to get in, it also meant she was trapped.

She heard the distant noise of someone moving around in the house. Her best bet was to stay quiet. She hoped whoever it was wouldn't look in here—at least not immediately. In the meantime, she had to figure out what to do... If the intruder wandered upstairs, perhaps she could make a dash for freedom and quietly call 911.

She heard the sound of a car on the gravel drive and almost sobbed with relief. Whoever it was must have known the security code at the front gate. Her heart jumped to her throat. *Rick?*

He didn't know about the intruder. He could be hurt, or worse, killed. She had to warn him.

Only a minute later, voices—angry and male—sounded in the house, but the confrontation was too indistinct for her to make out what was said.

"Chiara, if you're here, don't move!" Rick's voice came to her from the rear of the house.

She heard a scuffle. Something crashed as the combatants seemed to be fighting their way across the first floor.

Ignoring Rick's order, she wrenched open the door to the exercise room and dashed out in the direction of the noise. The sight that confronted her in the den made her heart leap to her throat all over again. Rick was pummeling Todd Jeffers, and while Rick appeared to have the upper hand, his opponent wasn't giving up the fight.

She looked around for a way to help and found herself reaching for a small marble sculpture that her interior decorator had positioned on a side table.

Grabbing it, she approached the two men. As her stalker staggered and then righted himself, she brought the sculpture down on the back of his head with a resounding thud.

Jeffers staggered again and fell to his knees, and Rick landed a knee jab under his chin. Her stalker sprawled backward, and then lay motionless.

Rick finally looked up at her. He was breathing heavily, and there was fire in his eyes. "Damn it, Chiara, I told you not to come out!"

As scared as she was, she had her own temper to deal

with. "You're welcome." Then she looked at the figure at their feet. "Sweet heaven, did I kill him?"

"Heaven is unlikely the place he'll be," Rick snarled.

"So I killed him?" she squeaked.

Rick bent to examine Jeffers and then shook his head. "No, but he's passed out cold."

She leaped for the phone even though what she wanted to do was throw up from sudden nausea. "I have to call 911."

"Do you have any rope or something else we can tie him up with?" Rick asked. "He's unconscious but we don't know for how long."

With shaky fingers, she handed him the receiver. While Rick called the police, she ran to get some twine she kept for wrapping presents. Her uninvited guest needed to be hog-tied, not decorated with a pretty bow, but it was all she had.

As she passed through the house, she noticed some picture frames had been repositioned—as if her stalker had stopped to admire them—and some of her clothes had been moved. Chiara shuddered. Likely Jeffers's obsession with her stuff had bought her time—time enough to stay hidden in the gym until Rick arrived.

Eleven

Chiara sat in her den attempting to get her bearings. Todd Jeffers was on his way to prison, not least because he'd violated a restraining order by scaling her fence, taking advantage of the fact that her alarm system had been off and she'd been ignoring the video cameras. Breaking and entering, trespassing... Thanks to Rick, the police would throw the book at him.

While Rick walked the remaining police to the door, she called Odele. She needed someone who would deal with the inevitable press attention. And even though she'd uttered the words *you're fired*, she and Odele were like family—and there was nothing like a brush with danger and violence to mend fences. She filled in her manager on what had happened, and Odele announced she would drive right over—both to get the fuller story, and perhaps because she sensed Chiara needed a shoulder to lean on.

Because Rick wasn't offering one—he continued to look mad as hell.

She knew she was lucky Rick had shown up at the right moment. She'd been in the shower when her father had attempted to reach her, and because he was worried she hadn't picked up, he'd called Rick. Michael Feran had done nothing for her...until today, when he may have saved her life. The ground beneath her had shifted, and there hadn't even been a major seismological event in LA. Forgetting about her scheduled call with her father had been a lucky break because minutes later she'd had an intruder in her house.

When Rick walked back in, Chiara hugged her arms tight across her chest as she sat on her couch.

He looked like a man on a short leash. The expression on his face was one she'd never seen before—not even in the middle of a difficult stunt. He was furious, and she wondered how much of it was directed at her.

"Thanks," she managed in a small voice.

"Damn it, Chiara!" Rick ran his hand through his hair. "What the hell? I told you to get extra security."

"You were it. I didn't have time to replace you...yet."

"You didn't have time? There's been a court order in place for weeks!"

She stood up. "Sarcastic stuntmen willing to moonlight as bodyguard and pretend boyfriend are hard to come by."

"Well, you almost gained an unwelcome husband!" Rick braced his hands at his sides. "According to the police, your Romeo had picked a wedding date and drafted a marriage announcement before he showed up today."

Chiara felt the hairs on the back of her neck rise. As a celebrity, she'd gotten some overzealous adulation in the past, but this was beyond creepy. "Don't lecture me."

She was frustrated, overwhelmed and tired—nearly shaking with shock and fear. She needed comfort but Rick was scolding her. It was all too much.

Rick crouched beside her. "We need to resolve this."

She raised her chin. "My stalker is behind bars. So that's another reason I don't need you anymore, I guess."

Except she did. She loved him. But he'd offered nothing in return, and she couldn't stay in a relationship based on an illusion. She'd learned this much from Tinseltown: she didn't want make-believe. She didn't want a relationship made for the press, and the false image of a happy couple expecting their first child. She wanted true love.

Rick stood up, a closed look on his face. He thrust his hands in his pockets. "Right, you don't need me. You'll never need any man. Got it. Your father may be back in your life, but you always stand on your own."

She said nothing. In her mind, though, she willed him to give her the speech that she really wanted. *I love you. I can't live without you. I need you.*

He braced his hands on his sides. "We're stuck playing out this drama, the two of us. The press junket for *Pegasus Pride* is coming up, and we don't want to be the story instead of the movie. I'll move back in with you here until my house is ready. We'll do promo for the movie and then nest until the baby arrives. All the while, we're back to Chiara and Rick, the happy expectant couple, as far as the press is concerned."

She lifted her chin again. "Got it."

The only thing that saved her from saying more was Odele breezing in the front door and descending like a mother hen.

"Oh, honey," her manager exclaimed.

Chiara looked at her miserably and then eyed Rick.

"I'm glad you're here because Rick was just leaving to pack. He's moving back in with me."

"I'll be back soon."

She'd dreamed about their getting back together, but it wasn't supposed to happen like this.

Rick looked around his West Hollywood rental, debating what to pack next. The movers could do the rest.

Chiara's stalker may have been arrested, but the threat to Rick's own sanity remained very real. He'd always prided himself on being Mr. Cool and Unflappable—with nerves of steel in the face of every stunt. But there was nothing cool about his relationship with Chiara.

"So the first Serenghetti grandbaby, and it was a surprise." Jordan shook his head as he taped a box together. "Mom must be beside herself."

His brother happened to be in town for another personal appearance, so he'd come over to help Rick pack. Together, they were surrounded by boxes in the small living room.

"Last I heard, she was trying three new recipes." Rick knew cooking was stress relief for his mother.

Damn it, he wished the news had broken another way. Yet, if Chiara was to be believed, it wasn't her doing that the cat was out of the bag.

Jordan shook his head. "Of course Mom is cooking. First Cole throws an unexpected wedding, now you hit her with a surprise grandchild. She's probably trying to figure out what went wrong with her parenting recipe— was she missing an ingredient?'

"Hilarious," Rick remarked drily. "She's got two more kids she can hang her hopes on."

Jordan held up his hands as if warding off a bad omen. "You mean, she has Mia to help her out."

Rick shrugged. "Whatever."

His brother looked around. "You know we could just throw this stuff in a van ourselves instead of using movers."

"Yeah, but I've got more pressing problems at the moment."

Jordan cocked his head. "Oh, yeah, daddy duty. But that doesn't start for another...?"

"Seven months or more," Rick replied shortly.

Chiara had gotten pregnant in Welsdale or soon after. There'd been plenty of opportunities. Once the floodgates had opened, they hadn't been able to keep their hands off each other.

"You know, I was debating what housewarming gift to get you. Now I'm thinking you need one of those dolls they use in parenting classes...to practice diapering and stuff."

"Thanks for the vote of confidence."

"Well, you and Chiara are definitely in the express lane of relationships," Jordan remarked.

"The relationship was a media and publicity stunt."

Jordan's face registered his surprise. "Wow, the work of a stuntman never ends. I'm impressed by your range."

"Put a lid on it, Jordan."

His brother flashed a grin. "Still, a publicity stunt... but Chiara winds up pregnant? How do you explain that one?"

"I was also supposed to protect her from her stalker friend. That was the real part."

Jordan picked up his beer and toasted him with it. "Well, you did do that. I suppose one thing led to another?"

"Yeah, but it could have gone better." The nut job had

already been in Chiara's house when he'd arrived. As for the relationship part…

"Or worse."

Rick's hand curled at his side. Damn it. Why hadn't Chiara listened to him and taken more precautions? Because she was hardheaded.

Jordan shook his head. "I can't believe I had to get the news from *Gossipmonger*."

"Believe it. Chiara's team has a contact there."

"Still, I figured I'd hear it from you. I thought the brotherly bond counted for something," Jordan said in a bemused tone.

"You didn't need to know it was a publicity stunt."

His brother shrugged. "It seemed real enough to me. So what are you going to do?"

"For the moment, I'm moving back in with her. What does it look like I'm doing?"

Jordan nodded, his expression blank. "So you're muscling back into her life. Do you know an approach besides caveman-style?"

"Since when are you a relationship expert?"

"This calls for a grand gesture."

Rick nearly snorted. "She's practically announced she doesn't need a knight on a horse."

Jordan shrugged. "She doesn't need you, you don't need her, but you want each other. Maybe that's what you have to show her." His brother's lips quirked. "You know, upend the fairy tale. Show up on a horse and tell her that she needs to save you."

Rick frowned. "From what?"

Jordan grinned. "Yourself. You've been bad-tempered and cranky."

"So says the Serenghetti family philosopher who only does shallow relationships."

Jordan placed his hand over his heart. "My guru powers only work with others."

Rick threw a towel at his brother, who caught it deftly. "Get packing."

Still, he had to admit Jordan had given him some ideas.

"You look like a miserable pregnant lady," Odele remarked.

"My best role yet." Chiara felt like a mess…or rather, her life was one. Ironically the situation with her father was the only part she'd straightened out.

After yesterday's drama, Odele had stayed over, feeling Chiara needed someone in the house with her. And Chiara was thankful for the support. She'd let herself cry just once…

Chiara toyed with her lunch of salmon and fresh fruit. Outside the breakfast nook, the sun shone bright, so unlike yesterday. Her mood should have picked up, too, but instead she'd been worried about spending the next months with Rick in her house—falling apart with need, so unlike her independent self.

"I hate to see you make a mistake," Odele remarked from across the table.

Was that regret in her manager's voice? "You sound wistful."

"I'm speaking from experience. There was one who got away. Don't let that be your situation."

"Oh, Odele."

"Don't *Odele* me," her manager said in her raspy voice. "These days there's a fifty-three-year-old editor at one of those supermarket rags who is just waiting for a date with yours truly."

Chiara managed a small laugh. "Now, that's more like it."

Odele's eyes gleamed. "He's too young for me."

"At fiftysomething? It's about time someone snatched him out of the cradle."

"I'll think about it...but this conversation isn't about me, honey. It's about you."

Chiara sighed. "So how am I supposed to avoid making a mistake? Or are you going to tell me?"

"I've got an idea. You and Rick are meant to be together. I've thought so for a long time." She shook her head. "That's why—"

"This pregnancy is a sign from the heavens?"

"No, your moping expression is."

Chiara set down her fork. "I guess I'm not as good an actress as I thought."

"You're a great actress, and I've lined up Melody Banyon at *WE Magazine*. She can come here for an interview tomorrow." Her manager harrumphed. "My second attempt at making you and Rick see reason."

"Another of your schemes, Odele?" she said, and then joked, "Haven't we had enough of the press?"

"Trust me, you're going to like this plan better than my idea of lighting a fire under your stuntman with the pregnancy news, but it's up to you what you want to say."

When Odele explained what she had in mind, Chiara nodded and then added her own twist...

By the next morning, Chiara was both nervous and excited. She felt as if she was jumping off a cliff—in fact, it was not so different from doing a movie stunt.

Sitting in a chair in her den facing Melody Banyon, she smoothed her hands down the legs of her slacks. It was

almost a replay of her last interview with the reporter...
except Rick wasn't here.

"Are you pregnant?"

There it was. She was about to give her confirmation
to the world. "Yes, I am."

"Congratulations."

"I'm still in my first trimester."

"And how are you feeling?"

Chiara sucked in a shaky breath. "Good. A little
queasy but that's normal."

Melody tilted her head and waited.

"Even though this pregnancy was unexpected," she
went on, "I've always wanted children. And, you know,
I've learned you can't plan everything in life."

"You were dating a stuntman working on one of your
movies. Rick Serenghetti?"

"Yes. Rick did me an enormous favor. It started as a
PR stunt. Rick was supposed to pose as my boyfriend to
distract the press from stories about my father and his
gambling. I know celebrities aren't supposed to admit
to doing things for publicity, but I want to clear the air."

This was *so* hard. But she had to do it. Odele had convinced her to talk honestly about her feelings for Rick,
but Chiara had thought it was important to come clean
publicly about the whole charade. Risky, but important.

"You say *started*..."

"Even though I didn't know it, Rick signed up for
our make-believe because he also wanted to protect me
from a stalker. It was a threat that I wasn't taking seriously enough."

"But Todd Jeffers is now charged with serious crimes.
Are you relieved?"

"Yes, of course. And I'm so grateful to Rick for tackling Jeffers when he broke into my house."

"And how is your father doing?"

"Great. We met, and he agreed to go into rehab for his addiction. I'm proud of him." She had Rick to thank there, too.

Melody leaned forward. "So with your father addressing his addiction, and your stalker behind bars, you and Rick are…?"

Chiara gave a nervous laugh. "Somewhere along the way, I fell in love with Rick. I love him."

Melody leaned forward and shut off her voice recorder. "Perfect."

Chiara blew a breath. "You think so?"

The reporter gave her a sympathetic look. "I know so. A headline will appear on the *WE Magazine* site in a few hours, and then we'll go to press with the print edition for the end of the week."

Hours. That's all she had before Rick and the world would know what lay in her heart.

Best to keep occupied. She still needed to put in motion the last part of the plan, which she'd suggested to Odele.

Rick nearly fell out of his seat. *I love him.*

He'd followed the news link to *WE Magazine* in Odele's text and got a sucker punch.

Looking around his now nearly bare and sparsely furnished rental, he felt the swoosh of air that he normally associated with a high-altitude stunt.

His cell phone rang, and it was Melody Banyon from *WE Magazine.*

"Do you have a public comment on Chiara Feran's interview with us? She confirmed her pregnancy."

Yes. No. I don't know. "I won't ask how you got my number."

"I think you know the answer," Melody replied, amusement in her voice.

Odele, of course.

And then with sudden clarity, he realized going for broke was the thing to do. His concerns about privacy, getting manipulated by the press, or even publicity-hungry actresses, flew out the window. He didn't have time to think about whether this was another of Odele's PR moves. He was done with charades, make-believe and pretend.

"Anything you'd like to say for the record?" Melody prompted again.

"Yes. My feelings for Chiara were real from the beginning. There was no pretending on my part."

"And the baby news?"

Yeah, wow. Somehow tomorrow was today...but he couldn't be more elated with every passing day. "It may not have been planned, but I'm happy about it."

"Are you Prince Charming?"

He laughed ruefully. "I've enjoyed my privacy up until now. And I've liked keeping my aliases under wraps, but things are becoming public knowledge."

Melody cleared her throat. "Okay, off the record now... I wouldn't let Chiara get away if I were you. She's scared, but I've seen you two together. You belong together."

"And here I thought Chiara and I had done a good snow job convincing you that we really were a couple."

"Not as good a snow job as you two have done on each other," Melody replied.

Yeah. And suddenly he knew he had to follow through on the idea that Jordan had given him...

"Give me until tomorrow before you publish my comment, Melody. I want Chiara to be the first to know."

"Of course!" the reporter responded with a smile in her voice.

Rick barely heard her. His mind was already buzzing with ideas for props for his next stunt.

Chiara was tense. Controlling one's image was paramount in Hollywood, and she'd just blown her cover. *I love him...* And the entire world knew. There was nowhere to hide.

She wrung her hands as she stared out her kitchen window. *WE Magazine* had published parts of her interview online late yesterday. It had been hours...and still no word from Rick.

He could humiliate her. He could issue a stunning rejection that handed her heart back to her.

Picking up the phone, she made a lifeline call to her manager.

"Oh, Odele, what have you gotten me into?" she moaned.

"Have you looked at social media?"

"Are you kidding? It's the last thing I can bring myself to peek at."

"Well, you should. The confirmation of your pregnancy has taken the internet by storm, of course."

"Great," she said weakly.

"Yup, but the viral storm is turning in your favor, sweetie. People are applauding your honesty."

"About being a fraud?"

"You were honest about the phoniness of celebrity culture."

Chiara closed her eyes. She'd gone viral as a recovering liar...and people loved it. "I'm afraid to leave the house."

"You weren't scared when you had a stalker, but now you are?"

Of course she was. She hadn't heard from Rick. The ax could still fall.

Then a distant sound reached her, and she frowned. "Hold on, Odele."

It sounded like hoof beats. *Impossible.*

She peeked out the window. A rider on a white horse was coming up the drive.

The *clomp* of hooves sounded louder as horse and rider came closer. It couldn't be...but her heart knew it was. "Odele... I've got to go."

"What's the matter, honey?" Chiara could practically hear the frown in her manager's voice. "Do I need to send the police?"

"Um, that won't be necessary. I think I'm being rescued..."

"What...?"

"It's Rick on a white horse...bye."

"Well, I'll be damned. And he didn't even give me a heads-up so I could send a photographer to snap the moment."

"We'll do the scene over for you."

"Great, because romances are my favorite."

"I'd never have known from the way you've pushed me to do action flicks—"

"And you met a hunky stuntman in the process."

"Odele, I have to go!"

Her manager laughed. "Good luck, honey."

Rushing to the front door, Chiara took a moment to glance at herself in the hall mirror. Her eyes were bright, but she wished she could have looked more polished than she did in stretch pants and a T-shirt. Still, at least these clothes continued to fit her.

She took a deep breath and opened the door, stepping outside.

Rick stopped his horse in front of her, a smile playing at his lips.

Chiara placed her hands on her hips. "You got a horse through my front gate...really?"

"I still have the code. You've got to change it if you don't want to keep having unexpected visitors."

She nodded at the animal that he sat astride, her insides buzzing. "And you rode him along canyon roads to my house?"

"Hey, I'm a stuntman."

She met his gaze head-on. "And this is one of your stunts?"

"Jordan told me to get on a horse. Before I could do it or go with the backup plan of coming by with a wood boyfriend for Ruby, you had your interview with *WE Magazine*," he said, not answering her directly. "But I thought I'd...accommodate you anyway."

She tilted her head. "Accommodate how?"

He swung down, all lithe physique, and then pulled her into his arms and kissed her.

She leaned into him, kissing him back.

When they broke apart, he said, "I love you."

She blinked back sudden emotion, and joked, "You should if you rode a horse here."

"It took me a while to recognize it, but then you were put in danger by Jeffers." His face blazed with emotion. "Damn it, Chiara, I could have lost you."

She nodded, swallowing against the lump in her throat.

"I let my experience with Isabel color my perspective even though it was becoming increasingly obvious you couldn't be more different."

She gave a watery smile. "Well, you can be forgiven

for that one. Thanks to Odele, I was using you to manipulate the press, too."

"In the beginning, yeah. But you had guts and determination. Plus more and more layers that I wanted to uncover even though I kept trying to pigeonhole you as just another evil starlet."

"Who, me? Snow White?" she said playfully.

He cracked a smile and then gave her another quick kiss.

She braced her hands on his chest. "Thank you for tackling Jeffers…twice. I didn't take the risk seriously enough because I wasn't going to let you tell me what to do. But you helped me save my father from himself." When he started to say something, she placed a finger on his lips to stop him. "Thank you for coming into my life and dealing with all the craziness of fame. I was so afraid of being vulnerable and getting hurt."

He grasped her wrist and kissed her hand.

"I love you. I was falling in love with you and it scared me to feel so much," she finished.

"We're getting married."

She gave an emotional laugh—happiness bubbling out of her. "Before or after the baby is born?"

"Before. Vegas, even. Your father can give you away."

"He doesn't want to give me away. He just got me back! And I can't be an actress eloping to Vegas. It's too clichéd," she protested.

"You're a pregnant Hollywood actress who'll be a few months along at the wedding. You're already a cliché." He winked. "We'll leave people guessing about whether we're taking our stunt to the extreme by actually getting married."

"So our love isn't real?"

"Snow, if my feelings were any more real, they'd be jumping around like the Seven Dwarves."

"Funny, Serenghetti."

And then he proceeded to show her just how real they were…

Epilogue

Two months later...

Chiara mingled with other Serenghettis who'd gathered for Serg's sixty-seventh birthday barbecue on a hot August afternoon in Welsdale. She was still getting used to these family get-togethers. They were a world apart from her past experiences with her own family. Serg and Camilla's home brimmed with animated voices and laughter.

Still, her relationship with her father had come a long way. Her father was in rehab, but he'd already announced he'd like to become an addiction counselor. And Odele had been and continued to be like a second mother. She'd already started shopping for baby clothes. And now, of course, Chiara had the Serenghettis, as well.

"The food is delicious," Marisa announced as she stepped onto the patio bathed in late-afternoon sun. "I feel even more like an overstuffed piñata."

Chiara smiled at her sister-in-law. "Now, there's a met-aphor for being pregnant I haven't heard before."

In a nice surprise, shortly after her own pregnancy had gone public, Cole and Marisa had quietly announced they were expecting, too. Her sister-in-law was only a month further along. Naturally, Chiara thought, there'd be another female Serenghetti to take this journey with.

Marisa sighed. "I know what a chicken cordon bleu feels like."

"A ham?" Jordan asked, having overheard.

His sister-in-law shot him a droll look. "Funny."

"Just don't have a surprise birth," Jordan teased. "Mom wants a chance to plan for a big event for once."

Chiara bit back another smile, and then looked down at her plain platinum wedding band and large canary di-amond solitaire engagement ring. She and Rick had had a quick wedding in Las Vegas with just immediate fam-ily present. It had been small, intimate and private, just like they'd wanted. There'd been no press, though they'd given Melody an exclusive after the fact.

Now as Marisa and Jordan stepped away, Rick came up and settled his hands on her shoulders, kneading them gently. Chiara nearly purred with contentment.

"How are you feeling?" Rick asked in a low voice.

"Like my next role should be as a pregnant stunt-woman," she responded.

"You'd be great. I've got just the vehicle."

"I feel like a starlet who has slept her way to the top with the studio boss."

He chuckled. "Snow, we're partners now."

At home and at the office. She and Rick were start-ing their own production company. He'd vowed to sup-port her career in any way he could, and that included helping her find appropriate acting roles. For her part, she wanted to respect Rick's preference to not be in the glare of celebrity. She'd done interviews herself, but he'd insisted that as her prince, he needed and wanted to be her escort to public events.

Just then, Serafina, Marisa's cousin, stepped onto the patio and then frowned as she spotted Jordan.

"Uh-oh," Rick said in a low voice for Chiara's ears only. "Trouble."

As if on cue, Jordan gave a lazy grin, and then sauntered toward Serafina with a gleam in his eye.

Chiara smiled. "Only the best kind for those two." Then turning, she snuggled against Rick as he draped an arm around her shoulders. "Don't you agree?"

Her husband winked and gave her a kiss. "Definitely. You're the best trouble I ever had, Snow. And then love had walked in for us."

* * * * *

HIS PRINCESS OF CONVENIENCE

REBECCA WINTERS

This book is dedicated to every woman who was once a little girl with a dream to be a princess.

CHAPTER ONE

August, Monte Calanetti, Italy

THE FLOOR-LENGTH MIRROR reflected a princess bride whose flowing white wedding dress, with the heavy intricate beading, followed the lines of her slender rounded figure to perfection. It probably weighed thirty pounds, but her five-foot-nine height helped her to carry it off with a regal air.

The delicate tiara with sapphires, the something-borrowed, something-blue gift from the queen, Christina's soon-to-be mother-in-law, held the lace mantilla made by the nuns. The lace overlying her red-gold hair, to the satin slippers on her feet, formed a whole that looked...pretty.

"I actually feel like a bride." Her breath caught. "That can't be me!" she whispered to herself. Her very recent makeover was nothing short of miraculous.

Christina Rose, soon-to-be bride of Crown Prince Antonio de L'Accardi of Halencia, turned to one side, then the other, as past memories of being called an ugly duckling, the chubby one, filled her mind.

From adolescence until the ripe old age of twenty-eight, she'd had to live with those unflattering remarks muttered by the people around her. Not that she really heard people say those things once she'd grown up and had been spending her time doing charity work on behalf of her prominent family. But she knew it was what people were thinking.

In truth her own parents were the ones who'd scarred her. They'd left her with nannies from the time she was born. And as she'd grown, her father had constantly belittled her with hurtful barbs by comparing her unfavorably to her friends. "Why is our daughter so dumpy?" she'd once heard him say. "Why didn't we get a boy?" They'd picked out the name Christopher, but had to change it to Christina when she was born.

His unkind remarks during those impressionable years had been wounds that struck deep, especially considering that Christina's mother had been a former supermodel.

Christina didn't know how her father could have said such cruel things to his daughter when she had loved both her parents so much and desperately wanted their approval. Between her unattractive brownish-red hair she'd always worn in a ponytail, to her teeth that had needed straightening, she'd been an embarrassment to her parents, who moved in the highest of political and social circles in Halencia.

In order to keep her out of sight, they'd sent their overweight daughter to boarding school in Montreux, Switzerland, where forty-five girls from affluent, titled families were sent from countries around the world.

Her pain at having to live away year after year until she turned eighteen had been her deepest sorrow. Christina was a poor reflection on her parents, whose world revolved around impressing other important people in the upper echelons of society, including the favor of the royal family of Halencia. Her father particularly didn't want her around when they were entertaining important dignitaries, which was most of the time.

If it hadn't been for Elena, the daughter of Halencia's royal family attending the French-speaking boarding school who'd become her closest friend, Christina didn't know how she would have survived her time there. With both of them being from Italian-speaking Halencia, their nationality and own dialect had immediately created a bond between the two women.

Though Elena bore the title of Princess Elena de L'Accardi, she'd never used it at school or behaved as if she were better than Christina. If anything, she was a free spirit, on the wild side, and good-looking like her older brother, the handsome Crown Prince Antonio de L'Accardi, who was the heartthrob of Halencia, beloved by the people. He'd had a hold on Christina's heart from the first moment she met him.

Elena never worried about breaking a few rules, like meeting a boyfriend at the local ice-skating rink in Montreux without their headmistress finding out. And worse, sneaking out to his nearby boarding school and going rowing on the lake at midnight, or sneaking her out for a joyride to Geneva in the Lamborghini his wealthy parents had bought him.

Christina had loved being with Elena and secretly wished she could be outgoing and confident like her dear friend. When the royal family went on their many vacations, Christina missed Elena terribly. It was during those times that Christina developed a close friendship with the quiet-spoken Marusha from Kenya.

Marusha was the daughter of the chief of the westernized Kikuyu tribe who'd sent his daughter to be educated in Switzerland. Marusha suffered from homesickness and she and Christina had comforted each other. Their long talks had prompted Christina to fly to Kenya after she turned eighteen and Marusha prevailed on her father to open doors for Christina to do charity work there.

Once she'd established a foundation in Halencia to deal with the business side, Christina stationed herself in Africa and lost herself in giving help to others. She knew she was better off being far away from home where she couldn't be hurt by her parents' dissatisfaction with her.

Caught up in those crippling thoughts, Christina was startled to hear a knock on the door off the main hallway.

"Mi scusi," sounded a deep male voice she hadn't heard since his phone call two months ago. "I'm looking for Christina Rose. Is she in here?"

What was Antonio doing up here outside the doors of the bridal suite?

In a state of absolute panic, Christina ran behind the screen to hide. She'd come up here to be alone and make sure her wedding finery fit and looked right. For him to see her like this before the ceremony would be worse than bad luck!

Her heart pounded so hard she was afraid he could hear it through the doors. Trying to disguise her voice to a lower pitch, she said, "Christina isn't here, *signor*."

"I think she is," he teased. "I think it's you playing a game with me."

Heat filled her cheeks. He'd found her out. "Well, you can't come in!"

"Now, *that's* the Christina I remember. Still modest and afraid of your own shadow. What a way to greet your intended beloved."

"Go away, Antonio. You should be at the chapel."

"Is that all you have to say after I've flown thousands of miles to be with my fiancée?"

The large four-carat diamond ring set in antique gold belonging to the L'Accardi royal family had been given to her at their engagement four years ago. Though she'd gone through the sham ritual for the most worthy reason, it had been a personal horror for Christina.

But when her parents had acted overjoyed that she'd snagged the crown prince, she felt she'd gotten their attention at last. Becoming a royal princess had made them look more favorably at her, and that had helped her enter into the final wedding preparations with growing excitement.

The minute Antonio had flown back to the States, she put the ring in a vault for safekeeping. To damage it out in Africa would be unthinkable. She'd only gotten it out to wear on the few times they were together in Halencia. Now it was hidden in her purse.

Christina had never felt like a fiancée, royal or otherwise. She knew Antonio had been dreading this union as much as she had, but he was too honorable for his own good. Therefore Christina had to follow through on the bargain they'd made for Elena's sake.

"I didn't really believe this day would come."

He'd stayed away in San Francisco on business. The press followed his every move and knew he'd only been with her a handful of times since the engagement. He'd flown home long enough to be seen with her at the palace when she flew in from Africa. They came together in order to perpetuate the myth that they were in love and looking forward to their wedding day.

"San Francisco is a long way from Halencia, Christina, but I should have made time before."

"I know you've been married to your financial interests in Silicon Valley. No fiancée can compete with that." Not when she knew he'd been with beautiful women who were flattered by his attention and couldn't care less that he was engaged.

"You want to marry a successful husband, right? We had an agreement for Elena's sake."

He was right, of course, and it had been a secret between her and Antonio. But no one knew how Christina had pulled off such an improbable coup. The press had dubbed her the Cinderella Bride.

"I know, Antonio, and I plan to honor it. But not one second before I have to go downstairs to the chapel. Don't you have something else to do?"

"I'm doing it right now. Do you mind if I put a little

gift on the bed for you?" He'd said it kindly. "I promise I won't look at you and I'll hurry back out."

"What gift? I don't want anything." She knew she sounded ungracious, but she couldn't help it. She'd never been so nervous in her life!

"It's your family brooch, the one that a Rose bride wears at her wedding to bring her marriage luck. One of the stones had come loose, so I had it repaired for you to wear and couldn't get it back to you until today."

The brooch?

Christina had heard the story behind the brooch all her life. It was supposed to bring luck, but she thought it had been lost a long time ago. She'd asked her wedding planner, Lindsay, to try and track it down for her, but to no avail. Her father's aunt Sofia certainly hadn't whispered a word about it during all the wedding preparations. Why hadn't she given it to Christina herself? Furthermore how did Antonio get hold of it?

"Thank you for bringing it to me," she said in a subdued voice. "It means a lot." In fact, more than he could know. A special talisman to bring her luck handed down in the Rose family. Now she felt ready.

"It was important to me that you have it. I want this day to be perfect for you."

She was thrilled by the gesture and heard the door open. If all he had to do was put it on the bed, she should be hearing the doors closing any second now.

"Are you still holding your breath waiting for me to go away, *bellissima*?"

Bellissima. Christina was not beautiful, but the way

he said it made her feel beautiful, and today was her wedding day. She imagined he was trying to win her around with all the ways he knew how. She had no doubts he knew every one of them and more.

He laughed. "I'm still waiting, but we don't need to worry, Christina. After all, this isn't a real marriage."

She took a deep breath, realizing he was teasing her. "Well, considering that this isn't going to be a real marriage, then I'd say we need all the luck we can get, so please leave before even the ceremony itself is jinxed by your presence here."

"A moment, *per favore*. It's a lovely bridal chamber. The balcony off this suite shows the whole walled village of Monte Calanetti—it's very picturesque. I do believe you have a romantic heart to have chosen the Palazzo di Comparino for our wedding to take place. All nestled and secluded in this place amongst the vineyards rippling over the Tuscan countryside. I couldn't imagine a more perfect setting to celebrate our nuptials."

"After living near the vineyards of the Napa Valley in California all these years, I doubt a spot like this holds much enchantment for you. I guess I should be thanking you for letting our wedding take place here instead of the cathedral in Voti. Now, will you please go so I can finish getting ready?"

Christina was still her vulnerable self. Antonio stopped the teasing for a minute. "If it's any solace to you, I'm sorry for the position I've put you in."

After a long silence she said in a defeated tone,

"Don't worry about it." He heard a sadness in her voice. "To be honest, it isn't as if I've had any other offers."

Her comment revealed a little of her conflict, the same conflict torturing him. There was a part of him that wanted to be crazy in love. If only he'd been an ordinary man like his best man, Zach, who could marry the woman who'd captured his heart. To choose a bride his heart wanted had never been a possibility.

When he thought about Christina, he realized she was having similar feelings that increased his guilt, but he couldn't dwell on that right now. It was too late for regrets. They would be married within the hour and he intended to be a good husband to her.

"Just remember we're doing this for Elena," he reminded her, hoping it would help her spirits. "She'll be up in a minute to escort you to the chapel." His eyes closed tightly for a moment. "Would it help if I told you I admire you more than any other woman I know?" It was the truth.

"Actually it wouldn't," she came back. "Thousands of women have entered into political unions disguised as marriage. We thought our engagement wouldn't last long. I thought that after four years you would fly to Africa and tell me in person we didn't have to go through with it."

"I'm afraid that wasn't our destiny, Christina. Everything has escalated out of control, the paparazzi have driven things to a higher pitch. Father's chief assistant, Guido, had me on the phone, urging me to marry you as soon as possible. The people are fed up with my parents. They want our marriage to take place for the good of the monarchy, reminding me of the danger of an abolished royal family if we wait."

"I know. That's because they want you for their king, and you need a queen. I understand that, but I'd rather you didn't start using meaningless platitudes with me."

"I was complimenting you," he asserted.

"I'm glad we could help preserve Elena's reputation along with your family's, but I don't want compliments. Your sister is doing much better these days and has a boyfriend who treats her well. Let's be happy for that and avoid any unnecessary pretense."

Antonio had come to the bridal suite already deeply immersed in troubled thoughts about their forthcoming marriage. Her last remark only added to his anxiety. He put the small velvet-lined box at the foot of the bed. After closing the doors quietly behind him, he left the bridal suite and walked down the corridor to the staircase of the three-storied palazzo.

Zach, his best friend, would be waiting for him in the bedroom just off the staircase of the second floor. By now some hundred and fifty guests had arrived for the ceremony, including his parents and their entourage. The small wedding Christina wanted had grown to royal proportions. It had been inevitable.

Antonio had met Christina when he went to Switzerland many times to visit his younger sister at boarding school. She always asked if her roommate, Christina, could come along with them when they went out for *fondue au fromage* or took the ferry to see the sights around Lake Geneva.

Though Antonio thought of Christina as his sister's pudgy friend, he'd found her sensible and soft-spoken, and probably the sweetest girl he'd ever met. That favorable impression of her grew deep roots when she'd phoned him in the middle of the night about Elena four years ago.

His sister had needed help because she and her loser addict boyfriend had been hauled off to jail on drug possession. Her boyfriend had been arrested and charged. What if Elena was next to be tainted with a jail record?

The paparazzi would have blown his sister's mistake into a royal scandal that would do great damage to the already damaged royal family. Antonio's parents hadn't been in favor with the country for a long time and were constantly being criticized in the press for their profligate ways.

In order to keep Elena's latest scandalous affair out of the news, Antonio had to think of something quick to take the onus off his wayward younger sister. Thankful beyond words for Christina's swift intervention with that phone call, he was able to turn things around and had talked her into entering into a mock engagement with him to create a new piece of news.

If the press focused on his stunning announcement, it would take up column space and deflect the paparazzi's interest in his sister's scandal, thus saving Elena's poor reputation and the family from further scrutiny and ruin.

After some persuasion Christina had agreed to fly to Halencia and become his fiancée because she loved

Elena and had believed the engagement wouldn't last long. They'd be able to go their own separate ways at some future date. Or so Antonio had thought...

But once he'd leaked the news of their engagement to the press and it had gone public, everything changed. Elena's problems with the paparazzi went away like magic. Even more startling, the news of his engagement to the unknown Christina Rose grew legs.

The country approved of the Cinderella fiancée doing charity work in Kenya, whom he'd plucked out of obscurity. Immediately there was a demand for a royal wedding to become front and center. Guido was insistent on it happening immediately.

Antonio understood why. The royal approval ratings had dropped to an all-time low. In particular, his and Elena's philandering parents drew criticism with their string of affairs. There were accusations of them dipping into the royal coffers to fund their extravagant lifestyle. To his chagrin, Elena was also becoming infamous for her wild party ways and uncontrolled spending habits.

The press had been calling for the king and queen to step down. It was the will of the people that the monarchy be turned into a republic. Or...put Antonio on the throne.

A lot had gone wrong with his family while Antonio was pursuing his studies and business interests in the US. To his amazement, the separation that had distanced him from all this scandal had endeared him further to his subjects, who saw him as the one person to save the royal dynasty! Christina's hope that there wouldn't be a wedding was dashed. So was his... Guido's phone calls to him had changed everything.

And had made him feel trapped.

Once Antonio reached the second floor of the palazzo, he entered the bedroom designated as the groom's changing room.

"There you are!" Zach declared with relief. "You have a letter from your father." He handed him an envelope.

Antonio opened it and after reading it, he put the note back in the envelope and slid it in his trouser pocket. What were his parents up to now, spending the taxpayers' money on a honeymoon he hadn't asked for? He couldn't say no, but this was the last time public money would be spent on private, privileged citizens of the royal family.

"It's getting late," Zach reminded him. "You have to finish getting ready now. Lindsay has the wedding planned down to the second."

Antonio looked at his best man through veiled eyes. "I had to deliver the brooch to Christina so she could pin it on her wedding dress before the ceremony."

"How did that go?"

"She was hiding behind a screen and told me to leave." Considering the fact that she'd been forced to go through with this marriage they hadn't planned on, he shouldn't have been surprised she sounded so upset.

"That was wedding nerves. Christina was a sweetheart when Lindsay and I met with her for her fittings," Zach said, helping him on with the midnight blue royal dress uniform jacket.

After their unexpected exchange upstairs, Antonio didn't exactly agree with his friend. "She's not happy about this wedding going ahead."

Zach attached the royal blue sash over his left shoulder to his right hip, signaling his rank as crown prince. "She's a big girl, Antonio. No matter how much she cares for Elena, she wouldn't have agreed to an engagement with you if deep down she hadn't wanted to. Christina doesn't strike me as a woman who would bow out on a commitment once she'd given her word."

Antonio grimaced. "She wouldn't," he admitted, "but she would have had every right. When I was talking to her upstairs, I heard a mournful sound in her voice. She thought our engagement would have ended before now and she wouldn't have to go through with a real wedding." He'd felt her pain. From here on out he'd do everything he could to make her happy.

"You both underestimated the will of the people who want you to be their ruler."

His jaw hardened. "But she didn't ask for this." He had a gut feeling there was trouble ahead.

"So use that genius brain of yours and look at your wedding as new territory. Think of it the way you do with every challenge you face at work. Think it and rethink it until it comes out right."

"Thanks for the advice, Zach."

His friend meant well, but Antonio couldn't treat it as he would a business problem. Christina wasn't a problem. She was a flesh-and-blood human being who'd sacrificed everything for her friend Elena. That kind of loyalty was so rare, Antonio was humbled by it. His concern was to be worthy of the woman whose selflessness had catapulted her to the highest rank in the kingdom.

Zach gazed at him with compassion. "Are you all right?"

He sucked in his breath. "I'm going to have to be. Because of you, I was able to give Christina that brooch. I can't thank you enough for getting it from Sofia."

"You know I'd do anything for you."

A knock on the outer door caused both of them to look around. "Tonio—" his sister called out, using her nickname for him. "It's time. You should be out at the chapel."

"I know. I'll be right there."

"I hope you know how much I love you, brother dear."

"I love you too, Elena."

"Please be happy. You're marrying the sweetest girl in the whole world."

"You don't have to remind me of that." He'd put Christina on a pedestal since she agreed to their engagement. But he'd heard another side come out of her in the bridal suite.

"Lindsay says you two have to hurry!"

Zach's wife had planned this wedding down to the smallest detail. The schedule called for a four-thirty ceremony to avoid the heat of the day. He checked his watch. In the next fifteen minutes Christina would walk down the aisle and become his unhappy bride.

"We're coming," Zach answered for them.

Antonio glanced at Zach. "This is it."

"You look magnificent, Your Highness."

"I wish I felt magnificent. Let's go."

Christina heard Elena's tap on the door of the suite. "Come in."

Her friend hurried in, wearing a stunning blush-colored chiffon gown. On her stylishly cut dark blond hair she wore a tiara. "You look like the princess of every little girl's dreams," Christina cried softly.

"So do you. The tiara Mother gave you looks like it was made for you." Elena walked all the way around her, looking her up and down. "Guess what? This afternoon all eyes are going to be on you, *chère soeur.*" They would be sisters in a few minutes. Tears smarted Christina's eyes. "Oh, la-la, la-la," she said. "My brother will be speechless when he sees you at the altar. Your hair, it's like red gold."

"I just had some highlights put in."

"And you got your teeth straightened. How come you didn't do it a lot earlier in your life?"

"Probably reverse snobbery. Everyone thought I looked pathetic, so why not maintain the image? I knew it irked my parents. It upset me that they couldn't accept me for myself. But when the wedding date was announced, I realized I would have to be an ambassador of sorts.

"Antonio deserves the best, so I knew I had to do something about myself and dress the right way. Until a month ago, I never spent money on clothes. It seemed such an extravagance when there are so many people in the world who don't have enough to eat. Elegant high fashion wouldn't have changed the way I looked."

"Oh, Christina." Elena shook her head sadly. "I always thought you were pretty, but now you're an absolute knockout! If all the girls at our boarding school could see you, they'd eat their hearts out."

Christina's cheeks went hot with embarrassment. "Don't be silly."

"I'm being truthful. You've lost weight since the last time I saw you. Your figure is gorgeous. With your height, the kind I wish I had, that tiara gives you the elegance of a young queen. I'm not kidding. Lindsay found you the perfect gown and I love the interlocking hearts of your brooch. Is there anything more beautiful than diamonds?"

"It's been in the Rose family for years and supposed to bring luck. Antonio brought it to the room earlier. Do you think I pinned it in the right place?"

"It's right above your heart where it should be. You look as pure and perfect as I know you are."

She averted her eyes. "You know I'm not either of those things."

"I know how much your parents have hurt you, but you *can't* let that ruin your opinion of yourself. One day they'll realize you're the jewel in their crown. Today my brother is going to see you as his prize jewel. I've never told you this before, but all the time we were in Switzerland together, I had the secret hope he would end up marrying you one day."

I had the same hope, Christina admitted to herself, but she'd never confess it to anyone, not even Elena.

"The day I met you at school, you became the sister I never had and you never judged me. That has never changed. After we left school, our friendship has meant more to me than you will ever know."

"I feel the same," Christina said with a tremor in her voice.

"That awful night I phoned you when Rolfe was arrested for drugs, I knew I could count on you to help me. I believe it's destiny you contacted Tonio. Now you're about to become his bride to save my reputation." Her eyes glistened with tears. "You have to promise me you'll be happy, Christina. Tonio's the best if you'll give him a chance."

Christina reached for Elena's hands. "I know he's the best because he was always kind to me when we were in Montreux. And because of his sacrifice for you, that takes brotherly love and goodness to a whole new level. He honors his family and his heritage. Who couldn't admire him?"

"But I want you to learn to *love* him!" Her eyes begged.

"You're talking a different kind of love." After he'd phoned to tell her the date they were going to be married, she was forced to accept her fate. "I haven't dated much, Elena. I did spend time with one doctor in Africa. But when I got engaged to Antonio, that ended any possibility of a relationship with him or any man, let alone potential love."

In a way, her engagement had helped her to hide

from love for fear that she would never be good enough for anyone. If she wasn't good enough for her parents, why would she be good enough for any man?

Still, her parents had been overjoyed with the engagement, which made her happy. And Christina had adored Antonio in secret for years, not only for the way he loved Elena, but for his hard-work ethic. In Christina's new position as his wife, the number of people she'd be able to help with her charities would be vastly increased. Was it worth giving up on the possibility of true love?

Christina had never felt worthy of love and so had never been hopeful of meeting "the one." At the end of the day she'd reconciled herself to this marriage.

"Can you honestly tell me you're not excited about your wedding night?"

"Oh, Elena—you're such a romantic and I know you feel guilty about what's happening, but don't let that worry you. Yes, I'm excited, but mostly I'm nervous. Antonio and I have never spent time alone together. You know what I mean. But Antonio has been with other women both before and probably after our engagement. My eyes are wide-open where he is concerned. After the women he has been with, I'm afraid I'm not going to compare."

A stricken look entered Elena's eyes. "Don't you dare say that! And don't think about any of his past relationships. He knew they would never amount to anything, and today he's marrying *you*."

"I know, but it's still hard to believe." Christina stared at her friend. "I wasn't convinced Antonio planned to go through with our nuptials. You can't imagine my surprise when he finally called me and said I needed to start making the wedding plans with Lindsay."

"He meant it, Christina. I know he got engaged to you to save my skin, but he could have chosen any number of eligible royal hopefuls. Why do *you* think he chose you?"

"I was…convenient."

"That's not the answer and you know it. There was something deeper inside that drove him to choose you. I think you need to think about that as you walk down the aisle toward him today looking like any man's dream. If you don't believe me, take one more look in the mirror."

"You're very sweet."

"It's true. Tonio came to Switzerland a lot during our days at boarding school. He liked you right off and enjoyed your company. He trusts you."

"But he's not in love with me."

"Give him a chance and he *will* fall in love with you. *I've* always loved you and feel all the more indebted to you for the sacrifice *you're* making to save me and our family from scandal. Will you promise me one thing?"

"If I can."

"Pretend that today you're going to get married to the man you've always loved and who has always loved you."

I have *always loved him…from a distance.* There was no pretense on Christina's part.

Elena rushed over to her and they hugged.

"What's wrong, Elena? Are those tears?"

"I just don't want anything to go wrong. This wedding is all my fault. I'll pray for you and Antonio to be happy."

Christina took a big breath, sensing that deep down Elena was really worried. Why? What wasn't she telling her, unless her guilt was working overtime?

"It'll be fine, Elena." She'd made up her mind about that. Today was her wedding day and she was living her fantasy of marrying the prince of her dreams. For once in her life she planned to enjoy herself. She could do it. She'd seen herself in the mirror and felt confident to be his bride.

"You'd better start working on it right now," Elena warned. "Otherwise you're going to give everyone a heart attack if you don't make an appearance in the chapel in the next minute."

"I'm ready."

"I love you, Christina."

"The feeling's mutual. You have to know that by now."

Elena blew her a kiss. "I do."

Together they walked down the stairs to the foyer of the palazzo and out the main entrance to the courtyard. The chapel faced the palazzo across the way with a beautiful fountain in the center. Lindsay was waiting for them inside the church doors of the foyer with their flowers.

She let out a gasp when she saw Christina. "You're perfect! Better than anything I'd imagined. So perfect, in fact, I can't believe my eyes."

Christina smiled at Zach's wife. "You outdid yourself, Lindsay. All the credit goes to you. This dress is divine."

Louisa, the owner of the palazzo, hurried toward her. "You're the most stunning bride I've ever seen."

"Thank you, Louisa. You look lovely too. I'm indebted to you for your generosity in letting us be married here. The Palazzo di Comparino is the most ideal setting for a wedding in all of Tuscany."

"It's been an honor for me. I told Prince Antonio the same thing."

Louisa had given Christina a tour of the newly renovated chapel yesterday. She'd met the elderly priest who would be marrying them. While he walked with her in private, they chatted about the renovations.

She'd been utterly enchanted with the fabulous unearthed fresco of the Madonna and child now protected by glass. The charming chapel had an intimacy and spiritual essence. It thrilled her to know she'd be taking her vows in here. She intended to make this the perfect wedding day.

"Everyone is inside waiting," Lindsay whispered. "Here's your bouquet, Christina."

"Oh—these white roses are exquisite."

"Just like you. And here's your bouquet, Elena." Lindsay had matched the flowers to the soft blush of her gown. "Zach will hand you the ring to give Antonio when the time comes during the ceremony. As we rehearsed, once you hear the organ, you and your father will enter the chapel with Elena five paces behind you.

The king and queen are seated on the right side with their retinue. Your family and friends are on the left."

Christina looked around. "Where's my father?"

"I'm right behind you."

As she turned, her heart thudded mostly in fear in case she saw rejection in his dark gray eyes. He had a patrician, distinguished aura and was immaculately dressed. His gaze studied her features for a moment. "I'm glad to see you've changed for the better. Today the Rose family can be proud of you."

"You look very handsome too, Father."

"Christina?" Lindsay reminded her. "Take your father's arm."

The organist had started playing Wagner's "Wedding March." There'd probably never been this many people inside. Her joy was almost full.

She clung to her father as they slowly made their way down the aisle of the ornate interior. The only eyes she searched for were her mother's, wanting her approbation. Her mother, who was in her midfifties, was still a beautiful brunette woman and the envy of many.

Just once Christina hoped to find a loving smile meant for her alone. As she passed the pew, she made eye contact with her. A proud smile broke out on her mother's perfectly made-up face. That acknowledgment made Christina feel as if she were floating as she walked toward her prince.

She focused her attention on the two men standing at the altar before the priest. Zach, as best man, stood several inches taller than the crown prince, who was six foot one, according to Elena. They were watching her progress.

A slight gasp escaped her lips when she looked into the startling blue eyes of the man she was about to pledge her life to. It had been several months since the last time she saw him at the palace. His visit had been brief.

In full dark blue ceremonial dress, Antonio looked so splendid she was shaken by her reaction to him. His light brown hair, smart and thick, was tipped with highlights from the sun, reflecting a healthy sheen. With such a lean, fit body, he was the epitome of a royal prince every little girl dreamed of marrying one day.

How incredible that Christina was about to become his wife. *If I were the type, I'd pass out at the feet of the most desirable man in all Halencia. But I'm not going to make any mistakes today. This is my wedding day. I love it already.*

Caught up in all the wedding preparations, she felt that she *was* his beautiful bride and she intended to be the woman he was excited to marry. Her teenage dream had come true. The only thing more she could ask of this day was that the fantasy would last forever.

CHAPTER TWO

MAYBE ANTONIO'S EYES were playing tricks on him. The stunning woman walking on the arm of her father with the grace of a queen had to be Christina, but it was a Christina he'd never seen or imagined.

When did the brownish-red hair, which he remembered she'd worn in a ponytail, turn out to be a spun red gold?

Had her body ever looked like an hourglass before now?

The lace veil against her smooth olive skin provided a foil for her finely arched dark eyebrows. Because of the light coming through the stained glass windows, her crystalline gray eyes had taken on a silvery cast. Her red mouth had a passionate flare he'd never even noticed.

His gaze fell lower to the brooch she'd pinned to the beaded bodice of her wedding dress. The diamonds sparkled in the light with every breath she took.

Elena approached her side to take the bouquet from her. When Christina smiled at his sister, Antonio caught its full effect and was blindsided by the change in her.

While he'd been talking to her earlier in the bridal suite, parts of her sounded like the woman he'd gotten engaged to four years ago. But she wasn't the same person on the outside. It threw him so completely that he felt a nudge from Zach to pay attention to the priest.

"Your Highness?" he whispered. "If you will take your bride-to-be by the hand."

Antonio reached for her right hand. Her cool, dry grip was decisive. If she was suffering wedding nerves, it didn't show. He didn't know if he was disappointed by her demeanor, which seemed unflappable.

In a voice loud enough to fill the interior, the priest began. "Welcome, all of you. Today we are gathered here for one of the happiest occasions in all human life, to celebrate before God the marriage of a man and woman who love each other. Marriage is a most honorable estate, created and instituted by God, signifying unto us the mystical union that also exists between Christ and the Church. So too may this marriage be adorned by true and abiding love. Let us pray."

Antonio bowed his head, but his burden of guilt over compelling Christina to follow through with this marriage weighed heavily on him. As Zach had reminded him, she'd entered into this union of her own free will because of her love for Elena, but the words *may this marriage be adorned by true and abiding love* pierced him to the core of his being.

In the past four years he'd done nothing to show her love. The only thing true about this marriage was their love for Elena, and on his part the need to preserve the monarchy. But at this moment Antonio made up his mind that their love for his sister would be the foundation upon which they built a life together.

Antonio's absence from her life except for those four quick visits had made certain she had no anticipation of love to come. To his surprise she sounded happy as she repeated the marriage covenant. He hadn't expected that.

When it was his turn to recite his vows, he felt the deep solemnity of the moment and said them with fervency.

"Who holds the rings?"

"I do," Zach responded.

"Grant that the love which the bride and groom have for each other now may always be an eternal round. Antonio? Take the ring and put it on Christina's finger saying, 'With this ring, I thee wed.'"

She presented her left hand while he repeated the words. Her hand trembled a little as he slid the wedding band next to the diamond from the royal family treasury he'd given her four years earlier. So she wasn't quite as composed as he'd thought, but it didn't make him feel any better. If anything, he felt worse because he'd done nothing to ease her into this union and lamented his selfishness.

Now it was her turn to present him with his ring. She took it and placed it on Antonio's finger. His new bride was suddenly so composed that again he marveled. "With this ring, I thee wed," she said in a steady voice.

They were married.

The deed was done.

"Antonio and Christina, as the two of you have

joined this marriage uniting as husband and wife, and as you this day affirm your faith and love for each other, I would ask that you always remember to cherish each other as special and unique individuals, that you respect the thoughts, ideas and suggestions of one another.

"Be able to forgive, do not hold grudges, and live each day that you may share it together. From this day forward you shall be each other's home, comfort and refuge, your marriage strengthened by your love and respect."

Antonio's shame increased. *I've shown her no respect.*

"You may now kiss your bride."

When Antonio turned to her, he saw a look of consternation in her eyes. *Oh, Christina. What have I done to you? You're so good. So sweet.* His eyes focused on her lovely mouth before he grasped her upper arms gently and kissed her.

Not only her lips but her whole body trembled. Her fragrance assailed him. He deepened the kiss, wanting her to know he planned to make their marriage work. Whether she was putting on a show for everyone, or responding instinctively to new emotions bombarding her as they were him, he didn't know. But she kissed him back and he found himself wanting it to go on and on.

The priest cleared his throat, prompting Antonio to lift his mouth from hers. A subtle blush had entered her cheeks. He removed his hands.

"Antonio and Christina, if you'll turn around."

When they'd done his bidding, he said in a loud voice, "May I present Crown Prince Antonio de L'Accardi and his royal bride, Princess Christina Rose. Allow them to walk down the aisle to the foyer of the chapel, where you can mingle outside."

Elena came forward to give Christina her bouquet, and then the organist played the wedding march. Taking a deep breath, Antonio grasped her free hand, still feeling the tingly effect of her warm, generous mouth on his. He guided her to the first pew where his parents were seated and stopped long enough for both of them to bow to the king and queen of Halencia.

To show Christina's parents his respect, he escorted her across the aisle to their pew to acknowledge them. He gave her a sideward glance. Her eyes glistened with unshed tears. He didn't know what that was about.

How could you know when you haven't spent any real time getting to know her?

More upset with himself and even more shaken by their kiss, he walked her slowly down the aisle. He darted her another glance, but this time she was smiling at everyone. She was so gracious it impressed the hell out of him. She could have been born to royalty.

He'd honored Christina's wishes by letting her plan the wedding here instead of the fourteenth-century cathedral in Voti. She'd insisted on a simple ceremony. If there'd been any royal formality or long traditional ceremony, she wouldn't have agreed. Antonio had been so thankful she hadn't backed out that he'd fallen in with her every wish.

In private he'd asked his parents to take a backseat

so this could be Christina's day. She was beloved of the people, but she couldn't have abided all the pomp and circumstance. Since his parents were resigned to their fate to put Antonio on the throne, they'd acceded to his wishes. He'd even heard them say they were relishing the idea of retirement and looking forward to more freedom in the future.

At his engagement four years ago, Antonio had vowed to sacrifice his personal freedom and return from California to take the throne at a later date with Christina at his side. He'd felt a strong loyalty to his country and had always been conscious of his royal duty. But he'd only been prepared to marry her on *his* terms, and hadn't considered her fears.

There were going to be a lot of changes after his coronation in another week. He had a raft of constitutional issues that would put the royal family in a figurehead role, with specific duties. There would be a much reduced civil list, no hangers-on supported by the state; all personal belongings and lifestyle choices and holidays would be paid for by personal business interests rather than the state.

The areas of change went on and on, which was why the monarchy had been on the brink of disaster. This marriage would hopefully turn the tide of criticism. Christina's values of hard work and true charity resonated with the people. Her example of selflessness was the big reason they'd embraced Antonio as their soon-to-be king. Antonio still had to prove himself equal to the task. And much more, like becoming the husband Christina deserved.

He walked her outside and across the courtyard to the terrace bedecked in flowers at the side of the palazzo. A small orchestra was playing a waltz at one end of the terrace with an area reserved for dancing. Hundreds of tiny lights strewn among the trees and flowers made it look like a true fairyland and had created a heavenly fragrance. The grand serving table with its fountain and flowers was surrounded by exquisitely set tables, an enchanting sight he'd always remember.

The late-afternoon Tuscan sunshine shone down on them. The picturesque setting and vineyard had an indescribable beauty, yet all he could see for the moment was the stunning bride draped in alençon lace, still clinging to his hand. Antonio swallowed hard.

She's my wife! She's the woman I promised to love and cherish.

Suddenly he seemed to see a whole new world ahead of them, uncharted as yet. Her faith in their marriage made him open his eyes to new possibilities. This was their wedding day. He wanted it to be wonderful for both of them. After their kiss at the altar, he was eager to feel her in his arms.

"Christina? Look this way."

She was so dazed by what had happened at the end of the ceremony that she was hardly aware of the photographers brought in to make a record of their wedding day. When Antonio had deepened their kiss, she felt a charge of energy run through her body like a current of electricity. She could still feel his compelling mouth on hers.

Maybe this was how every bride felt when kissed on her wedding day. But Antonio wasn't just any man. He was her husband, for better or worse.

Before everyone could crowd around to congratulate them, Antonio pulled her close. "Do you mind if we talk to our guests later? I'd like to dance with you first," he said in his deep voice.

Her heart thumped hard before she looked at him. "I'd love it."

His hot blue eyes played over her features. "Let me put your bouquet on this table."

After he laid it down, Christina felt his arm go around her waist. The contact reminded her of the kiss they'd shared at the altar. She hadn't been the same since and was more aware of him than ever as he led her to the dance area.

She couldn't help thinking back to the time she'd been at boarding school. Never in her wildest imagination would she have believed she'd eventually become the wife of Elena's dashing older brother. This moment was surreal.

As he drew her into his arms she said, "You need to know I haven't done much dancing in my life."

He held her closer. "Didn't they teach you to dance at boarding school?"

"Are you kidding? Whatever you think goes on at boarding school simply doesn't happen. We were all a bunch of girls who'd rather be home. We all had a case of homesickness and waited for the letters that didn't arrive. We ate, studied and slept four to a room in an old freezing-cold chateau. You don't even want to know how frigid the water closet could be."

He laughed out loud, causing everyone to look at them.

"Once a week we were allowed to go to town with the chaperone. She chose the places we could visit. Elena managed to scout out the dancing places we weren't supposed to visit, then dragged me with her where we met guys who flocked around her."

"Sounds like my sister."

"She taught me the meaning of *fun*. The rest of the time we went to a symphony or an opera, and other times we went to a play, always on a bus. I liked the plays, especially one adapted from Colette's writings about a dog and cat."

Antonio started moving them around the terrace decorated with urns of flowers. "Tell me about them," he whispered against her hot cheek. His warm breath sent little tingles of delight through her body.

"Elena and I bought the books and studied the lines to help us with our French. Both animals loved their master and mistress. Their battles were outrageous and hilarious."

"You'll have to lend me the book to read."

"Anytime. Wouldn't it be fun if animals really could talk? I used to love the *Doctor Doolittle* books as a child. When I first got to Africa, I thought I really had arrived in Jollijinki Land."

He lips twitched and he held her a little tighter, but her gown provided a natural buffer. "I have a feeling you could entertain me forever."

She moved her head so she could look into his eyes. Marrying Antonio felt right. She felt like a princess. The feeling was magical. She was living her fantasy and never wanted it to end. Her parents were proud of her today. Everything was getting better with them. "This is a new experience for both of us, Antonio. Forever sounds like a long time. Let's just take it one step at a time."

His lips brushed hers unexpectedly, creating havoc with her emotions. "One step at a time it is. Since everyone is watching us, let's put on a show, shall we?"

She smiled at him. "I thought we'd already been doing that."

"They haven't seen anything yet."

Her adrenaline gushed as he waltzed them around the terrace. It didn't surprise her that he knew what he was doing. She followed his lead as he dipped her several times, causing people to clap. Dancing with him like this was a heady experience she hadn't anticipated. He must have been enjoying it too, because one dance turned into another.

"This is fun," he murmured against her lips. "Your idea for having our wedding here at the palazzo has turned out to be sensational. I remember once when the three of us climbed into the mountains above the vineyards lining Lake Geneva and came to an old farmhouse that had been turned into a quaint inn.

"You said it was your favorite place and went there often on your hikes and bicycle rides with Elena for fondue bourguignonne. I think you must have had it in mind when you chose the Palazzo di Comparino for our wedding. I see similarities."

Her head tilted back in surprise. "I can't believe you remembered that hike, let alone made the association with this place."

His gaze played over her features. "I've remembered all our outings. The truth is, I found you and my sister more entertaining than most of my friends, with the exception of Zach." His comment made her smile.

"When I did fly to Switzerland, I came because I wanted to. Being with you two was like taking a breath of fresh air and kept me grounded. I've never told you this, but I was always relieved to know you were there to help temper my sister. She's always had trouble with boundaries."

"And I was the insipid, boring tagalong, afraid to break out of my shell, right?"

He frowned. When he did that, he looked older and quite fierce. "You were shy, but amazingly kind to my sister. Even when she got herself into impossible situations you never judged her."

"You were kind to me too by including me. Remember the day we visited the Chateau de Chillon? We'd climbed up on the ramparts and I was taking a picture when I dropped my camera by mistake and it fell into the lake several hundred feet below."

"You should have seen the tragic look on your face," he teased.

"I was so upset, but you turned everything around when you bought me a new one just like it and gave it to me before you left us at the school." She felt her eyes smart. "That was the kindest thing anyone had ever done for me."

"Then we're even because Elena needed a constant friend like you and you were there for her in her darkest hours. You have no idea what that meant to me. I knew I could always count on you. I wish I could say the same for our parents. They've been so caught up in a lifestyle that has cost them the confidence of the people that they've neglected Elena, who needed a strong hand."

Christina sucked in her breath. "I needed her friendship too."

"Elena told me you had problems with your parents."

"Yes, but I don't want to talk about them right now. We were talking about your sister. She's so sweet. Elena cared about me when no one else did. She made me believe in myself."

"The two of you have an unbreakable bond. Otherwise you wouldn't have stayed close over all these years. You don't know how lucky you are. How rare that is."

"According to Elena, you have that kind of relationship with Zach."

He nodded. "But I didn't have a friend like you while I was at boarding school and college. It wasn't until I moved to San Francisco. If you want to know a secret, I envied you and Elena."

She heard a loneliness in his admission that went deep. "Because you're the prince, it was probably hard for you to confide in someone else during those early years. With you being expected to rule one day, you had to watch every step."

Antonio stopped dancing and grasped her hands in both of his. "You understand so much about me, Christina." His blue eyes had darkened with emotion. "But you paid a price by agreeing to get engaged to me."

Giddy with happiness she said, "What price is that when I'm having the wedding of my dreams?"

Her thoughts flew back to their engagement. The king and queen had thrown the supposedly happy couple a huge, glossy engagement party, but it had been the worst night of Christina's life. To have to be on show, self-consciously standing next to the most gorgeous man she'd ever known, she'd never felt so unglamorous in her life. Especially when she knew her parents considered her a failure.

Yet they'd acted thrilled over the engagement and made such a fuss over her that it made her happy that they showed her that kind of attention. She'd been starved for it. But once she saw the photos, she'd been unable to bear the sight of herself looking so dull and plump. But that was a long time ago and she refused to dwell on it.

The guests had been going through the buffet line before finding their seats at individual linen-covered tables with baskets of creamy roses and sunflowers. Christina had to admit the estate and grounds looked beautiful. A fountain modeled after the one in the courtyard of a draped nymph holding a shell formed the centerpiece. Everything looked right out of a dream-world, including the beautifully dressed people.

Antonio drew her even closer as they walked past the guests to get their food. He handed her a plate and they moved back and forth, choosing a delicious tidbit here and there. But she was too happy and stimulated to sit down to a big meal with him at a table reserved for them alone.

Several of the guests had started to dance. Among them Louisa, who was being partnered by Nico. According to Louisa, the two of them weren't on the best of terms, but the way he was looking at her right now, Christina got the feeling they had a strong attraction. Well, well. It appeared the festive party mood had infected everyone.

Antonio finished what was on his plate. Since hers was empty, he put them both on the table. When he looked at her she was filled with strong emotion and said, "Today I'm so happy to be your wife, Antonio. I mean that with all my heart."

"Christina," he said in a husky voice, squeezing her hand. "Because of your sacrifice for me—for the country—I trust you with my life." He said it like a vow and kissed her fingers in a gesture so intimate in front of the wedding guests that she made up her mind to be the best wife possible.

Just then Louisa happened to pass by her. "You look radiant," she whispered.

Christina was still reacting to Antonio's gesture as well as his words. "So did you out there dancing with Nico."

"Who knew he could waltz?"

Her comment made Christina chuckle. Antonio

smiled at her. "I want to dance the whole evening away with you, but I think we need to say something to our parents."

They walked hand in hand toward the king and queen and they all chatted for a moment. Christina's parents were seated by them. While Antonio was still talking with his parents for a minute, her mother, dressed in an oyster silk suit, got up from the table to greet Christina with a peck on the cheek.

Though Christina had known this began as a publicity stunt, she'd tried to win her parents' affection. Four years later she was still trying and had hopes that her marriage to the future king had softened their opinion of her.

Her mother stared into her eyes. "You look lovely, Christina. I do believe that tint on your hair was the right shade."

A compliment from her mother meant everything. "I'm glad you like it."

"It's a good thing Lindsay planned everything else, including your new royal wardrobe. You'll always want to look perfect for Antonio."

"I plan to try."

"I know you will. Certainly today you've succeeded." Her voice halted for a minute before she added, "You've never looked so attractive."

Christina's eyes moistened. She couldn't believe her mother was actually paying her another compliment. In fact, she sensed her mother wanted to say more but held back.

"*Grazie*, Mama," she said in a tremulous voice, and kissed her mother's cheek.

Marusha stood nearby. Christina hugged her. She'd flown in for the wedding. Her family would be coming for the coronation. For this ceremony, only their closest friends and relatives made up the intimate gathering.

Next came Christina's great-aunt Sofia. "You look enchanting." The older woman embraced her. "Working in Africa has made all the difference in you," she said quietly. "You have a queenly aura that comes naturally to you."

Christina craved her aunt's warmth and hugged her extra hard. "I'm thrilled to be wearing the brooch." She was glad Antonio had sneaked up to the bridal chamber to give it to her.

"It suits you. I'm so proud of you I could burst."

"Don't do that!" she said as they broke into gentle laughter.

"I've been watching your handsome husband. He's hardly taken his eyes off you since we came outside." Her brown gaze conveyed her sincerity. "I can see why. You're a vision, and you're going to help Prince Antonio transform our country into its former glory. I feel it in these old bones. I have the suspicion that you didn't need the brooch to bring you good luck. You and your prince are special, you know?"

No, Christina *didn't* know, but she loved her aunt for saying so. "I love you."

Her great-aunt kissed her on the cheek before Elena rushed in to hug her hard. "Ooh—you're the most gorgeous bride I ever saw. I do believe you've knocked the socks off Tonio. All the time he's been talking to the parents, he's had his eye on you."

Sofia had said the same thing. From the mouths of two witnesses…

"The two of you looked so happy out there it seemed like you were sharing some great secret. By the way, in passing I heard your mother tell your aunt Sofia that she'd never been so proud of you."

"Thank you for telling me. Things seem to be better with Mother," she whispered. "It is a beautiful wedding, isn't it?"

"It's fabulous, and you know why? Because you're Tonio's wife and will make him a better man than he already is. Meeting you was the best thing that ever happened to me. He's going to feel the same way once he gets to really know you the way I do."

Tears glistened on Christina's eyelashes. She hugged her again. "We're true sisters now," she whispered.

CHAPTER THREE

"YOUR HIGHNESS, THE photographer is waiting for you and your bride to cut the wedding cake."

Antonio switched his gaze to Zach, but his mind and thoughts had been concentrated on Christina and it took a moment for him to get back to the present. "Thanks, Zach. We're coming."

"I hope you love wedding cake," she whispered as they made their way to the round table holding the fabulous three-tiered cake.

He flashed her a quick smile. "Is this the moment you're going to get your revenge on me for past misdeeds?"

"If you're referring to the chocolate you fed me full of cherry cordial that dripped down my blouse on one of our outings, I wouldn't be surprised." The impish look in her beautiful gray eyes was so unexpected that his heart skipped a beat.

"Be gentle," he begged, putting his arms around her from behind to help her make the first cut with the knife. Another chuckle escaped her lips. With great care she picked up the first piece and turned to him, waving it in the air as if trying to decide how to feed it to him. This produced laughter from the guests.

"Just take your best shot, whatever you have in mind."

"So I *do* have you a little bit worried."

"Please, Christina."

"I tell you what. I'll have a napkin ready." She plucked one off the table. "Now open sesame."

He closed his eyes and obeyed her command.

"You have to keep your eyes open, coward," she said in a low teasing voice.

"I can't do both," he teased back.

"Then I'll eat it instead."

Shocked by her response, he opened his eyes only to be fed the cake, part of which fell onto his chin into the napkin she held for him. The wedding guests laughed and clapped their hands. Of course everything had been caught by the videographer.

Christina cleaned him up nicely, then kissed his chin. "Thanks for being a good sport, Your Highness."

"Don't call me that."

She looked surprised. "No?"

"Not ever."

She flashed him a smile. "Are we having our first fight?"

Her question caught him off guard. Before he could respond, Lindsay came up to Christina with her bridal bouquet. "When you're ready to leave the party, you can toss it behind you."

"Thank you, Lindsay. All your planning has made

this the most beautiful wedding party in the world. I've never been happier."

"You look radiant, Christina." She gave her a hug, and Antonio saw his wife whisper something to her in private.

"It's already being taken care of," Lindsay whispered back, but Antonio read her lips.

Intrigued, he couldn't wait to get his bride alone, but no one was ready to leave the reception yet and Zach had snatched her away to dance. He decided now was the time to dance with his mother, then his mother-in-law.

The queen gave him a hug before he danced her around the terrace. "You're going to have to keep an eye on that one," she said, eyeing Christina, who was still whirling around with Zach. "She isn't quite as docile as I remember."

"She's her own person," Antonio replied with the sudden thrilling realization that his new bride might mean more to him than he could have imagined.

"Indeed she is. You both look perfectly marvelous together. She's changed so much since the engagement that I hardly recognize her. You have no idea how glad I am that you've come home for good to settle down. A man needs marriage, and your marriage is good for the monarchy. I'm very happy with you today."

"Thank you, Mama." Except that marriage hadn't stopped his parents from having their offstage affairs.

He twirled her back to the table and asked Christina's mother to dance. She had been a former fashion model and was still a very attractive woman. But as he gazed at Christina, who was laughing quietly with Zach, he thought she was the *real* beauty. Not only in her appearance, but in her character.

"Are you sorry our daughter wanted the wedding here instead of at the cathedral in Voti?"

"Anything but. Don't you think every woman should be able to have the wedding of her dreams where she wants it?"

"But you're the crown prince."

Antonio smiled at her. "Tonight I'm a new bridegroom and I can't imagine a more perfect setting for Christina and me than this delightful spot in Tuscany."

"Then I'm glad for both of you. You make a stunning pair."

"Grazie."

He could still hear Christina's words when she'd told him what it was like at boarding school. *We were all a bunch of girls who'd rather be home. We all had a case of homesickness and waited for the letters that didn't arrive.* The emptiness in her voice had conveyed pain, even after all these years.

If he didn't do anything else, he would make certain she didn't feel pain because of him. "Did you visit her in Africa?"

"We made it over once and were guests in the palace of Marusha's parents. They're very westernized there."

"Your daughter has made a big contribution. It's no small thing she has done to help those in poverty."

"I'm very proud of her."

He was glad to hear it. On that note he danced her back to the table. After thanking her, he went over to the table where Marusha was seated and asked her to dance with him. The charming woman had come with her husband. He gave her a turn around the terrace.

"You honor me, Your Highness. I'm very happy Christina is your bride. We hope you'll both come to Kenya and stay with us."

"I've always wanted to travel there and promise to visit you when the time is right. You honor us by coming. Christina thinks the world of you and your family."

"We feel the same. Thank you."

Once she was seated, Antonio hurried to find Christina, who was talking to Elena. His sister smiled at him. "It's about time you paid attention to your bride."

"First I want a dance with you, little sister, if it's all right with my wife."

Christina darted him a serious glance. "She's the reason we even know each other. You're welcome to enjoy her for as long as you want."

He knew she meant that and moved Elena around the terrace. She had a gleam in her eye. "Having fun, brother dear? More than you thought?"

"Much more," he confessed.

"Christina has that effect on people. Mother can't get over the change in her. I told her that Christina is like the woman in the stone. All Michelangelo had to do was chip away at the marble until her beauty emerged for all to see."

His sister had just put the right words to his thoughts. "It's a perfect analogy."

She studied his features. "It's growing dark. Are you ready to leave the party?" she asked with a sly smile.

"The truth?"

"Always."

"I feel like I did the first time I had to jump out of a plane during my military service."

Elena chuckled. "Since you survived, I'm not worried."

"In all honesty, I haven't made this easy for Christina by maintaining distance between us over the last four years."

"Don't worry about it. She married you today and I think you've both met your match. I'm so happy for both of you I could burst. Don't let me keep you from whisking your bride away." She kissed his cheek and hurried off.

He was left standing there while her last comment sank in. Antonio hated to admit he felt nervous for what was to come. He'd be taking his wife upstairs to the bridal chamber. This was a new experience for him. Taking a fortifying breath, he made a beeline for Christina, who was talking to more guests.

Lindsay came up to him. "Christina still needs to throw her bridal bouquet to the crowd. If you're ready, take her to the front of the palazzo and I'll make the announcement to the guests to follow you."

"Thank you for all you've done."

"It has been my pleasure."

He kissed her cheek before reaching for his wife. Christina's gaze flicked to his. "What is it?"

"We have one more ritual to perform." He picked up the bridal bouquet. After putting it in her hands, he slid an arm around her slender waist. Her lovely body was a perfect fit for him.

"I already know where I'm going to throw it," she whispered as they left the terrace and walked around to the front entrance of the palazzo.

"So do I," he drawled.

"Antonio?" She eyed him with surprising tenderness. "Thank you for dancing with Marusha. To dance with the future king had to be one of the big highlights of her life."

"I wanted a chance to thank her for coming. She's been your true friend all these years. I have a feeling you two are going to miss each other."

"That's something I want to talk to you about, but we'll discuss it later."

An alarm bell went off in Antonio's head. Did Christina want to go back to Africa? She'd lived a whole period of her life there that he knew nothing about. In fairness, she didn't know details about his former life either. While he stood there filled with new questions that needed answers, the guests had congregated in the courtyard.

Before he knew what she was doing, his wife cleared her throat and faced the crowd. "Antonio and I want to thank you all for coming to share in our beautiful wedding day. I'm one of the lucky girls in the world who actually got to marry a real prince. His kindness to his sister, Princess Elena, my dearest friend, proved his princely worth to me years ago. I can honestly say there's not another man like him, prince or otherwise.

So this is for you, Elena. May you find your own wonderful prince too!"

Christina turned her back to the crowd and threw the bouquet in a southeasterly direction that was no mistake with Elena standing there. It was no accident that everyone made room around his sister so she could catch it. Then a roar of approval and clapping burst from the crowd. Antonio's breath caught. With that speech she'd ensured her place in everyone's heart as their queen-to-be.

Filled with emotion, he put his arm around her shoulders and pressed a kiss to her lips. She kissed him back and it felt convincing, but was this a show for the camera? He'd felt a distinct spark when they kissed at the altar. But if it had only been on his part, he didn't want to believe it right now. Was she nervous too?

Without asking her permission, he grasped her hand and drew her along with him to the inside of the palazzo. He leaned back against the closed door, still holding her hand. Now that the moment was here to be alone with her, he felt slightly breathless. The wedding night was upon them.

"Are you up to climbing to the third floor?"

The bridal suite.

Their bridal suite now. The kiss Antonio had given her in front of the palazzo felt…hungry. In that moment she'd experienced an answering rush of desire that took her by storm. Her fantasy had taken on a new dimension. What was going on with her?

"I think I can about make it," she teased, and started

her ascent. But after a few steps she picked up her gown to give her the freedom to hurry the rest of the way. His footsteps followed, keeping pace with the thundering of her heart.

She almost ran down the hallway to the bridal suite. Before she reached the doors, he caught up to her and picked her up in his arms. "Oh—" she half squealed, surprised her gown didn't hinder him. She knew her husband was strong, but being held close to him like this made her realize what a rock-hard physique he possessed, and he smelled wonderful.

Their faces were only inches apart. He smiled into her eyes. The blue of his irises had a depth of brilliance that ignited every pulse point in her body. "I don't know about you, but I've been looking forward to this all day." He slowly lowered his mouth to hers and began kissing her.

A burst of desire swept through her. Things were moving much faster than she'd anticipated and she found herself kissing him back with an urgency she couldn't seem to suppress. What was happening was perfectly natural for a grown man and woman on their wedding night, but they had come to this marriage as friends from a long time ago. He'd never held her, or danced with her or kissed her, in Switzerland.

When she could take a breath she said, "If you keep this up, our dinner will get cold."

"What dinner?" His gaze was focused on her mouth.

"The one we didn't eat. It's waiting for us out on the terrace of our suite."

"Was that what you were whispering to Lindsay about?"

She nodded.

"I must say I'd much prefer eating with you alone up here. I like the way my wife thinks."

Christina was glad he felt that way, because she needed time to get used to him. A meal would give both of them a chance to unwind while they antici- pated their wedding night. Now that the moment was here, she didn't know what to do and felt so awkward she hoped he couldn't sense it.

Antonio gave her another swift kiss on the lips and managed to open the door. He walked through the foyer of the semidark suite and made it as far as the bed- chamber before putting her down. She eased away far enough to remove the veil and tiara.

He knew she needed some privacy before they did anything else. "I'll be back in a few minutes." He pressed a kiss to her lips. "Don't start dinner with- out me."

"I won't. Your bags should be in the sitting room."

"I'll find them."

Much as he was reluctant to let her go, he needed to make her more comfortable. After giving her upper arms a quick squeeze, he left the bridal chamber for the other part of the suite. Spotting his bags, he went into the bathroom down the hall to freshen up. It was a relief to discard his sash and ceremonial dress jacket. This was a brand-new experience for both of them. To- night he wanted to do everything right for her.

Hoping he'd given her enough time, he left the bathroom and started back to the bridal suite. He'd undone his shirt at the neck and rolled his sleeves up to the elbows.

Against the darkened sky, the candles flickering from the terrace table bathed Christina in soft light. As she leaned over in her exquisite wedding dress to pour their wine, he noticed the glory of her midlength hair where the strands of gold gleamed among the red. It looked so thick and sleek he longed to run his hands through it.

She must have sensed his presence and gave him a sideward glance. Again the candles flickered, turning her eyes to a shimmery silver. His bride had come to this earth with her own unique color scheme, one that resonated with him in ways he hadn't noticed at the age of eighteen. His fifteen-year-old sister and her friend had been too young for him to appreciate the sight he was being treated to tonight.

Between her classic features with those high cheekbones and passionate red mouth, the blood was pounding in his veins. His gaze fell lower to the feminine outline of her body in her gown. While they'd danced, she filled his arms in all the right places and was the perfect height for him.

Her choice of wedding gown had pleased him immensely. She looked demure, but her coloring added the dash of sensuality he'd noticed the first moment he saw her in the chapel.

Christina might not have been aware of it, but he'd

watched the males in the crowd admiring her all evening long.

For the first time he wondered how many men she'd known who'd more than admired her. Though it was a little late to question what her love life had been like prior to the actual preparations for their wedding, he couldn't help but wonder. He felt as if he were swimming in waters over his head.

Her eyes played over him as he moved toward her. He liked the way she was looking at him. When she reached for her wineglass, he picked up his. "This wine comes from the Brunello grapes grown in this vineyard."

Antonio swirled it around in his glass. "That's very fitting. I'm sure it will be delicious. A toast to my wife, who has already made my life infinitely richer by simply agreeing to marry me. *Salud!*" He touched his glass to hers before they both drank some.

She unexpectedly raised her glass again and touched his. "To my husband. You never let your sister down or betrayed her trust. Because of that you've won mine. To you, Antonio. *Salud!* You'll make the finest king our country has ever known."

"If that happens, it's because you're at my side." His throat swelled with emotion, making it difficult to swallow his second taste of the fruity wine.

"Shall we sit down to eat? I'm sure you're as ravenous as I am." She seated herself before he could help her.

They both tucked in to the heavenly food. She ate with an appetite. He liked that. Most women of his acquaintance ate rabbit food—whether to impress him or not—but not Christina. There was nothing fake about her. *That* was what impressed him.

When she lifted her eyes to him he said, "The little speech you gave in front of the palazzo blew me away."

"It did?"

"How could it not? I thought no other man could be luckier than I am to have you for my wife."

"I feel the same way about you."

"Christina—I know I've put you in an impossible situation."

"You don't have to say anything, Antonio. I understand. That's behind us now."

"No, it isn't. Not until I tell you why."

She had hold of her wineglass stem, but she didn't lift it to her lips while she waited for his explanation. Looking at her right now, he didn't think he'd ever seen so beautiful a woman.

"In a word, I was afraid."

Her delicate eyebrows frowned. "Of what?"

"That once I was in Africa where we could really be alone, you might tell me the engagement was off and send me packing."

She sounded aghast and let go of the glass to put a hand to her throat. "I would never have done that to you."

"Then you're a woman in a million. Who else would have sacrificed her personal happiness for the greater good of someone, something else?"

"Our circumstances were very unusual, but I *am* happy."

He shook his head. "You don't need to pretend with me. This is truth time. I did something terribly selfish to ask you to marry me."

A pained look entered her eyes. "Is this your way of telling me you wish we hadn't gone through with the wedding?"

"No, Christina, no—" He reached across the table and grasped both her hands. "I'm just thankful you consented to be my bride. If you'll let me, I'd like us to start over again. Through Elena we've been friends for years, but you and I don't know each other. I want to get to know all about you. What are the things you love to do? What are the things you hope to do?"

Her silvery gaze enveloped him. "Besides grow old with you?"

"Yes. I'd like to learn it all."

"I'm a pretty normal woman, Antonio. I like reading books and eating chocolate. I like spending time with my friends, especially your sister. I love Africa and the time I spent there helping others. But I suppose my greatest wish would be to have a family of my own. When I first visited the Kikuyu villages with all the adorable children, I hungered for a child of my own. How do you feel about children?"

"I want them too, Christina."

"But I want to take care of them myself. Even if I'll be queen, I want to be their mother in the truest sense of the word."

"So you don't want to send them away to boarding school?"

"Why? It doesn't make sense to me that if you have a child, you would send it away as soon as possible."

He released her hands. "You're talking about yourself."

"Yes."

He saw her eyes glaze over.

"I wanted my mother and father during my growing-up years. If you and I have a baby, would you want it to leave us before it was time to let him or her go? Did you like being sent away to boarding school?"

"I didn't have a choice."

"But did you like it?"

"No. I've never admitted that out loud."

"Neither did Elena."

"I know."

"But *we'll* be the parents," Christina said, then added in an anxious tone, "Will our son have a choice? You say you want to know all about me. If you tell me our children will have to leave home before I'm ready to see them go, I couldn't bear it. Why have them at all?"

Antonio got out of the chair and went around to hunker down beside her. He grasped the hand closest to him. "Look at me." She finally did his bidding. "I was wrong not to come to Africa. We did need time to talk about all these things so I could reassure you."

He heard her heavy sigh before she spoke. "I'm sorry I've turned this beautiful night into something else. Forgive me."

"There's nothing to forgive. You have my word that we'll keep any children we have with us for as long as they want to be with us. The only time they'll have a nanny is if you need to attend a royal function with me."

Her eyes lit up again. "Honest? Is that a promise?"

He could deny her nothing. "I swear it."

"Oh, Antonio. You've made me so happy."

To crush her in his arms was all he had on his mind, but he wanted to give her time and feel comfortable with him. "I was afraid you were going to tell me that you wanted to live in Africa part of the year."

"My life is with you, but I'd love it if we took some trips there together one day. Maybe when our children are old enough to enjoy the animal life? But we've been talking about me. What is one of your dreams?"

"I'm a pretty normal man too. I want a family. I want to be a success at what I do. Because I'll be king, I want to change the country's impression of a monarchy that has shown a breakdown in the old values."

"Like what for instance?"

"The excess spending for one. There are so many areas that need change. But I'm boring you."

"Never."

"Spoken like my queen already." He got to his feet and drew her over to the terrace railing with him. He looked out over the peaceful Tuscan landscape. His pulse throbbed with new life. He wasn't the same man who'd slipped the brooch into the bedchamber earlier in the day.

If he had to describe his feelings at this minute, he was excited for what was to come. When he'd anticipated his wedding weeks ago, he didn't count on being thrilled by this woman who surprised him at every turn. He no longer felt trapped.

Things were going so well he didn't dare make the wrong move until she was ready for the physical side of their marriage. For them to get through the wedding without problems when they were virtual strangers led him to believe they could turn their marriage into something strong, maybe even wonderful given enough time.

He already felt strong feelings for her, which surprised him. They'd discussed one crucial element concerning their marriage by talking about the children they would have. But as near to each other as they were physically right now, they were still worlds apart.

"Christina?" He turned to her and cupped her face in his hands. "Tonight I'm happier than any man has a right to be." He lowered his head and closed his mouth over hers. The taste and feel of her set his pulse racing. "You're the most wonderful thing to come into my life."

Antonio pressed kisses over every feature. "I need to get closer to you. Would you like me to undo the buttons at the back of your wedding dress before I change?"

He saw a little nerve jump at the base of her throat. His bride was nervous. That was his fault for not visiting her and letting her get comfortable with him.

"Yes, please."

She turned, reminding him of a modest young maiden. It brought out his tenderest feelings as he began undoing them from the top of her neckline to the bottom, which ran below her waistline. His fin-

gers brushed her warm skin as he set about freeing
her trembling body. Never had he enjoyed a task more.

"A-are you finished?" she stammered.

He smiled to himself. "Not quite." When he was
done, he lifted her hair and kissed the nape of her neck.
Her mane felt like silk. "There. You're free," he whispered, and turned her around. The sleeves and bodice
of her gown were loose. All he had to do...

But he didn't dare. "I don't think you have any idea
how lovely you are. I want to kiss you, *esposa mia.*
Really kiss you." He found her trembling mouth and
began to devour her. The few kisses they'd shared up
to now bore little resemblance to the desire he felt for
her as she responded with growing hunger.

He clasped her against him, feeling her heart thundering into his. Antonio had an almost primitive need
to make love to her, but not this stand-up kind of loving. He wanted her in his bed and was so enthralled
by her he moaned when she unexpectedly tore her lips
from his and eased away from him.

"Christina?" He had to catch his breath. "Have I
frightened you?"

"No." She shook her head, clutching her gown to
her.

He could tell she was as shocked as he was by what
had just happened. He needed to reassure her. "This
has been a huge day, especially for you. I'm going
to let you go right now. Since we have to be up early
to leave on our honeymoon, I'll bid you *buonanotte,
bellissima*, and make myself a bed on the couch in the
sitting room."

CHAPTER FOUR

CHRISTINA STARED AFTER her new husband, so startled by his sudden departure she could weep. She'd been on fire for him and had been ready to go wherever he led. But in the moment that she'd tried to catch a breath, Antonio left her in a dissatisfied condition.

Was it possible a groom could have nerves like the bride? Confused over what had happened, she blew out the candles and walked to the bedroom. After stepping out of her wedding dress, she laid it over a chair with the veil on top. She put her satin slippers on the floor and placed the tiara on the dresser. They were remnants of the happiest day of her life.

She slipped on a nightgown before brushing her teeth. Then she turned out the lights and got into bed. How could she possibly sleep when her body was throbbing with needs she'd never felt before? He'd awakened a fire in her, but she hadn't known how to handle it when he told her he'd make a bed on the couch for the night. She hadn't had the temerity to go after him.

Sleep must have come, but she awakened early and finished her packing. Making use of the time until

Antonio joined her, she'd touched up her pedicure and manicure. Her nails were done in a two-toned nude shade that matched everything and did justice to her royal antique-gold wedding band and diamond ring.

Since they'd be flying to Paris and would be the target of the paparazzi, Christina had chosen to wear an elegant-looking white two-piece suit from her new royal trousseau. The jacket with sleeves to the elbow fit at the waist. The high neck was half collared and there were pockets on the jacket as well as the skirt. She wore the brooch above the left pocket.

It was the perfect lightweight summery outfit to wear while walking around the City of Lights. Low-heeled off-white pumps and an off-white jacquard designed clutch bag with gloves completed her ensemble.

She'd worn her hair parted sideways into a high bun with one loose, hanging side longer than the other. Two white sticks for her hair with pearl tips matched her pearl stud earrings. Christina hadn't worn perfume in Africa in order to avoid attracting insects. Back home now, she used a soap with a delicious flowery scent. Her makeup consisted of a tarte lip tint. She needed no other color.

When she was ready, she walked to the door of the sitting room and knocked. "Antonio? Our breakfast is waiting."

"*Grazie*. I'll be right out." His deep-timbred male voice curled through her. It sounded an octave lower than usual. He must have barely awakened.

She wandered out to the terrace to wait for him. Her eyes filled with the beauty of the Tuscan countryside. The peaceful scene reminded her of a picture in a storybook where the rows of the vineyard formed perfect lines. All around it the gold and green of the landscape undulated off in the distance dotted with a farmhouse here and a red-roofed villa there.

Too bad she felt anything but peaceful inside.

All of a sudden she sensed she wasn't alone and turned to discover a clean-shaven Antonio studying her from the doorway wearing a casual summer suit in a tan color with a cream sport shirt unbuttoned at the throat. With his olive skin and rugged features, he was so gorgeous she couldn't believe she was married to him.

"Buongiorno, esposo mio," she said softly.

His blue gaze roved over her body from her hair to her heels, missing nothing in between. She'd never felt him look at her that way before, as if she were truly desirable. Her legs went weak because she hadn't expected that look after he decided not to sleep with her last night. She honestly didn't know what to expect.

"How are you this morning?" he asked in a husky tone of voice. A small nerve throbbed at the corner of his mouth. What were his emotions after having gone to his own bed last night instead of spending it in hers?

"I'm fine, thank you. I'm excited that we'll be walking along the Champs-élysées later on today. Aren't you?"

A strange smile broke the line of his mouth. "Shall we eat while we talk over our itinerary?" A question instead of an answer. Something was wrong.

He held out a chair for her. When she sat down, his

hands molded to her shoulders for a moment. Warmth from his fingers coiled through her body. "As bewitching as you were to this man's eyes last night, I find the sight of you right now even more beguiling."

Because of the way he'd been looking at her when no one else was around, she believed he'd meant what he just said. But she hadn't been beguiling enough to go to bed with her. She decided to accept the compliment graciously instead of throwing it back in his face.

"Thank you."

"You're welcome." His hands left her shoulders and he took his place across the table from her. They both started eating the rolls and fruit. After drinking some coffee he said, "How did you sleep?"

"The truth?"

"Always."

"Probably as poorly as you. I doubt that couch was long enough to accommodate your feet." She was glad to hear a chuckle come from him. His eyes lit up with amusement. "When everyone sees us, they'll think we're sleep-deprived because of a passion-filled wedding night and they'll be happy to think that a new royal heir could be on the way already. You know that's what's on everyone's mind."

He flashed her a piercing glance through narrowed lids. "But our business is our own."

"Of course."

After eating another roll, he sat back in the chair. "My mother left it to my father to give me some last-minute advice."

That didn't surprise Christina. "What did he have to say?"

"It isn't what they said. It's what they did."

"I'm not following you."

"Read this." He handed her a note from his suit jacket pocket.

She opened it.

Dear Antonio, your mother and I want you to have the perfect honeymoon. We know you wanted to spend a few days touring Paris and the environs before the coronation next week. But we've thought of something much better and it has all been arranged. All you have to do is be ready by eight in the morning. A helicopter will fly you to Genoa, where you'll take the royal jet to a dream spot for your vacation. It's a place neither you nor Christina has been to before. As always we remain your devoted parents.

They weren't going to Paris?

Her pulse raced. She'd thought there would be so much to do there and they'd have time to get to know each other while seeing the sights. Just what kind of dream vacation did his parents have in mind?

To be gone for a whole week together alone— It worried her that in a week's time he might find out she was unlovable. That old fear never quite went away.

What was Antonio's reaction to the news? Christina's first impulse was to tell him she didn't want to go on any dream vacation. But she couldn't refuse to do the first thing he was asking of her, especially when it was a wedding present from the king and queen themselves.

"I can hear every thought running through your head, Christina. The look in your eyes is all I need to see to know this is the last thing you expected or wanted. If it's any help, it's a surprise to me too. The idea of our honeymoon being scripted by my parents at the taxpayers' expense is typical of the lavish way they've lived their lives and expected me to do the same. If you still want to go to Paris, that's what we'll do."

"And hurt your parents?" It took a courageous man to say that to her. She was touched that he would put her feelings first. Her watch said it was almost eight now. "No, Antonio. We have the rest of our lives to plan our own vacations when we can get away. I don't want us to start off our marriage by alienating your parents. What difference does it make where we go?"

Something flickered in the recesses of his eyes. "Thank you for saying that. I like it that my new bride is adaptable and sensitive enough not to hurt their feelings. Have you done all your packing?"

"Yes." It was a good thing Elena had done some shopping with her and had insisted on her buying a couple of bikinis. "You never know when you need beachwear," her friend had confided. Maybe Elena had known about the location of the vacation spot her parents had planned for them and wanted Christina prepared for any eventuality. "How about you, Antonio?"

"I'm ready as I ever will be."

"Then I'll freshen up and meet you downstairs." She got up from the table and hurried into the bathroom for one last look in the mirror. After applying a new coat of lipstick, she walked into the bedroom and noticed her suitcase was missing. She could count on Lindsay and Louisa to make certain her wedding things were packed and returned to the royal palace in Voti.

All she needed was her purse and gloves. When she left the bridal suite and started down the stairs, she discovered Antonio waiting for her in the foyer of the palazzo.

He stood there looking tall and heartbreakingly handsome. His brilliant blue gaze swept over her in a way that sent her pulse racing. "Will you accuse me of using a platitude to tell you how beautiful you look this morning?"

"Even with bags under my eyes from lack of sleep?" But she smiled as she said it.

"Even then," he murmured. A tiny smile lifted one corner of his lips. "As you said earlier, any onlookers will speculate on the reason why and consider me the luckiest of men."

She took the last step, bringing her closer. "You're good, Antonio. I'll give you that."

He cocked his head. "What do you mean?"

"I think you know. Aren't you afraid all these compliments are going to turn my head?"

The smile disappeared. "If you want to know the truth, I'm afraid they won't."

While she stood there confused again and wondering how much truth was behind his statement, Guido, his father's chief of staff, opened the doors. "Your Highness? Princess Christina?"

Guido had addressed her as *Princess*. She'd better get used to the title, but the appellation was still foreign to her.

"If you're both ready, your cases are stowed in the limousine. Your helicopter is waiting in Monte Calanetti to fly you to Genoa."

"*Grazie*, Guido. We're coming."

She preceded Antonio out to the smoked-glass black limousine with the royal crest on the hood ornament. Guido held the rear door open for her so she could climb in, then shut the door. Antonio went around the other side and got in, shutting the door behind him. He slid close to her while they both attached their seat belts.

"This is nice," he murmured, and grasped her hand. "I'm excited to be going off on a trip with my new wife. I only wish I knew where."

She glanced at him out of the corner of her eye. "Your sister may have given me a hint, but I didn't realize it at the time."

"What did she say?"

"She made sure I bought some bathing suits when we went shopping. Did you pack one?"

"I'm sure mine is in my case somewhere."

"Do you think Hawaii or the Caribbean? I've never been to either destination."

"I have." He released her hand long enough to pull the note from his pocket. "According to this, it's someplace where neither of us has been before."

"That's right. I forgot."

"Our parents probably collaborated. It ought to be interesting."

"I agree. From what Elena has told me, you've been all over the world."

He smiled. "Let's put it this way. I've traveled over many countries without ever landing."

Christina returned his smile. She'd taken many helicopter trips with Marusha into the more inaccessible areas of Kenya's forested interior, so she was no stranger to the sensation of liftoff or landing. Before she knew it, they'd arrived on the outskirts of the village where their helicopter was waiting.

Antonio helped her out of the limo into one of the rear seats of the helicopter. He climbed in next to her while Guido placed their cases inside, then got in the copilot's seat for the short flight to Genoa. Passing over the Tuscan countryside was a constant delight.

Once they boarded the royal jet with its insignia in huge gold lettering, Christina was introduced to the pilot and copilot before being given a tour. She was struck by the staggering opulence inside and out. To her mind, the platinum curving couches, mirrored ceilings and ornate bathroom were out-of-this-world outrageous.

With an office, a gourmet kitchen and two bedrooms, all extravagant to the point of being ridiculous, she imagined the plane that contained a cockpit meant for the emperor of the universe must have cost in the region of millions upon millions of dollars.

Antonio must have been watching her, because he

said in a quiet voice, "Is there any question in your mind why our country is outraged by the unnecessary spending of my own parents? Papa bought this off an oil-rich sheik. When I'm king, I have every intention of selling it to the highest bidder and using the money to bolster Halencia's economy and put more funds in your charity foundation."

When she thought of the relief that money could bring to the Kikuyu people, she wanted to throw her arms around his neck in joy, but she didn't dare with Guido and the steward in hearing distance.

After they sat down on one of the couches, Guido made a surprising announcement. "This is where I leave you, Your Highnesses. When you reach your destination, you'll be met and taken to your vacation paradise. After the plane lands, you'll be flown in a helicopter to your own private paradise. There'll be no phone, television or internet service there."

What?

While she sat there stunned, she could tell by the lines around his mouth that Antonio wasn't amused either. "Guido? You've gotten us this far, but I refuse to travel any farther until you tell me where we're going."

"I suppose it couldn't hurt to say that you'll be arriving on the other side of the world in approximately twenty-one hours from now."

"That's not much help," Antonio said in a clipped voice.

"I'm only following the king's orders. Is there anything I can do for you before I leave?"

Antonio turned to her. "How about you, Christina?"

She had compassion for Guido, who was loyal to his king first. "I don't need anything. Thank you for everything you've done."

"You're welcome. Enjoy your honeymoon." He bowed to Antonio before leaving the plane.

In a few minutes the engines screamed to life and the fasten-seat-belts sign flashed on. Before long the jet headed into the sun. Once they'd achieved cruising speed, they got up from the couch and moved to sit in the lavish dining area where the steward served them a fabulous lunch.

"Don't be upset with Guido. It's obvious your parents' big surprise is important to him and to them."

One eyebrow lifted. "Twenty-one hours one way takes a lot of fuel. Round-trip means thousands more dollars being paid out from the public coffers. It isn't right."

She sat back while she sipped her coffee. "I agree, and I admire your desire to change the dynamics of the L'Accardi family's spending habits. But for now, why don't we decide to be Jack and Jill, two normal people who got married on a whim, and have just been given a windfall from their oil-rich uncle in Texas who wants to make us happy."

"Oil?"

"Why not? When we return to civilization, that's the time to start trimming the budget."

When she didn't think it was possible, he chuckled. "Jack and Jill, eh?"

She nodded. "One of the American girls from Texas

at the boarding school had the name Jill, and her brother's name was Jack."

By now his eyes were smiling. "I'll go along with that idea. What do you say we go to one of the bedrooms and watch a movie where we can be comfortable?"

Each bedroom had a built-in theater. She wiped her mouth with a napkin. "I'll find my suitcase and change my clothes."

He reached across the table and grasped her hand. "I'm sorry you're not able to show off that lovely white outfit in Paris."

A warm smile broke out on her face. "Don't be." She wouldn't forget the way he'd stared at her when he walked out on the terrace earlier that morning. Christina had seen a glint of genuine male appreciation in his eyes that brought her great pleasure. "We'll do Paris one of these days."

Feeling his gaze on her retreating back, she walked through the compartment and found the bedroom where both their cases had been placed. She took hers and crossed the hall into the other bedroom.

After putting it on the queen-size bed, she found a pair of lightweight pants in dusky blue and a filmy long-sleeved shirt with a floral pattern of light and dark blues combined with pink. It draped beautifully against her body to the hips.

The white suit went in the closet before she slipped into her casual clothes and put on bone-colored leather sandals. After removing the pearl tipped sticks from her hair, she exchanged the pearl studs for gold earrings mounted with star-shaped blue sapphire stones. As she was applying a fresh coat of lipstick, she heard a knock on the door.

"Antonio?"

He opened it but didn't enter. "Come on over to the other bedroom when you're ready."

Her heart started to thud. "I'll be there in a minute."

Antonio had changed into jeans and a sport shirt. Normally he would have put on the bottoms of a pair of sweats and nothing else for the twenty-one-hour flight. But out of consideration for Christina, he needed to make his way carefully for this journey into the unknown. Their honeymoon was in the process of becoming a fait accompli.

He'd experienced two heart attacks already: one at the altar when his fiancée appeared in her white wedding dress and lace veil. The other attack happened this morning when he first saw her on the terrace ready for their trip to Paris wearing a stunning white outfit. When he heard her call out his name just now, he should have known to brace himself for the third attack.

"Enter if you dare," he teased. Antonio had stretched out on the bed with his head and back propped against the headboard using a pillow for a buffer.

"Ready or not," she countered, and came into the room. The incredibly beautiful woman dressed in blue appeared, and the sight almost caused him to drop the remote. With her shiny hair, she lit up any room she entered. How could he have ignored her for so long?

The few phone calls and visits to her had been made out of duty. The busy life he'd been leading in California had included hard work *and* one certain woman when he had the time.

Thoughts of his future marriage for the good of the country had only played on the edge of his consciousness, as did the woman who'd been thousands of miles away in Kenya. He couldn't go back and fix things, but he could shower her with attention now. They didn't know each other well yet, but had made a start last night when their passion ignited.

Antonio recognized that he needed to treat her the way he would any beautiful woman he'd just met and wanted to get to know much better. He patted her side of the bed. "Come and join me. We have a choice of five films without my having to move from this spot."

She laughed and pulled a pillow out from under the quilt. The next thing he knew she'd thrown it at the foot of the bed and lain down on her stomach so she could watch the screen located on the other side of the bedroom. "Why don't you start the one you'd like to see without telling me what it is?" she said over her shoulder.

Christina made an amazing sight with those long legs lying enticingly close to him. "What if you don't like it?"

"I like all kinds of movies and will watch it because I want to know what makes my husband tick."

His heart skipped a beat. "You took the words out of my mouth." He clicked to the disk featuring a Neapolitan Mafia gangster film. "I only saw part of this when it first came out."

"I'm sure I haven't seen it. Italian films are hard to come by when you're out in the bush. This is fun!"

He found it more than fun to be watching it with the woman he'd just married. She made the usual moans and groans throughout. When it concluded she turned on her side and propped her head to look back at him. "I heard that the Camorra Mafia from Naples was the inspiration for that film. Were there really a hundred gangs, do you think?"

"I do."

"Did any cross the water into our country?"

"Three families that we know of."

"Do they still exist?"

"Yes, but were given Halencian citizenship at a time when our borders were more porous. They're no longer a problem. What I'm concerned about is creating high-tech jobs. Tourism and agriculture alone aren't going to sustain our growing population. I have many plans and have been laying the groundwork to establish software companies and a robotics plant, all of which can operate here to build Halencian industry."

"So *that's* what you've been doing in San Francisco all these years. No wonder you didn't come home often."

"Are you accusing me of being a workaholic?"

Her eyelids narrowed. "Are you?"

"I make time to play."

"Since I won't be able to go to sleep for a long time, what can I do for you, my husband?"

"How about reading to me?"

The question pleased her no end. "You'd like that?"

"I saw a book in your suitcase. Have you read it already?"

"I'm in the middle of it."

"What's it called?"

"*Cry, the Beloved Country* by Alan Paton. He wrote about South Africa and the breakdown of the tribal system. It's not the part of Africa I know, but it's so wonderful I'm compelled to finish the book."

"I never got around to reading it," he said.

"Tell you what. I'll read you the blurb on the flyleaf. If it interests you, I'll read from the beginning until you fall asleep."

"I'm surprised you don't carry a Kindle with you. Aren't physical books heavy to carry when traveling?"

"They can be, but I really like to hold a book in my hands. They're like an old friend I can see peeking at me from the bookshelf, teasing me to come and read again."

"I've decided you're a Renaissance woman, Christina."

"That's a curious word."

"It really describes you. You're a very intelligent woman. I see in you a revival of vigor and an interest in life that escapes most people. You're more intriguing than you know."

If she was intriguing, that was something. "When did you discover that?" she asked without looking at him.

"It happened when you were just fifteen. I drove

you and Elena to an old monastery in the woods above Lake Geneva. When we went inside, you were able to translate all the Latin inscriptions in those glass cases. I detested Latin and at eighteen I still needed a tutor for it. To hear you translating for us, I was so stunned at your expertise, it left me close to speechless. Do you remember that time?"

He remembered that? It caused her pulse to pick up speed. "Yes. I was showing off to you so you wouldn't think that your sister was spending time with a complete numbskull. My mother hated it that I was such a bookworm and would rather read than go to tea with a bunch of girls who only talked about boys and clothes."

"This conversation is getting interesting. When *did* you first become interested in boys?"

"Actually I was crazy about them at a very early age." Pictures of Prince Antonio and Princess Elena were constantly in the news. From the time she was about eight, she always liked to see photos of the famous brother and sister in the newspaper accompanying their family on a ski trip or some such thing.

He was the country's darling. By the time she met him in person, she'd already developed a crush on him that only grew after being with him. Of course all the silliness ended when she left Montreux and had new experiences in Africa. Once in a while she and Marusha would see him in the news, but until Elena's brush with the law he'd been as distant to her as another galaxy.

Antonio broke into laughter. "The secret life of Christina Rose. How scandalous."

She chuckled. "Marusha had plenty to tell me about tribal mating rituals of the Kikuyu. In fact, she kept me and Elena royally entertained most nights after lights went out. We'd stay up half the night talking. She had a crush on this security guard who was guarding a VIP at the Montreux Palace Hotel.

"You know how beautiful Marusha is. Well, we'd walk past him and she'd say things to him to capture his interest. He never spoke, but his eyes always watched her. He was tall, maybe six foot five, and he kept his arms folded. He was the most impressive figure I ever saw and I think he was the reason she could handle being in Montreux when she'd rather be home in Africa."

Laughter continued to rumble out of Antonio.

"Your sister had other interests. There was a drummer in the band that played at this one disco we were ordered not to visit. He was crazy about her and kept making dates with her. She only kept one of them. It was through him she met other guys, the kind she finally ended up with who got thrown in jail for drugs."

"Let's be thankful she has grown up now, but don't stop talking," Antonio murmured. "I could listen to you all night. What masculine interest did *you* have?"

Christina didn't dare tell him that there was no male to match Antonio. His image was the one she'd always carried in the back of her mind. "Oh... I always loved men in the old Italian movies. You know, Franco Nero, Marcello Mastroianni, Vittorio De Sica."

"No Halencian actors?"

"No. I've liked a couple of British actors too. Rufus

Sewell...*ooh-la-la*." She grinned. "Now, there is a male to die for! So, which actress did it for you?"

"That would be difficult to answer."

"You don't play fair. You manage to get a lot of information out of me, but I ask you one question and suddenly you play possum."

"What does that mean?"

"It means you play dead like a possum when you don't want to reveal yourself. The possum does it for protection. It's a very funny American expression and it describes you right now. What are you hiding from? Is the truth too scary for you?"

"Have a heart, Christina. I'm not nearly so terrible a womanizer as some of the tabloids have made me out to be. They're mostly lies."

"That's all right. You just keep telling yourself that. When I married you I forgave you for everything. But I've talked your ear off, so excuse me for a minute."

She hurried into the other bedroom and grabbed the book from the table, and then she returned to Antonio. "Are you still in the mood to be read to, or are you ready to confess your sins?"

"Yes and no."

He was hilarious.

"All right, then. Here's the quote from it. 'Cry, the beloved country, for the unborn child that is the inheritor of our fear.'" She read the rest.

A long silence ensued before Antonio murmured, "That's very moving. Tell me something honestly. Are you going to miss Africa too much?"

"What do you mean?"

"You've spent ten years of your life there. So many memories and friends you've made."

"Well, I'm hoping that from time to time I'll be able to fly to Nairobi to keep watch over the foundation, which I plan to continue with your permission."

"There's no question about that."

Good. "But our marriage is my first priority, and your needs come first and always will with me."

"You're wonderful, Christina, but that isn't what I asked, exactly. Did you leave your heart there?"

"Certainly a part of it, but I could ask you the same thing. Do you feel a strong tug when you think of San Francisco and the years you spent there?"

"I'd be a liar if I didn't say yes."

"I didn't expect you to say anything else. As for me, I've decided I have two homes. One there, where I've always been comfortable, and now the new one with you. I see them both being compatible. When you long for San Francisco and want to do business there, I'll understand."

"You'd love it there. I want to take you with me and show you around."

He couldn't have said anything to thrill her more. "And maybe you can fly to Africa with me for a little break from royal business."

"We'll make it happen."

She studied him for a long time. "Is there a woman you had to leave who's missing you right now? Maybe I should rephrase that. Is there someone you're missing horribly?"

Antonio should have seen these questions coming,

particularly since he hadn't slept with her last night. "I haven't been a monk. What about you?"

A quick smile appeared. Her appeal was growing on him like mad. "I'm no nun."

For some odd reason he didn't like hearing that.

You hypocrite, Antonio. Did you want a bride as pure as the driven snow? Did you really expect her to give up men while she waited four years for you to decide when to claim her for your wife?

"Who was he?" His parents' affairs had jaded him.

"A doctor who'd come to Kenya to perform plastic surgery on some of the native children. Once I came back to Africa with the engagement ring on my finger, he left for England three days later."

"I kept you waiting four years," Antonio muttered in self-disgust.

A frown marred her features. "Antonio, none of that matters. I'm your wife! But you still haven't answered my question. Is there a woman who became of vital importance to you before you had to fly home to get married?"

He got off the bed. "The only woman of importance was one I got involved with before our engagement, Christina."

"Then you've known her a long time. If there'd been no engagement, would you have married her?"

"That's hard to say. I might have if I'd decided to turn my back on my family and wanted to stay in California for the rest of my life. But when your call came telling me about Elena's problems and I talked to her, I realized how binding those family ties really are right from the cradle."

"I know that all too well," she whispered. Christina had obviously been talking about the relationship with her parents.

"The accident of my being born to a king and queen set me on a particular path. To marry a foreigner and deviate from it might bring me short-term pleasure. But I feared I'd end up living a lifetime of regret."

She shook her head. "How hard for both of you."

Her sincerity rang so true he felt it reach his bones. "Though I continued to see her after the engagement party, nothing was the same because we knew there would have to be an end. We soon said goodbye to each other.

"In a way it was a relief because to go on seeing her would not only have made a travesty of our engagement, but the situation was totally unfair to her and you. My sources at the palace confirmed that the country was suffering and there were plans afoot to abolish the monarchy. I knew it was only a matter of time before—"

"Before you had to come home and marry me to save the throne," she broke in. "I get it."

"Christina—" He approached her and grasped her hands. "Do you think it's possible for us to forget the past? You know what I mean. When I said my vows in the chapel, I meant what I said. I will love you and honor you all the days of my life. Can you still make that same commitment to me after knowing what I've told you?"

Her marvelous eyes filled with tears. "Oh, Antonio, I want you to know that when I made my vows at the altar, I was running on faith. Now that faith has been strengthened by what you've just admitted to me. If we have total honesty between us, then there's nothing to prevent us from trying to make this marriage work. You've always been the most handsome man I've ever known, so my attraction to you isn't a problem."

He kissed her fingers. "Can you forgive me for staying away from you before the wedding?"

"We've already had this discussion."

He slid his hands to her upper arms. "No woman but an angel like you would have sacrificed everything to enter into an engagement that didn't consider your own personal feelings in any way, shape or form. Forgive me, Christina. I don't like the man I was. I can only hope to become the man you're happy to be married to."

Her eyes roved over his features. "I liked the man you were. That man loved his sister enough to save her and their family from horrible embarrassment and scandal. She wasn't just any sister. She was the princess of Halencia, my friend. I loved you for loving her enough to help her.

"You have no idea what she did for me. She was the only person in my world besides my great-aunt Sofia who was good to me. Elena was the person I cried to every time I was hurt by my parents, especially my father, who wished I'd been born a boy." The tears trickled down her flushed cheeks.

Antonio sucked in his breath. "*Grazie a Dio*, you're

exactly who you are." He started kissing the tears away. When he reached her mouth he couldn't stop himself from covering it with his own. The taste of her excited him. Without her wedding dress on, he could draw her close and feel the contours of her beautiful body through the thin fabric of her shirt. Her fragrance worked like an aphrodisiac on his senses, which had come alive.

"Bellissima."

CHAPTER FIVE

THE FIRST TIME Christina had heard Antonio use the word *bellissima*, he'd said it in a teasing jest outside the door of the bridal suite. Just now he'd said it because she could sense his physical desire for her. After last night, there was no mistaking their attraction to each other. But she needed to use her head and not get swept away by passion until they'd spent more time together.

He'd wanted to put off making love to her last night. She was glad of it now. They did need more time to explore each other's minds first. Antonio might have walked away from the love of his life in San Francisco, but that didn't mean the memories didn't linger.

Christina could make love with him and pretend all was well, but she knew that until she held a place in his heart, then making love wouldn't have the same meaning for either of them. She wanted their first time to happen when it was right.

As soon as he lifted his mouth, she eased out of his arms. Avoiding his gaze she said, "I'm going to freshen up before dinner. Where do you want to eat?"

"How about the other bedroom? There'll be other

films to pick from. Your choice. I'll tell the steward to bring it in ten minutes."

"Good. After our fabulous lunch, I can't believe I'm hungry again."

When he didn't respond, she left him to use the restroom. Some strands of her hair had come loose. It was smarter to just undo it and brush it out. Before he brought their dinner, she pulled out the pillows and propped them against the headboard. After taking off her sandals, she reached for the remote and got up on the bed. Before long Antonio walked in carrying a tray.

"Put it here between us." She patted the center of the bed.

"The steward still won't breathe a word of where we're going." He put the tray down. Sandwiches and salad.

"Loyal to the end." She smiled at him. "In the meantime this looks good."

"I think so too." He joined her on the bed and they began to eat.

"Do you mind if we talk? We haven't discussed how we're going to live. In the fairy tales the prince takes his bride to his kingdom and they live happily ever after, but we never get to see *how* they live."

He smiled. "I have my own home in one wing of the palace. Our bedroom and living room overlook the Mediterranean. It's totally private and will be our home. My office is on the main floor adjoining my father's. My parents have their own suite. You've already visited Elena in her suite, which is in the other wing. But we're far enough apart to lead separate lives."

She poured them both more coffee, then sat back to drink hers. "Is it going to feel terribly strange bringing a wife into your world?"

He finished off the rest of his sandwich. "I thought it would. In fact, I couldn't comprehend it. But after being with you, I'll feel strange if you're not with me. I've discovered that I've slipped into the husband role faster than I would have thought and I'm enjoying every minute of it."

Christina studied him for a moment. "Today I feel like we're beginning to get to know each other and aren't afraid to be ourselves. That was my greatest fear, that you'd be different from the man I knew as Elena's brother. I've worried that in living with the man you've become, I'd feel invisible walls that kept us strangers. But I don't feel that way at all when I'm around you."

"That's good to hear. I have no idea if I'm easy to live with, Christina, and beg your forgiveness ahead of time."

A gentle laugh escaped her lips. "That goes for me too. So far I have no complaints. I hope you don't mind if I ask you a few more questions."

"Why would I mind? This is all new. You can ask me anything."

She put down her empty coffee cup. "Is Guido going to be your chief of staff when you take over?"

"At first, yes. But he's been loyal to my father for years and when he sees how I intend to rule the country, he may have trouble supporting me."

As he was lying in bed, he'd worried about how everything would go while he was away on his honeymoon. If something went wrong before the coronation, he wouldn't be there to smooth things over. His father's note said no phone, no TV or internet while they were on vacation. He'd never been without those things and couldn't comprehend it at the time.

"*I'll* support you, Antonio. I believe in the changes you're going to make."

He heard the fervor in her voice and smiled at her. She was too good to be true. "If things get bad, how would you like to be my new chief of staff?"

Christina broke into laughter. "Now, there's a thought. The media will claim that Princess Christina is running the show."

"Better you than anyone else I can think of. But seriously, let's not worry about the future of the monarchy today. Look—" He sat forward. "I know everything will be strange at first."

"Elena said your mother has her own personal maid. I don't want one, Antonio. I find it absurd to ask someone to fetch and carry when I'm perfectly capable of doing those things myself. And I'd like to cook for you, go shopping at the markets. I can balance homemaking with the time spent at the charity foundation office in town."

The more she talked, the more he liked the sound of it. "We're on the same wavelength. All the years I lived in the States I did most things myself and prefer it, so I get where you're coming from. We'll make this work."

Her silvery eyes glistened with unshed tears. "Thank you for being so understanding." When she spoke, her heart was in her eyes and it touched a part of his soul.

"Thank *you* for marrying me." He meant it with all his heart.

A shadow crossed over her face. "Antonio—if I'd told you I didn't want to get married when you called, what do you think you would have done?"

"I don't know. What saddens me is that you weren't sure I'd follow through and marry you. Christina, I swear not to do anything consciously to hurt you or bring you grief. Do you believe that?"

"Of course I do," she answered in a trembling voice. "Now I'll stop pestering you and hand you the remote. Here are half a dozen movies. Choose whichever one you want. I'm loving this.

"When we get back to Halencia, I'm afraid everything will change. Elena told me your father's daily schedule is horrendous, so I consider this time precious to have you all to myself. Tomorrow we'll reach our destination, so I'm taking advantage of the time to talk to you."

"You've always been so easy to be with, Christina. You still are." More than ever… He clicked the remote and flipped slowly through the titles so she could have time to choose.

"Stop!" she cried out. "*The African Queen* in Italian? Half of that film was filmed in the Congo!"

Antonio grinned. "I never saw it."

"I bet we have Elena to thank for this one." She smiled. "Trust her to find me a film I'd enjoy. Do you mind if we watch it?"

"Not at all. It will give me a feel for where you've lived and worked all these years."

"I never worked in the Congo. The Kikuyu tribe lives on the central highlands, but it doesn't matter. The part in the Congo is authentic. Just don't forget it's an old, old movie, Antonio."

He flashed her a smile that turned her heart over. "I like old if it's good."

"This is good. I promise."

Christina settled back to watch the film while she finished her sandwich. She could tell Antonio liked it. He kept asking questions as if he was truly interested. Maybe he was. But if she continued to wonder when his reactions were natural or made up to please her every time he spoke, their marriage didn't have a hope of succeeding.

"The actress is a redhead like you."

"The poor thing. She probably suffered a lot as a child."

"She became a movie star, Christina. It obviously didn't hurt her."

He lay back on the bed and slid his hand into her hair splayed on the pillow. He lifted some strands in his fingers. "I love your hair. It gleams like red gold and smells like citrus."

"My shampoo is called Lemon Orange Peel. When I'm in Africa I have to use a shampoo with no scent so the tsetse flies and mosquitoes won't zero in on me."

"You'd be a target all right. Do you love it there so much?"

"Yes."

"You're wonderful, you know that?"

Her eyes filled with telltale moisture.

His hand moved to her face. He traced the outline of her jaw with his fingers. "You have flawless skin and a mouth I need to kiss again." Without asking her permission his lips brushed hers over and over until he coaxed them apart and began drinking deeply.

A moan escaped her throat as she felt herself falling under his spell. He rolled her into his rock-hard body. A myriad of sensations attacked her as she felt him rub her back, urging her closer. With every stroke, her body continued to melt as the heat started building inside her, making her feverish. Antonio was taking her to a place she'd never been before.

She wasn't cognizant of the fasten-seat-belt sign flashing until the captain's voice came over the intercom. "We've started to experience turbulence. For your safety, you need to come forward and sit until we get through this."

On a groan Antonio released her, much more in control than she was. "Come on. Let's go." He got off the bed and helped her to her feet.

She couldn't believe how bumpy it had become and clung to him while they made their way out of the bedroom and down the hallway to the couches. Christina had so much trouble fastening her seat belt that Antonio did it for her and then fastened his own.

"It's going to be all right." He reached for her hand.

The incident didn't last long. When the sign went off, she undid her seat belt and got up before Antonio did. "It's late. If you don't mind, I'm going to get ready for bed. Last night I hardly slept and now I'm exhausted."

After he undid his seat belt, he stood up. "You go ahead. I'm going to have a chat with the captain and will see you in the morning." He put a hand behind her head and pressed a firm kiss to her mouth before releasing her. "Get a good sleep."

"You too," she whispered before walking back to the bedroom she'd just left. Her legs felt like mush, but this had nothing to do with the bumpy flight. The kiss he'd just given her was able to reduce her to a trembling bride. A little while ago she'd experienced the kind of passion that would have rendered her witless and breathless given another minute in his arms.

Frightened because she'd almost lost control, she showered and got ready for bed. Once under the covers she had a talk with herself. It *was* too soon in their marriage for the physical side to take over. She didn't doubt Antonio's intentions. He was doing his best to be a considerate husband. There was nothing wrong with that, not at all. But she wanted to know his possession and realized this was what she got for entering into a marriage of convenience.

I don't want to be his convenient bride.

Christina wanted him to make love to her because he was in love with her and couldn't live without her. She wanted Antonio in every way a woman wanted her husband. From the age of fifteen she'd been attracted to him. All it had taken was that kiss at the altar to turn her inside out.

What have you done to me, Antonio?

She closed her eyes, reeling from that torturous question until she fell into oblivion. The next time she was aware of her surroundings, her watch indicated she'd slept ten hours. All in all, they'd been flying twenty hours with refueling stops she hadn't been aware of. That meant they were close to their unknown destination.

If Antonio had come to her in the night, she didn't know about it. Chances were he'd been exhausted too and needed sleep as much as she did. She threw off the covers and went to the bathroom to brush her teeth and arrange her hair back in a French twist.

The more she thought about it, the more she believed they were flying to a beach vacation. After some deliberation, she chose to put on a pair of white pants and toned it with a filmy white top of aqua swirls that looked like sea spray. The short sleeves and round neck made it summery. Once she'd put on lipstick, she packed her bag so it would be ready to carry off the jet.

Antonio must have had the same thoughts, because when she walked through the plane to the dining area, she discovered him dressed in white pants and a white crew-neck shirt with navy blue trim. His virility took her breath.

As she approached, he broke off talking to the steward. "I was just about to come and wake you for breakfast. We'll be landing pretty soon. I've been told we don't want to miss the view before we touch down."

"That sounds exciting. How did you sleep?" She sat down at one of the tables.

He took his place opposite her. "I don't think as well as you."

"I'm sorry."

"Don't be. I'm a restless sleeper when I travel. When we touched down to refuel, I got out of the jet to stretch my legs. I peeked in on you to see if you wanted some exercise too, but you were out like a light."

She felt Antonio's admiring gaze before the steward served them another delicious meal that started off with several types of chilled melon balls in a mint juice. "Mmm. This is awesome."

"I agree," he said, still eyeing her face and hair over his cup of cappuccino until she felt a fluttery sensation in her chest.

They ate healthy servings of eggs, bread and jam. If she ate like this for every meal, she'd quickly put on the weight she'd slowly lost over the past year.

The steward came to their table. "The pilot will be addressing you in a minute. When you're through eating, please take your seats in the front section. He'll start the descent, allowing you a bird's-eye view."

"Thank you," Antonio said, exchanging a silent glance with her. By tacit agreement, they got up from the table and walked forward to one of the couches, where they sat together and buckled up.

In a minute the fasten-seat-belt sign flashed and they heard the captain over the intercom. "Your Highness? Princess Christina? It's eleven a.m. Tahitian time."

"Tahiti—" she blurted in delight, provoking a smile from Antonio who reached for her hand.

"We'll be landing at the airport built on the island next to Bora Bora. From there you'll be taken by helicopter to a nearby island that is yours exclusively for the next four days. The sight you're about to see is one of the most glorious in the world. Start watching out the windows."

Christina felt the plane begin to descend. Pretty soon she saw a sight that was out of this world. The captain said, "Bora Bora has been described as an emerald set in a sea of turquoise blue with a surrounding necklace of translucent white water."

"Incredible!" she and Antonio cried at the same time.

"There are dark green islands farther out in the lagoon that face the mountain. This lagoon is three times the size of the land mass."

"Oh, I can't believe this beauty is real." She shook her head. "No wonder sailors from long ago dreamed of reaching Bora Bora."

"To the southeast you'll see a coral garden with waters swimming with manta rays, barracudas and sharks. You can watch them at their feeding time."

She turned to her husband. "I'm not sorry your parents gave us this beautiful gift, Antonio. They couldn't have planned a more glorious honeymoon retreat for us."

"You're right." He squeezed her hand.

The jet circled lower and before long they touched down. Antonio undid both their seat belts. "I'll grab our suitcases. What else?"

"My white purse on the dresser."

He nodded. "I'll be right back." His excitement matched hers. They'd come to paradise and couldn't wait to get out in it.

She walked toward the galley to thank the steward.

"It's been my pleasure, Princess."

Antonio caught up to her with her purse. The steward carried their cases to the entrance of the jet where their pilot was waiting. He shook his hand. "Thank you for a flawless flight."

"It has been an honor for me to serve you and the princess. There's a helicopter waiting to fly you to your private resort where every need will be met. In four days I'll be here to fly you back to Halencia. Enjoy your honeymoon."

She left the jet with Antonio following her and made her way to the helicopter. The pilot, an islander, greeted them warmly and explained they'd be flying to one of those dark green islands in the distance.

Christina sat in one of the backseats. The second Antonio joined her and buckled up, the rotors screamed to life and they lifted off, flying low over the aquamarine water. The pilot spoke to them over the mic.

"Welcome to Tahiti. The resort has heard that the future king and queen of Halencia are our guests. Word has come that you are much beloved, Princess. No one else will disturb your vacation, but you have a staff to wait on you. Ask for anything."

"Thank you."

When she looked back at Antonio, he was staring at her. "Do you know everyone who meets you is so charmed by you that you have them eating out of your hand? I noticed it as we were walking down the aisle after the ceremony. All eyes and smiles were focused on you."

A blush seeped into her cheeks. "A bride is always the center of attention at a wedding. It's the way of things."

"But my bride is exceptional and loved by the people already. If I'm to gain any credibility with the country when I'm king, it will be because of you."

"Thank you, but you don't need to say things like that to me."

"Yes, I do." The sincerity in his voice convinced her.

Before she knew it, the pilot set down the helicopter on a stretch of the purest white beach she'd ever seen. Another man in shorts and T-shirt was there to take their bags.

"Welcome to Bora Bora, Your Highnesses. I'm Manu and will be serving you. If you want anything, it will be at your disposal. With the powerboat you can go where you wish to fish, scuba dive, hike. Anything you want."

They shook his hand and followed him to their resort. It turned out to be a massive island bungalow of traditional Polynesian design with a vaulted ceiling situated on stilts over their private lagoon of turquoise water. As they walked inside, the living room looked like a sumptuous palace suite with windows on all sides and glass floors throughout to watch the fish.

There were windows on all sides and two different sundecks facing Bora Bora with platforms so they could step off directly into the lagoon.

Outside were oversize chairs and more glass floor panels. Manu showed them the dining room and kitchen with a refrigerator stocked with snacks and drinks. "There's food here to enjoy inside or to make a picnic. The spacious bathroom has two tubs and walk-in showers."

They followed him to the fabulous bedroom, also with a vaulted ceiling, where he put down their cases. Then he showed them out to one of the platforms. "The powerboat is ready and filled to capacity to take you where you want. Come with me to the other platform."

They followed him. "You have your own two-seater kayak, snorkeling equipment, rubber rafts, whatever you want including towels and sunscreen. The lagoon water is eighty degrees and the nighttime temperature is the same."

Warmer than a bathtub?

Christina marveled that everything you could ever want had been provided. She thanked Elena silently for taking her to buy some swimming suits.

"I'll be the person waiting on you. Pick up the phone to order your food or when you need clothes washed or ironed. There's one in the living room and another one in the bedroom. There's no internet, no television. If there's an emergency, you call me on the house phone and I'll take care of it. Can I answer any questions?"

"Not right now." Antonio shook his hand. "Thank you, Manu."

After the islander disappeared, she looked around in wonder. "All of this just for us?" she murmured to her husband. "Only a king could afford to pay the resort enough money to keep the world away."

He chuckled and turned to her. "What do you want to do first?"

"Let's unpack and then go for a swim. That water is calling to me."

Antonio couldn't help but admit that this had to be the ultimate getaway. His parents had gone over-the-top on this one, but he'd promised Christina they'd enjoy this outrageous luxury and not count the cost.

It didn't take long to put their things in closets and drawers. Then she disappeared in the bathroom. While she was out of sight he changed into his boxer-style black bathing trunks. Wanting to create a mood, he went into the living room and searched in the entertainment center for the radio.

When he turned it on, he got Tahitian music, exactly what he wanted. There was a switch that said Outside. He flipped it and suddenly they were surrounded with island music that no doubt could be heard out on the beach.

A smiling Christina came hurrying in wearing a lacy peach-colored beach robe over what looked like a darker peach bikini. Her gorgeous long legs took his breath away. "That's such romantic music, I think I'm dreaming all this."

"Fun, isn't it? Let's go try out the water."

He opened the door that led to the platform off the living room. She leaned over the railing to look down at the water. "It's clear as crystal." When she reached the edge of the platform, she removed her beach coat and put it over the railing.

"Wait, Christina. You need some sunscreen or you'll pick up a bad sunburn."

"You're right."

"I'll get it." He went over to the basket and brought it to her. "I'll put some on your back and shoulders."

She turned her back toward him without hesitation. Her skin felt like satin and he loved rubbing the cream over her. The legitimate excuse to touch her made him wish he didn't have to stop. Summoning all the self-control he could muster, he handed her the tube so she could do the rest herself.

"Thank you," she said in a shaky voice. "Now it's my turn to put some on you, although you're already tanned."

He longed to feel her hands on him. His pulse throbbed as he felt her spread the cream over his shoulders and back. After putting the tube on the railing, she jumped in the shallow water and shrieked with joy.

"Oh, Antonio— This is divine!" She splashed the water with her hands and laughed in delight before lying back while her legs did the work of keeping her afloat.

One look at her and he couldn't reach her soon enough. Bathtub was right. The temperature here stayed around eighty day and night. He swam up next to her, infected by her sounds of excitement. With the Polynesian music filling the air, they were like children who'd discovered the fount of pure pleasure.

Together they moved out deeper into the blue lagoon. He swam under and around her. The glimpses of her exquisitely molded body set his heart pounding.

"Look at that darling little sea turtle!"

Spectacular as it was, he would rather look at her. As they trod water, they caught sight of other types of small fish including a clown fish with orange and white stripes. One discovery turned into another. They played and darted through the water for several hours, concocting silly games to identify the fish they saw. Her prowess as a swimmer was going to make this the adventure of a lifetime.

Since there was no one else around, Antonio felt as if they were the last two people on earth…or the first. Adam and Eve?

He loved the idea of it, loved being with her like this where her guard was down. Her sense of fun was already making this trip unforgettable. "What do you say we go back and drink something icy cold while we sunbathe on the lounge chairs?"

"That sounds perfect. I'll race you back."

Together they did the crawl. He slowed his pace to stay even with her. When they reached the platform he climbed up first, then helped her. She put on her beach robe and headed for one of the loungers.

"I'll order some drinks and be right back."

"No alcohol for me. Even a little wine can give me a headache."

"Did you suffer from one on our wedding night?"

"No, because I only sipped a little, but I know to be careful."

That was something he didn't know. He rarely drank himself and was pleased to learn she didn't care about it. His parents constantly overindulged.

A few minutes later and Manu appeared with two frosted glasses of juice topped with a flower.

"I could get used to this in a hurry," Christina commented after they'd given him their order for dinner and were alone again. Antonio handed her some of the brochures from the table in the living room. He looked over one, but would study the rest of them later. Right now he was content to study her and look at the white clouds moving slowly across the sky.

He finished his drink. "It'll be several hours before dinner, but it's already late in the day. How would you like to go exploring in the powerboat? We'll follow the directions in that brochure and make our plans for tomorrow."

"That's exactly what I want to do. While we were descending in the plane, I longed to spend more time just to get acquainted with this glorious place."

A few minutes later they undid the ropes and Antonio idled them out into the lagoon. He reached into one of the lockers. "Here—put this lifesaving belt on." He handed it to her.

"But the water isn't that deep."

"It doesn't matter. If we got into trouble, you'd be glad of it."

"I'll wear it if you wear one too."

"Nag, nag." But he smiled as he put one on.

"Now that I think about it, can you imagine the media storm if we had an accident and word got out that the future king and queen of Halencia had almost drowned because they hadn't been wearing preservers? People would wonder what kind of ruler they had."

He chuckled. "Point taken. It would never do."

Off Point Matira they came across a group of huge manta rays. There were spotted and gray rays. Antonio swam near their boat while they watched in fascination.

"We should be marine biologists," she exclaimed. "Just think, we could come out to places like this and spend all day long for weeks on end."

Antonio nodded. "Being out here, you can understand the appeal for that kind of work. Are you interested in watching the locals feed the sharks? We're not far from there."

"I guess it's safe or they wouldn't advertise it, but I think I'll want to stay in the boat."

He drove them to the spot where the local divers stood chest deep in the water. Four-and five-foot sharks circled around them to get their food.

"That's scary to me," Christina said. "I've changed my mind about being a biologist."

"Instead you'd rather be in Kenya where you can be dragged off by a lion."

"No—" She grinned at him.

For their last destination they took off and headed for the coral garden, an underwater park southwest of Bora Bora Island. For an hour they were spellbound by the amount of colorful fish and coral. Like an excited child she squealed over the varieties.

"I'm going to take a quick dip before we head back."

Antonio couldn't have stopped her. She was too anxious to get closer. Off came her belt and she lowered herself in the water. The sight of her going underwater made him nervous. He watched her like a hawk.

To his relief she came back up a few minutes later, but she looked distressed.

"I stepped on something, but I don't know what."

Diavolo. "Does it sting?"

"No. It's just kind of sore on the pad of my foot."

Antonio leaned over and helped her into the boat. He set her down on the banquette so he could inspect it. "You made contact with a sea urchin, but luckily I only see two spines." *Thank heaven.* "They'll need to come out. Keep your leg on the banquette and I'll get us back home." He wrapped the life belt around her, kissed her lips and got behind the wheel.

"Do you think it's serious?"

"No. I once got a whole foot full of them, but I was fine. Still, we'll ask the doctor to check you."

"Oh no—I didn't mean for this to happen."

"Accidents can happen anytime in the water, as you reminded me."

The sky was darkening fast. He was glad when they reached their island. After tying up the boat, he undid the life belts and carried her from the deck into their bedroom.

After setting her down on top of the bed, he phoned Manu and asked for a doctor to come. "I'll get you some ibuprofen after we've talked to the doctor."

"Will you carry me to the bathroom? I need to get out of my suit and into a robe."

"Of course." He lifted her in his arms once more and let her hang on to him while he reached for her robe hanging on the door. "Can I help you?"

"I'll be all right." He waited until she said she was

ready, and then he carried her back to the bed. In another moment he heard Manu's voice coming from the main entrance. "The doctor is here."

"Will you show him into the bedroom, Manu?"

Within seconds the two men came in. "Princess Christina? This is Dr. Ulani."

He brought his bag with him. "Thank you for coming, Doctor. As you can see, my wife stepped on a sea urchin. She's in pain."

"Hush, Antonio. It's not that bad at all. More of a discomfort."

The native doctor smiled. "Accidents like this happen every day, even to someone like Your Highness. Let me check your foot. I'll try not to add to your pain."

Antonio placed a chair for him to sit while he worked on her. Relieved as he was that she was getting medical attention, it suddenly hit him how frightened he'd been when she first surfaced. In very little time she'd become so important to him that he couldn't bear the thought of anything truly serious being wrong with her.

The doctor opened his bag and proceeded to get rid of the two spines. He put ointment on the sores and a dressing. "You'll be fine tomorrow. Just make sure you wear some kind of shoe in the water if you're not snorkeling with fins. I'll give you a tablet for you to sleep that will kill the pain. Tomorrow if you're still too sore, take some ibuprofen."

"Thank you so much. It feels better already."

"It's a privilege to help you, Princess." When he'd finished, he stood up. "Take care, now."

"I'll make sure of it," Antonio muttered. He shouldn't have let her slip into the water like that. The action had caught him off guard.

"Here's the pill. Tomorrow you can take off the dressing."

Antonio walked him out to the living room. "I can't tell you how grateful I am you came."

"It is my pleasure to wait on the future king and queen of Halencia. Our people are aware of your presence here and they are delighted. Don't hesitate to get hold of me through Manu if you are alarmed by anything."

Manu stood by. "You want your dinner in the bedroom, Your Highness?"

"Yes. Thank you. Will you bring a glass of water so she can take her medicine?"

He nodded and hurried to the kitchen. Antonio headed back to the bedroom. "Christina? It's my fault you got hurt this evening."

"Nonsense. I wasn't thinking. When I saw those fish, I just had to get in closer."

"Please tell me you'll give me a heads-up next time before you do a disappearing act."

His mermaid was resting against the headboard with a sore foot. "I'm sorry to be the one at fault for not having the sense to get in the water prepared. But, Antonio, you don't have to try to be perfect with someone as imperfect as I am. I did a stupid thing, but the situation really is funny, don't you think? Your parents planning for every contingency to bring us joy? And I blew it. At least for tonight. Now you have to give me my medicine and be stuck with your ball and chain until morning."

"Don't say that! Not ever! I don't feel that way about you and never could. Promise me!" He sounded truly upset.

"I promise," she said as Manu appeared with their dinner. Antonio thanked him and put the tray of food on the side of the bed next to her. He handed her the glass of water and the pill. "Take this first."

After she did his bidding, he sat in the chair the doctor had used and they ate their dinner. He heard her sigh.

"It's another beautiful night, so balmy. I'd wanted to go walking on the beach with you."

"We'll do that tomorrow night. For now, you need to try and fall asleep."

"You won't leave me?" Her eyes beseeched him.

"As if I would," he murmured, experiencing a hard tug of emotion. It came to him that his new wife had become of vital importance to him. "I'll join you as soon as I change out of my swimming suit."

"Good. Don't be long."

Christina, Christina.

He put the tray on the table and went into the bathroom to change. After putting on a robe, he turned out the lights, then got into bed beside her. The pill must have been powerful, because her eyelids were drooping. Antonio rolled her into him and she let out a deep sigh. Soon she was asleep. Before long, oblivion took over.

Around six in the morning he felt the bed move. She'd gotten up to use the bathroom.

He eyed her through sleep-filled eyes. When she returned he said, "How's the pain?"

"There's hardly any at all. I can walk fine as long as I'm careful."

"That's wonderful news. Come back to bed and rest that foot some more. It's still early."

CHAPTER SIX

CHRISTINA EYED HER HUSBAND, who'd kept a vigil over her all night. She got back in bed, lying on her side so she could watch him sleep. He was such a gorgeous man. Dawn was sneaking into the bedroom with the morning breeze. Through the open windows she could see the unique shape of the mountains on Bora Bora. If she could be anywhere in the world, she wanted to be right here with the man she'd married.

When next she came awake, she found herself the object of Antonio's blue gaze. She propped her head up with her hand. "How long have you been awake?"

"Long enough to watch my lovely wife. You've been sleeping so peacefully."

Without hesitation he leaned over to kiss her. "Good morning, *esposa mia*. I dreamed about kissing you all night long."

"I had the same dream."

Before she could blink he put his arm around her and kissed her deeply, not letting her go until she had to breathe.

He sighed. "I needed that."

"I'm pretty sure you need something else after taking care of me all night. I'll ring Manu to bring our breakfast tray." She reached for the phone and put in their order. After hanging up, she turned to her husband.

"How did you know?"

"That you're starving?" she quipped. "I'm hungry too."

He raised himself up and leaned over her. "You have no idea how beautiful you are, do you? I could eat you up."

But at that moment Manu appeared at the door. "Shall I put your breakfast on the table?"

"No, Manu," Antonio said. "I think we'll have it right here in bed."

The other man smiled and set it on the end of the bed before making a discreet departure.

She smiled at her husband. "We're spoiled rotten. You know that."

He moved to put the tray between them. Christina propped her head with a couple of pillows and bit into a croissant. "If the famous French impressionist Gauguin were here to paint us, he'd entitle it *Petit Déjeuner au Lit Tahitien*."

His lips twitched. "Breakfast in a Tahitian bed is far too mundane. I think a more appropriate title would be *Le Mari Amoureux*."

The Amorous Husband? Christina laughed to cover the quiver that ran through her. She'd forgotten he'd attended a French/Swiss boarding school too and was fluent in French besides Halencian, Italian, English and Spanish.

"What do you want to do today?"

"I'm up for anything."

"Honestly?"

"My foot doesn't hurt and I don't want us to miss out on anything while we're here. We don't have that much time before we have to go back."

"I don't want to go back."

Her pulse raced. "Neither do I."

"What do you say we take out the kayak and just paddle around for fun?"

"That sounds perfect. I'll get my suit on and wear a T-shirt so I don't pick up any more sun on my shoulders." With a kiss to his jaw, she slid out of bed. "I'll be back in a minute."

He'd been worried about that. The need to touch her was growing. A bad case of sunburn could make her feel miserable for several days. Relieved that her foot was healing well, he got excited to think about spending another glorious day with her. It was pure selfishness on his part to want her able to do everything with him waking or sleeping.

There was only one bed, but a number of couches. He had no intention of sleeping on a couch or a sun lounger tonight. He wanted his wife in that oversize bed clinging to him while the scented breeze from Bora Bora wafted through their bedroom.

"Antonio? I'm ready when you are."

He looked up to see her standing there with a white T-shirt pulled over her suit. "I'm glad you're wearing your tennis shoes."

There was no doubt his bride had one of the most

beautiful faces and bodies he'd ever seen, starting with her glorious hair. She'd fastened it on top with a clip. He wanted to reach up and pull her down to him, but right now it was important they keep having fun while breaking down walls.

Levering himself out of bed, he hurried to the bathroom to put on his trunks. Then he joined her at the edge of the platform. The Sevylor inflatable plastic kayak had been secured to the post with cords. Once they were undone he reached down to hand her a belt life preserver. While she put hers on, he fastened his.

"I'll go first." After getting in the front seat, he held out his hands to her and eased her into the backseat.

"Ooh—" She laughed. "It's tippy. I'm used to a canoe."

"You'll soon get the hang of it."

They unloosened their oars and started paddling. He led them around in circles to get her used to the motion. Over his shoulder he said, "According to the brochure, there's no surf here because of the reef across the lagoon. When you're ready, we'll head out to that other island in the distance."

"I can see you're an old pro at this."

"During my boarding school days in Lausanne, some friends that my parents didn't approve of flew home with me on breaks. We'd go kayaking around Halencia on weekends. But as you know, the Mediterranean can be choppy when the wind comes up. This lagoon is like glass in comparison."

They started paddling together and headed out. "I

wonder if I ever saw you out there during the few times I came home from boarding school."

"I've been wondering the same thing myself. Do you believe in destiny, Christina?"

"To be honest, until I received the phone call from you that we were really getting married, I believed that I was meant to—" She broke off abruptly. "Oh, it doesn't matter what I believed."

He stopped paddling and turned to look at her. "Tell me. I want to know."

She shook her head. "If I told you, you'd see me as a pitiful creature who feels sorry for herself."

"You're anything but pitiful. I want to know what you were going to say."

Christina rested her oar. She cast her gaze toward Bora Bora. "My parents didn't want me, Antonio. They really didn't. The only genuine love I felt came from my great-aunt Sofia, but I wasn't her daughter and didn't see her very often.

"I believed it was my lot always to live on the outside of their lives. This became evident when they didn't put up a fuss about my working in Africa. I was crushed when they sounded happy about my doing charity work there. They didn't miss me, not at all. Marusha's parents have been more like parents to me than anyone."

Her suffering had to be infinite. "That's tragic about your parents."

"I was afraid you'd say that, but I don't want you to feel sorry for me. They were warmer to me at the wedding, especially Mother. You asked for the truth and I've told you. As for believing in destiny, despite my pain, I was happy with my life in Africa and decided I'd probably live there forever. The ability to help other people brought me a lot of peace I hadn't known before."

"Until I turned your world upside down," he bit out in self-deprecation.

"It wasn't just you, Antonio. Elena had already become family to me. When she got into real trouble, I felt her pain. Like you, she led a life of isolation being royal. I can understand why she took up with guys from my world. In your own way, you and Elena have led a life of loneliness. It's a strange world you two inhabit and always will be. But I was lucky enough to be the friend Elena let in. If I could have had a sister, I would have wanted her."

"You're very perceptive, Christina. I originally went to San Francisco to learn business. It was there I worked with normal people. Zach became a true friend and I enjoyed it so much I didn't want to go home. My parents' lifestyle was a personal embarrassment to me. But when I heard of the trouble Elena was in, I couldn't turn my back on her. Forgive me for using you."

"By phoning you, I used you too," Christina came back. "Did you really have a choice to do anything but try to draw the paparazzi's attention away from her? I was the perfect person to help. After all, we were an unlikely threesome, yet no one knew me or knew about me. What I want to know is, why didn't you break off our engagement a few years later and ask the woman you loved to marry you?"

His jaw hardened. "I wouldn't have done that to you."

"You see what I mean?"

Her sad smile pierced him.

"You tried to be like everyone else, but in the end, the prince in you dominated your will. The princess in Elena let you fall on your sword because you were both born to royalty and knew your duty. She wanted you to be king one day.

"Before I phoned you, did you know she wanted to admit everything to the police and take the blame so there'd be no reflection on you or your family? But I wouldn't let her. I told her I was going to phone you because I knew you could fix things and you found a way."

"Which involved you." His voice throbbed. His emotions hovered near the surface. "Let me ask you a question. Why didn't you tell me to go to hell when I called you to give you the wedding date? You would have had every right."

She breathed in deeply. "Because your royal dust had blown on me years before. I'm not a Halencian for nothing. My country means everything to me. The engagement we entered into was very bizarre, but it made a strange kind of sense. In fact, the only kind of sense that would satisfy the people.

"I'm positive it would have been hard for them to accept your marriage to a woman from a different nationality as you pointed out. But if you'd wanted it badly enough, you could have made it happen."

He eyed her for a moment. "When it came down to

it, I didn't want her badly enough to break my commitment to you."

"Thank you for saying that. I want you to know I'm not sorry, Antonio."

His heart skipped a beat. "Do you honestly mean it? Even though it meant ending an important relationship with the doctor you met in Kenya?"

"It wasn't that important. I didn't want to break my commitment to you either. You and Elena have trod a treacherous path all your lives. You always will because you were born to the House of L'Accardi.

"Elena and I were friends from the age of fifteen. I knew her sorrows. She bore mine. Her greatest fear was that you might end up living in California one day and giving up the throne so she would have to be queen. That was one of her greatest nightmares."

Good heavens. So much had gone on that he hadn't known about behind the scenes because of his selfishness in pursuing his own dream. "I didn't realize…"

"How could you if she never said anything? At our reception, Elena acted so happy we got married that she could hardly contain herself." Even though there was still something she seemed to be holding back.

"Her happiness went much deeper than that because it meant she wasn't going to lose the best friend she's ever had."

Christina flashed a full, radiant smile at him, stunning him. "Now she's got both of us and our threesome can go on forever."

Forever.

* * *

Antonio turned around and started paddling again. There'd been a time when the thought of being married forever stuck in his throat. But no longer. When they returned to the hut, Manu had served their dinner on the deck.

"Tonight you are eating freshly caught mahimahi with coconut rice and mango salsa."

"It looks fantastic, Manu."

After he left them alone Christina said, "They've gone all out for us. Now I know the true meaning of being treated like a king."

His blue eyes glinted with amusement as they sat down to eat.

Christina took her first bite. "The fish is out of this world."

"This is Bora Bora mahimahi," he quipped. "We won't be getting anything this good in Halencia. If I could put off the coronation for a while, I'd like us to stay here for a month at least! I'm thinking our first-year anniversary. What do you say?"

"But we'll fly commercial. And we'll stay in a little bungalow over the water and play tourist like everyone else."

"And climb the mountain and scuba dive. Have you ever been?"

"No."

"Then you've got to take lessons. I'll go with you."

"You mean you'll take time out of your busy day?"

"You'll need a buddy. I don't want anyone else buddying up with *my* wife."

The possessive tone in his voice thrilled her.

Once dinner was over Christina showered and washed her hair. After toweling it, she used the blow dryer until it swished against her shoulders. She put on a pale lemon-colored nightgown. Her skin had picked up some sun, adding color to her complexion. To her relief her injury was barely noticeable.

Her lamp was the only light on in the room. There were more brochures for her to read on the side table, but she wasn't ready for bed yet. Antonio had turned on more romantic music. The thought of him made her heart thump out of control. She'd just spent the most heavenly day of her life with the man who was now her husband.

Before long he came into the bedroom wearing a robe. Without a shirt he had an amazing male physique with a dusting of dark hair on his chest. Her mouth went dry just looking at him. When he came closer, she could smell the soap he'd used in the shower. "The night is calling to us. Let's go out on the deck. I want to dance with you."

He grasped her hand and they walked out into the balmy night. Christina gasped softly to see millions of stars overhead. "Antonio—have you ever seen the heavens this alive? I just saw a shooting star."

"We don't need a telescope when the universe seems so close. It's even in your eyes. They are shimmering like newly minted silver. Combined with the red gold of your hair, you're an amazing sight. A new heavenly body to light up this unforgettable night."

His words overwhelmed her before he wrapped his

arms around her and started dancing with her. Not the kind of dancing they did at the reception. This was slow dancing. She melted into him. The night had seduced her. There was a fragrance in the air from the flowers on the deck that intoxicated her. Being held against his hard body like this was pure revelation.

Her womanhood had come alive in his arms. She liked being taller because their bodies fit together. He'd buried his face in her hair. She could feel the warmth of his breath, tantalizing her because she longed to feel his mouth on hers. On their wedding night she'd thought the fantasy was over. How could she have known they would come to this paradise where she was finding rapture beyond her dreams?

"Give me your mouth, Christina," he murmured. "I'm aching for you."

She had the same ache and lifted her head. Their mouths met and they kissed for a long time, giving and taking, back and forth. She clung to him, needing the pleasure he gave her with every caress of his hands roaming over her back. When he moved his mouth lower, she moaned as he slowly kissed her neck and throat. Everywhere his lips touched, it brought heat that spread through her body like fire.

Without her realizing it, he'd danced them back inside. Then he swept her into his arms and followed her down on the bed. "I could eat you alive," he whispered against her lips, and once again Christina was consumed by his kiss, hot with desire. A *husband's* desire. She hadn't known it could be like this.

"*Bellissima?* Tell me something. Have you ever been to bed with a man?"

The question jolted her. "No. Does my inexperience show so much?"

"Not at all. But I worried that if I'm the first man to make love to you, then I don't want to rush you into anything. You're so sweet, Christina. I didn't need Elena to tell me just how sweet you really are. I want our first time to be everything for you."

"Everything has been perfect so far," she whispered, fearing something had to be lacking in her for him to bring it up. When he didn't say anything, she eased away a little, but he drew her to him with her back resting against his chest.

"I'm glad, but I want to give you time to get used to me. Until you're truly ready, let's simply hold each other tonight. If I'd gone to Africa to see you, this is what we would have done. We have the rest of our lives and don't need to be in a hurry." He kissed her neck. "This is heavenly, you know? You smell and feel divine to me."

To be held in his arms was heavenly, but little did he know she *was* ready! Though she loved him for trying to make their first time perfect, she was dying inside. Still, by his determination to ease her into marriage, it showed a tender side of his nature that proved what a wonderful man she'd married. How many men would care enough about their brides' feelings to go to these lengths?

"This has been my idea of heaven, Antonio. I can't wait until tomorrow." Maybe tomorrow night he'd realize she didn't want to wait a second longer.

When she awakened the next morning, she discovered her husband fast asleep. They'd slept late. Christina slid out of bed without disturbing him and rushed into the kitchen to phone Manu and order breakfast. Then she showered to get ready for the day.

With that accomplished she put on another bikini. This one had an apple-green flutter top. Both she and Elena had loved the crocheted look of the top and bottom overlying a white lining. It was more modest than many of the suits.

Since they'd probably be out in the water most of the day, she decided the best thing to do with her hair was to sweep it on top and secure it with her tortoiseshell clip. She removed her gold studs and put on a pair of tiny earrings the shape of half-moons in a green that matched her bikini.

Before going in to Antonio, she threw on a lacy white beach jacket that fell to just below her thighs. Now she was ready to greet her husband. But when she entered the bedroom, he'd turned onto his stomach and was still out for the count. Only a sheet covered his lower half. What a fabulous-looking man! She was still pinching herself to believe he was her husband.

He would need a shave, but she loved the shadow on his hard jaw. He looks were so arresting that his state of dress or his grooming didn't matter. She'd loved the handsome eighteen-year-old prince. But over the years he'd grown into a breathtaking man no woman could be immune to.

While she sat feasting her eyes on him, she heard sounds coming from the kitchen. She got up from the side of the bed and went back to bring him their breakfast tray. She brought it in and put it on the end of the bed.

The aroma of the coffee must have awakened him. He turned on his side and opened his eyes. Between the dark fringe of his lashes, their brilliant blue color stole her breath. Antonio raised himself up on one elbow. "Well, what do we have here? Could it be the nymph from the fountain holding the seashell?"

She loved the imagery. He'd noticed the fountain sculpture in the courtyard in front of the palazzo. "Yes, sire." His eyes darkened with emotion. "I'm here with your breakfast. Your wife told me you would awaken with a huge appetite."

"My wife told you that? Her exact words?"

"I never lie."

"Then will you tell her that spending the day with her yesterday was more than wonderful? But I'll tell her just how wonderful when we're alone again today. Those will be words for her ears only."

Christina couldn't prevent the blush that rose into her cheeks. "I'll be happy to do that after I've served you your breakfast." She got up and put the tray in front of him. "Do you wish me to leave? You have only to command me."

"Then I command you to bring that chair over to the side of the bed and we'll enjoy this food together."

She smiled secretly and moved it next to the bed. "Your wife won't mind?"

He flicked her an all-encompassing gaze. "She might. A woman serving me breakfast who looks as gorgeous as you might worry, so I think we'll keep this moment to ourselves. How does that sound to you?"

She reached for a roll and bit into it. "You flatter me, sire."

"I haven't even started. That's quite an outfit you're wearing."

Christina drank some orange juice and reached for a strip of bacon. "You like it?"

"I can't keep my eyes off you. Do you serve all the men like that?"

"What men? You're the only one on this whole island."

He ate his food in record time. "That's good because if I found out otherwise, I'd have to confine you to a room in the palace where I have the only key."

Their conversation was getting sillier and sillier, but she loved it. She loved *him*.

"What are your plans for today, sire?"

"This and that."

"Does your wife know about that?"

His eyes narrowed on her mouth. "She'll find out."

"I see." Her heart jumped. "Well, if you've finished your breakfast, I'll take the tray back to the kitchen."

"*Grazie*. When you see her, tell her I want her to come to me. *Now*. I don't like to be kept waiting."

She trembled as she reached for the tray. "*Si*, Your Highness."

The second his wife left the bedroom on those long, shapely legs, Antonio headed for the shower and freshened up. Since she'd already put on her bikini, he pulled on a fresh pair of white bathing trunks. When he'd told her last night he could eat her alive, he hadn't been kidding.

"*Ciao*, Antonio." She was looking at one of the brochures while waiting for him.

"I understood you wanted to see me?" Her smile curved so seductively he wanted to throw her on the bed and stay there all day, but he resisted the urge. She was a fetching siren. Who would have guessed?

"How would you like to go to the nearby island with the waterfall? Manu says it's a short hike, but worth it if you're wearing tennis shoes."

"I love hikes. I did it all over Switzerland and Kenya."

She was amazing. "Manu told me it's off-limits to everyone else while we're here on our honeymoon."

Her eyes lit up. "A whole island to ourselves? Let's do it! I'll pack us some food so we don't have to come back for dinner."

"Why not pack enough food in case we want to stay there overnight?"

"You mean sleep by the waterfall?"

He smiled at her. It was all he could think about. "Why not? Haven't you ever wondered what it would be like to be Tarzan and Jane?"

She chuckled in response. "Yes. Many times."

"We'll take the speedboat."

With their day decided, they packed things in the backpacks supplied by the resort, including light blankets, food and water. Antonio rang Manu to let him know where they were going. Then they left their retreat and took off for one of the dark green islands they could see in the distance that was taller than the others.

"The lagoon never changes, Antonio. It's like eternal beauty all the time. I've never been this excited to do anything."

She was reading his mind. They skimmed across the gorgeous blue water before reaching the white beach. Once they'd drunk some bottled water, they headed for the trail Manu said would be visible. Sure enough, they found it and started up the incline.

"The vegetation is so lush!" she exclaimed.

"Our own rain forest." Their gazes clung before they got going on their trek. It took them less time to reach their destination than to have kayaked over there. Flowers grew in abundance. They spotted terns and swallows. The water came down in a stream, small at first, then widening before they reached the waterfall itself.

"Oh, Antonio—it reminds me of a waterfall scene in an old movie I once saw, but I think it was filmed in Hawaii."

"This is as primitive as it gets." He helped her off with her pack and gave her a long kiss. Then he removed his.

"Isn't that spray marvelous? Look up there. If we can get on those rocks, we can ride the water down to the pool," she said.

"Let me test the depth of it first." He walked over to the edge and waded in the swirling water. He discovered that after a few steps there was a drop-off, but when he swam underwater he found it was only about twenty feet deep. When he emerged, he waved to her. "Come on in. It's safe but a little cooler than the lagoon. Keep your tennis shoes on."

For several hours they played in the water like children. Eventually they climbed up the side to reach the spot where the water from the mountain poured over the top of the rocks. He turned to his wife. "Shall we do it?"

"Yes."

"Scared?"

"Terrified."

"Take my hand."

Together they moved onto the slippery rocks and before long the strength of the waterfall washed over them, plunging them down into the pool. Christina came up laughing. "Oh, Antonio—talk about a rush! This just couldn't be real."

He swam to her and kissed her over and over again while keeping them afloat. "We've found paradise, *innamorata*. How about one more jump, and then we'll make camp for the night?"

Once again they hiked up the side to the top. Before they went out on the rocks, he plucked a white flower with a gardenia scent, growing on a nearby vine. He tucked it behind her ear. "Now you're my Polynesian princess."

Her eyes wandered over him. "I don't ever want to go home."

"Then we won't." He grabbed her hand and they inched their way onto the rocks until the force of the water took them over the edge. It was like free-falling into space until the water caught them and brought them to the surface.

Together they swam to the edge of the pool where they'd left their packs. He helped her out of the water and they proceeded to set up camp. After they'd made their bed, they put out the food. The exertion had made them hungry. They sat across from each other and ate to their hearts' content.

He finally stretched. "I've never felt so good, never tasted food so good, never been with anyone I enjoyed more. In truth, I've never been this happy in my life."

"I feel the same way," she responded. "I want it to last, but I know it's not going to."

He shook his head. "Shh. Don't spoil this heavenly evening. We have two more days and nights ahead of us."

"You're right."

"You've lost your gardenia. I'm going to pick another one." He got up and walked a ways until he found one. When he returned, he hunkered down next to her and put it behind her ear. "This is how I'm always going to remember you."

Antonio couldn't wait to get close to her again and cleaned up their picnic. When everything had been put away, she started to leave, but he caught her by the ankle. "Stay with me."

"I was just going to get out of my bathing suit."

"But I want to hold you first." He pulled her down and rolled onto his side so he could look at her. "I've been waiting all day for tonight to come."

"So have I." Her voice throbbed.

He pulled her into him and claimed her luscious mouth that had given him a heart attack last night. "You could have no idea how much I want you. Love me, Christina. I need you."

"Would it shock you if I told I wanted you to love me on our wedding night?" she admitted against his throat.

He let out a slight groan. "Why didn't you tell me?"

"I was afraid you would think I was too eager. I decided you needed time."

Laughter broke from him. When he looked down at her, those fabulous silvery eyes were smiling. "I think that from here on out we each need to stop worrying about what the other one is thinking, and do more doing."

"I couldn't agree more. You drove me crazy on the way over in the jet."

"Maybe that was a good thing," he teased, kissing every feature on her face.

"It was painful!"

"Tesora mia," he cried in a husky voice before starting to devour her. "I love your honesty. Come here to me."

Christina melted in his arms and kissed him with the kind of passion he'd never imagined to find in this marriage. His heart jumped to realize he had such a loving, demonstrative wife.

CHAPTER SEVEN

ANTONIO HAD CALLED her his treasure. Christina felt cherished and desirable. His hunger aroused her to the depth of her being. This was her husband bringing her to life, shocking her, thrilling her as they found new ways to worship each other with their bodies.

His long legs trapped hers. "Why did I wait four years?"

She couldn't have answered him if she'd wanted to. Enthralled by the things he was doing to her, Christina was too consumed by her own hunger for him. Like the spiral constellations lighting the canopy above, he sent her spiraling into another realm of existence. Throughout the hours of the night they loved fully until they finally fell asleep, only temporarily sated.

After their passion-filled night of ecstasy, she couldn't believe they were still on earth. During the night he'd swept her to a different place, so intimate she'd wanted to stay on that sphere of euphoria forever.

She lay there wondering if last night's lovemaking had resulted in a baby. Stranger things had happened to other women. She suddenly realized that she wanted his baby so badly she could hardly stand it.

Heat washed over her to remember what had happened between them last night. Christina wasn't sorry that he hadn't made love to her at first. Far from it. Last night had been magical.

Taking great care not to wake her husband *and* lover, she lay there looking at him. The sun was already high in the morning sky. They'd slept in late again, but it didn't matter.

Oh, Antonio—I love you so much, you have no idea.

Antonio heard his wife sigh and glanced at her in sleep. She was the most unselfish lover he could ever have imagined. Last night she'd made him feel totally alive. Whole. When had he ever felt like this? Long after the stars had come out, they'd made love again and early this morning, again. He'd found paradise with her.

The next time he had cognizance of his surroundings, the sun was high in the sky. His wife lay on her side facing him. For a while he lay there studying her, then got to his feet and took a dip in the pool before pulling on his bathing trunks. He opened the backpack to get out some rolls and fruit. They'd need more food to stay on this island. He drank half a bottle of water while he ate.

She must have heard him and opened her eyes. "Oh—you're up!"

"Just barely. Loving you has given me a ferocious appetite."

She laughed. "I'm getting up, but you'll have to turn your head."

"Why?" he teased.

Christina blushed beautifully. "You know why."

"I'm your husband."

"I know, but—"

"All right. I'll close my eyes, but I'll give you to the count of ten to reach the water before I open them again."

"Antonio—" she squealed.

"One, two." He could hear the blanket rustle before she got up. A second later he heard water splashing and turned to watch her treading water. "You see? You made it."

"If you'll please put my bikini near the water and turn around, I'll get dressed."

Antonio's deep laughter resounded through the forest. She could feel it reverberate inside her. "Anything to oblige." He did her bidding. "I hate to tell you this, but the water is so transparent I can see you perfectly."

"You're no gentleman to say that to me."

"Is that what you thought I was?" he mocked before turning his back.

She climbed out and dressed as fast as she could. When she reached him, he crushed her in his arms and gave her a kiss to die for. Then he handed her food and drink.

"Thank you."

"You're welcome."

"I wish we could stay here longer. Last night—"
Her voice caught.

Their eyes met. "Last night will be burned in my memory forever, *tesora*."

"Mine too." She finished eating and started putting everything in their packs.

He worked with her. "Are you about ready?"

"Yes."

After slipping on their tennis shoes, they started down the trail to the beach. In some parts she walked behind him, enjoying the play of muscle across his back and shoulders. Antonio had great legs for a man. In fact, there wasn't a part of him that wasn't perfect.

They reached the boat and loaded it. Christina helped him push it into the water, and then he helped ease her up and in before he took his place at the front. Before they took off across the lagoon, he looked back at her. As far as he could see, they were the only people out on this part of the lagoon.

"What do you want to do after we get back to the hut?" he called over his shoulder.

"I'd love to go to that coral sea garden and do some more snorkeling."

"That makes two of us. When in our lives will we ever have a chance to see fish like this up close?"

"Probably never. I'm still pinching myself to believe there's a spot like this on earth."

"We'll eat a meal and then go out for the rest of the day. Do you know what?"

"What?"

"You're more fun than any of my friends."

"Thank you."

"I mean it. I don't know anyone, male or female, who loves what I love and can do everything with me and keep up."

"I'm afraid I didn't turn out to be like my social-ite parents."

"Thank heaven!"

Those two words warmed her heart all the way back to their island. After putting things away, they sat down to a meal, then went back out to the deck. Antonio covered her in sunscreen. His touch made her knees buckle. "Shall we stay in bed the rest of the day instead?"

Christina could hardly talk. "I'd love it, but our time here is so short, we need to take advantage of it." She couldn't believe she'd worried that in a week Antonio might be bored with her. Maybe it was because all the time they'd spent together in Switzerland had prepared her to be more comfortable with him where everything felt so natural.

"Just remember we'll have all night," he whispered against her neck. His breath sent tendrils of delight through her system. While she was still trying to re-cover, he got out the snorkels and fins. Once again they got into the boat and went looking for fish. The lagoon was home to so many species they had the time of their lives viewing everything.

She lost track of the time. So did Antonio. It wasn't until they suffered hunger pains that she realized it was time to go in. When they returned to the island and were tying up the boat, Manu was there to greet them.

"You two must have had a good day to be out so long."

Christina smiled at him. "Every day is a good day here." But she sensed he had something else on his mind. So did Antonio.

"What's wrong, Manu?"

"There was a call from the palace in Halencia. You are to call your sister as soon as you can. You can use the phone here and I'll put it through for you."

Both Christina and Antonio exchanged worried glances. Any number of things could be wrong for her to interrupt their honeymoon. "Thank you. I'll do it as soon as we're finished here."

"Your dinner is in the kitchen when you want to eat."

"You're terrific, Manu," she said.

After he disappeared, Antonio helped her out of the boat and they put their gear away. Already there was a change in her husband. Lines darkened his features, making him look older. They'd had an unforgettable night of loving and had been so carefree she could have cried to see that anxious look cross over his face.

Together they walked inside the bedroom of the hut, both of them still wearing their bathing suits. He turned to her. "I'm going to put on a robe, then make the call."

While he went into the bathroom to change, she pulled out some underwear and dressed in a pair of tan shorts and a cream top. Then she hung her bikini over the outside rail to dry, all the time frightened something serious had happened back home. An accident, or worse?

Antonio came out of the bathroom and walked over to the side of the bed to the phone. She sat down next to him. He put the phone on speaker and grasped her hand while he waited for Manu to connect the call.

"Tonio?"

"Elena?" His heart was racing. "What's wrong?"

"I'm so sorry to bother you on your honeymoon, but—"

"Is anyone ill?"

"No, no. Everyone's fine, but there's something you need to know. I hope you're sitting down to hear this."

Antonio looked at his wife, anxious for what was coming. "Go ahead."

"I—I have to give you some background first," she stammered. "You know that guy Rolfe? The drug addict I wish I'd never met?"

He sucked in his breath. "Yes?"

"Last week he was arrested on heavier drug charges. He called me from the jail and told me that if I didn't help him out of the new charges, he'd tell the press everything about what happened when he was jailed the first time."

"What?" he and Christina cried out at the same time. His thoughts were reeling.

"I thought he was high on drugs when he called me and I hung up on him. But he phoned me on the morning you were getting married and threatened me again. I told him there wasn't anything I could do. He hung up on me telling me I'd be sorry.

"Oh, Tonio—he leaked the news about your fake engagement to the press. It's all over the media that you thought up the bogus alliance with Christina to get me out of trouble with the police. He claimed I used drugs too and should have been jailed along with him.

"It's gone viral too. The internet is alive with rumours that you were having an affair in California while Christina was in Africa having an affair with the doctor. He made it all up, but it's done its damage.

"Marusha phoned me and told me she and her family are sick about this and want to know what they can do to stop it getting any worse. I don't know what to do.

"The palace is in an uproar. Both sets of parents are beside themselves. Guido's trying to help everything by preparing a new list of princesses. In case you can somehow salvage your reputation and get your marriage annulled, you'll have a list of royal hopefuls to choose from. I'm fighting for you, Tonio, but I can't do it alone."

Pain ripped him apart. His arm went around his wife. He could only imagine how Christina was feeling right now.

"I heard Father give immediate orders for the jet to be flown to Tahiti to bring you home. It's on its way now and will arrive at the airport at six in the morning Tahitian time. You need to be ready with a plan and come home as quickly as you can to help sort out this disaster, because that's what it is!

"There's a groundswell from people who don't believe you should be crowned because of the lie. I've been labeled a drug addict and am the result of my parents who aren't worthy of ruling the country. The people are afraid the lack of integrity on both your part and Christina's has compromised everything.

"If feelings reach tipping point, the people could withdraw their support for the monarchy and this could be the end of it. The coronation has been called off until further notice."

"No," Christina cried out.

"Oh, Christina, I didn't know you were listening. Let's face it. I'm the one responsible for all this. I'm the reason any of this has happened and I feel so horrible about it I want to die. I never realized how vindictive Rolfe could be. How cruel and heartless after what you did to get him a light sentence. I spent time with him when I was at my most rebellious and wasn't careful with the information I let out without realizing it. You and Christina have every right to hate me."

"Of course we don't hate you," he ground out. "For now you'll just have to hang on until we get back to Halencia. Trust me. We're going to sort this out. I'll talk to you tomorrow in person. And, Elena, never forget that we love you."

Christina had buried her face in her hands. *"Bellissima—"* He took her in his arms.

Hearing that word applied to her produced a groan from her. She was so horrified over the news she felt physically ill and couldn't form words.

His body stiffened. "I wondered what form of chicanery has been underfoot while we were on our honeymoon. It's what I expected. I just didn't know in the exact manner it would explode. Christina? Look at me."

She tried, but his image was blurry.

"I know this has come as a shock, but we're going to get through this because there's been total honesty between us, *grazie a Dio*. Remember Elena needs our protection more than ever. She's very fragile right now."

"You're right. I knew there was something wrong when she kept saying she hoped we'd be happy. Throughout our wedding she was terrified and had to keep all that bottled up inside. The poor thing."

He kissed her lips. "I'll make arrangements for the helicopter to be here at five a.m. Then you and I are going to have a long, serious talk."

His composure under these precarious circumstances was nothing short of miraculous. The affairs of the kingdom were falling apart, yet his mastery in dealing with it was a revelation. As far as she was concerned, this was Antonio's finest hour.

Whether she ever became queen or not, she would act like one right now because Antonio had never needed her help more to present a unified front. She knew deep down he wanted to be king in order to save his country from possible ruin. More than anything, Christina wanted that for him, whatever it took.

She grabbed two bottles of water from the refrigerator and hurried through the hut to their bedroom. While she waited for him to come, she started the packing for both of them. Five o'clock would be here soon enough. They needed to be ready to leave.

Christina lifted her head when he came into the bedroom with their dinner tray. "Did you get through to Manu?"

He nodded. "Everything is set. Since you've packed the bags, we can eat." He put it on the bed. "Come on."

She took a shaky breath. "I—I couldn't."

"You have to. I don't want my wife getting sick on me. We're on our honeymoon and I intend to enjoy it for the next six hours."

Christina actually laughed despite her agony.

Together they got on the bed and ate. When they'd finished eating, he got up to put the tray on the table. "Excuse me a moment. I'll be right back."

She wondered what he was doing until she heard Tahitian music from the radio piped into their room. Once he reappeared, he turned off the lamps and crawled onto the bed beside her.

"This music is enchanting, isn't it?" she said.

"I love it. Come here to me," he whispered. "I need you."

The blood pounded in her ears before she moved into his arms. "What are we going to do, Antonio?"

"We're going to stay just like this."

"You know what I mean."

"Yes, but there's nothing to do about anything until we reach Halenica, so you're stuck with me."

"That's no penance. You smell wonderful."

"So you've noticed."

She swallowed hard. "I notice everything."

"So do I. You're a warrior under that fiery mane."

"What a compliment."

"It is, because you're going to be queen and now I know you have the steel to help me. Any other woman would have gone into hysterics a little while ago. Not you."

She smiled in secret pleasure. "You wouldn't let me. That's the sign of a great king."

"The priest's words never had as much meaning to me until now."

"Which words were those?"

"The part where he said 'From this day forward you shall be each other's home, comfort and refuge.' Whatever we have to face when we get back home, Christina, I'm not worried because you've become my refuge in a very short time."

Tears stung her eyelids. He kissed them. "I didn't mean to make you cry."

"It's the good kind. When I'm happy, I often cry."

"I saw tears when you looked at your parents in the chapel. What was going on in your mind?"

"That I didn't always want to be a disappointment to them. Now that there's a national scandal, they'll consider that I've hit rock bottom."

"If they can't see beyond the end of their noses and recognize a hatchet job of major proportions, how sad for them. But I couldn't be happier that you turned out just the way you are. My one regret is that we're going to have to leave our paradise far too soon. I've had you all to myself since the wedding ceremony and I love the privacy so much I'm loath to give it up."

"I feel the same. We've been living most people's fantasy."

He suddenly held her tighter and burrowed his face in her neck. "I want this fantasy to go on and on." The longing in his voice echoed the desire of her heart. "I want you to know I'll treasure this time together for the rest of my life."

"I've loved every second of it too. Isn't this place wonderful?"

"Yes, but it would be a waste without the right person along. We'll come back again one day and spend time over at the coral garden. We'll do a lot of things, but right now I just want to make love to you."

Once again the age-old ritual began. This time Christina took the initiative to show her husband how much she loved him. She loved him in every atom of her body and poured out her feelings, wanting to take away any pain he was feeling tonight. At one point he pulled her on top of him. It was heaven to cover his face with kisses and play with his hair. He was such a beautiful man, there were no words.

"Christina? We only have a few hours before we have to return to Halencia and deal with the mess. If I'd known it was going to happen, I would have insisted we get married sooner and enjoy a month's honeymoon at least. Now it's too late for that."

But before their wedding, neither of them had a clue that they would come to care for each other in so short a time. Christina was positive that flare of desire she'd felt when he kissed her at the altar had been unexpected for him too.

"Are you happy?" His voice sounded anxious. "Because I want you to be happy."

She heard the longing and drew in a breath. "I'm happier right now than I've ever been in my life."

"*Grazie a Dio*, because I am too. I hope our daughter has red hair like her mother."

"Would you mind if our son has red hair instead?"

"Your hair is glorious. Why would I mind?"

"Mother wanted to turn me into a brunette."

"It's a good thing you didn't listen to her. When the time came, I wanted you for my bride."

Yes. And he wound up with Christina to save his sister from disgrace. And now that the news had leaked, it was a national scandal, but he didn't seem worried.

Their trust was on solid ground. More than ever she understood the deeper words of the priest. *Be able to forgive, do not hold grudges, and live each day that you may share it together. From this day forward you shall be each other's home, comfort and refuge, your marriage strengthened by your love and respect.*

So far they'd shared each incredible day together. Their nights had been euphoric. This bedroom had become their home and refuge. She'd been able to comfort him in a way she wouldn't have imagined. Living with Antonio was already changing her life and it frightened her that the happiness she was experiencing might be taken away from her after they returned home.

The next morning they awakened for breakfast. It had arrived with a newspaper. He pored over it.

Her heart thudded. "Anything to report about us?"

"There's a photo of me taken at the airport. No matter how hard my father tried, the word still got out. But so far Manu has managed to keep our exact location a secret. He's worth every Eurodollar he's being paid."

"Do you think your father will be upset?"

"Yes." He flicked her a searching glance. "Are you in with me?"

"All the way. You know that."

He put the newspaper down and moved himself away from the table. "Come out on the deck with me. I crave a walk along the beach with you before it rains."

Her husband reached for her hand as they stepped down to the edge of the water and started walking. "With Bora Bora appearing and disappearing mystically through the clouds this morning, it looks surreal, Antonio. I feel like we're in some primordial world. The air is so balmy it's unreal."

After they'd gone a ways, he stopped and grasped her arms so she faced him. "You're so lovely *you* seem unreal. I need to know if I'm with a phantom wife." In the next breath he lowered his mouth to hers and gave her the husband's kiss she'd been dying for. Fire licked through her veins as she was caught up in his embrace. She knew he had to be in pain, but the way he was kissing her had her senses reeling.

Their bodies clung. She could feel the powerful muscles in his legs and melted against him. He released her mouth long enough to kiss her face and neck. His hands plunged into her hair before he kissed her throat, in fact, all the area of skin exposed by the sundress she was wearing home.

"Touch me," he whispered in a ragged voice.

Succumbing to his entreaty, she wrapped her arms

around his waist and heard his moan of pleasure as his mouth began devouring hers. The rain had started and was so ethereal in nature it felt more like a mist, adding to the rapture building inside her. Antonio was doing the most amazing things to her with his hands and mouth.

Too soon Manu arrived to tell them the helicopter had arrived. It was time to go.

CHAPTER EIGHT

THIRTY HOURS LATER the royal jet landed at Voti International Airport, where a helicopter was waiting to fly them to the palace. To their relief, no press was allowed on the tarmac.

During the times throughout the flight while Christina napped, Antonio had talked with his sister at length to get her to stop blaming herself. During the night his wife had been restless and couldn't sleep. They were flying home to a hornet's nest. She was holding her own, but he knew the emotions of his brave, beautiful wife were in turmoil.

At one o'clock that afternoon the helicopter landed on the back lawn of the palace closed to the public. He helped her down and they hurried toward the south entrance with several staff members bringing their luggage.

They rushed up the grand staircase to the second floor of the east wing. When he reached the doors of his apartment, he picked her up again like a bride.

"Antonio—" She hid her head against his shoulder. "We've already done this once."

"I don't care. I might feel like doing it every time we come in." Before she could say another word, he silenced her with a kiss because he couldn't help himself. She'd become the drug in his system. Her response electrified him. At this point he needed to be with her inside their home away from the world and make love to his wife.

After managing to open one of the two tall, palatial doors, he swept her through the apartment to the bedroom and followed her down on the bed. The staff knew better than to do anything but place the suitcases inside the main doors and leave them alone.

"Welcome to my world, Christina de L'Accardi. Besides family, you're the first and only woman I've ever brought here. It's always been a lonely place for me. Now it's going to be our home." It was liberating to crush her against him. One kiss turned into another. She wanted him as much as he wanted her.

Like clockwork both his cell phone and room phone started ringing. He moaned aloud before continuing to kiss her, but the ringing persisted until she tore her lips from his. "Of course everyone knows we're back, Antonio," she said out of breath. "You at least have to say hello."

"That's all I'll say." He sat up and reached for the bedside phone first, impatient because of the interruption of civilization. Being away from technology for a few days had been the best thing that could have happened to them. *"Pronto—"*

"Come sta, figlio mio?"

He looked at his wife, whose silvery eyes fastened on him still had the glaze of desire burning in their depths. His fingers ran over her lips. "Christina and I have been to heaven thanks to your generosity, Papa. But we were called back to earth too soon."

"I'm thrilled you've had a wonderful time, but now we must talk."

"Not now, Papa. My wife and I need the rest of this day together."

"But there's a crisis."

His muscles clenched. "So I've been informed, but nothing's more important than my time with her. I promise I'll take care of things starting tomorrow. Give my love to Mama. *Ciao*."

Christina chuckled. "You'll have to answer your cell phone or it will never stop." Letting out another sound of frustration, he reached in his pants pocket and pulled it out. When he saw the caller ID, he didn't mind answering.

"Zach!"

"I'm glad you answered. Where are you?" His friend sounded more than anxious.

He smiled down at Christina. "We've just entered our humble home after being flown to paradise and back." She kissed his fingers.

"I've never thought of Paris as paradise."

"No. Bora Bora. A surprise wedding gift from my parents. You should take Lindsay there. You'd never want to come back."

"Antonio? Is this really you? You sound strange, like you're on something."

He grinned. "I've been drugged all right." A laugh came out of his wife. "Listen, I'll call you tomorrow."

"But you've got problems, buddy. Big problems."

"My other half is going to help me solve them."

"But she's part of the problem, if you get my meaning," Zach said, lowering his voice.

"You've got that wrong. She's the solution, but I appreciate your concern. You're the best friend a man ever had next to his wife. *Ciao.*"

No sooner had he hung up to indulge himself with his beautiful bride than Christina's cell phone rang. She had to get off the bed for the purse she'd accidentally dropped on the inlaid wooden flooring while her husband was carrying her.

She didn't need to look at the caller ID to know who it was. Might as well get this over now. *"Pronto?"*

"Christina?" Her mother sounded mournful rather than angry. "Is it true that you had an affair while you were engaged to Antonio?"

She held her breath. "If I tell you that was a lie, would you believe me?"

"Yes."

"Would Father?"

"I—I can't speak for him. What are you going to do?"

Her mother sounded as though she really cared. "It's up to Antonio."

"Just remember I'm here for you if you need me."

For her mother to say that was astounding to Christina. "Thank you, Mama. We'll talk later."

Antonio's arms were locked around her from behind. But for once she didn't feel like crawling into a dark hole never to come out again. She turned to Antonio. "Mother just gave me her support."

"It's about time, but don't forget you've got me now."

"I know." She lifted her mouth to kiss him, but there was a knocking on the outer doors, loud enough to reach their ears in the bedroom. "Tonio? It's me," Elena cried. "Can I come in? It's an emergency!"

"Tell her to come," Christina urged him. "She's been waiting for us."

He gave her another hug before they both hurried through the apartment to greet his sister.

When he opened the door, they barely recognized Elena, who'd been crying for so long her blue eyes were puffy and her face had gone splotchy. "I'm so glad you're home." She threw herself into Antonio's arms and sobbed.

Christina closed the door and the three of them went into the living room. When he let her go, she turned to Christina. As they hugged, his sister had another explosion of tears.

"Elena—it's going to be all right. Come and sit down on the couch." She drew her by the hand. Antonio sat in the love seat near them.

She brushed the tears from her cheeks. "I have something to tell both of you. Marusha and I have had a long talk. Her husband found out through another doctor that before Roger left Africa, he got drunk and told things to the doctor that were supposed to be kept quiet. But the other doctor was unscrupulous and leaked it to the news."

Christina shook her head. "I should never have gone out with him."

Antonio stood up. "If we all keep blaming ourselves for everything, nothing will be accomplished. What's done is done."

"There's more," Elena admitted.

He took a deep breath. "Go on."

"I broke down and told our parents why you and Christina got engaged. I also told them Christina had never slept with that doctor. It was pure fabrication."

"It's all right, Elena. The truth will free all of us."

His wife was so right!

He'd already known that Christina hadn't given herself to the doctor. Antonio had been stunned at the time and overjoyed.

"They think you're both so noble," Elena kept on. "Our parents are prepared to do anything to help you. But as you know, they've lost Guido's respect and he has powerful friends in the council who are ready to abolish the monarchy altogether. Some of the others wanting to keep the monarchy alive have prevailed on the archbishop to grant an annulment so you can re-marry. There's a list of titled women they're vetting now with Princess Gemma at the top."

Filled with joy that Christina was his wife, Antonio stopped pacing. "No. That isn't going to happen. I've got plans, ideas to build the economy. Christina and I plan to enlarge the African charity to make it far-reaching. I have a new jobs initiative to help us become a leader in technology. Scandal has rocked this nation for years, but we'll weather it. We have to."

Elena stared at him as if she'd never seen him before.

His wife got up from the couch and stood in front of him, wearing the same white suit she'd worn on the plane to Tahiti. *"We will."*

Two beautiful words from the mouth of the woman he couldn't imagine living without. He kissed her in front of his sister before walking over to Elena and pulling her to her feet. "I'm glad the truth is out, all of it." He gave her a hug. "Everything is going to work out."

"It's got to, because I love you two so much."

Antonio looked at his clever, adorable wife. She was so remarkable he couldn't believe he was lucky enough to be married to her.

He brushed his sister's cheek with his finger. "So, what is the latest between you and Enzio?"

"We're good."

"Just good."

"Um, very good."

"I'm glad to hear it."

"But you don't need to hear about my love life right now. I'm going to leave you to your privacy and will talk to you later."

They both hugged her before she hurried out of the apartment. He put his arm around Christina's waist and walked her back to the bedroom. "Before we do anything else, I need to take another look at your foot. Why don't you get undressed first? I want to make certain it is healing properly."

"This is almost like déjà vu."

While she started to take off her top and pants, her phone rang again. She'd left it on the end of the bed. "Let me get this first." The caller ID said it was her great-aunt calling.

She clicked on. "Sofia?"

"Welcome home, darling. How was your trip?"

"Heavenly."

"But you've come home to a viper's nest. I know something that you don't and I'm calling to warn you."

Antonio came to stand next to her.

She gripped the phone harder. "What is it?"

"I've spent part of the day with your parents. Your father has left for the palace to talk to you. I tried in my own way to ask him to wait until tomorrow, but you know how he is."

Yes... Christina knew exactly.

"For once in your life, darling, stand up to him and don't let him bully you. He's like his father and grand-father, born mean-spirited."

This conversation meant her father was furious. "He's a hard man to confront because he doesn't have a soft side."

"Unfortunately your mother has always been too afraid of him to intercede for you."

Her eyes filmed over. "I always had you, Aunt Sofia."

"And you've been one of my greatest joys."

"Thank you for alerting me."

"If there's anything I can do…"

Christina turned to Antonio. "My husband and I are prepared to face whatever is coming. I love you so much for caring. Talk to you again soon." She clicked off.

"What's going on?" he murmured.

"My father is on his way over to talk to me."

"I won't leave you alone with him."

She loved Antonio for saying that. "Knowing his style of quick attack, he won't be here long. Do you mind if we talk in the living room?"

"Of course not. This is our home. You can have anyone you want here, anytime."

"Thank you." She rose on tiptoe and kissed him.

"I'll go downstairs to my office and talk to my executive assistant. If you need me, I'll be here in an instant." She nodded. He put on a fresh sport shirt and left the apartment. Antonio was far too handsome for his own good.

This was her first chance to walk around her new home. The palace was a magnificent structure. Antonio's apartment was bigger than any home she'd ever been in. Already she knew her favorite place would be the terrace overlooking the water.

To think Antonio had been born here and had lived here until he was old enough to be sent away to schools and college. There was so much to learn about him as a child as well as an adult, but she couldn't concentrate when she knew her father would be coming any minute.

The phone on the bedside table rang. She walked over to pick it up. "Yes?"

"Princess Christina? This is the office calling. Your father is here to speak to you."

"Can you send him to our apartment?"

"Si, signora."

"Grazie."

"Prego."

Five minutes later she heard the knock on the door and opened it to see her father standing there. "Come into the living room, Papa."

He looked around while he followed her, but he didn't take a seat when she suggested it.

"Where's your husband?"

"In his office downstairs."

"What I have to say won't take long."

It never does.

His eyes glittered with anger. "If you want to do one thing to restore the name Rose in people's estimation, you'll leave Antonio for the good of the monarchy."

"I thought you wanted a king for a son-in-law."

He stared at her. "Not when his queen dishonored him by being with another man during the engagement. The people will forgive him, but they'll never forgive you."

She lifted her chin. "I didn't dishonor him. Is that all you came to say?"

His lips thinned. "Use the one shred of decency left in you to allow Antonio to rule with the right queen at his side. He may stand by you now, but in time doubts will creep in, and doubt can ruin a marriage faster than anything else. Let him marry Princess Gemma."

"Antonio didn't want her the first time around. He chose me."

Her father's cheeks grew ruddy. "The archbishop

will sanction a divorce since the marriage was fraudulent and your behavior during the engagement has painted you an immoral woman. You have one more opportunity in your life to right a tremendous wrong. Then public sentiment will end up being kind to you."

"So if I do that and bow out of his life, will you forgive me for being born a woman instead of a man and be kind to me?"

"The one has nothing to do with the other."

Her breath caught. "You mean that no matter what I do, there can be no forgiveness from you in this life?"

"You always were a difficult child."

She stiffened and fought her tears. "I'm your daughter. Yours and Mother's. I wanted your love. I wanted your acceptance. I tried everything under the sun to be the child you could love."

"We gave you everything, didn't we?" He turned to leave.

"Papa—"

Halfway out the door he said, "Has he told you he loves you? Because if he hasn't, then you need to do the right thing. If you don't know what is in Antonio's heart, why take the risk?"

Beyond tears, she walked out to the terrace, clutching her arms to her waist. The warning phone call from her aunt Sofia hadn't helped. She'd been thrown into a black void. Antonio had never said he loved her. She hadn't expected him to love her, but that was before they'd gone to Tahiti together and she'd found rapture with him.

If she truly didn't know what was in Antonio's

heart, then was it a risk to stay in the marriage as her father said?

After standing there for a while, she went back to the bedroom and called the palace switchboard. "Would you connect me with the palace press secretary please?"

"*Si.*"

In a minute a male voice came on the line.

"This is Princess Christina. I have a statement to come out on the evening news. I'll have it sent to your office by messenger. If you value your job, you'll tell no one. I mean, not a single soul."

"*Capisco*, Princess."

She hung up and went into the den, where she wrote out what she wanted to say. It didn't take long. After putting the note in an envelope and sealing it, she phoned the charity foundation in Voti. Arianna, the manager, answered the phone. Thank heaven she was still there.

"Christina? I can't believe you're calling. I thought you were on your honeymoon."

"We're back. I need a favor from you. A big one. Can you stop what you're doing right now and drive to the west gate of the palace?"

"Well, yes."

"I'll be waiting. This is an emergency."

"I'll be there in five minutes."

"Bless you."

She hung up and started throwing the things she'd need for overnight in her large tote bag. There was always money in her bank account and she had her passport. Without stopping to think, she left the apartment and hurried down the long hall of the west wing to the staircase.

When she reached the main doors, she stopped to talk to one of the guards. "Would you see that the palace press secretary receives this immediately?"

"Of course."

"Thank you."

Then she passed through the doors to the outside where another guard was on duty. "If the prince wonders where I am, tell him that an emergency came up at the charity foundation in town. One of my head people is picking me up so we can deal with it. I'll phone the prince later, but he's in meetings right now and can't be disturbed."

"Capisco."

So far, so good. She rushed outside and waited under the portico until she saw Arianna's red Fiat. Christiana hurried around the passenger side and got in. "You are an angel, Arianna, and I'll give you a giant bonus."

"Where do you want to go?"

"Back to the foundation." She put on her sunglasses. It only took a few minutes to reach the building. "Why don't you go on home? I'll be working late and will lock up again."

"All right."

"This is for your trouble." She handed her a hundred Eurodollars and got out of the car. When her friend drove off smiling, Christina hailed a taxi and asked to be driven to the ferry terminal. There were ferries leaving on the hour for Genoa during the summer.

She paid the driver, then hurried inside and bought

a ticket. Within twenty minutes she walked onto the ferry and sat on a bench as it made its way to the port in Genoa. From there she transferred to the train station and caught the next train going to Monte Calanetti via Siena. So far no one had recognized her because pictures of her wedding to Antonio hadn't been given to the press.

When it pulled in to the station, she phoned Louisa.

"Dear friend?" she said when Louisa answered.

"Christina?"

"Yes. I'm in Monte Calanetti. Do you have room for a visitor?"

"Did I just hear you correctly?"

"Yes."

"Of course I have room!" No doubt Louisa figured correctly that there'd been trouble since their flight back from Tahiti. "You can stay in the bridal suite for as long as you want."

"Thank you from the bottom of my heart. I'll be there soon and tell you everything."

As the taxi drove her to the Palazzo di Comparino, she turned off her phone. No one knew where she'd gone and that was the way she wanted things to stay.

Antonio had spent more time in his office than he'd meant to. He'd given Christina as much time as she needed to be with her father. After taking care of some business matters, he hurried to his wing of the palace. He planned to order a special dinner for them and eat out on the terrace. Having to come home early had robbed them of another precious night in Bora Bora, but tonight he intended to make up for everything. The need to make love to his wife was all he could think about.

"Christina?" There was no answer. He walked through to their bedroom. She wasn't there. Maybe she'd gone exploring, but she hadn't left a note. It was possible that after being with her father she'd gone to visit Elena. He phoned his sister. "Does Christina happen to be with you?"

"No."

"Hmm. I was doing a little business, but she's not here."

"She loves the outdoors. Maybe she took a walk outside to the kennel. That's what we usually do when she visits me. You know how much she adores animals."

"Thanks for the tip."

He put through a call to the kennel, but no one had seen her.

Angry with himself for not putting a security detail on her first thing, he phoned the head of palace security. "Alonzo? I'm looking for Princess Christina. Find out where she is and let me know ASAP. I want surveillance on her twenty-four-seven starting now."

"Yes, Your Highness."

He put off ordering dinner and hurried downstairs to the palace's main office. "Did anyone here see Princess Christina's father arrive?"

One of them nodded. "The princess asked that he be shown to your apartment. About twenty minutes later he passed by the office and left the grounds in a limousine."

More than frustrated at this point, Antonio headed for Alonzo's office. "Any news about her yet?"

Alonzo shook his head. "We're still vetting everyone on the force. Some of them went off shift at five o'clock and we're still trying to reach them for information."

He frowned. She wouldn't have gone to his parents' apartment, would she? He called them on the chance that she was there for some reason. But they had nothing to tell him.

Definitely worried now, he put through a call to Christina's parents. He should have tried there first. Her father got on the other extension. "Your Highness?"

"I'm looking for my wife. If you have any idea where she is, I'd like you to tell me now. The last anyone saw of her was you."

"You mean she's missing?"

His anger was approaching flash point. "What did you say to her?"

"The only thing a good father could say to his daughter. Do the right thing."

Antonio saw red. He clicked off and spun around in fury. It was almost nine o'clock. Could she have flown to Nairobi without telling him?

Frantic, he asked Alonzo for his men to check the airport to see if she'd flown out. Within a few minutes the news came back that she hadn't boarded any planes going anywhere.

"Hold on, Antonio. There's another report coming in. The guard at the west gate saw her leave the palace grounds in a red Fiat before he went off duty just before five. He had no idea you were looking for her. She told him she was going to the charity foundation to take care of an emergency and didn't want you to worry."

His hands balled into fists. "Find out if she's still there! We need to call all the girls working there to find out who drove the Fiat."

Before long the report came back that the building was closed for the night. No sign of Princess Christina anywhere. In another minute they had a woman on the line. Antonio took the call. "Arianna?"

"Your Highness. I didn't realize you were looking for her. When I dropped her off in front of the building, she said she was going to work in there for a while and that I should go home."

"So you have no idea where she went, or if she even went inside."

"No. I'm so sorry."

"What state was she in?"

"She definitely had an agenda and asked me to hurry, but that's all."

"Thank you, Arianna."

He handed the phone back to Alonzo.

Where are you, Christina. What did your father say to turn you inside out?

While he stayed there in agony, wondering where to turn next, the press secretary, Alonzo, came hurrying into the office. "Your Highness?"

Antonio turned to him. "Do you have news about the princess?"

His face had gone white. "I do. She told me if I

said anything I'd lose my job, but I can't let you suffer like this."

"What do you know?"

"She handed me an envelope and wanted the television anchor to read her statement during the ten o'clock news."

"She *what*?"

He nodded. "It'll be on every network in five minutes in every country in the world."

Alonzo turned on the big-screen television in his office. Antonio felt so gutted he started to weave.

"Better sit down, Your Highness."

"I'll be all right." His heart plummeted to his feet as he saw the words *breaking news* flash across the screen.

Suddenly the female news anchor appeared. "There's huge news breaking from the royal palace in Voti, Halencia, tonight, threatening to rock the already shaky monarchy decimated by scandal. It is struggling to stay alive in a nation so divided that one wonders what the ultimate outcome will be.

"I have in front of me a statement that Princess Christina, recently married in a private ceremony to Crown Prince Antonio de L'Accardi, has asked the press to read. These are her words and I quote. 'Dear citizens of Halencia. It is with the greatest sadness that I, Princess Christina de L'Accardi, am removing myself from the royal family to end the bitter conflict. I confess that although my relationship with Prince Antonio started out as a publicity stunt for reasons I don't intend to go into, I want everyone to know I love my new husband with every fiber of my being. A man with his integrity doesn't come along every day, or even in a lifetime. I knew him when we were both teenagers. Even then he showed a love and loyalty to his country that put others to shame. I want everyone to know he's the light of my life and my one true love. But I'm sorry that it isn't enough for the people of Halencia.'"

Christina...his heart cried.

"Wow! How's that for a heartfelt confession from the 'Cinderella Bride' as the nation has called her? Her charity in Africa has gained international attention. I have to admit I'm moved by her sacrifice and graciousness. That doesn't happen to me very often. Stay tuned for news coming from the palace as the fallout from her surprising statement is felt throughout the country and the world.

"There's no word from the prince or his family about this shocking development. You'll have to stayed tuned when more news will be forthcoming."

The television was shut off. Alonzo eyed Antonio with concern. "We'll find her. Just give us time."

"Thank you, Alonzo." But he knew the damage had been done when her father talked to her. He'd done such an expert job of destroying her that Antonio doubted Christina might ever come out of hiding.

As he left the office and started up the staircase for his apartment on legs that felt like lead, his phone started ringing. He looked down. Good old faithful Zach. He clicked on.

"Antonio?"

"Si?"

"What a hell of a mess."

"That doesn't even begin to cover it," he half groaned.

CHAPTER NINE

September, Voti, Halencia

AFTER HIS SPEECH, Antonio stood before the divided government assembly to answer questions.

"With all due respect, Your Highness, Princess Christina has graciously stepped aside to appease those voices who still want you to rule, but with someone more befitting to be your consort. Why won't you listen to reason?"

His anger was acute. "What princess on your short list has devoted half her life to charity and worked among the poverty-stricken in Africa with no thought for herself? What princess would willingly give up the title of queen in order not to stand in the way of her husband?"

The room grew quiet.

"My wife hasn't made excuses or defended herself, so I'll do it for her. This so-called affair of hers was in truth a friendship, nothing more, but trust evil to find its way to do its dirty work. She remained true to our engagement. So I'll say it again. If I can't rule with Christina at my side, then I have no desire to rule. Therefore I've given orders that there'll be no coronation."

A loud roar of dissent from that part of the council loyal to him and the crown got to their feet, but he was deaf to their cries.

"But, Your Highness—"

Antonio ignored the minister of finance, his good friend, who was calling to him and stormed out of the council meeting. He walked out of chambers and headed straight for his office down the hall of the palace.

"Roberto?" he barked.

"Your Highness?" His assistant's head came up.

"Call the press secretary and ask him to come in here right away. No one is to disturb us, do you understand?"

"Si." He picked up the phone immediately.

Antonio went into his private suite and slammed the door, but he was too full of adrenaline to sit. With Christina's stunning press statement read over the airwaves three weeks ago, plus her disappearance that had come close to destroying him, the joy he'd experienced on his honeymoon had vanished. He felt as if he'd been shoved down a pit and was falling deeper and deeper with no end in sight.

Within a few hours of searching for her that night, Alonzo's security people had tracked his wife to the Palazzo di Comparino. Apparently Louisa had taken her in. His clever, resourceful wife had made her getaway so fast by car, taxi, ferry and train that it had knocked the foundation from under him.

There'd been no word from her for the past desolate three weeks, but he hadn't expected any. Her father had made certain of that. With her press statement ringing out over the land, she would never come to him now. Meanwhile, Antonio had made a firm decision. He'd meant what he'd just said before the council. If he didn't have her at his side, he didn't want to be king at all.

For the first time in his life he was doing what he wanted, and he wanted Christina. No amount of argument could persuade him to change his mind. Being reminded by Guido that Christina had decided to sacrifice her own heart for Antonio's reputation and the country had only made him fall harder for his wife, if that was possible.

Roberto buzzed him that the press secretary was outside. Antonio told him to send him in.

When the other man entered the room looking sheepish, Antonio said, "Do you want to redeem yourself?"

"Anything, Your Highness."

"I want you to arrange a press conference for me on the steps of the palace in approximately one hour."

"I'll do it at once, Your Highness."

Louisa had turned the sitting room at the palazzo into a TV room. Christina was grateful, since it was the only way she got information from the outside world. The rest of the times she took long walks and coordinated charity business with the foundations in both Halencia and Nairobi.

Between Marusha and Elena, she was kept apprised of their news. Marusha was pregnant after suffering two miscarriages. Christina couldn't be happier for her. Elena's boyfriend, Enzio, wanted to marry her, but it meant talking to her parents first and she was nervous about that.

Though there was plenty of talk because Louisa had constant visitors, no one mentioned Antonio in her presence. Her aching heart couldn't have handled talking about him. Marusha begged her to come back to Africa. She would always have a home waiting. Christina told her she'd be coming in a few days. She'd outstayed her welcome with Louisa. It was time to go.

This afternoon both love-smitten Daniella and Marianna had come over for an evening with the girls. Christina had the suspicion Louisa was trying to cheer her up. She loved her for it and it was fun for all of them to get together.

Louisa poured wine from the vineyard and showed off her expertise about the vintage. Christina was impressed that she knew so much about it. Nico definitely had something to do with it.

Dinner wouldn't be for another couple of hours. Christina wasn't a wine drinker, but this afternoon was special, so she joined in with the others to take a sip.

Marianna smiled. "Hey, you guys—want to know a little gossip? I overheard Connor and Isabella talking wedding plans with Lindsay."

"I knew it!" Louisa said while everyone cheered. "Oh—it's time for the six o'clock news."

"Do we care?" Daniella interjected.

"I do," Louisa exclaimed. She hurried over to the TV and turned it on. Christina was secretly glad, since it was the only way she had of knowing what was going on at the palace. Her heart was broken for Antonio, who was having to carry on through the fight to determine the destiny of his country.

"*Buonasera*. Tonight we have more breaking news coming from the royal palace in Voti, Halencia. Crown Prince Antonio de L'Accardi has broken his long silence and has prepared a statement, which we will bring to you from the front steps of the royal palace."

The image flashed to a somber Antonio in a dark blue suit who was so gorgeous that Christina feared her heart would give out. The girls grew quiet as all eyes were focused on him.

"Fellow countrymen and women, these have been dark times for the crown and it's time for the conflict to end. I'll be brief. As I told the National Council this morning, I dare any tabloid to come after me or my wife again."

What? Christina shot to her feet.

"I admit that our engagement was originally a strategic move, but having spent time with Christina, I realize what an amazing person she is, how kind, generous and charitable she is, and how lucky this country is to have her as queen! I defy anyone to call our marriage a fake. To me it's the most real and true relationship I've ever had. So I'll tell you what I told the council.

I'm in love with my wife and will *not* be giving her up, even if it means losing the throne!"

Christina was shaking so hard she might have fallen if she'd hadn't been holding on to the chair. The girls stared at her in wonder.

Louisa smiled at her. "Every woman in the world with eyes in her head would love to be in your shoes right now, Christina Rose."

She nodded. "I'd like to be in them too, but he's not here."

Footsteps coming from the hall caused them to turn. Christina came close to fainting when Antonio walked in. "Who says I'm not?"

"Antonio," she gasped. "But you were just on television." He was dressed in a sport shirt and chinos instead of his dark suit.

"That was taped at noon. This afternoon the council reassembled and voted unanimously for our marriage to stand. The coronation will take place in two weeks. Once I was given the news, I flew here in the helicopter. It's standing by for me to take you back to the palace."

By now the girls were on their feet, hugging her and each other for joy.

Christina watched as her husband in all his male glory walked over to her. His brilliant blue eyes blinded her with their heat.

"H-how did you know I was here?"

"Palace security traced you once we heard from the guard that you'd left the grounds with Arianna."

"I thought I was being so careful."

"You were. For a few hours your disappearance gave me a heart attack. Since we'd barely returned from Bora Bora, I hardly think that's fair. Don't you ever do that to me again."

Her love for him was bursting out of her. "I promise."

In front of everyone he picked her up in his arms as he'd done twice before. "Excuse us, ladies. We have very personal matters of state to discuss and must get back to the palace. The limo is waiting for us."

Heat flooded her body as he carried her out of the room and the palazzo. After helping her into the car, he told the driver to head for Monte Calanetti before crushing her in his arms. "You don't have to worry about the state of our marriage, *cara*. I'm madly in love with you and this is a new day."

Christina was euphoric during their flight to Voti. Once they touched ground and were driven to the palace, he swept her along to their home on the second floor. Again he gathered her in his arms and carried her through to their bedroom.

After following her down onto the bed, he began kissing her. They were starving for each other. Christina couldn't get enough of him fast enough. Everything that had kept them apart had been cleared away. She was able to give him all the love she'd stored up in her heart and body.

The next morning she heard a sound of satisfaction as he pulled her on top of him. Their night of lovemaking had appeased them for a little while. She sat up and looked at their clothes strewn all over the floor.

Antonio pulled her back down. "I'm in love with you, Christina. So terribly in love with my red-haired beauty I'll never get over it. You believe me, don't you?"

There was a vulnerability about the question that touched her heart. "I feel your love in every atom of my body, my darling. Is there any doubt how I feel about you after last night? I need you desperately and want your baby."

"Anything to oblige the woman who has made me thankful I was born a man."

"I loved you from the time I was fifteen, but I never dared admit it to myself because—"

Another kiss stifled any words. "We're never going to talk about past sadness. When I called your father to find out what he said to you, he gave me the answer and I had a revelation of what it was like to grow up with him. All we can do is feel sorry for him. I believe your mother has always been afraid of him."

"I know you're right." Just when Christina didn't think she could love him anymore, he said or did something that made her love for him burn hotter. "I can't wait to thank your parents for Bora Bora."

"They've always lived their life over-the-top, but there's one thing they did I'll always be thankful for. They wanted us to find love."

"Yes, darling, and we found it there."

He kissed her neck and shoulders. "I'm the happiest man alive."

"Are you ready for a little more happy news?"

"What?"

"Enzio has asked Elena to marry him."

Antonio grinned. "He's a brave man to want to take her on."

"She's worth the risk. Guess what else? Marusha is expecting a baby." Christina kissed every feature. "I can't wait until we can announce we're having our own baby."

"I'm going to do my best to make that happen. I know now the one thing missing in my life was you and the family we're planning to have. We should have gotten married instead of engaged."

"I think about that too, all the time. But I don't think we were destined to get together until the time was right. We both had work to do first."

Antonio rolled her over and looked down at her. "You're the most beautiful sight this man has ever seen. I love you, *tesoro mio.* Never leave me."

"You *know* why I did."

A pained look entered his eyes. "The last three weeks have been the worst of my entire life."

"For me too. But as you said, no concentrating on past sorrows. We're together now and I'm able to live every day and night with the prince of my heart."

While they were talking, the house phone rang. She eyed her husband. "That's probably Guido wanting to know when you're free to discuss royal business. You better put him out of his misery."

Antonio grinned and picked up. *"Pronto."*

"Your Highness, Princess Christina's mother is asking if she can talk to her daughter in private."

He covered the mouthpiece. "Christina?" Curious,

she looked at him. He stared into her eyes with concern. "Your mother wants to talk to you."

She swallowed nervously. "Is she on the phone?"

"No. It's Guido. What do you want to do?"

"I'll take the call."

He handed her the receiver. "Guido?"

"Your mother asks if she can come to your apartment to talk to you."

She blinked. "Now?"

"She's says it's of vital importance."

"Then have someone show her up."

"Very well."

Antonio had picked up on the conversation. "Are you sure you want to do this?"

"Yes. My mother let me know she's on our side. Why don't you order breakfast while I talk to her in the living room? She won't be here very long, no matter what is on her mind."

He pressed a swift kiss to her lips and did her bidding. As for herself, Christina could have changed into an outfit, but she decided the robe was perfectly presentable. Before long she heard a knock on the main door.

Sucking in her breath, she opened it. Her mother always looked impeccably dressed and coiffed. But Christina knew right away something was wrong when she saw the tears in her eyes. "Come in."

But she just stood there.

"Mother?"

She shook her head. "I thought I could do this, but I can't." She started to turn away.

"Can't do what?" Christina asked, causing her mother to stop.

"Ask your forgiveness, but I don't have the right. I lost the right years ago. I knew your father must have had emotional problems when you were born. He wanted to give you up for adoption because you weren't a boy. I purposely prevented any more pregnancies in case I had another girl."

Christina was aghast at what she was hearing, but it made sense when she considered what her great-aunt Sofia had told her about the Rose men.

"I bargained with him that I wanted to keep you, and he wouldn't be sorry. That's why I kept you away. But you'll never know my shame for what I've done." She hung her head.

"I may have given birth to you, and your father may have provided you with everything, but you didn't have parents who showed you the love and devotion you deserved."

Christina stood there in shock as her mother broke down and sobbed.

"I'll never be forgiven for what I did to you. I don't deserve forgiveness, but you're my sweet, darling girl. I love you, Christina. My pride in you is fierce. Just know that I loved you from the moment you were born and I wanted you to hear it from me. I won't bother you again."

"Mother? Don't say that. I want us to have the relationship we never had. It's never too late," Christina said in a tremulous voice. "What you've told me about Papa changes everything."

Her mother turned to her with a face glistening in tears. "You mean you don't hate me with every fiber of your being? I would, because I'm not the great person you are."

"Oh, Mama—"

Christina reached for her and hugged her until her mother reciprocated. They clung for a long time. With every tear her mother shed, Christina felt herself healing. "We'll invite you over for dinner in a few weeks. I'll be cooking." She kissed her mother on both cheeks. "Dry your tears and I'll see you soon."

"Bless you, *figlia mia.*"

On Coronation Day bells rang out through the whole of Voti as Antonio and Christina left the cathedral and climbed into the open carriage. The massive throng roared, "Long live King Antonio and Queen Christina! Long live the monarchy!" They chanted the words over and over as the horses drew the carriage through the street lined with cheering Halencians.

The day had turned out to be glorious. Christina thought her heart was going to burst with happiness. Every few minutes someone called out, "Queen Christina!" When she turned, people were taking pictures.

Antonio sat next to her and squeezed the hand that wasn't waving. "You know what they want, *bellissima.*"

She looked back at him. "You mean a kiss? I want it much more." Showing breathtaking initiative that would probably cause her to blush later, she kissed him several times to the joy of the crowds.

The capital city of Halencia teemed with joyful faces and shouts of "Long live the monarchy."

"Your country loves you, darling. You don't know how magnificent you looked when the archbishop put that crown on your head."

"It's a good thing I didn't have to keep wearing it. How does yours feel?"

"I like the tiara. It's light."

"Your hair outshines its gleam."

They were both wearing their wedding clothes. The only thing different was the red sash on Antonio proclaiming him king.

"We made a lot of promises today." She kept waving. So did he.

"Are you worried?"

"No, but the sun is hot," he muttered. Their procession went on for over an hour.

Christina laughed. "I feel it too. But don't worry. We'll make it through and be alone later."

"I can't wait."

Eventually the carriage returned them to the palace. On their way up to the balcony off the second floor, Antonio summoned Guido to bring them a sandwich and a drink. The chief of staff, who'd chosen to stay on with Antonio, looked shocked, but he sent someone for the food.

Antonio whispered in her ear, "Did you see that look he gave us?"

"We're breaking royal protocol, darling."

"We'll be breaking a lot of rules before my reign has come to an end."

She shivered. "Don't talk about that. I can't bear the thought of it."

When the sandwich arrived, they both ate a half and swallowed some water. Feeling slightly more refreshed, they walked out onto the balcony to the roar of the crowd.

To please them her husband kissed her again with so much enthusiasm she actually swayed in his arms. A thunderous roar of satisfaction broke from the enormous throng that filled every square inch of space.

Once the royal photographers had finished taking pictures, Antonio grasped her hand. "Come with me."

"Where are we going?"

"To our home for some R and R until the ball this evening."

"But we're supposed to mingle with all the dignitaries."

"There'll be time for that tonight."

She hurried along with him, out of breath by the time they reached their apartment. When they entered, they discovered a lavish meal laid out for them in the dining room.

"Who arranged for this, darling?" she asked.

"My mother. She said it would be an exhausting day and we'd need it."

"I think she's wonderful."

Once in the bedroom, she removed her tiara and asked him to undo the buttons of her wedding dress. "That didn't take long. You did that so fast I'm afraid you've lost interest already. Last time you took forever."

"I hope it drove you crazy." He bit her earlobe gently when he'd finished. "Did it?"

"I'll never tell."

Antonio caught her to him and rocked her in his arms for a long, long time.

"Your capacity to love is a gift," he whispered against her cheek. "I don't know how I was the one man on earth lucky enough to be loved by you. I'm thankful your mother came to see you on the day we got back from Tuscany. She was able to answer the question that's always been in your heart. The sadness in your eyes has disappeared."

Christina threw her arms around his neck and looked into those blue eyes filled with love for her. "You're right. And now I have one more secret to disclose. You were always the man for me. When you asked me to get engaged, I jumped, *leaped* at the opportunity. To be honest, deep down I was petrified you *would* come to Africa and call it off. So I played it cagey, and it paid off!"

After enjoying a meal, they made love again before it was time to go out to greet their guests and enjoy the royal celebration. Guido looked frantic as they approached the balcony.

"Your Highness, we've been waiting for your appearance to start the fireworks."

Antonio hugged her waist. "We're here now."

No sooner had they stepped out so everyone could see them than a huge roar of excitement from the throng of people filled the air. Suddenly there was a massive fireworks display that lit up the sky, burst-

ing and bursting, illuminating everything. Antonio
looked into Christina's eyes. Her heart was bursting
with happiness.

"Ti amo, Antonio."

He stared at her. "Darling, you're crying. What's
wrong?"

"I'm so happy tonight I can't contain it all."

Giving the crowd what they wanted by kissing her,
he whispered, "My beautiful wife. This is only the beginning. *Ti amo, bellissima.* Forever."

* * * * *

A VERY EXCLUSIVE ENGAGEMENT

ANDREA LAURENCE

To my series mates – Barbara, Michelle,
Robyn, Rachel and Jennifer

It was a pleasure working with each of you.
Thanks for welcoming a newbie to the club.

And our editor, Charles

*Sei fantastico. È stato bello lavorare con voi.
Grazie per il cioccolato le sardine.*

One

Figlio di un allevatore di maiali.

Liam Crowe didn't speak Italian. The new owner of the American News Service network could barely order Italian food, and he was pretty sure his Executive Vice President of Community Outreach knew it.

Francesca Orr had muttered the words under her breath during today's emergency board meeting. He'd written down what she'd said—or at least a close enough approximation–in his notebook so he could look it up later. The words had fallen from her dark red lips in such a seductive way. Italian was a powerful language. You could order cheese and it would sound like a sincere declaration of love. Especially when spoken by the dark, exotic beauty who'd sat across the table from him.

And yet, he had the distinct impression that he wasn't going to like what she'd said to him.

He hadn't expected taking over the company from

Graham Boyle to be a cakewalk. The former owner and several employees were in jail following a phone-hacking scandal that had targeted the president of the United States. The first item on the agenda for the board meeting had been to suspend ANS reporter Angelica Pierce for suspicion of misconduct. Hayden Black was continuing his congressional investigation into the role Angelica may have played in the affair. Right now, they had enough cause for the suspension. When Black completed his investigation—and hopefully uncovered some hard evidence—Liam and his Board of Directors would determine what additional action to take.

He was walking into a corporate and political maelstrom, but that was the only reason he had been able to afford to buy controlling stock in the company in the first place. ANS was the crown jewel of broadcast media. The prize he'd always had his eye on. The backlash of the hacking scandal had brought the network and its owner, Graham Boyle, to their knees. Even with Graham behind bars and the network coming in last in the ratings for most time slots, Liam knew he couldn't pass up the opportunity to buy ANS.

So, they had a major scandal to overcome. A reputation to rebuild. Nothing in life was easy, and Liam liked a challenge. But he'd certainly hoped that the employees of ANS, and especially his own Board of Directors, would be supportive. From the night janitor to the CFO, jobs were on the line. Most of the people he spoke to were excited about him coming aboard and hopeful they could put the hacking scandal behind them to rebuild the network.

But not Francesca. It didn't make any sense. Sure, she had a rich and famous movie producer father to support her if she lost her position with ANS, but charity was her *job*. Surely she cared about the employees of the company as much as she cared about starving orphans and cancer patients.

It didn't seem like it, though. Francesca had sat at the conference room table in her formfitting flame-red suit and lit into him like she was the devil incarnate. Liam had been warned that she was a passionate and stubborn woman—that it wouldn't be personal if they bumped heads—but he wasn't prepared for this. The mere mention of streamlining the corporate budget to help absorb the losses had sent her on a tirade. But they simply couldn't throw millions at charitable causes when they were in such a tight financial position.

Suffice it to say, she disagreed.

With a sigh, Liam closed the lid on his briefcase and headed out of the executive conference room to find some lunch on his own. He'd planned to take some of the board members out, but everyone had scattered after the awkward meeting came to an end. He didn't blame them. Liam had managed to keep control of it, making sure they covered everything on the agenda, but it was a painful process.

Oddly enough, the only thing that had made it remotely tolerable for him was watching Francesca herself. In a room filled with older businesswomen and men in gray, black and navy suits, Francesca was the pop of color and life. Even when she wasn't speaking, his gaze kept straying back to her.

Her hair was ebony, flowing over her shoulders and curling down her back. Her almond-shaped eyes were dark brown with thick, black lashes. They were intriguing, even when narrowed at him in irritation. When she argued with him, color rushed to her face, giving her flawless tan skin a rosy undertone that seemed all the brighter for her fire-engine red suit and lipstick.

Liam typically had a thing for fiery, exotic women. He'd had his share of blond-haired, blue-eyed debutantes in private school but when he'd gone off to college, he found he had a taste for women a little bit spicier. Francesca, if she hadn't been trying to ruin his day and potentially his year, would've been just the kind of woman he'd ask out. But complicating this scenario with a fling gone wrong was something he didn't need.

Right now, what he *did* need was a stiff drink and some red meat from his favorite restaurant. He was glad ANS's corporate headquarters were in New York. While he loved his place in D.C., he liked coming back to his hometown. The best restaurants in the world, luxury box seats for his favorite baseball team...the vibe of Manhattan was just so different.

He'd be up here from time to time on business. Really, he wished it was all the time, but if he wanted to be in the thick of politics, which was ANS's focus, Washington was where he had to be. So he'd set up his main office in the D.C. newsroom, as Boyle had, keeping both his apartment in New York and the town house in Georgetown that he'd bought while he went to college there. It was the best of both worlds as far as he was concerned.

Liam went to his office before he left for lunch. He put his suitcase on the table and copied Francesca's words from his notebook onto a sticky note. He carried it with him, stopping at his assistant's desk on his way out.

"Jessica, it's finally over. Mrs. Banks will be bringing

you the paperwork to process Ms. Pierce's suspension. Human Resources needs to get that handled right way. Now that that mess is behind me, I think I'm going to find some lunch." He handed her the note with the Italian phrase written on it. "Could you get this translated for me while I'm gone? It's Italian."

Jessica smiled and nodded as though it wasn't an unusual request. She'd apparently done this in the past as Graham Boyle's assistant. "I'll take care of it, sir. I have the website bookmarked." Glancing down at the yellow paper she shook her head. "I see Ms. Orr has given you a special welcome to the company. This is one I haven't seen before."

"Should I feel honored?"

"I don't know yet, sir. I'll tell you once I look it up."

Liam chuckled, turning to leave, then stopping. "Out of curiosity," he asked, "what did she call Graham?"

"Her favorite was *stronzo*."

"What's that mean?"

"It has several translations, none of which I'm really comfortable saying out loud." Instead, she wrote them on the back of the note he'd handed her.

"Wow," he said, reading as she wrote. "Certainly not a pet name, then. I'm going to have to deal with Ms. Orr before this gets out of control."

A blur of red blew past him and he looked up to see Francesca heading for the elevators in a rush. "Here's my chance."

"Good luck, sir," he heard Jessica call to him as he trotted to the bank of elevators.

One of the doors had just opened and he watched Francesca step inside and turn to face him. She could see him coming. Their eyes met for a moment and then she reached to the panel to hit the button. To close the doors faster.

Nice.

He thrust his arm between the silver sliding panels and they reopened to allow him to join her. Francesca seemed less than pleased with the invasion. She eyeballed him for a moment under her dark lashes and then wrinkled her delicate nose as though he smelled of rotten fish. As the doors began to close again, she scooted into the far corner of the elevator even though they were alone in the car.

"We need to talk," Liam said as the car started moving down.

Francesca's eyes widened and her red lips tightened into a straight, hard line. "About what?" she asked innocently.

"About your attitude. I understand you're passionate about your work. But whether you like it or not, I'm in control of this company and I'm going to do whatever I have to do to save it from the mess that's been made of it. I'll not have you making a fool out of me in front of—"

Liam's words were cut off as the elevator lurched to a stop and the lights went out, blanketing them in total darkness.

This couldn't really be happening. She was not trapped in a broken elevator with Liam Crowe. Stubborn and ridiculously handsome Liam Crowe. But she should've known something bad was going to happen. There had been thirteen people sitting at the table during the board meeting. That was an omen of bad luck.

Nervously, she clutched at the gold Italian horn pendant around her neck and muttered a silent plea for good fortune. "What just happened?" she asked, her voice sounding smaller than she'd like, considering the blackout had interrupted a tongue lashing from her new boss.

"I don't know." They stood in the dark for a moment before the emergency lighting system kicked on and bathed them in red light. Liam walked over to the control panel and pulled out the phone that connected to the engineering room. Without saying anything, he hung it back up. Next, he hit the emergency button, but nothing happened; the entire panel was dark and unresponsive.

"Well?" Francesca asked.

"I think the power has gone out. The emergency phone is dead." He pulled his cell phone out and eyed the screen. "Do you have service on your phone? I don't."

She fished in her purse and retrieved her phone, shaking her head as she looked at the screen. There were no bars or internet connectivity. She never got good service in elevators, anyway. "Nothing."

"Damn it," Liam swore, putting his phone away. "I can't believe this."

"So what do we do now?"

Liam flopped back against the wall with a dull thud. "We wait. If the power outage is widespread, there's nothing anyone can do."

"So we just sit here?"

"Do you have a better suggestion? You were full of them this morning."

Francesca ignored his pointed words, crossed her arms defensively and turned away from him. She eyed the escape hatch in the ceiling. They could try to crawl out through there, but how high were they? They had started on the fifty-second floor and hadn't gone very far when the elevator stopped. They might be in between floors. Or the power could come back on while they were in the elevator shaft and they might get hurt. It probably was a better idea to sit it out.

The power would come back on at any moment. Hopefully.

"It's better to wait," she agreed reluctantly.

"I didn't think it was possible for us to agree on anything after the board meeting and that fit you threw."

Francesca turned on her heel to face him. "I did not throw a fit. I just wasn't docile enough to sit back like the others and let you make bad choices for the company. They're too scared to rock the boat."

"They're scared that the company can't bounce back from the scandal. And they didn't say anything because they know I'm right. We have to be fiscally responsible if we're going to—"

"Fiscally responsible? What about socially responsible? ANS has sponsored the Youth in Crisis charity gala for the past seven years. We can't just decide not to do it this year. It's only two weeks away. They count on that money to provide programs for at-risk teens. Those activities keep kids off the streets and involved in sports and create educational opportunities they wouldn't get without our money."

Liam frowned at her. She could see the firm set of his jaw even bathed in the dim red light. "You think I don't care about disadvantaged children?"

Francesca shrugged. "I don't know you well enough to say."

"Well, I do care," he snapped. "I personally attended the ball for the past two years and wrote a big fat check at both of them. But that's not the point. The point is we need to cut back on expenses to keep the company afloat until we can rebuild our image."

"No. You've got it backward," she insisted. "You need the charity events to rebuild your image so the company can stay afloat. What looks better in the midst of scandal than a company doing good deeds? It says to the public that some bad people did some bad things here, but the rest of us are committed to making things right. The advertisers will come flocking back."

Liam watched her for a moment, and she imagined the wheels turning in his head as he thought through her logic. "Your argument would've been a lot more effective if you hadn't shrieked and called me names in Italian."

Francesca frowned. She hadn't meant to lose her cool, but she couldn't help it. She had her mother's quick Italian tongue and her father's short fuse. It made for an explosive combination. "I have a bit of a temper," she said. "I get it from my father."

Anyone who had worked on the set of a Victor Orr film knew what could happen when things weren't going right. The large Irishman had a head of thick, black hair and a temper just as dark. He'd blow at a moment's notice and nothing short of her mother's soothing hand could calm him down. Francesca was just the same.

"Does he curse in Italian, too?"

"No, he doesn't speak a word of it and my mother likes it that way. My mother grew up in Sicily and met my father there when he was shooting a film. My mother's Italian heritage was always very important to her, so when I got older I spent summers there with my *nonna*."

"Nonna?"

"My maternal grandmother. I picked up a lot of Italian while I was there, including some key phrases I probably shouldn't know. I realized as a teenager that I could curse in Italian and my father wouldn't know what I was saying because he's Irish. From there it became a bad habit of mine. I'm sorry I yelled," she added. "I just care too much. I always have."

Francesca might take after her mother in most things, but her father had made his mark, as well. Victor Orr had come from poor beginnings and raised his two daughters not only to be grateful for what they had, but also to give to the less fortunate. All through high school, Francesca had volunteered at a soup kitchen on Saturdays. She'd organized charity canned food collections and blood drives at school. After college, her father helped her get an entry level job at ANS, where he was the largest minority stockholder. It hadn't taken long for her to work her way up to the head of community outreach. And she'd been good at it. Graham had never had room to complain about her doing anything less than a stellar job.

But it always came down to money. When things got tight, her budget was always the first to get cut. Why not eliminate some of the cushy corporate perks? Maybe slash the travel budget and force people to hold more teleconferences? Or cut back on the half gallon of hair gel the head anchor used each night for the evening news broadcast?

"I don't want to hack up your department," Liam said. "What you do is important for ANS and for the community. But I need a little give and take here. Everyone needs to tighten their belts. Not just you. But I need you to play along, too. It's hard enough to come into the leadership position of a company that's doing well, much less one like ANS. I'm going to do everything I can to get this network back on top, but I need everyone's support."

Francesca could hear the sincerity in his words. He did care about the company and its employees. They just didn't see eye to eye quite yet on what to do about it. She could convince him to see things her way eventually. She just had to take a page from her mother's playbook. It would take time and perhaps a softer hand than she had used with Graham. At least Liam seemed reasonable about it. That won him some points in her book. "Okay."

Liam looked at her for a moment, surveying her face as though he almost didn't believe his ears. Then he nodded. They stood silently in the elevator for a moment before Liam started shrugging out of his black suit coat. He tossed the expensive jacket to the ground and followed it with his silk tie. He unbuttoned his collar and took a deep breath, as if he had been unable to do it until then. "I'm glad we've called a truce because it's gotten too warm in here for me to fight anymore. Of course this had to happen on one of the hottest days of the year."

He was right. The air conditioning was off and it was in the high nineties today, which was unheard of in early May. The longer they sat in the elevator without air, the higher the temperature climbed.

Following his example, Francesca slipped out of her blazer, leaving her in a black silk and lace camisole and pencil skirt. Thank goodness she'd opted out of stockings today.

Kicking off her heels, she spread out her coat on the floor and sat down on it. She couldn't stand there in those pointy-toed stilettos any longer, and she'd given up hope for any immediate rescue. If they were going to be trapped in here for a while, she was going to be comfortable.

"I wish this had happened after lunch. Those bagels in the conference room burned off a long time ago."

Francesca knew exactly what he meant. She hadn't eaten since this morning. She'd had a cappuccino and a sweet *cornetto* before she'd left her hotel room, neither of which lasted very long. She typically ate a late lunch, so luckily she carried a few snacks in her purse.

Using the light of her phone, she started digging around in her bag. She found a granola bar, a pack of *Gocciole* Italian breakfast cookies and a bottle of water. "I have a few snacks with me. The question is whether we eat them now and hope we get let out soon, or whether we save them. It could be hours if it's a major blackout."

Liam slipped down to the floor across from her. "Now. Definitely now."

"You wouldn't last ten minutes on one of those survival reality shows."

"That's why I produce them and don't star in them. My idea of roughing it is having to eat in Times Square with the tourists. What do you have?"

"A peanut butter granola bar and some little Italian cookies. We can share the water."

"Which is your favorite?"

"I like the cookies. They're the kind my grandmother would feed me for breakfast when I stayed with her. They don't eat eggs or meat for breakfast like Americans do. It was one of the best parts of visiting her— cake and cookies for breakfast."

Liam grinned, and Francesca realized it was the first time she'd seen him smile. It was a shame. He had a beautiful smile that lit up his whole face. It seemed more natural than the serious expression he'd worn all day, as though he were normally a more carefree and relaxed kind of guy. The pressure of buying ANS must have been getting to him. He'd been all business this morning and her behavior certainly didn't help.

Now he was stressed out, hungry and irritated about being trapped in the elevator. She was glad she could make him smile, even if just for a moment. It made up for her behavior this morning. Maybe. She made a mental note to try to be more cordial in the future. He was being reasonable and there was no point in making things harder than they had to be.

"Cake for breakfast sounds awesome. As do summers in Italy. After high school I got to spend a week in Rome, but that's it. I didn't get around to seeing much more than the big sites like the Colosseum and the Parthenon." He looked down at the two packages in her hand. "I'll take the granola bar since you prefer the cookies. Thank you for sharing."

Francesca shrugged. "It's better than listening to your stomach growl for an hour." She tossed him the granola bar and opened the bottle of water to take a conservative sip.

Liam ripped into the packaging. His snack was gone before Francesca had even gotten the first cookie in her mouth. She chuckled as she ate a few, noting him eyeing her like a hungry tiger. Popping another into her mouth, she gently slung the open bag to him. "Here," she said. "I can't take you watching me like that."

"Are you sure?" he said, eyeing the cookies that were now in his hand.

"Yes. But when we get out of this elevator, you owe me."

"Agreed," he said, shoveling the first of several cookies into his mouth.

Francesca imagined it took a lot of food to keep a man Liam's size satisfied. He was big like her *nonno* had been. Her grandfather had died when she was only a few years old, but her *nonna* had told her about how much she had to cook for him after he worked a long shift. Like *Nonno,* Liam was more than six feet tall, solidly built but on the leaner side, as though he were a runner. A lot of people jogged around the National Mall in D.C. Or so she'd heard. She could imagine him down there with the others. Jogging shorts. No shirt. Sweat running down the hard muscles of his chest. It made her think maybe she should go down there every now and then, if just for the view.

She, however, didn't like to sweat. Running during the humid summers in Virginia was out of the question. As was running during the frigid, icy winters. So she just didn't. She watched what she ate, indulged when she really wanted to and walked as much as her heels would allow. That kept her at a trim but curvy weight that pleased her.

Speaking of sweating…she could feel the beads of sweat in her hairline, ready and waiting to start racing down the back of her neck. She already felt sticky, but there wasn't much else to take off unless she planned to get far closer to Liam than she ever intended.

Although that wouldn't be all bad.

It had been a while since Francesca had dated anyone. Her career had kept her busy, but she always kept her eyes open to the possibilities. Nothing of substance had popped up in a long time. But recently all of her friends seemed to be settling down. One by one, and she worried she might be the last.

Not that Liam Crowe was settling-down material. He was just sexy, fling material. She typically didn't indulge in pleasure without potential. But seeing those broad shoulders pulling against the confines of his shirt, she realized that he might be just what she needed. Something to release the pressure and give her the strength to hold out for "the one."

Francesca reached into her bag and pulled out a hair clip. She gathered up the thick, dark strands of her hair and twisted them up, securing them with the claw. It helped but only for a moment. Her tight-fitting pencil skirt was like a heavy, wet blanket thrown over her legs. And her camisole, while seemingly flimsy, was starting to get damp and cling to her skin.

If they didn't get out of this elevator soon, something had to come off. Taking another sip of water, she leaned her head back against the wall and counted herself lucky that if nothing else, she'd worn pretty, matching underwear today. She had the feeling that Liam would appreciate that.

Two

"Sweet mercy, it's hot!" Liam exclaimed, standing up. He felt as if he was being smothered by his crisp, starched dress shirt. He unfastened the buttons down the front and whipped it off with a sigh of relief. "I'm sorry if this makes you uncomfortable, but I've got to do it."

Francesca was sitting quietly in the corner and barely acknowledged him, although he did catch her opening her eyes slightly to catch a glimpse of him without his shirt on. She looked away a moment later, but it was enough to let him know she was curious. That was interesting.

He'd gotten a different insight into his feisty executive vice president of Community Outreach in the past two hours. He had a better understanding of her and what was important to her. Hopefully once they got out of this elevator they could work together without the animosity. And maybe they could be a little more than friendly. Once she had stopped yelling, he liked her. More than he probably should, considering that she worked for him.

"Francesca, take off some of your clothes. I know you're dying over there."

She shook her head adamantly, although he could see the beads of sweat running down her chest and into the valley between her breasts. "No, I'm fine."

"The hell you are. You're just as miserable as I am. That tank you're wearing looks like it will cover up enough to protect your honor. The skirt looks terribly clingy. Take it off. Really. I'm about ten minutes from losing these pants, so you might as well give up on any modesty left between us."

Francesca looked up at him with wide eyes. "Your pants?" she said, swallowing hard. Her gaze drifted down his bare chest to his belt and then lower.

"Yes. It's gotta be ninety-five degrees and climbing in this oven they call an elevator. You don't have to look at me, but I've got to do it. You might as well do it, too."

With a sigh of resignation, Francesca got up from the floor and started fussing with the latch on the back of her skirt. "I can't get the clasp. It snags sometimes."

"Let me help," Liam offered. She turned her back to him and he crouched down behind her to get a better look at the clasp in the dim red light. This close to her, he could smell the scent of her warm skin mixed with the soft fragrance of roses. It wasn't overpowering— more like strolling through a rose garden on a summer day. He inhaled it into his lungs and held it there for a moment. It was intoxicating.

He grasped the two sides of the clasp, ignoring the buzz of awareness that shot through his fingertips as he brushed her bare skin beneath it. With a couple of firm twists and pulls, it came apart. He gripped the zipper tab and pulled it down a few inches, revealing the back of the red satin panties she wore.

"Got it," he said with clenched teeth, standing back up and moving away before he did something stupid like touch her any more than was necessary. It was one thing to sit in the elevator in his underwear. It was another thing entirely to do it when he had a raging erection. That would be a little hard to disguise.

"Thank you," she said softly, her eyes warily watching him as she returned to her corner of the elevator.

As she started to shimmy the skirt down her hips, Liam turned away, although it took every ounce of power he had to do so. She was everything he liked in a woman. Feisty. Exotic. Voluptuous. And underneath it all, a caring soul. She wasn't one of those rich women that got involved in charity work because they had nothing better to do with their time. She really cared. And he appreciated that, even if it would cost him a few headaches in the future.

"Grazie, signore," she said with a sigh. "That does feel better."

Out of the corner of his eye, he saw her settle back down on the floor. "Is it safe?" he asked.

"As safe as it's going to get. Thank you for asking."

Liam looked over at her. She had tugged down her camisole to cover most everything to the tops of her thighs, although now a hint of her red bra was peeking out from the top. There was only so much fabric to go around, and with her luscious curves, keeping them all covered would be a challenge.

"You might as well just take those pants off now."

Liam chuckled and shook his head. Not after thinking about her satin-covered breasts. He didn't even have to touch her to make that an impossibility. "That's probably not the best idea at the moment."

Her brow wrinkled in confusion. "Why—" she started, then stopped. "Oh."

Liam closed his eyes and tried to wish his arousal away, but all that did was bring images of those silky red panties to his mind. "That's the challenge of being trapped in a small space with a beautiful, half-naked woman."

"You think I'm beautiful?" her hesitant voice came after a long moment of silence between them.

He planted his hands on his hips. "I do."

"I didn't expect that."

Liam turned to look at her. "Why on earth not? I think a man would have to be without a pulse to not find you desirable."

"I grew up in Beverly Hills," she said with a dismissive shrug. "I'm not saying I never dated in school—I did—but there was certainly a higher premium placed on the Malibu Barbie dolls."

"The what?"

"You know, the blond, beach-tanned girls with belly button piercings and figures like twelve-year-old boys? At least until they turn eighteen and get enough money to buy a nice pair of breasts."

"People in Hollywood are nuts," he said. "There was nothing remotely erotic about me as a twelve-year-old. You, on the other hand..." Liam shook his head, the thoughts of her soft curves pressing against the palms of his hands making his skin tingle with anticipation. He forced them into tight fists and willed the feeling away.

"It takes everything I've got not to touch you when I see you sitting there like that."

There was a long silence, and then her voice again. "Why don't you?"

Liam's jaw was flexed tight, and his whole body tensed as he tried to hold back the desire that was building inside for her. "I didn't think it was a good idea. I'm your boss. We have to work together. Things would get weird. Wouldn't they?"

Please let her say no. Please let her say no.

"I don't think so," she said, slowly climbing to her knees. "We're both adults. We know what this is and what it means." She crawled leisurely across the elevator floor, stopping in front of him. Her hands went to his belt buckle as she looked up at him through her thick, coal-black lashes. "What happens in the elevator, stays in the elevator, right?"

Liam didn't know what to say. He could barely form words as her hands undid his belt buckle, then the fly of his pants. But he didn't stop her. Oh, no. He wanted her too badly to let good sense interfere. Besides, they had time to kill, right? Who knew how long they'd be trapped in here.

His suit pants slid to the floor and he quickly kicked out of them and his shoes. Crouching down until they were at the same level, he reached for the hem of her camisole and pulled it up over her head. Francesca undid the clip holding her hair and the heavy, ebony stands fell down around her shoulders like a sheet of black silk.

The sight of her body in nothing but her red undergarments was like a punch to his guts. She was one of the sexiest women he'd ever seen—and she was mostly naked, and on her knees, in front of him.

How the hell had he gotten this lucky today?

Unable to hold back any longer, he leaned in to kiss her. They collided, their lips and bare skin slamming into one another. Francesca wrapped her arms around his neck and pulled her body against him. Her breasts pressed urgently against the hard wall of his chest. Her belly arched into the aching heat of his desire for her.

The contact was electric, the powerful sensations running through his nervous system like rockets, exploding at the base of his spine. He wanted to devour her, his tongue invading her mouth and demanding everything she could give him. She met his every thrust, running her own silken tongue along his and digging her nails frantically into his back.

Liam slipped his arm behind her back and slowly eased her down onto the floor. He quickly found his place between her thighs and dipped down to give attention to the breasts nearly spilling from her bra. It didn't take much to slip the straps from her shoulders and tug the bra down to her waist. The palms of his hands quickly moved in to take its place. He teased her nipples into firm peaks before capturing one in his mouth.

Francesca groaned and arched into him, her fingertips weaving into his thick, wavy brown hair. She tugged him back up to her mouth and kissed him again. There were no more thoughts of heat or sweat or broken elevators as he lost himself in the pleasurable exploration of her body.

And when he felt her fingers slide down his stomach, slip beneath the waistband of his underwear and wrap around the pulsating length of his erection, for a moment he almost forgot where he was, entirely.

Thank heavens for power outages.

* * *

Francesca wasn't quite sure what had come over her, but she was enjoying every minute of this naughty indulgence. Perhaps being trapped in this hot jail cell was playing with her brain, but she didn't care. There was just something about Liam. Sure, he was handsome and rich, but she'd seen her share of that kind of man in Washington, D.C. There was something about his intensity, the way he was handling the company and even how he handled her. She'd been fighting the attraction to him since she first laid eyes on him, and then his shirt came off to reveal a wide chest, chiseled abs and a sprinkle of chest hair, and she lost all her reasons to resist.

When he told her that she was beautiful, a part of her deep inside urged her to jump on the unexpected opportunity. To give in to the attraction, however inappropriate, and make a sexy memory out of this crazy afternoon.

She still wanted a solid, lasting relationship like her parents had. They'd been happily married for thirty years in a town where the typical wedding reception lasted longer than the vows. But having a fun fling in an elevator was in a totally different category. Liam would never be the serious kind of relationship, and she knew it, so it didn't hurt. This was a release. An amusing way to pass the time until the power was restored.

Francesca tightened her grip on Liam until he groaned her name into her ear.

"I want you so badly," he whispered. He moved his hand along the curve of her waist, gliding down to her hip, where he grasped her wrist and pulled her hand away. "You keep doing that and I won't have the chance to do everything I want to do to you."

A wicked idea crossed her mind. Francesca reached out with her other hand for the half-empty bottle of water beside them. "Let me cool you off then," she said, dumping the remains over the top of his head. The cool water soaked his hair and rushed down his face and neck to rain onto her bare skin. It was refreshing and playful, the cool water drawing goose bumps along her bare flesh.

"Man, that felt good," Liam said, running one hand through his wet hair as he propped himself up with the other. "I don't want to waste it, though." He dipped down to lick the droplets of water off her chest, flicking his tongue over her nipples again. He traveled down her stomach to where some of the water had pooled in her navel. He lapped it up with enthusiasm, making her squirm beneath him as her core tightened and throbbed in anticipation.

His fingertips sought out the satin edge of her panties and slipped beneath them. Sliding over her neatly cropped curls, one finger parted her most sensitive spot and stroked her gently. She couldn't contain the moan of pleasure he coaxed out of her. When he dipped farther to slip the finger deep inside her body, she almost came undone right then. The muscles tightened around him, the sensations of each stroke building a tidal wave that she couldn't hold back for much longer.

"Liam," she whispered, but he didn't stop. His fingers moved more frantically over her, delving inside and pushing her over the edge.

Francesca cried out, her moans of pleasure bouncing off the walls of the small elevator and doubling in volume and intensity. Her hips bucked against his hand, her whole body shuddering with the feeling running through her.

She had barely caught her breath when suddenly there was a jarring rattle. The silence was broken by the roar of engines and air units firing up, and the lights came back on in the elevator.

"You have got to be kidding me," he groaned.

And then, with Liam still between her thighs and their clothes scattered around the elevator, the car started moving downward. Francesca threw a quick glance to the screen on the wall. They were on the thirty-third floor and falling. "Oh, no," she said, pushing frantically at his chest until he eased back.

She climbed to her feet, tugging on her skirt and yanking her bra back into place. She didn't bother tucking in her camisole, but shrugged into her jacket. Liam followed suit, pulling on his pants and shirt. He shoved his tie into his pants pocket and threw his coat over his arm.

"You have my lipstick all over you," she said, noting less than ten floors to go. Liam ran his hand through his still wet hair and casually rubbed at his face, seeming to be less concerned than she was with how he looked when they walked out.

By the time the elevator came to the first floor and the doors opened, Francesca and Liam were both fully dressed. A bit sloppy, with misaligned buttons and rumpled jackets, but dressed.

They stepped out into the grand foyer where the building engineers and security guards were waiting for them. "Are you two—" one of the men started to speak, pausing when he saw their tousled condition "—okay?"

Liam looked at Francesca, and she could feel her cheeks lighting up crimson with embarrassment. He still had some of her Sizzling Hot Red lipstick on his face, but he didn't seem to care. "We're fine," he said. "Just hot, hungry and glad to finally be out of there. What happened?"

"I'm not sure, sir. The whole island lost power. Wouldn't you know it would be on such a hot day. Might've been everyone turning on their air conditioners for the first time today. Are you guys sure we can't get you anything? Three hours in there had to be miserable."

"I'm fine," Francesca insisted. The engineer's expression had been a wake-up call from the passionate haze she'd lost herself in. She'd very nearly slept with her boss. Her new boss. On his first day after they'd spent the morning fighting like cats and dogs. The heat must've made her delirious to have thought that was a good idea.

At least they'd been interrupted before it went too far. Now she just wanted to get a cab back to her hotel. Then she could change out of these clothes, shower and wash the scent of Liam off her skin. "Just have someone hail me a taxi to my hotel, would you?"

The engineer waved to one of the doormen. "Sure thing. It might take a minute because the traffic lights have been out and there's been gridlock for hours."

Without looking at Liam, Francesca started for the door, stepping outside to wait on the sidewalk for her car.

"Talk about bad timing," Liam said over her shoulder after following her outside.

"Fate has a funny way of keeping you from doing things you shouldn't do."

Liam came up beside her, but she wouldn't turn to look at him. She couldn't. She'd just get weak in the knees and her resolve to leave would soften.

"I'd like to think of it more as a brief interruption. To build some anticipation for later. Where are you headed?"

"To where I was going before my whole day got sidetracked—back to my hotel. To shower and get some work done. Alone," she added if that wasn't clear enough.

"Do you have plans for dinner tonight?"

"Yes, I do." She didn't. But going out to dinner with Liam would put her right back in the same tempting situation, although hopefully without power outages. She'd given in to temptation once and she'd been rescued from her bad decision. She wasn't about to do it again.

Liam watched her for a minute. Francesca could feel his eyes scrutinizing her, but she kept her gaze focused on the passing cars. "You said things wouldn't get weird. That we both knew what this was and what happened in the elevator stayed in the elevator."

Francesca finally turned to him. She tried not to look into the sapphire-blue eyes that were watching her or the damp curls of his hair that would remind her of what they'd nearly done. "That's right. And that's where it will stay. That's why I don't want to go to dinner with you. Or to drinks. Or back to your place to pick up where we left off. We've left the elevator behind us and the opportunity has come and gone. Appreciate the moment for what it was."

"What it was is unfinished," he insisted. "I'd like to change that."

"Not every project gets completed." Francesca watched a taxi pull up to the curb. It was empty, thank goodness.

"Come on, Francesca. Let me take you to dinner tonight. Even if just to say thank-you for the granola bar. As friends. I owe you, remember?"

Francesca didn't believe a word of that friend nonsense. They'd have a nice dinner with expensive wine someplace fancy and she'd be naked again before she knew it. As much as she liked Liam, she needed to stay objective where he was concerned. He was the new owner of ANS and she couldn't let her head get clouded with unproductive thoughts about him. They'd come to a truce, but they hadn't fully resolved their issues regarding her budget and the way forward for the network. She wouldn't put it past an attractive, charming guy like Liam to use whatever tools he had in his arsenal to get his way.

She stepped to the curb as the doorman opened the back door of the taxi for her.

"Wait," Liam called out, coming to her side again. "If you're going to leave me high and dry, you can at least tell me what you called me today in the board meeting."

Francesca smiled. If that didn't send him packing, nothing else would. "Okay, fine," she relented. She got into the cab and rolled down the window before Liam shut it. "I called you *figlio di un allevatore di maiali*. That means 'the son of a pig farmer.' It doesn't quite pack the same punch in English."

Liam frowned and stepped back from the window. The distance bothered her even though it was her own words that had driven him away. "I'd say it packs enough of a punch."

She ignored the slightly offended tone of his voice. He wasn't about to make her feel guilty. He'd deserved the title at the time. "Have a good evening, Mr. Crowe," she said before the cab pulled away and she disappeared into traffic.

Three

Liam had just stepped from his shower when he heard his cell phone ringing. The tune, "God Save the Queen," made him cringe. Had he told his great aunt Beatrice he was in Manhattan? She must've found out somehow.

He wrapped his towel around his waist and dashed into his bedroom where the phone was lying on the comforter. The words "Queen Bee" flashed on the screen with the photo of a tiara. His aunt Beatrice would not be amused if she knew what the rest of the family called her.

With a sigh, he picked up the phone and hit the answer key. "Hello?"

"Liam," his aunt replied with her haughty Upper East Side accent. "Are you all right? I was told you were trapped in an elevator all afternoon."

"I'm fine. Just hungry, but I'm about to—"

"Excellent," she interrupted. "Then you'll join me

for dinner. There's an important matter I need to discuss with you."

Liam bit back a groan. He hated eating at Aunt Beatrice's house. Mostly because of having to listen to her go on and on about the family and how irresponsible they all were. But even then, she liked them all more than Liam because they kissed her derrière. And that was smart. She was worth two billion dollars with no children of her own to inherit. Everyone was jockeying for their cut.

Everyone but Liam. He was polite and distant. He didn't need her money. Or at least he hadn't until the ANS deal came up and he didn't have enough liquid assets to buy a majority stake quickly. Other people also were interested in the company, including leeches like Ron Wheeler, who specialized in hacking businesses to bits for profit. To move fast, Liam had had to swallow his pride and ask his aunt to invest in the remaining shares of ANS that he couldn't afford. Together, they had controlling interest of the company, and by designating her voting powers to him, Aunt Beatrice had put Liam in charge.

Liam had every intention of slowly buying her out over time, but he wouldn't be able to do so for quite a while. So now, at long last, Aunt Beatrice had something to hold over his head. And when she snapped, for the first time in his life, he had to jump.

"Dinner is at six," she said, either oblivious or unconcerned about his unhappy silence on the end of the line.

"Yes, Aunt Beatrice. I'll see you at six."

After he hung up the phone, he eyed the clock and realized he didn't have long to get over to her Upper

East Side mansion in rush hour traffic. He'd do better to walk, so he needed to get out the door soon.

It was just as well that Francesca had turned down his dinner date so he didn't have to cancel. That would've pained him terribly, even after knowing what she'd called him.

"Son of a pig farmer," he muttered to himself as he got dressed.

He opted for a gray suit with a pale purple dress shirt and no tie. He hated ties and only wore them when absolutely necessary. Today, he'd felt like he needed to look important and in control at the board meeting. He didn't want the ANS directors to think they were in the hands of a laid-back dreamer. But as soon as he had a strong foothold in the company, the ties would be gone.

Tonight, he left it off simply because he knew to do so would aggravate Aunt Beatrice. She liked formal dress for dinner but had given up long ago on the family going to that much trouble. She did, however, still expect a jacket and tie for the men and a dress and hosiery for the ladies. It was only proper. Leaving off the tie would be a small but noted rebellion on his part. He didn't want her to think she had him completely under her thumb.

It wasn't until he rang the doorbell that he remembered her mentioning something about an important issue she wanted to discuss. He couldn't imagine what it could be, but he sincerely hoped it didn't involve him dating someone's daughter. Aunt Beatrice was single-minded in her pursuit of marriage and family for Liam. He couldn't fathom why she cared.

"Good evening, Mr. Crowe," her ancient butler Henry said as he opened the door.

Henry had worked for his aunt Liam's entire life and a good number of years before that. The man was in his seventies now but as spry and chipper as ever.

"Good evening, Henry. How is she tonight?" he asked, leaning in to the elderly man and lowering his voice.

"She's had a bee in her bonnet about something all afternoon, sir. She made quite a few calls once the power was restored."

Liam frowned. "Any idea what it's about?"

"I don't. But I would assume it involves you because you were the only one invited to dinner this evening."

That was odd. Usually Aunt Beatrice invited at least two family members to dinner. She enjoyed watching them try to one-up each other all night and get in her good favor. It really was a ridiculous exercise, but it was amazing what the family would do just because she asked. His grandfather, Aunt Beatrice's brother, had never had much to do with her, so neither did that branch of the family. It was only after all the others of the generation had died that she took over as matriarch. Then, even Liam's part of the family was drawn back into the fold.

Liam held his tongue as Henry led him through the parlor and into the formal dining room. When a larger group was expected, Aunt Beatrice would greet her guests in the parlor and then adjourn to the dining room when everyone had arrived. Apparently because it was just him they bypassed the formalities and went straight to dinner.

Aunt Beatrice was there in her seat at the head of the long, oak table, looking regal as always. Her gray hair was curled perfectly, her rose chiffon dress nicely accented by the pink sapphire necklace and earrings she paired with it. She didn't smile as he entered. Instead, she evaluated him from top to bottom, her lips tightening into a frown when she noted his lack of tie.

"Good evening, Aunt Beatrice," he said with a wide smile to counter her grimace. He came around the table and placed a kiss on her cheek before sitting down at the place setting to her right.

"Liam," she said, acknowledging him without any real warmth. That's why he'd always thought of her as royalty. Stiff, formal, proper. He couldn't imagine what she would have been like if she had married and had children. Children would require laughter and dirt—two things unthinkable in this household.

Henry poured them each a glass of wine and disappeared into the kitchen to retrieve their first course. Liam hated to see the old man wait on him. He should be in a recliner, watching television and enjoying his retirement, not serving meals to privileged people capable of doing it themselves. The man had never even married. He had no life of his own outside of this mansion.

"When are you going to let Henry retire?" he asked. "The poor man deserves some time off before he drops dead in your foyer."

Aunt Beatrice bristled at the suggestion. "He loves it here. He wouldn't think of leaving me. And besides, Henry would never die in the foyer. He knows how expensive that Oriental rug is."

Liam sighed and let the subject drop. Henry placed bowls of soup in front of them both and disappeared again. "So, what have you summoned me here to discuss tonight?" He might as well just get it over with.

There was no sense waiting for the chocolate soufflé or the cheese course.

"I received a phone call today from a man named Ron Wheeler."

Liam stiffened in his seat and stopped his spoon of soup in midair. Ron Wheeler was in the business of buying struggling companies and "streamlining" them. That usually involved laying off at least half the employees and hacking up the benefits packages of the ones who were left. Then he'd break the company up into smaller pieces and sell them off for more than the price of the whole. No one liked to hear the mention of his name. "And what did he have to say?"

"He heard I'd bought a large portion of Graham Boyle's ANS stock. He's made me an extremely generous offer to buy it."

At that, Liam dropped his spoon, sending splatters of butternut squash all across the pristine white tablecloth. Henry arrived in an instant to clean up the mess and bring him a new spoon, but Liam didn't want it. He couldn't stomach the idea of food at this point.

"Aunt Beatrice, your holding is larger than mine. If you sell him your stock, he'll gain majority control of the company. The whole network will be at risk."

She nodded, setting down her own spoon. "I realize that. And I know how important the company is to you. But I also want you to know how important this family is to me. I won't be around forever, Liam. This family needs someone strong and smart to run it. You don't need me to tell you that most of our relatives are idiots. My two sisters never had any sense and neither did their children. My father knew it, too, which is why he left most of the family money to me and your grandfather. He knew they'd all be broke and homeless without someone sensible in charge."

Liam didn't want to know where this conversation was going. It couldn't be good. "Why are you telling me this? What does it have to do with Ron Wheeler?"

"Because I think you're the right person to lead the family after I'm gone."

"Don't talk like that," he insisted. They both knew she was too mean to die. "You have plenty of years ahead of you."

Her sharp blue gaze focused on him, an unexpected hint of emotion flashing in them for a fleeting second before she waved away his statement. "Everyone dies, Liam. It's better to be prepared for the eventuality. I want you to take my place and be family patriarch. As such, you would inherit everything of mine and serve as executor of the family trusts."

The blood drained from Liam's face. He didn't want that kind of responsibility. Two billion dollars and a family full of greedy suck-ups chasing him around? "I don't want your money, Aunt Beatrice. You know that."

"Exactly. But I know what you do want. You want ANS. And as long as I have my shares, you won't truly have it. I could sell at any time to Ron Wheeler or anyone else who gives me a good offer."

Liam took a big swallow of wine to calm his nerves. Aunt Beatrice had never held anything over him. She couldn't because until now he hadn't needed her or her money and she knew it. But he'd made a critical error. He never should've agreed to this stock arrangement with her. He'd given her the leverage to twist him any way she wanted to. "Why would you do that? I told you

I would buy that stock from you at what you paid or the going rate, if it goes higher."

"Because I want you to settle down. I can't have you leading this family while you play newsman and chase skirts around D.C. I want you married. Stable. Ready to lead the Crowe family."

"I'm only twenty-eight."

"The perfect age. Your father married when he was twenty-eight, as did your grandfather. You're out of school, well established. You'll be a prize to whatever lucky woman you choose."

"Aunt Beatrice, I'm not ready to——"

"You will marry within the year," she said, her serious tone like a royal decree he didn't dare contradict. "On your one-year wedding anniversary, as a gift I will give you my shares of ANS stock and name you my sole beneficiary. Then you can truly breathe easy knowing your network is secure, and I can know this family will be cared for when I'm gone."

She couldn't be serious. "You can't force me to marry."

"You're right. You're a grown man and you make your own decisions. So the choice is entirely yours. Either you marry and get the company you want and more money than most people dream of…or you don't and I sell my shares to Ron Wheeler. Tough choice, I understand." At that, she returned to her soup as though they'd been discussing the weather.

Liam didn't know what to say. He wasn't used to anyone else calling the shots in his life. But he'd given himself a vulnerability she had been waiting to exploit. She'd probably planned this from the very moment he'd come to her about buying ANS. Liam leaned his head into his hand and closed his eyes.

"If you don't know any suitable ladies, I can make a few recommendations."

He was sure she'd just love that, too. Thankfully she'd stopped short of deciding who he should marry. "I think I can handle that part, thank you. I've been seeing someone," he said quickly, hoping she didn't ask for more details about the fictional woman.

Aunt Beatrice shrugged off the bitter tone in his voice. "Then it's time the two of you got more serious. Just remember, you have a year from today to marry. But if I were you, I wouldn't dawdle. The sooner you get married, the sooner ANS will be yours."

Francesca had deliberately avoided Liam since they'd returned to D.C., but she couldn't put off speaking to him any longer. She needed to know if they were going to be sponsoring the Youth in Crisis gala or not. It was a week and a half away. It was already too late to pull out, really, but if he was going to insist they couldn't do it, she needed to know now.

She waved as she passed his assistant's desk. "Afternoon, Jessica."

The woman looked up at her with a wary expression. "You don't want to go in there."

Francesca frowned. Did she mean her specifically, or anyone? Liam couldn't still be mad about the whole elevator thing. Could he? "Why?"

"He's been in a foul mood since we left New York. I'm not sure what happened. Something with his family, I think."

"Is everyone okay?"

Jessica nodded her head. "He hasn't had me send flowers to anyone, so I would assume so. But he's not taking calls. He's been sitting at his desk all morning flipping through his address book and muttering to himself."

Interesting. "Well, I hate to do it, but I have to speak with him."

"As you wish." Jessica pressed the intercom button that linked to Liam's phone. "Mr. Crowe, Ms. Orr is here to see you."

"Not now," his voice barked over the line. Then, after a brief pause, he said, "Never mind. Send her in."

Jessica shrugged. "I don't know what that's all about, but go on in."

Francesca gripped the handle to his office door and took a deep breath before going inside. She'd dressed in her most impressive power suit today and felt confident she would leave his office with what she wanted. The emerald-green pantsuit was striking and well-tailored. Her black hair was twisted up into a bun, and she had a silk scarf tied around her neck. Not only did she feel good in the outfit, she felt well-covered. Liam had already seen too much of her body. She intended to keep every inch out of his sight from now on.

As she opened the door, she saw Liam sitting at his desk just as Jessica had described. He was flipping through an address book, making notes on his desk blotter. As she came in he looked up and then slammed the book shut.

"Good morning, Ms. Orr." His voice was a great deal more formal and polite than it was the last time they'd spoken. Of course, then they'd been recently naked together.

"Mr. Crowe. I wanted to speak to you about the Youth in Crisis gala. We don't have much time to—"

"Have a seat, Francesca."

She stopped short, surprised at his interruption. Unsure of what else to do, she moved to take a seat in the guest chair across from his desk. Before she could sit, he leaped up and pointed to the less formal sitting area on the other side of his office.

"Over here, please. I don't like talking to people across the desk. It feels weird."

Francesca corrected her course to sit in the plush gray leather chair he'd indicated. She watched him warily as he went to the small refrigerator built into the cabinets beside his desk.

"Would you like something to drink?"

"I don't drink at work."

Liam turned to her with a frown and a bottle of root beer in his hand. "At all? I have bottled water, root beer—my personal favorite—and some lemon-lime soda. I don't drink at work, either, despite the fact that if anyone wanted to be in a drunken stupor right now, it would be me." He pulled a bottle of water out of the fridge and handed it to her. "To replace the one we... *used up* in the elevator."

Francesca started to reach for the bottle, then froze at the memory of water pouring over his head and onto her own bare chest. Damn, he'd said that on purpose to throw her off her game. Pulling herself together, she took the bottle and set it on the coffee table unopened.

Liam joined her, sitting on the nearby sofa with his bottle of root beer. "I have a proposition for you."

She didn't like the sound of that. "I told you that I wasn't interested in dinner."

Liam watched her intently with his jewel-blue eyes as he sipped his drink. "I'm not asking you to dinner. I'm asking you to marry me."

Francesca was glad she hadn't opted to drink that water or she would've spit it across the room. She sat bolt upright in her seat and glared at him. "Marry you? Are you crazy?"

"Shhh…" he said, placing his drink on the table. "I don't want anyone to hear our discussion. This is very important. And I'm dead serious. I want you to be my fiancée. At least for a few months."

"Why me? What is going on?"

Liam sighed. "I've put myself in a vulnerable position with the company. I couldn't afford all of Graham Boyle's stock, so my aunt owns the largest share of ANS, not me. She's threatening to sell it to Ron Wheeler if I don't get married within a year."

Ron Wheeler. That was a name that could send chunks of ice running through her veins. Charity didn't help the bottom line in his eyes. Francesca, her staff and the entire department would be out the door before the ink was dry on the sale. And they would just be the first, not the last to go if he were in charge. "Why would she do that?"

"She wants me married and settled down. She wants me to be the strong family patriarch when she's gone and doesn't believe my playboy ways are appropriate. I think she's bluffing, really. I'm hoping that if I get engaged, that will be enough to soothe her. In the meantime, I'm going to work with my accountant and financial advisor to see if I can arrange for a line of credit large enough to buy her out. I have no expectation that we'll actually have to get married."

"I should hope not," she snapped. Francesca had some very strong ideas about what a good marriage was made of and blackmail was not the ideal start. "Don't you have anyone else you can ask? You've known me less than a week."

Liam looked over to the book on his desk and shook his head. "I've gone through every woman's name in my address book and there's not a single suitable candidate. All those women would look at this as a romantic opportunity, not a business arrangement. That's why you're my ideal choice."

A business arrangement? That's just what a girl wanted to hear. "So if this is just a business arrangement, that means you have no intention of trying to get me into bed, right?"

Liam leaned closer to her and a wicked grin spread across his face. "I didn't say *that,* but really, that's not my first priority here. I'm asking you for several reasons. First, I like you. Spending time with you shouldn't be a hardship. My aunt will expect the relationship to appear authentic and she'll sniff out the truth if she thinks we're faking it. After our time in the elevator, I think you and I have enough chemistry to make it realistic. And second, I know I can count on you because you want something from me."

Francesca opened her mouth to argue with him and then stopped. She knew exactly where this was going. Tit for tat. "The Youth in Crisis gala?"

He nodded. "If Ron Wheeler gets a hold of this company, everything you've worked for will be destroyed. The only thing I can do to protect this company and its employees is to get engaged as soon as I can. For your assistance, I'm offering the full financial support of ANS for the Youth in Crisis charity ball. I'll even pledge to top the highest private donation with my own money. I look at it as an investment in the future of the network. And all you have to do is wear a beautiful diamond ring and tolerate my company until my aunt backs down."

It felt like a deal with the devil and there had to be a catch. "You said it had to appear authentic. Define *authentic*."

Liam sat back in his seat and crossed his leg over his knee. "No one is going to follow us into the bedroom, Francesca, and I won't make you do anything that you don't want to do. But everything we can do to convince people we are a couple in love would be helpful."

She shook her head and looked down at her lap. This was all so sudden. The idea of being Liam's fiancée, even if just temporarily, wasn't so bad. She'd be lying to herself if she said she hadn't thought about their time in the elevator as she lay alone in bed each night. But his fiancée? Publicly? What would she tell her family? She couldn't tell them the truth. And her friends? She would have to lie to everyone she knew.

But the alternative was unthinkable. She cared too much about ANS and its employees to let the company fall into Ron Wheeler's hands. Going along with Liam's plan would protect the company and earn her the charity gala she wanted so badly. When the arrangement was no longer necessary, her friends and family would just have to believe that things had soured between them and they broke it off. She could live with that. It wasn't as though they were actually going to get married.

She looked up in time to see Liam slide off the couch to his knees and crawl across the floor until he was kneeling at her feet. He looked so handsome in his navy suit, his dark, beautiful blue eyes gazing into her own. He took her hands into his, his thumb gently stroking her skin. With him touching her like that, she'd probably agree to anything.

"Francesca Orr," he said with a bright, charming smile. "I know I'm just the humble son of a pig farmer, but would you do me the honor of being my temporary fiancée?"

Four

Liam watched Francesca's terrified expression, waiting for her answer. He could see the battle raging in her head. He understood. He was having to make sacrifices for the company and what he wanted, too. He felt guilty for dragging her into his mess, but she really was the perfect choice. If she could walk away from that elevator like nothing happened, she could do the same with this engagement. In the end, they could go their separate ways, both having gotten what they wanted.

Her dark brown eyes focused on him for a moment, then strayed off to his shoulder. Her expression of worry softened then, her jaw dropping with surprise.

Confused, Liam turned to look at his shoulder. Perched there on the navy fabric was a lone ladybug. He'd opened the window of his office this morning when he was suffocating from the pressure and needed some fresh air. The tiny insect must've been a stowaway.

Francesca untangled her hands from his and reached out to scoop the ladybug from his shoulder. She got up from her seat and walked over to the window. Opening it wide, she held her palm out to the sun and watched the bug fly out into the garden outside the network offices.

She stood looking out the window for several minutes. Liam was still on his knees, wondering what the hell had just happened, when he heard her speak.

"Yes, I will be your temporary fiancée."

He leaped to his feet and closed the gap between them in three long strides. "Really?"

She turned to him, her face calm and resolute. She looked really beautiful in that moment. Serene. The dark green of her suit looked almost jewel-like against the tan of her skin. It made him want to reach out and remove the pins from her hair until it fell loose around her shoulders. He liked it better that way.

"Yes," she said. "It's the right answer for everyone."

Liam was elated by her response yet confused about what had changed. There had been a moment when he had been absolutely certain she was going to tell him no. He'd already been mentally putting together a contingency plan. He was going to offer her obscene amounts of cash. And if that didn't work, he was going to find out if Jessica, his secretary, was married. "What helped you decide?"

"The ladybug. They're an omen of good luck. Having one land on you means you are a blessed soul. It was a sign that I should accept your proposal."

Liam knew better than to question her superstitions as long as they ruled in his favor. "Well, remind me to thank the next ladybug I come across."

Francesca chuckled. "I think you owe the entomology department at Georgetown a nice check."

"And I will get right on that. After I take my fiancée to lunch and let her pick out her engagement ring."

Her head snapped up to look at him. "So soon?"

"Yes," he insisted. "The sooner my aunt hears about this, the better. That means ring shopping, an announcement in the paper here and in New York and public sightings of the happy new couple. I intend to update my relationship status on Facebook before the day is out."

Her eyes widened with every item on his list. She wasn't sold on this arrangement, ladybug or no. "Before it hits the papers, I need to make a few calls. I don't want my family to find out from someone else. This is going to come out of the blue."

Liam nodded. That was understandable. He had a few calls of his own to make. First, to his mother and younger sister, both living in Manhattan.

His family was miserable at keeping in touch, but this was big enough news to reach out to them. They had always been like ships passing in the night, waving to one another as they went along their merry way. His parents were very outgoing and traveled quite a bit his whole life. But that changed after his father died three years ago when his car hit black ice on the highway coming home from a late business meeting. Since then, his mother had kept to her place in Manhattan, nearly becoming a recluse. He just assumed she was bad about calling until she stopped altogether—then he knew something was really wrong. His sister had moved in with her to keep an eye on the situation, but it hadn't helped much.

When he spoke with them, it was because he was

the one to reach out. Maybe the news of the engagement would be exciting for her. He felt bad lying to his mother about something like that, but if it got her up and out of the apartment, he didn't care.

Liam had often wondered, even more so in the past week, how things would be different if his father hadn't been in that accident. Where would everyone be now? Perhaps Aunt Beatrice would've wanted to hand the family to him instead, and Liam wouldn't be in this mess.

That was a pointless fantasy, but it reminded him of his next call. Once he was done with his mother, he had to inform Aunt Beatrice of the "happy" news. He didn't have many people to tell, but he could see by the expression on Francesca's face that she had the opposite problem. She must have a large, close family. An out-of-the-blue engagement would send up a hue and cry of mass proportions.

"I know this is a big deal. And not at all what you were expecting when you walked in here today. But it's all going to work out." He moved closer to her and put his arms gently around her waist. She reluctantly eased into his embrace, placing her hands on his lapels and looking up into his eyes. "I promise."

The dark eyes watching him were not so certain. He needed to reassure her. To make her feel more at ease with their new situation and prove they were compatible enough to pull this off. He only knew of one way to comfort a woman. He slowly lowered his lips to hers, giving her time to pull away if she needed to. She didn't. She met his lips with her own, her body leaning into his.

The kiss wasn't like the one in the elevator. They had come together then in a passionate and desperate rush. Two people in a stressful situation looking for any way to deal with their nervous tension. This kiss was soft, gentle and reassuring. They were feeling their way around each other. Her lips were silky against his, the taste of her like cinnamon and coffee. She made a soft sound of pleasure that sent a warm heat running through his veins. It reminded him of the cries she'd made beneath him that first day. It beckoned him to explore further, but he didn't dare push this moment too far. At this point, she could change her mind and no one would know the difference.

He couldn't risk running her off. They both needed this fake engagement to work. And if it did, he would eventually have his chance to touch her again. The thought gave him the strength to pull away.

Francesca rocked back onto her heels, her cheeks flushed and her eyes a little misty. She took a deep breath to collect herself and took a full step back from him. "Well," she said with a nervous laugh, "that authenticity thing shouldn't be an issue."

Liam smiled. "Not at all. Are you hungry?"

She straightened her suit coat and shrugged. "A little."

"Okay. You're not starving, so let's go ring shopping first. Then if we run into anyone at lunch, we'll have it and can share the news like a happy couple would."

"I need to get my purse from my office before we leave. I'll meet you at…" Her voice trailed off.

"The elevator?" he said with a grin.

She blushed. "Yes, I'll meet you at the elevator."

They strolled out of Pampillonia Fine Jewelry two hours later and, frankly, Francesca was exhausted. Who knew jewelry shopping could be so tiring? She almost wished that Liam had just popped the question with ring in hand like most men would and saved her the trouble of choosing.

Instead, they had spent the past couple of hours quibbling. She was worried that Liam was spending too much, especially considering it was a fake engagement. Liam insisted that Francesca needed to choose a ring large enough for people to see from a distance. Fake or not, the engagement needed to be splashy so people like his aunt would take notice.

They finally came to a compromise when she got tired of arguing and just let herself choose the ring she'd want if this were a real relationship and she had to wear the ring every day for the rest of her life. By the time they left, she was certain there was no doubt in the jeweler's mind that they were a real couple getting a head start on a lifetime of fussing at one another.

When it was all over, Francesca was the proud owner of a two-carat emerald-cut diamond solitaire framed with micro-pavé set diamonds in a platinum split band with diamond scrollwork. It was a stunning ring, and as they walked to the restaurant where they had lunch reservations, she almost couldn't believe it was on her hand. The weight of it pulling on her finger kept prompting her to lift her hand to look at it.

Francesca had dreamed her whole life of the day a man would give her a ring like this. The ring was right. But everything else was so wrong. Her life had taken a truly surreal turn since she had woken up this morning.

"Are you hungry now?" he asked as they approached the bistro with outdoor seating. It was perfect for an early May lunch; luckily, the Manhattan heat wave had not affected the D.C. area. It was pleasant and sunny in the high seventies with a breeze.

She still wasn't really hungry. Her stomach hadn't come to terms with the day's events. But she needed to eat or her blood sugar would get low and she'd spend the afternoon eating cookies out of the network vending machines. "I could eat. I think."

They followed the hostess, who took them to a shaded table for two on the patio. As nice as it was outside, she'd secretly hoped to get a table indoors. The street was so busy with foot traffic that she was certain to see someone she knew. Of course, she could just as easily run into someone inside. Between her and Liam, they knew a lot of people in this town. Francesca wasn't sure she was ready to play the gushing new fiancée for them yet.

Liam pulled her chair out for her and saw that she was comfortably seated before taking his own seat.

"I'm starving," he said, picking up the menu.

Francesca had to admit she wasn't surprised. Liam seemed to be constantly hungry when she was around him. "No breakfast?"

He shook his head. "I really haven't eaten much since I had dinner at my aunt's house. Killed my appetite, you know?"

"I do," she agreed. Nothing on the menu looked appealing, so she settled on a spinach salad with chicken. At the very least she was eating something figure-friendly.

She had a wedding dress to fit into, after all.

The thought crept into her brain, startling her upright in her seat. Where had that come from?

"Are you okay?" Liam asked.

"Yes," she said dismissively. "I just remembered something I need to do when we get back to the office."

Liam nodded and looked back at the menu. Francesca shook her head and closed her eyes. There would be no wedding and no wedding dress. It didn't matter how real their kisses seemed or how quickly her whole body responded to Liam's touch. It didn't matter that she had a luxury condo's worth of diamonds on her hand. Because she wasn't really engaged. She was Liam's fake fiancée. It was a business arrangement, nothing more, despite what she had to tell her friends and family.

The waiter took their orders and left with their menus. Feeling awkward, Francesca sipped her water and eyeballed her ring. She didn't know what to say to her new fiancé.

"Now that all the engagement stuff is arranged, I wanted to talk to you about something else, too."

She looked up at him with a sense of dread pooling in her stomach. She couldn't take any more surprises today. "No, Liam, I will not have your baby to make your aunt happy."

He laughed, shaking his head. "No babies, I promise. This is strictly work-related. I've been kicking around this idea for a few days, but the nonsense with my aunt sidetracked me. I wanted to ask…you're friends with Ariella Winthrop, aren't you?"

Francesca sighed. Her friend Ariella had been the media equivalent of the Holy Grail since the inaugural ball in January where it was revealed that the successful events planner was the newly elected president's long-lost daughter. How many journalists and garden-variety busybodies had asked Francesca about her friend since the scandal hit? More than she could count. Yes, they were friends. They had been for several years. That didn't mean she had anything useful to share with the press, even if she would tell—and she wouldn't. Ariella was adopted. She hadn't even known who her birth father was for sure until the DNA test results came back a little more than a month ago.

"I am," she said, her tone cautious.

"I was wondering if you could talk to her for me. I've got an idea that I think she might be interested in, but I wanted to run it by you first. I know ANS reporters and old management were responsible for the whole mess with President Morrow and her. I was hoping we could make a sort of goodwill gesture to them both."

"A fruit basket?" she suggested.

"A televised reunion show with Ariella and the president."

Francesca groaned aloud. That was a horrible idea. "Go with the fruit basket. Really."

Liam held up his hand. "Hear me out. I know lots of rumors and misinformation are swirling around on the other networks, especially because everyone involved isn't talking to the press. ANS obviously has stayed out of the story after everything that happened. I want to offer them the opportunity to publically set the record straight. Give them a chance to meet and clear the air without any spin or dramatic angles."

"That has 'exploitive' written all over it."

"And that is why I would give you total control over the show. You're her friend and she trusts you. You could work directly with the White House press secretary and see to it that no one is even remotely uncomfortable. No other network will offer them an opportunity like this, I guarantee it."

Francesca couldn't hold back her frown. She didn't like the sound of this at all. If it went badly and ANS ended up with mud on its face, there would be no coming back from it and Ariella might never forgive her. "I don't know, Liam."

"This is a win-win for everyone involved. Ariella and the president get to tell their story, their way. ANS will get the exclusive on their interview and it will help us make amends for the hacking scandal. It can't go wrong. You'll see to it that it doesn't turn into a circus. It's perfect."

Perfect for ratings. But Francesca wasn't so sure television was the right environment for her friend to be reunited with her famous birth father. That was an important moment for them both. A private moment. Ariella hadn't spoken much to her about the situation, but Francesca knew it was hard for her friend.

"Just promise me you'll ask her. If she doesn't want to do it, I'll let the whole idea drop."

The waiter came with their lunches, placing them on the table and briefly interrupting their conversation.

"I'll talk to her," Francesca agreed after he left. "But I can't promise anything. She made one short statement to the press, but aside from that, she's turned down every interview request she's received."

"That's all I ask. Thank you."

Francesca speared a piece of chicken and spinach with her fork. "At last, the dirty truth comes out. You're just marrying me for my political connections."

"A completely unfounded accusation," he said with a wicked grin. "I'm marrying you for that slammin' body."

Francesca met his gaze, expecting to see the light of humor there, but instead she found a heat of appreciation for what he saw. It was the same way he'd looked at her in that elevator when she'd had only a camisole to cover her. Today, she was deliberately covered head to toe, but it didn't matter. Liam apparently had an excellent memory.

A warmth washed over her, making her squirm uncomfortably in her seat with her own memories of that day. She had wanted him so badly in that moment, and if she was honest with herself, she still did. Things were just so complicated. Would giving into her desire for him be better or worse now that they were "engaged"?

She wished she hadn't opted for the silk scarf around her neck. It was strangling her now. Her left hand flew to her throat and started nervously tugging at the fabric. "I…well, I uh…"

A voice called to them from the sidewalk, interrupting her incoherent response. "Francesca, what is that I see on your hand?"

So much for not running into anyone she knew. On the other side of the wrought-iron railing that separated the bistro seating from the sidewalk was her friend Scarlet Anders. The willowy redhead owned a party planning company with Ariella that specialized in weddings and receptions. She could smell a new diamond from a mile away.

"Scarlet!" she said, pasting a smile on her face and hoping Scarlet didn't see through it. "How are you feeling?" she asked to distract her from the ring. Her friend had suffered a head injury earlier in the year and had temporarily lost her memory. It was a reasonable question that might buy Francesca a few minutes to get their engagement story straight.

Scarlet wrinkled her nose. "I'm fine, really. The doc-

ANDREA LAURENCE 61

tors say there's not a single, lingering side effect from my accident. Now stop fussing over me, you staller, and let me see that hand."

Reluctantly, Francesca held out her left hand, letting the flawless diamond sparkle in the sunlight. Scarlet looked at the ring, then at Liam and back at her. "You are engaged to Liam Crowe. *Liam Crowe.* You know, when Daniel proposed to me, I told you and Ariella almost the moment it happened."

That was true, Francesca thought guiltily. And under any other circumstances, she would've done the same thing. This just didn't feel like a real engagement. Because it wasn't. "It just happened," she insisted, grinning widely with feigned excitement at her groom to be. "We just picked out the ring before lunch."

Scarlet smiled. "It's beautiful. You two are so sneaky. I didn't even know you guys were dating. How did this happen?"

"We, uh…" Francesca realized she had no clue what to say. They hadn't really gotten around to deciding what they're relationship history was. Certainly the truth wouldn't do, or people would think they were crazy. "Actually, um…"

"We started seeing each other a while back when I first started looking to buy ANS," Liam interjected. "With everything going on, we wanted to keep it quiet for a while. But after being trapped in that elevator with Francesca, I knew I had to spend the rest of my life with her."

Francesca swallowed her snort of contempt as Scarlet sighed with romantic glee. "That is so sweet. I can't believe you didn't tell *me,* of all people, but you two are just adorable together. So when is your engagement party? You have to let Ariella and I do it for you."

"No," Francesca insisted. "You've been so busy with Cara and Max's wedding and now, planning your own big day." The former newscaster and the public relations specialist for the White House press secretary had married at the end of March. Scarlet's beau, Daniel, had proposed to her at the wedding reception. "Don't worry about us. We're probably not going to—"

"Nonsense," Scarlet said. "I insist. I'm on my way back to the office right now. I'll tell Ariella the good news and we'll get right to work on it. When would you like to have it?"

"Soon," Liam interjected, cutting off another of Francesca's protests. "This weekend, if at all possible. We can't wait to share our excitement with all our friends and family."

Scarlet's eyes widened, but she quickly recovered with a pert nod. She was used to dealing with the unreasonable demands of powerful D.C. couples. "I'm sure we can make that happen. Short notice makes it harder to find a venue, but I've got a couple of people who owe me some favors. For you, I'm thinking an afternoon garden party. Something outdoors. Light nibbles, champagne punch. Maybe a gelato bar. How does that sound?"

Francesca choked down a sip of her water. "That sounds beautiful." And it did. It was just what she would've chosen for her engagement party. Her friend knew her well. She just wished they weren't wasting their efforts on an engagement that wouldn't lead to a loving marriage.

Scarlet was bursting with excitement. Francesca could see the lists being made in her head. Flowers, caterers, maybe even a string quartet to serenade the guests. Scarlet did everything with a stylish flair that was famous in elite D.C. society. "I will give you a call tomorrow and work out some details."

"Just tell me where to send the check." Liam smiled.

"Absolutely," Scarlet said. "Talk to you soon." She swung her bag over her shoulder and disappeared down the sidewalk with an excited pep in her step. She really did live for this stuff.

Francesca wished she could work up as much enthusiasm. And she needed to if they were going to pull this off. Because this was really happening. Really, *really* happening.

What on earth had she done?

Five

Liam hadn't planned on their having dinner that night, but seeing Francesca with Scarlet had made it absolutely necessary. They really knew nothing about each other. They had no relationship backstory. Once the news of their engagement got out, people would start asking questions and they needed to get their stories straight.

Usually this kind of discussion happened before the engagement, but they were working on a steep learning curve, here. After the waiter took their orders, Liam settled back into his seat and looked at his fiancée. He knew she was beautiful, feisty, caring and exciting. He knew that he desired her more than any other woman he'd ever known. And yet, he knew almost nothing about who she was and where she'd come from. That was a problem.

"So, Francesca, tell me all about yourself. I need to know everything to play this part properly and convince everyone we're really together."

"I feel like I'm trying to get a green card or something." She took a sip of wine as she tried to determine where best to start. "I grew up in Beverly Hills. My father is a Hollywood movie producer, as you know. He met my mother on a film set in Sicily and they eloped within a month of meeting."

"So they have no room to complain about our quick engagement?"

"Not at all." She smiled. "Although that didn't stop my father from giving me an earful on the phone this afternoon. I had to assure him that we would have an extended engagement to keep him from hopping a jet over here and having a chat with you."

"The longest engagement in history," Liam quipped.

"My parents are my model for what a marriage should be. It's what I've always hoped to have one day when I get married."

Liam took note. Francesca wanted the real deal for herself, just like her parents. This was probably not what she thought her engagement would be like. He felt bad about that. But she still had her chance to have the fairy tale with the next guy. This was just a temporary arrangement.

"I have a younger sister, Therése," she continued, "who lives in San Francisco. She's a fashion photographer. I moved to D.C. after graduation to go to Georgetown."

"I went to Georgetown, too. Maybe we were there at the same time." Francesca recited the years and, thankfully, they partially overlapped with his own. He'd graduated two years before she had. "That's excellent," he said. "I think if we tell people that we dated back in college and then met up again this year, it will make the speed of this relationship more palatable. What did you study?"

"I got a degree in communications with a minor in political science. I'd originally intended to become a political news commentator."

"It's a shame you didn't. I would've loved to have you on my big screen every night. It's funny we didn't meet until now. I had a minor in communications. I'm surprised we didn't have a class together."

Francesca shrugged. "Maybe we did. A lot of those classes were pretty large."

Liam shook his head. There was no way he could've been in the same room with Francesca and not have seen her. Even in one of those freshman courses they held in the huge auditoriums. His cocky, frat boy self would've picked up on those curves and asked her out in a heartbeat. "I would've noticed you. I'm certain of that."

Francesca blushed and started fidgeting with the gold pendant around her neck that looked like some kind of horn. For dinner, she'd changed into a burgundy wrap dress with a low V-cut neckline and an abundance of cleavage. He'd noticed the necklace earlier, but every time he thought to ask about it, he'd been mentally sidetracked by the sight of her breasts.

"So what's that necklace about? You seem to have it on whenever I've seen you."

She looked down at it before holding it out a little for him to see it better. "It's a *corno portafortuna*. My *nonna* gave it to me. It's Italian tradition to wear one to ward off the evil eye. You never know when someone might curse you, especially in this town. I wear it for good luck."

The way the horn rested right in the valley of her

breasts was certainly lucky for him. It gave him an excuse to look at the firm globes of flesh he could still feel in his hands and pretend he was admiring her jewelry. "In the elevator you mentioned spending summers in Italy with your grandmother."

"Yes, I spent every summer in Sicily from when I was about five until I graduated from high school. My mother would travel with me when I was younger, but once I reached junior high, I got to fly alone. My mother said it was important for me to keep in touch with my culture. My *nonna* would teach me authentic Italian recipes and tell me stories about our family. My sister and I both learned a good bit of Italian over the years. I don't remember as much as I should now."

"You know all the dirty words," Liam noted.

"Of course." She laughed. "You always remember the words and phrases that you shouldn't know."

"You picked up all your superstitions there too?"

"Yes. Italians are a very superstitious people. My *nonna* told me she only taught me a few of them. It's amazing. My mother never really cared for all that, but it was something special I shared with *Nonna.* She died last year, but the superstitions keep her alive in my mind."

"Thank goodness she told you the one about ladybugs or I might be in big trouble right now. Any bad luck omens I should keep an eye out for?"

"Hmm…" Francesca said thoughtfully. "There are the ones most people know about—broken mirrors and such. Never leave your hat on the bed. Never set a loaf of bread upside down on the table. Birds or feathers in the home are bad luck. If you spill salt, you have to toss some over your shoulder. The most unlucky number is seventeen. Never marry on a Friday. There are a million of these."

"Wow," Liam said. "I'm probably doomed. I've been running around for years, cursed, and never knew it."

Francesca smiled, easing back in her seat to let the waiter place their food on the table. "I think you've done pretty well for yourself without it."

That was true. He'd taken the seed money from his father and built quite a name for himself in broadcast media. He was only twenty-eight. Who knew what else he could accomplish with most of his career still ahead of him? Closing the deal with his aunt and taking full control of ANS could be the launching pad to bigger, better things. Especially if the two-billion-dollar inheritance came through.

His brain couldn't even comprehend having that much money. He tried not to even think about it. He could only focus on one thing at a time and right now, it was pulling off this engagement and buying ANS outright. He'd put his financial manager on the task before he even sat down to look for a bride. Hopefully, it would all work out. But even his worries were hard to concentrate on with such a beautiful woman sitting across the table from him.

"How about some more random trivia about you? Likes and dislikes," Liam said.

"My favorite color is red. I adore dark chocolate. I'm allergic to cats. I can cook, but I don't. I hate carrots and yellow squash. My middle name is Irish and impossible to spell or pronounce properly."

Liam had to ask. "Wait, what is it?"

"My middle name? It's pronounced *kwee-vuh,* which is Gaelic for *beautiful.* Unfortunately, in English it's pronounced absolutely nothing like it's written. *C-A-O-I-M-H-E.*" She spelled out the name for him and then said it again. "Try explaining that to the woman at the DMV."

Liam laughed, not trusting himself to repeat the name without slaughtering it. "My middle name is Douglas. Not very exciting or hard to spell."

"I envy you."

"What about your dad's side of the family? You haven't mentioned much about them."

"My dad isn't that close with his family, which is silly considering they live in Malibu, only about thirty miles from Beverly Hills. I only ever saw my grandparents on holidays and birthdays. I'm much closer with my mother's side of the family."

"Sounds more like my family. I almost never see them. Tell me something else about you."

"What else? I never exercise—I hate to sweat. And I enjoy luxurious bubble baths and long walks on the beach." She finished with a laugh. "This is turning into a lame personal ad."

"It's not lame. If I ran across it, I'd be messaging your in-box in an instant."

"Thanks. But enough about me. What about you?" Francesca asked. "Your turn to tell me all about Liam Crowe."

Dinner had been very nice. The conversation flowed easily and Francesca had to admit she had a good time. She enjoyed spending time with Liam. Honestly, she liked him. He was handsome, smart, funny and easy to talk to. It was nice to hear him talk about his family and his work. He was so passionate about his career; it made her understand just how important the success of ANS was to him. A part of her wished she had met him in college. Who knows what would've happened then?

Well, that wasn't true. She knew what would've happened. They would've dated, she would've fallen for him and he would've broken it off at some point, breaking her heart. Liam wasn't much of a long-term guy. They were only engaged now because his aunt had recognized that in him and twisted his arm.

Despite that, he seemed to be taking the whole thing pretty well. She wasn't exactly sure how Liam felt about their forced proximity, but he didn't let it show if he wanted to be someplace else. Actually, he'd been quite complimentary of her, listening to her when she spoke and watching her over his wineglass with appreciative eyes.

Liam pulled up his gray Lexus convertible outside her town house and killed the engine. He turned in his seat to face her, a shy smile curling his lips. He watched her collect her purse and sweater, not speaking but also not making a move to let her out of the car, either.

Their plotting dinner suddenly felt like a date and it made her a little nervous. It was silly considering he'd not only seen her naked, but they were engaged. Technically.

"I had a good time tonight," she said, feeling stupid the moment the words left her lips.

"Me, too. I, uh, wanted to say thank-you again for doing this for me. And, you know, for the company. I feel like I've hijacked your entire life today."

Francesca tried to think about what she was supposed to have done today. She certainly had plans of some kind, but Liam had wiped her memory clean along with her calendar. "I'm sure I didn't have anything important planned and if I did, it will still be around for me to do tomorrow."

"Do you have time on your schedule to have some engagement portraits taken? I wanted a picture to put with the newspaper announcement."

"I think so. Just have Jessica look at my calendar in the morning. Do I need to wear anything in particular or do something special with my hair or makeup?"

Liam watched her, shaking his head. "You're perfect just as you are. I couldn't ask for a more beautiful fiancée."

Francesca blushed. She couldn't help it. To hear him talk, she was the most beautiful woman in the world. It was ridiculous. She was a pretty enough woman but nothing special. He had a knack for making her feel special, though. "You're just sucking up so I don't change my mind."

"Absolutely," he admitted. "But it's easy when it's true. You don't know how much I've thought about you since that afternoon we spent together. And now, spending all day with you, I've been struggling with myself. I've spent the past three hours trying not to kiss you. I'm not sure I can hold out much longer."

Francesca couldn't help the soft gasp of surprise when he spoke so honestly about his desire for her. Before she could think of something intelligent to say, he leaned across her seat and brought his lips to hers.

It wasn't their first kiss. Or even their second, but somehow it felt like it. It lacked the raw heat of their time in the elevator and the reassuring comfort of this morning's kiss. This one felt like the kiss of a blossoming romance. His hand went to the nape of her neck, pulling her closer to him and gently massaging her with his fingertips.

His mouth was demanding but not greedy, coaxing her to open to him and give in to the pleasure he promised. She felt herself being swept up in his touch. It was so easy, just like letting herself flow with the current of a river. It felt natural to let her tongue glide along his, to let her fingers roam through the thick strands of his wavy hair.

His lips left hers, traveling along the line of her jaw to nibble the side of her neck. The sensation of it sent a wave of desire through her whole body. When his hand cupped her breast through the thin microfiber of her dress, she leaned into his touch, moaning softly in his ear.

It wasn't until her eyes peeked open and she saw the giant diamond on her hand that she came to her senses. This relationship was supposed to be for show. One that appeared authentic to friends and family. But as Liam had said, no one would follow them into the bedroom. Somehow, Francesca knew that if she crossed that line, it would be hard for her to keep this relationship in perspective.

Liam was her fiancé, but he would never be her husband. He wasn't in love with her, nor was she in love with him. Sex would just blur the lines.

Francesca gently pushed at Liam's shoulders. He pulled away, watching her with eyes hooded with desire. His breath was ragged. That was one hell of a kiss. And it was begging for one hell of a night together. She could tell that he intended to come inside. A nice dinner, a bottle of wine, good conversation, a dynamic kiss... now she was supposed to invite him in for coffee and take off her dress. That was all too much too soon, no matter how badly she might want him.

Francesca reached for the door handle. "Good night, Liam."

"Wait," he said with a frown as he reached out to her. "Good night?"

She nodded, clutching her purse to her chest as a sub-par barrier between them. "It's been a long day filled with a lot of excitement. You went from my boss to my fiancé just a few short hours ago. I think adding 'lover' to the list tonight is a bad idea."

Liam sighed but didn't try to argue with her. Instead, he opened his car door and came around to help her out. He escorted her to her doorstep.

Francesca paused, clutching her keys in her hand. Right or wrong, she couldn't help leaning into him and placing a quick but firm kiss on his lips.

"I'll see you tomorrow at the office."

"Yes, I'm engaged." Liam sat back in his office chair and looked at the newly framed photograph of Francesca and himself that sat on the corner of his desk. They'd had it taken for the newspaper announcement, and Liam couldn't help sending a copy to the Queen Bee herself. When the phone rang the next afternoon, he wasn't surprised.

"Congratulations to you both. I didn't expect you to move so quickly on my offer," she noted, her tone pointed. She obviously thought that Liam was trying to pull one over on her somehow. She missed nothing. "I did give you a year, not a week, to get engaged."

"Well," Liam began, "I told you I had been seeing someone. You helped me realize that I needed to move forward in my relationship. Francesca and I are perfect for each other—I was just hesitant to take that last step. Thank you for the encouragement." He hoped he'd managed to work out the bitterness from his voice after practicing this speech several times before her call.

"That is wonderful, Liam. The picture of the two of you is lovely. I've sent Henry to have it framed for the mantle. She's quite the striking young lady. Where did you meet her?"

She was fishing for details. Thank goodness they'd worked all this out at dinner. "We met the first time in college through mutual friends and dated for a while." He recalled their fabricated past, linking it together with what he'd told Scarlet at lunch. "When I started looking into buying ANS, we ran into each other at a media event. She works there doing community outreach programs and we started seeing each other again."

Liam had no doubt that his aunt was taking notes and would have someone look into the fact that they had both attended Georgetown at the same time. "What a lovely coincidence that you two would find each other again. It must be meant to be."

"I think so."

"I hope both of you will be very happy together. I can't wait to meet her. In fact, I'm coming to D.C. later this month to speak to Congress. I'd love for the three of us to have dinner and celebrate while I'm there."

Liam frowned at the phone, glad for the miles between them and the lagging technology of camera phones that prevented her from seeing his pinched expression. He'd never known his aunt to have any political involvement before beyond writing checks. If she was coming to D.C., it was to check on him. She didn't trust

Liam a bit and rightfully so. They would have to perfect their lovey-dovey act before she arrived. Frankly, Francesca had been miserable at it when they ran into Scarlet.

It wasn't just the details of their relationship that had tripped her up. Her smile of engaged bliss had looked a little pained. She'd lacked the excited glow. She had had to be asked to show the engagement ring, whereas any other woman would thrust it out at anyone that would look.

Despite her hesitation to embark on a physical relationship the other night after dinner, something had to be done. She needed some real romantic inspiration to draw on because she couldn't fake it. Liam was all too happy to provide it.

He may have told Francesca that he didn't choose her with the intention of seducing her, and that was true. If they did become lovers, it would simply be a pleasant bonus to a potentially unpleasant scenario.

Heaven knew, he wanted Francesca. Every time he closed his eyes he saw her in the elevator. Red panties. Flushed cheeks. Soft, passionate cries of pleasure echoing in the small space. Yes, he didn't need a romantic entanglement complicating this arrangement, but he'd be lying if he said he didn't want to pick up where they'd left off.

Sex wouldn't be a problem as long as they both knew that's all it was. Given the way Francesca had writhed beneath him and walked away like nothing happened, she knew how to play that game. He just had to coax her into taking another spin at the wheel.

Gripping the phone, Liam struggled to remember what his aunt had just said. The mere thought of Francesca's red panties had completely derailed his train of thought. *Dinner.* Aunt Beatrice was coming to town and wanted to have dinner. "Absolutely," he said. "Francesca is very excited to meet you."

"I'm sure she is. I hope you two have a lovely engagement party tonight. I'm going to let you go. I need to call Ron Wheeler and let him know I'm turning down his proposal. For now," she added, making it clear they weren't out of the woods quite yet.

"It was good to speak with you," he said between gritted teeth. "I'll see you soon."

Hanging up the phone, he spun in his chair to look back at the photo of Francesca and him. His aunt made him absolutely crazy, but if this scheme landed that voluptuous, feminine form back in his arms, he just might have to send the Queen Bee a thank-you card.

Six

Francesca was fastening on her last earring when the doorbell rang. Giving herself one final look in the mirror, she was pretty pleased with how her outfit turned out. She'd purchased something new for the engagement party—a pale turquoise dress that was strapless and hit just below the knee. Around the waist was a cream-colored sash with a fuchsia flower for a pop of color. It came with a crocheted cream shrug to keep her shoulders warm when the sun went down.

She'd opted to wear her hair half up, with the front pulled back into a stylish bump and the rest loose in long waves down her back. Wearing her hair back highlighted her face and the sparkling aquamarine jewelry she was wearing at her ears and throat. And, of course, she was wearing the most important piece of her ensemble—her engagement ring.

Satisfied, she went down the stairs to the front door.

She watched Liam waiting patiently through the peephole. He was looking very handsome in a light gray suit, ivory dress shirt and turquoise tie to coordinate with her outfit.

Even though he'd dropped her off the other night after dinner, he hadn't been inside her town house yet. They'd decided he should pick her up and get familiar with her home just in case someone asked questions.

So far, no one had, and it was likely no one would. None of their friends in D.C. were remotely suspicious about their quick engagement. Romance seemed to be in the air this spring. So many of her friends had gotten married or engaged, so they were on trend. It was only Liam's crafty aunt they had to please.

"Hello," she said as she opened the door and gestured for him to come inside. "Come on in. This is my place."

"Very nice," he said, strolling into the living room and admiring his surroundings.

Francesca had always liked her home. She'd bought the small, red-brick town house near the university while she was a student. It was only two bedrooms, but the floor plan was open and the walled courtyard off the living room was the perfect oasis from the world. When she'd first bought it, nearly every room in it was white. She'd painted each room a warm, inviting color and filled them with lush fabrics and comfortable fixtures. That was her biggest update over the years. She loved her place.

She led him into the two-story living room so he could see out into her little garden and to the nicely remodeled kitchen she rarely used. "It's not very big, but it suits me. I love the location—right across from the park."

"You've done a lot with the place," he said. "It looks comfortably lived in. Very much what I'd expect for you. My town house still looks like a showroom model. I never got around to hiring a decorator. Who did yours?"

"I did," Francesca said, her nose wrinkling. "I couldn't let someone else decorate my house. That's too personal."

Liam shrugged. "You've got the eye for it. Maybe while we're engaged, I'll let you decorate mine."

She turned away from him without answering and went in search of her clutch instead. She didn't like the sound of that at all. It wasn't as though she would be moving into his house one day. She didn't need to put her own personal stamp on his space or leave anything behind of her once all this was over. That made things seem more permanent than they were. But she wasn't going to make much of it. They had a long night to get through without her adding more worries to the pile.

"Are you ready?" she asked.

"Absolutely."

Liam followed her out and then escorted her to the curb, where his convertible was waiting for them. Once he merged into traffic, they didn't have far to go. Scarlet and Ariella had secured a location at one of the large historical mansions in Georgetown. The two-hundred-year-old estate had acres of gardens with fountains and an overabundance of spring flowers this time of year. It was the perfect location for a sunny, happy engagement party.

As they pulled onto the property, the valet opened the doors, pointed them to the garden entrance and took the car around back to park it with the others.

Standing on the lawn, facing her engagement celebration, Francesca was more nervous than she cared to admit. Her knees were nearly shaking. She'd done okay enduring the excited hugs and fielding questions from her friends and coworkers, one by one. But this was almost everyone she knew at one time. It made her wonder if she could pull this off. An engagement party. *Her* engagement party.

Liam sensed her hesitation and approached her. Putting his hands on the back of her upper arms, he stroked her gently, reassuringly. "Everything will be fine. You look beautiful. I'm sure Scarlet and Ariella did a great job with all the arrangements. There's no need to be nervous."

"I know," she said with a shake of her head. She looked down toward the grass, but Liam's finger caught her chin and turned her face up to him.

"You can do this. I know it. But I have to say you are missing something."

Her eyes widened in panic. What had she forgotten? Ring? Check. Lipstick? Check. Overwhelming sense of paranoia? Check. "What did I forget?"

"You don't have the rosy blush of a young woman in love. But I do believe I can fix that." Liam leaned in and pressed his lips to hers.

As much as she had tried to deny her attraction to Liam, her body always gave her away. The heat of his touch immediately moved through her veins and she could feel the tingling of the kiss from the top of her head to the tips of her toes. She suddenly felt flush under her dainty sweater. Her knees were still shaking, although for different reasons than before. She gripped at his lapels to keep steady and pull him closer to her.

Liam's kisses were dangerous. She should've learned

that the very first day. A girl could get lost in one if she wasn't careful. And right now, it seemed like the perfect escape from everything else. Couldn't they just stay in each other's arms here on the front lawn? That seemed like the kind of thing a new couple might do, right?

When Liam finally pulled away, he held her close to keep her from swaying. She felt a definite heat in her cheeks as she looked up at him. "No lipstick on you this time," she noted.

"I was being more cautious today. But it worked—you officially have the bridal glow. Let's get in there before it wears off."

He looped her arm through his and escorted her down the stone pathway that led into the garden reception.

At first the party was a blur. There were easily a hundred and fifty people there, which was impressive on such short notice. Someone announced their arrival, and a rush of people came over to hug and congratulate them. There were pictures and toasts to the happy new couple. Francesca worried it would be hard to keep up the act, but after a little practice and a little champagne, showing people her ring and gushing about how beautiful the party was became easier and easier.

It wasn't long before Francesca was able to slip away from Liam and the crowds to get herself a drink and admire her friends' party-planning handiwork. Scarlet and Ariella really did an excellent job. The garden itself was beautiful, but she could spot the touches they'd added, like white paper lanterns in the trees and a gauzy fabric and flower arch behind the string quartet. The layout of the food and seating areas generated the perfect traffic pattern through the space. It was those details that made what her friends did special. Hassle-free events were their forte.

She picked up a glass and filled it at the four-foot-high silver punch fountain. Just as the lifted the frothy pink drink to her lips, she heard a woman's voice from behind her.

"That's got champagne in it, you know."

Francesca turned to find Ariella with a silver tray of pastel petit fours in her hands. "Am I not allowed to have champagne at my own engagement party?"

Her friend smiled and passed the tray off to one of the catering staff. "That depends on why you and Liam Crowe are in such a rush to get married."

"I am not pregnant," Francesca said with a pout. She should've known that rumor would be one of the first to start circulating. They liked nothing better than juicy gossip in these circles and they weren't above making some up if it was in short supply. She swallowed the whole glass of punch just to prove the rumor wrong.

"Good." Ariella refilled Francesca's glass and filled one of her own, then gestured over to a few chairs under a wisteria tree dripping with purple flowers. "So, just between you and me, what's going on?" she asked once they were seated.

Francesca knew her friend would grill her, although not in the same way that Aunt Beatrice probably would. She just wanted the details so she could understand and be happy for her. Or concerned, depending on if she thought she was being stupid or hasty. That's what good girlfriends did. They kept your head on straight. "It all happened so quickly, I can hardly tell you. The moment I saw him, it was like the last few years we've been apart never happened. There were fireworks." That wasn't exactly a lie. It was more like armed missiles, but there were explosions nonetheless.

Ariella looked into her eyes, searching her face for a moment. Then, satisfied, she smiled and patted Francesca on the knee. "Then I'm happy for you. I just wish you had told us what was going on."

Francesca wished she could really tell her what was going on. She could use a sounding board, but Liam had been adamant that no one know about their arrangement. No one. That was tough for her, considering how close she was with her friends and family.

"Everyone has been so busy with their own lives. I just decided to keep things quiet until there was something to tell."

"How'd your dad take the news?" Ariella asked.

"Ah." She sighed, "you know Dad. He'll adjust eventually. He's concerned that we're rushing things, and that he had no idea who my groom even was. I had to remind him that he and my mother met and eloped within a month. He didn't want to hear that."

Ariella smiled. "I imagine not."

Hoping to shift the subject, Francesca decided to use the topic of fathers to fulfill her first obligation to Liam. "Can I talk to you about something?"

"Sure," Ariella said. "Anything."

Francesca nodded. "Okay. Now I want you to tell me 'no' the moment you're uncomfortable with the idea, but I told Liam I would ask. Now is as good a time as any."

"He wants an interview?" she said wearily. Francesca could tell the last few months were really wearing on her friend.

"Not exactly. He wants to offer you and President Morrow the opportunity to meet and get your story out there. A televised reunion show. No spin, no intruding interview questions. Just you and your father, however you want to do it. Liam has even said he'd put me in charge of the show to make sure you'd be comfortable with it. I told him that I thought it was—"

"Okay."

Francesca's head shot up and she stared at Ariella. Surely she'd heard that wrong. "What?"

She shrugged. "I said okay. If the president is okay with doing the show, I think it's a great idea. We've gone too long without saying anything publicly, and I think it's starting to hurt both of us in the court of public opinion. Neither of us has done anything wrong, but the silence makes us look like we have something to hide."

"But do you think television is the right place for you to be reunited with your birth father? Won't that be hard for you?"

"Not any harder than anything else that's happened this year. Frankly, I'd be relieved to clear the air so the news networks can find some other story to sniff out. Tell Liam I'm in."

Francesca took another large sip of her champagne punch and sighed. Everyone had lost their minds—she was certain of it. "Okay, great," she said, feigning enthusiasm. "I'll let Liam know."

Liam had to admit that it was an excellent engagement party. One of the better ones he'd been forced to attend over the years. He was exhausted and well-fed, as he should be. If and when he did get married, he intended to keep D.C. Affairs Event Planners in his address book.

It was dusk now. The party was winding down, with

guests making their way out amid glowing paper lanterns and white twinkle lights.

He'd lost track of Francesca a little while earlier as he started talking politics with a few other men. Now, he picked up his champagne glass and went in search of his elusive fiancée. That sounded so odd to say, even just in his head.

He found her sitting alone at a table near one of the cherub fountains.

"Hey, there," he said as he approached. "Thought you'd run off on me."

Francesca smiled wearily and slipped off one of her heels. "I'm not running anywhere right now."

"Are you ready to go?"

"Yes. I think the party is over. And was successful, I might add. I got several people to agree to buying tickets to the Youth in Crisis gala next week."

"You're not supposed to recruit at our engagement party."

She shrugged. "Why not? It's what I do, just like you talk politics all the time with folks." She slipped her shoe back on and stood gingerly. *"Ahi, i miei piedi."*

Liam watched her hobble a few steps and decided the walk to the car would be too far for her. "Stop," he insisted, coming alongside her and sweeping her up into his arms.

"Oh!" she hollered in surprise, causing a few people left at the party to turn and look their way. They immediately smiled at his romantic gesture and waved good-night to them.

Francesca clung to his neck, but not with a death grip. "You didn't have to do this," she said as he walked the path to the front of the house.

"I don't have to do a lot of things, but I do them because I want to. Gray Lexus convertible," he said to the valet, who immediately disappeared to the car lot.

"I think I can manage from here."

"What if I'm doing this for selfish reasons? What if I just like holding you this way?" he asked. And he did. He liked the way she clung to him. The way her rose perfume tickled his nose and reminded him of their time together in the elevator. His body tightened in response to the press of her breasts against his chest and the silk of her bare legs in his arms. He didn't want to put her down until he could lay her on a plush mattress and make love to her the way he'd wanted to for days.

Francesca's only response was a sharp intake of breath as she turned to look into his eyes. She watched his face with intensity, reading his body's reactions through his expression. He saw an acknowledgment in her eyes—something that told him she was feeling the same way. She opened her mouth to say something when the car pulled up beside them.

Liam wanted to know what she was about to say, but instead, she turned away and struggled in his arms. He reluctantly set her down in the grass and went around to his side of the car and got in. The moment had passed and whatever she had to say was left unspoken.

It wasn't until the car pulled up outside her town house that they spoke again. And when they did, it was all at once in a jumble of words.

"Would you like to come in?"

"I had a great time today."

"So did I."

"Yes."

Francesca smiled at the way they'd talked over each

other. "Now that we have that all cleared up, come in and I'll make us some coffee."

Liam was thrilled to get an invitation inside tonight. He got out and opened her door, following her up the brick stairs to her entranceway. He laid a gentle hand at the small of her back as she unlocked the dead bolt and he felt her shiver beneath it, despite the warm evening. She couldn't help responding to his touch, he noted. If he had anything to say about it, they wouldn't worry too much about coffee until the morning.

They went inside and he followed her to the kitchen, where she dropped her purse on the counter and slipped out of her heels. "So much better," she said with a smile. "Now, coffee." Francesca turned to the cabinets and started pulling out what she needed to brew a pot.

While she scooped beans into the machine, Liam slipped off his coat, draped it on one of the bar stools and came up behind her. He wrapped his arms around her waist and pressed the full length of his body against her. He swept her hair over one shoulder and placed a warm kiss on the bare skin of her neck.

The metallic coffee scoop dropped to the counter with a clank as Francesca reached out to brace herself with both hands. "You don't want coffee?" she asked, her voice breathy as his mouth continued to move across her skin. She pressed into him, molding her body against his.

Liam slipped her sweater down her shoulders. "Coffee would keep me awake. I think I'd like to go to bed." He pushed the firm heat of his arousal against her back and let his hands roam over the soft fabric of her dress. "What about you?" he asked. He knew Francesca had been in a war between her body and her mind since they met. She'd practically run from him the other night, yet when he kissed her, he could tell she wanted more.

But tonight, this step had to be her decision. Playing the happy couple would be much easier the next few weeks if he wasn't battling an erection whenever they were together. Sex wasn't required in their arrangement, but damn, being engaged was a really great excuse to indulge.

"No," she said.

Her words caused Liam's hands to freeze in place. *Had she just said no?* Damn. He must've been reading her wrong. Did she really only invite him in for coffee? Maybe she was a better actress than he thought.

Before he could pull away, Francesca turned in his arms to face him and wrapped her arms around his neck. She looked up at him with her large dark eyes, a sly smirk curling her pink lips. "I don't want to go to bed," she explained. "I want you right here."

Liam was all too happy to grant her wish. With a slide of his arm, he knocked her bag to the floor and cleared the countertop bar. He encircled her waist with his hands and lifted her up to sit at the rounded edge of the granite slab. His hands slid up the smooth length of her legs, pushing the hem of her turquoise dress high enough to spread her thighs and allow him to settle between them.

"How's this?" he asked, gripping her rear end and tugging her tight to him.

Francesca smiled and wrapped her legs around his waist. *"Perfetto."*

She leaned in to kiss him, and the floodgates opened. The moment their lips met, everything they'd held back for the past week came rushing forward. Their hands moved frantically over each other, pulling at zippers and buttons until they uncovered skin. Their tongues glided along one another, tasting, tempting and drinking it all in.

Liam couldn't get enough of her. The feel of her skin, the soft groans against his mouth as he touched her. He tried to be gentle as he unzipped her dress and pushed the hem up to her waist, but his patience was coming to its end. Especially when Francesca pulled the dress up over her head and he caught a glimpse of the hot pink lace panties and strapless bra she was wearing.

He took a step back to appreciate the view of her body and give himself a moment to recover. As badly as he wanted her, he wasn't going to rush this. Francesca delicately arched her back, reaching behind her to unfasten the bra and toss it aside. The sight of her full, round breasts was his undoing. His palms ached to cover them.

"Touch me," Francesca whispered, noting his hesitation. "I want you to."

"Are you sure? The other night..."

"That was then. Now I'm ready and I don't want to wait any longer."

He was ready too, but first things first. With his eyes focused on hers, he slipped off his unknotted tie and shrugged out of his shirt. The belt, pants and everything else followed until the only stitch of clothing on the two of them were those pink panties. Stepping back between her thighs, he put a condom on the counter and let his hands glide up her outer thighs to her lace-covered hip. "Are these your favorite pair?" he asked.

Francesca shook her head. He was glad. He was at the point of not caring if they were. He'd order ten pair to replace them tomorrow. His fingers grasped the fabric and gave it a hard tug. There was a loud rip, and the panties gave way as scraps in his hands.

At last. Her beautiful nude body was on full display in front of him. This time there was no power restoration to interrupt them, no reason for them to hold back.

Liam placed one forearm across the small of her back and used the other to press down on her chest until she was lying across the breakfast bar. He leaned over her and his lips joined both hands as they made their way over her breasts and down her stomach. His mouth left a searing trail down her belly, pausing at her hip bone as one hand sought out the moist heat between her thighs.

Francesca gasped and squirmed against him. Her back arched off the counter, her hands clawing futilely at the cold stone beneath her. She was ready for him, and as much as he wanted to take his time, he had to have her now. They had all night to savor one another.

Slipping on the condom, Liam gripped her hips and entered her in one, quick movement. Sinking into her hot, welcoming body was a pleasure he'd rarely experienced before. A bolt of sensation, like lightning, shot down his spine and exploded down his arms and legs, making his fingertips tingle where he touched her. He gritted his teeth, balancing on the edge of control as he eased out, then buried deep inside her again.

Francesca pushed herself up, wrapping her legs around his waist and her arms around his neck. Pressing her bare breasts against his chest, she whispered, "Take me," into his ear, flicking the lobe with her tongue.

Gripping at her back and pulling her so close to the edge she might fall without his hold, he did as he was told. He filled her again and again, losing himself in her until she cried out with pleasure and his legs began to shake. It was only then that he let go. Moving quickly, he gave in to the sensation of her body wrapped around his own and flowed into her with a deep growl of long-awaited satisfaction.

Seven

Francesca rolled over and snuggled into her blanket, opening her eyes only when a weight kept the covers from moving the way she wanted. The sunlight was streaming in through her bedroom window, illuminating the wide, bare back of Liam beside her.

What had she done?

She'd had a night of fantastic, passionate sex with her fake fiancé—that's what she'd done. Giving up on the blanket, she moved slowly onto her back, hoping not to wake him. She wasn't quite ready to face the morning after with the man she wasn't going to marry.

She glanced under the sheet at her nude body and cursed that she didn't think to slip into *something* once it was over. Bringing her hand up to her head, she swallowed a groan. This situation was complicated enough. Feigning an engagement wasn't for the faint of heart. Had she really added sex to the mix? On her kitchen counter, of all places? It was a good thing she didn't cook.

Now things were going to go from complicated to downright tricky. Liam was her boss. Her pretend fiancé. She had no business sleeping with either, much less both. And yet she was undeniably attracted to him. She couldn't help it.

He was handsome, wealthy, powerful…. He had a wicked sense of humor and a boyish smile that made her heart melt a little when he looked at her. And most important, he cared about his employees. They'd gotten off on the wrong foot over the budget, but that issue aside, she respected him for what he was doing. She respected him even more for the lengths he was willing to go to protect the network.

Liam was just the kind of man she could fall for—and hard. The only problem was that he wasn't the kind of man that would feel the same about her.

Francesca took relationships seriously. She wasn't one for flings, despite losing her sense in the elevator, and she certainly didn't make a habit of sleeping with men when she didn't see any relationship potential.

She wanted a marriage like her parents had. Victor and Donatella Orr had been married thirty years. When she was growing up, they'd set a good example of what a relationship should be. They argued, but they compromised and never held grudges. They were affectionate and understanding. They allowed each other their space, yet were always certain to spend quality time together as a family and as a couple.

At twenty-seven, Francesca had yet to run across a man she could have that kind of relationship with. Some were too clingy; others were too self-absorbed. Some were quick-tempered or arrogant. Then there were the kind like Liam—work-focused dreamers who looked at marriage as something they'd do later. They indulged in a variety of women, never taking anything but their jobs seriously. They were the kind of men who would wake up at fifty and realize they had missed out on their chance for a family unless they could find a willing younger woman with a fondness for expensive gifts.

Despite being engaged to Liam, he was the last man on Earth she would marry. And that's why she knew sleeping with him was a mistake. As a passionate woman, she put her heart in everything she did. But she couldn't put her heart into this. She couldn't look at her engagement ring and their portrait together and imagine it was anything more than a well-crafted fantasy.

Francesca turned to look at Liam as he grumbled in his sleep and rolled onto his back. The blankets fell across his torso, his hard, muscular chest exposed to the early-morning sunlight. She wanted to run her fingertip along the ridges of his muscles and bury her hands in the patch of dark hair across his chest. She wanted to reach under the covers and wake him up in the most pleasant way possible.

This sure didn't feel like a business arrangement.

Turning away, she spied her robe hanging on the knob of her closet door. Easing silently out of bed, she snatched the silk wrap off the handle and slid into it. She gave another glance to Liam, still sleeping, and slipped out of the room.

Downstairs, she found she could breathe a little easier. At least until she saw the scraps of her pink underwear on the kitchen floor. She snatched them off the tile and dumped them in the trash, and then went around gathering other bits of their clothing. She tossed the pile onto her sofa and went to the front door to pick up the paper. Laying it onto the kitchen table, she decided to make coffee. The caffeine would help her think so she could sort all this out.

The last few drops were falling into the pot when she heard Liam's shuffling footsteps across her hardwood floors. A moment later, he appeared in the kitchen wearing nothing but the suit pants she'd just gathered up.

"Morning," she said, pouring a cup for both of them.

"You snuck out on me," Liam complained, his voice still a touch low and rough with sleep. He ran his fingers through his messy hair and frowned at her with displeasure.

"I promised you coffee last night," she explained. "I had to come down here and make it so it was ready when you woke up." That sounded much better than saying she'd gotten weirded out and had to leave. "How do you take it?"

"One cream, one sugar," he said, sitting at the small round table in her breakfast nook. He unfolded the paper and started scanning the articles, oblivious to the nerves that had driven her to the kitchen.

Francesca busied herself making their coffee and grabbed a box of pastries from the counter. She set the two mugs and the carton on the table and plucked two napkins from the container in the center of the table. "Breakfast is served."

"Thank you," he said, looking up from the paper. "Our party made the society pages in the Sunday edition." Liam slid the section with their photo across the table to her. "I should clip it out and send it to the Queen Bee."

"I'm sure she hated missing it. My friends throw parties even she couldn't find fault with. Oh—" Francesca said, pausing to take a sip of her hot drink. That had reminded her of the important information she hadn't shared with Liam yet. "I forgot to tell you that Ariella said yes."

Liam looked up from the paper. "Ariella said yes to what?"

"I got a chance to talk to her at the party about the televised reunion show. I can't fathom why, but she's agreed to do it if the president is willing."

Liam's eyes grew wide, and he folded the paper back up as he grinned. "That's excellent. Wow. How could you forget to tell me something like that? We've been together since the party."

Francesca looked at him over her cup with an arched eyebrow. "Yes. We were together *all* night. And highly occupied, if you recall."

Liam grinned. "Indeed, we were. It's just as well because there was nothing I could do about it last night." He picked a pastry out of the box and set it on his napkin, sucking some icing from his thumb. "Well, now you'll need to contact the White House press secretary to see if President Morrow will participate."

"Me?"

"Yes. I told you that you would be in charge of the event. That means the ball is in your court."

"The Youth in Crisis gala is Saturday night. I've got my hands full with that."

"I have every confidence," he said with a meaningful gaze, "that you can handle everything I'm giving you and more. It's likely the ball won't really get rolling on the show until after the gala, and you just need to get White House buy-in. By the time everything is in place, the show will probably air in June."

Francesca could handle June. "I'll call over there Monday morning," she agreed. Part of her hoped the president and his staff would see what a bad idea this was. She knew it would mean good ratings, and maybe a boost in public opinion for ANS, but it felt wrong. If she had been adopted, she didn't think she'd want those first reunion moments captured for the world to see.

"Sounds great." Liam set aside the folded paper and reached his hand across the table to rest on hers. "Thank you for asking her. I know you felt uncomfortable about it."

"It's Ariella's decision to make, not mine. If she thinks it's the right choice, far be it for me to tell her no. It's her life."

"I think you'll do a great job running the show. I know it isn't something you've handled at the network before, but you'll do a bang-up job. Everything has been so crazy since I started at ANS, but I really believe that we can bring this network back. If all goes well, I'll get absolute control of the stock and we can end the fake engagement. The exclusive with the president and his daughter will earn us Brownie points and market share for our time slot. I know I can rebuild this network— with your help. So thank you for everything you've done so far."

"Don't thank me yet," she said, fidgeting with her coffee mug. A lot of pieces had to click together for these miracle scenarios to work out. And deep in her heart, Francesca worried that eventually, things would start to go awry.

* * *

Monday morning, Francesca breezed into Liam's office without Jessica's usual announcement. He looked up from his computer as she entered and a wide grin broke out across his face. He *should* be smiling after the weekend they'd spent together. "I see you're enjoying the new privileges of being the owner's bride-to-be."

"Exclusive access, anytime," she said with a grin.

Liam was glad to see her relaxed and happy. At first, he wasn't sure they could pull this off. Liam would never admit to that out loud; this had to work or he'd lose the network. And he knew Francesca had her own worries. She wore every emotion on her face. But after their time together this weekend, he was certain they both had sunnier outlooks on the arrangement. The lines of doubt were no longer wrinkling her brow, replaced with a contented smile that suited her much better.

Francesca set a to-go cup of coffee and a bag of Italian breakfast cookies in front of him. She was going to get him addicted to those things and he'd never be able to find them without her help.

"Grande drip with one cream, one sugar," she announced.

"Just how I like it," he said, turning in his chair to give her a hello kiss.

Francesca leaned into him but pulled away before his hands roamed too far. As much as it annoyed him to not be able to touch her when and where he wanted, he understood. Their relationship might be for the sake of the company, but public displays of affection at the office were a little much. She sat down in the guest chair with her own cup.

"Have you called the White House yet?" he asked.

"It's nine in the morning and I just handed you a hot, fresh coffee from the bakery. No. I haven't been to my office yet."

"Okay, sorry," he said, taking a sip. "You know I'm excited to move this plan forward."

"I know. I'll call once I get to my desk. Hopefully it won't take very long. I have a million things to wrap up this week before the gala on Saturday."

Liam nodded, but the details of the event didn't really interest him. The gala was really just a blip on his radar. And they were only doing it because she had agreed to be his fiancée. He couldn't have justified the expense given the state of the network. As it was, every mention of centerpieces and orchestras made dollar signs run through his mind.

"Now about the gala," she continued. "I've got most everything in place. Ticket sales have gone well and our sponsorship will see to it that it's the best year we've had yet. You'll need to make sure your tuxedo goes to the cleaners."

Liam made a note on his blotter so he wouldn't forget to ask Jessica about that later. "Check."

"And write a speech."

"What's that?" Liam looked up, his brow furrowed. He didn't like public speaking. As a matter of fact, he hated it. Avoided it at all costs and had since prep school debate class. Not even his aunt's declaration of mandatory matrimony made his stomach turn the way approaching a crowd of people with a microphone could do. There was a reason he preferred to be behind the camera instead of in front of it.

"As the major event sponsor, it's your job to give the

evening's welcome speech and encourage everyone to donate well and often."

"I don't remember Graham ever doing that." He tried to remember the times he'd gone. Maybe Graham did speak, but Liam was far too interested in his date for the evening to pay much attention. "Shouldn't that be the responsibility of the Youth in Crisis people?"

Francesca's red lips turned up with a touch of amusement. He must look like a damn deer in the headlights. "They do speak but not for long. Graham did it every year. And without bellyaching, I might add."

Liam grumbled under his breath and made another note to write a speech. This wasn't in their original agreement, but he could make concessions. Sleeping with him wasn't in their agreement either, but that had worked out splendidly. He would get something out of this. "Fine. I'll write a speech. But you'll have to go out to dinner with me tonight then."

"Why?"

Liam leaned across the desk, his most seductive gaze focused on her. "Because I'm going to ply you with sushi and expensive sake, and once you're drunk, I'm going to…talk you into letting me off the hook or writing the speech for me."

Francesca laughed. "I'm no speechwriter. But you do have several in your employ. I suggest you bribe them instead."

That wasn't a bad idea. Being a media mogul had its perks. If only he could get one of his news anchors to deliver the speech, too. He made another note on his blotter. "Does that mean you don't want to have sushi with me tonight?"

"I do. And I will. But first I have a president to cajole

and a charity ball to throw." She got up from her chair and leaned down to give him a goodbye kiss.

This time, because they were alone, Liam wasn't about to let her get away with just a peck. When she leaned down to him, he quickly reached for her and tugged her waist to him. She stumbled in her heels and fell into his lap. He clamped his arms around her so she couldn't get away.

Before she could complain, his lips found hers. He really enjoyed kissing her. He enjoyed kissing women in general, but there was something about Francesca's lips that beckoned him to return to them as soon as he could. Maybe it was the way she clung to him. Or the soft sighs and moans against his mouth. Maybe it was the taste of her—like a sweet, creamy sip of coffee. But he couldn't get enough of her.

Francesca indulged him for as long as she could, then pulled away. "I've got to get to work," she insisted, untangling herself from his arms. She straightened her skirt and rubbed her fingers along the edge of her lips to check for smeared lipstick.

"You look beautiful," he assured her. And she did. Dressed up, not dressed at all, perfectly styled or fresh from bed. He liked it all.

Liam wanted to tug her into his lap again and maybe make better use of his desk than he had since he'd moved into this office. But Francesca wouldn't hear of it—he could tell. As it was, that kiss guaranteed she would be on his mind all day. He probably wouldn't be able to focus on anything until after dinner, when he could get his hands on her again. But it had been worth it.

"You can flatter me all you want, but you're not getting out of this speech, Liam." She pulled away and sauntered out of his office, closing his door behind her.

Liam sat in his chair for a moment after she left. If he breathed deeply, the scent of her rose perfume still lingered in his office. Was there anything about this woman he didn't like?

He thought for a moment, then shook his head. Not yet. He'd been physically attracted to her the moment he laid eyes on her, but getting to know her had made the attraction that much stronger. She was beautiful. And smart. And thoughtful.

He picked up the coffee she'd brought him and took another sip. Her flaring temper could be a handful to deal with, but there were two sides to that passionate coin and he was certainly enjoying the other half at the moment.

The situation Aunt Beatrice had forced him into was unfortunate. But he couldn't regret asking Francesca to be his fiancée. Drawing her into this circus wasn't fair, but she was the right woman for the job. He couldn't imagine it going nearly as well with any of the women in his address book.

He liked being around Francesca. Working with her last week had been nice. Liam had gotten very comfortable having Francesca around, and that was saying a lot. He'd dated his share of women, never for more than a few months at a time. But he had boundaries. He very rarely had them over to his house and if he did, it wasn't overnight. They didn't meet any of his family or at least hadn't gotten to a point in the relationship where he thought it would be appropriate.

And he absolutely never brought them into his workplace. His romantic life and his work were two wires that never crossed. He usually didn't date at work, Francesca being a notable exception. He even tried to date outside the business. It took a bit of effort when you lived in D.C. not to date someone in media or politics—his usual circles—but he liked it that way. Usually.

Francesca was changing everything. This fake engagement was growing into something else with every passing moment. He didn't just want Francesca to come to his house; he also wanted her to help him decorate it. He liked starting his mornings chatting with her over coffee in his office or at her kitchen table. She may not have met his family yet, but if Aunt Beatrice had anything to say about it, she would—and soon. If the engagement went on for long, maybe he could convince his mother and sister to come to D.C. for a visit. He actually liked the idea of introducing them. He was certain his sister would really like Francesca.

All his rules were being broken. Stomped on with a red stiletto was more like it.

Normally, that would make Liam cringe. This woman he'd lassoed and pulled into his life was blurring all his boundaries. And he liked it.

A gentle rap at the door made him look up from their engagement photo. "Yes?"

Jessica came in, a couple of files stacked in her arms. "Good morning, sir."

"Good morning, Jessica."

She smiled as she approached his desk. "You're looking quite chipper this morning. Love looks good on you, sir. As does Ms. Orr's lipstick."

Liam grinned sheepishly and got up to look in the mirror over the minibar. He spotted a touch of reddish-pink lipstick, which he quickly wiped off. "Thanks, Jessica. She would've let me walk around like this all day, I bet."

"Of course. I've got those things you asked for this morning." Jessica set the stack of paperwork on his desk. "Last month's ratings numbers for the 5:00 to 7:00 p.m. weekday time slots, the budget breakout for the gala this weekend and the copy of *Italian for Idiots* you asked me to order came in from Amazon."

"Excellent. Thank you, Jessica. I've got a meeting with the CFO today, right?"

"At four."

Liam nodded. "Would you call and make reservations for Francesca and me at that nice sushi place in Dupont Circle? At six? I should be done with my meeting by then."

"I'll take care of it. Anything else?"

"That should do it for now."

When Jessica turned to leave, Liam thought of something. "Wait, one more thing. I'd like to send something to Francesca. An unexpected gift. Any suggestions?"

His secretary thought for a moment. "Well, for most men, I would suggest flowers or candy."

"Am I not most men?"

"Not at all, sir."

At least she was honest. "Then what would you recommend for the smaller minority of men?"

"Perhaps something for the gala this weekend? Do you know what dress she's wearing? Maybe something sparkly to go with it?"

Liam seemed to remember her saying something about that yesterday. That she had to go find a dress, but she didn't know when she would have the time. Perhaps he could help with that. Aunt Beatrice had the per-

sonal shoppers from Saks Fifth Avenue and Neiman
Marcus come to her when she was choosing an outfit
for an event. His aunt rarely left her mansion anymore.

"Check Ms. Orr's calendar for tomorrow afternoon
and move anything she has to another time. Then call
Neiman Marcus and have them send over a personal
shopper."

"They'll need her size, colors and any other preferences."

Liam wrote down a few things on a Post-it note and
handed it to her. "This is a fairly solid guess on her
size, although tell them to bring a few things larger and
smaller in case I'm wrong. I want the whole outfit, so
shoes too. She wears an eight." He'd seen the label on
her shoe as he'd carried her from the engagement party.

"Anything else, sir?"

"Yes. I want her to be the most stunning woman
there. She is gorgeous on her own, but I'd like her to
have a dress almost as beautiful as she is. And as such,
let them know there's no price limit."

Eight

Liam had wanted to escort Francesca to the gala, but she'd insisted she had to go early and that she would just meet him there. He anticipated that she would be running around for most of the evening. That meant loitering on his own. Normally that wouldn't bother him, but lately being separated from Francesca brought on an awkward tightness in his chest. The only thing that would cure it was holding her in his arms.

As he walked through the front doors of the hotel's grand ballroom, he was greeted by the sound of a ten-piece orchestra accompanied by the dull roar of several hundred people mingling. The light was dim, but his eyes quickly became accustomed to it. He searched around the room for Francesca, but he began to think it was a lost cause. She was a needle in a haystack.

Despite the fact that he'd paid for the outfit she had chosen for tonight, he had no idea what she would be wearing. She had been exceedingly pleased with the gift and had thanked him in several ways over the past week, but the only details she would share was that it was a Marchesa and "*molto bellisima.*"

Then the crowds parted near the bar and he saw her. There was no mistaking this needle in any size haystack. The personal shopper from the department store had certainly taken Liam's requests into consideration. Francesca was the most stunning woman in the room tonight. He didn't even have to look around to check. He knew it in his gut.

The gown was black and gray with a swirling design. It was off the shoulder and clung to each curve all the way to the knee, where it fanned out into a delicate cascade of black marabou feathers. Her breasts were tastefully showcased by the neckline of the gown, which was trimmed with more feathers—there wasn't so much showing as to make him jealous of other men looking at her, but it was enough to make *him* notice. Her hair was swept up, making her neck look impossibly long and ready for his kisses. Her only jewelry was a pair of sparkling diamond dangles at her ears and a bracelet on one wrist.

When she turned to speak to someone, he noticed the feathers continued into a short train that draped behind her. It was grand, elegant and extremely sexy. And the best part was that *his* fiancée was wearing it.

He'd tried not to think too much of her that way. It implied more than there was between them, but he felt a surge of territoriality rush through him when she started talking to another man. He had the urge to rush to her, kiss her senseless and stake his claim before anyone got any ideas.

Then she held up her hand to show off her engagement ring. Even across the room, he could see the massive gem sparkle as her hand turned and she smiled. At long last, she radiated joy like a future bride should. The man said a few things, then they parted ways and she started walking in his direction.

The second her eyes met his, she stopped in her tracks. With a seductive grin curling her ruby lips, she held out her arms to showcase the gown and did a little turn for him. Lord, he thought, curling his hands into fists at his side. It was even more incredible from the back, where it dipped low to showcase her flawless, tanned skin.

Liam closed the gap between them as fast as he could without running across the ballroom. Up close, the dress sparkled as the lights hit little crystals sprinkled across the fabric, but it didn't shine as radiantly as she did.

"What do you think? Did I spend your money wisely?"

Not caring if he ruined the look she'd so carefully crafted, he leaned down and kissed her. He couldn't help it.

When he pulled away, Francesca smiled. "I guess so."

"Incredible," he said.

"Thank you for buying it for me. Having the woman from the department store just show up with gowns was perfect. I felt like I was an Oscar nominee with designers fighting for me to wear their looks on the red carpet."

"Hollywood is all the poorer for you not being on the big screen."

"Oh, stop," she said, smacking him lightly on the arm. "There's no one around to hear us, so you don't have to lay it on so thick."

Liam shook his head. "I mean every word. It wouldn't matter if we were all alone. I'd say the same thing. Of course, I'd be saying it as I unzipped you from the gown."

Francesca smiled and slipped her arm through his. "Let me show you where we're sitting. People are still milling around the silent auction tables, but the event should be starting shortly. You'll give your speech after the video plays about the youth facilities."

The speech. He'd almost forgotten about that weight dragging him down when he saw her looking so stunning. "Hooray," he said flatly.

"Did you bring it?"

He patted his lapel. "Got it right here. And I wrote it myself, I might add. No bribery was involved."

"I'm looking forward to hearing it."

They approached a round banquet table front and center, just beside the steps that led up to the stage. He helped her into her seat and took his own just as the orchestra music increased in intensity and the lights on the stage shifted to indicate the program was about to start.

Salads were brought to every place setting as the director of Youth in Crisis welcomed everyone and introduced the short video about their program.

Liam could only pick at his salad. With every minute of the video that went by, he felt more and more nauseated by the idea of speaking to three hundred people.

When the credits started rolling, Francesca sought out his hand and squeezed it gently. "It's time," she said, looking over to him. "You'll do great."

Liam took a large sip of wine and got up from the table. He made his way to the stairs and up onto the stage, where he was bathed in blinding white lights. He reached in his pocket for his speech, adjusted the microphone and tried to keep the frantic beating of his heart from being audible to the crowd. It was now or never.

"Thank you and welcome, everyone, to the eighth annual Youth in Crisis charity gala. As some of you may know, I recently bought the ANS network, which has a longstanding commitment to this organization. It's a partnership I'm proud of, and there are many people who work hard to make it possible."

He looked down in front of the podium, where he could see Francesca's dim silhouette. Her excited expression fueled his courage to continue. His heart seemed to slow and the subtle shaking of his hands subsided. He just might make it through the speech with her sitting there, silently cheering him on.

"First, I would like to thank ANS's Executive Vice President of Community Outreach and organizer of tonight's grand event, my beautiful fiancée, Francesca Orr. For those of you that don't know Francesca, she cares so deeply about this cause. With everything that has happened with our network in the past few months, there was some uncertainty about whether or not we could sponsor this event like we have for the past seven years.

"Well," he corrected, "I should say everyone *but* Francesca had some uncertainty. Come hell or high water, this gala would go on as far as she was concerned. The woman would give back her own salary to fund this event if she had to. I hope everyone rewards her determination by writing a big, fat check. I have agreed to match the largest private donation tonight as an engagement present for my bride, so feel free to stick it to me for a good cause."

The crowd laughed and Liam felt his confidence

boost. He shuffled to the next index card, gave Francesca a wink and continued in his bid to get the attendees to part with their money.

Francesca loved her dress. She really did. But after a long night, she was just as happy to change into a breezy slip dress and zip the gown into the garment bag she'd brought with her to the hotel. She couldn't stuff all those feathers into her little BMW and drive around. With that done, she stepped into the comfortable black flats she'd stashed away with her change of clothes and sighed in relief. Not only did her feet feel better, but the gala was a roaring success and—more important—it was over.

The ballroom was nearly empty by the time Liam found her gathering up the last of her things. "That was a very painful check to write," he said. "Remind me to kick Scarlet's fiancé for donating that much the next time I see him."

She smiled, standing and turning to look at him. His bow tie was undone, his collar unbuttoned. He managed to look casually sexy yet elegantly refined at the same time. "Daniel knows that it's for a good cause, as should you. And an excellent tax deduction," she added.

"It was worth it to see the look on your face when they announced how much money we raised."

"I can't believe it, really. We blew last year's donations out of the water. Everyone was buzzing about ANS tonight—and for a good reason." Francesca slipped her bag over her shoulder and took Liam's arm.

"It's about time," he said, leading them back to the front of the hotel where the party had been held. He approached the valet and handed him his ticket.

"I parked over there," she said, pointing to an area she didn't really want to walk to.

"We'll get your car in the morning," he said. "I want you to come home with me tonight."

That was an interesting development. Liam had yet to have her over to his place. She figured that it was a personal retreat for him. They'd always gone to her town house instead. And tonight, she really wished they were sticking with that arrangement. She had no change of clothes. She had what she had worn to the hotel and her dress. The designer gown, while fabulous, would look ridiculous in the morning.

"I don't have any clothes for tomorrow," she said.

"You won't need any," he replied with a wicked grin as the valet brought the car out.

Francesca gave up the fight. She was too exhausted after a long day to argue. They loaded her things into his convertible and she sat back in her seat, going with the flow. It wasn't until they reached his place that she perked up.

Liam had described where he lived as a town house, just a little bigger than hers, but he'd lied. As they pulled up the circular brick driveway, she found herself outside what looked like a two-story home. It was detached with a courtyard out front. Two stories of red brick with an elegantly arched front doorway and dormer windows on the roof.

"I thought you said you lived in a town house."

Liam shrugged and pulled the car into the attached garage. "It's close."

He came around the car and opened the door for her, escorting her toward a few steps leading up into the house. They entered through the kitchen. The cabinets were a stark white with glass fronts, set against stainless appliances and gray granite countertops. There wasn't a single dish in the sink and not a piece of mail sitting on the counter.

Liam took her garment bag and led her through to the front entryway, where he hung it in the closet. She set her bag containing the other items she'd needed tonight on the floor beside the door and wandered into the living room.

"It's a beautiful place," she said, walking over to the staircase and running her hand along the wood railing. The space had so much potential. It was a stunning home, but as he'd said before, it was probably just as it was when he'd moved in. White walls, hardwood floors, minimal furniture. There wasn't a single piece of art on the walls or personal item on a shelf. It looked like a model home or one stripped to sell. "But it does need a woman's touch," Francesca admitted.

"I told you I needed you to help me decorate."

"I didn't realize it would be such a large task."

Liam shrugged out of his tuxedo jacket and laid it across the arm of the couch. "Not what you were picturing?"

"I guess I was anticipating this place as more of a reflection of you. You seemed to guard it so fiercely that I thought coming into your home would give me some insight into who you are as a person."

"You don't see me in this place?"

Francesca glanced around one last time. "Not really. But I see what I should've expected to see. A house owned by someone too wrapped up in his work to make it a home. That speaks volumes about you, I think."

Liam's eyes narrowed at her. "My work is more important to me than the color of the walls."

"My work is important to me. But I make time for other things, too. I want to get married and have a family someday soon. When I do, I want not only a successful man, but also one that can take a step back from his job to enjoy family life. You'll burn out without that."

As Francesca said the words aloud, she realized she may have made a grave tactical error with Liam. He might not read much into what she'd just said, but it struck a painful chord with her. When she'd said the words, when she'd mentally envisioned getting married and having a family, she'd seen Liam in her mind. She had pictured this place filled with color and life and toddlers who looked like him.

She had let her heart slip away, piece by piece. It had happened so slowly over the past few weeks that she'd barely noticed the change until it was too late. Liam didn't know it, but Francesca had given her heart to him.

The man she could never really have.

It was unexpected, really. She was passionate about everything she did, but she knew from the beginning that this was business. There was no future for her with a man like Liam.

And yet she could see more now. Their future together was as crystal clear as the illuminated swimming pool she caught sight of from his living-room window.

"There's plenty of time for all that," he insisted.

This man, this workaholic, had so many layers to him she was anxious to explore. She knew there was more to him than he showed the world. The way he cared about his employees. The way he was handling the interview with Ariella. He had an attention to detail that went beyond just doing quality work. He was just as passionate about what he did as she was.

How could she not love that about him?

Love. Francesca swallowed hard and turned away from him to look out the window at his darkened yard and glowing turquoise pool. She couldn't look him in the eye with these kinds of thoughts in her mind. He'd know. And he could never know. Because it would never work between them.

Despite the future she could envision, there was a critical piece missing between them. He didn't love her. He wouldn't even be with her right now if it wasn't for his aunt and her demands. That was a bitter dose of reality to swallow, but the sooner she reminded herself of that, the better off she'd be when this "arrangement" came to an end.

"Would you like to see the upstairs?"

Pulling herself together, Francesca turned and nodded with a smile. Liam led the way up the stairs, showing her his home office, the guest room and finally, his bedroom.

Knowing they'd reached their final destination, she slipped out of her shoes and stepped onto the plush carpeting. She ran her hand over the soft, blue fabric of his duvet as she made her way to the window. She watched the glow of the city lighting the black night above the tree line, hiding any stars from her view of the sky. On a night like this, she really needed a sign to help her. Something to tell her she was making the right choices with Liam.

She reached for the *corno portafortuna* necklace she always wore and realized she'd taken it off tonight. It was in a pouch in her purse. She suddenly felt exposed without it, as though something could get through her protective armor without it. Looking down, she saw a rabbit sitting on Liam's front lawn. Before she could move, something startled it and the bunny shot across the yard, crossing her path.

A sign of disappointment to come.

Francesca took a deep breath and accepted the inevitable. She was in love with a man she couldn't have. She didn't need a rabbit to tell her disappointment was on the horizon.

The heat of Liam's body against her back was a bittersweet sensation. Just as her mind began to fight against it, her body leaned back into him. His bare chest met her back, his fingertips sliding beneath the thin straps of her dress to slide them off her shoulders.

The flimsy sundress slid down her body, leaving her completely naked with it gone. Liam's hands roamed across her exposed skin, hesitating at her hip.

"No panties?" he asked.

She hadn't worn any undergarments tonight. The dress was almost sheer and wouldn't allow for them. Besides, she knew how the night would end. "I can't have you ripping up all my nice lingerie," she said.

"That's very practical of you. I find that sexy. Everything about you just lures me in. I don't know that I'll ever be able to get away."

Francesca closed her eyes, glad her back was still to him. She wished he wouldn't talk that way sometimes. It was nice to hear, but it hurt to know it wasn't really true. The minute his aunt let him off the hook, this whole charade would end. At least now she wouldn't have to worry about faking the heartbreak when their engagement was called off. The tears she would shed on Ariella's shoulder would be authentic.

"Look at me," Liam whispered into her ear.

She turned in his arms, wishing away the start of tears in her eyes that had come too early. They weren't done just yet. She needed to make the most of her time with him.

When her gaze met his dark blue eyes, she felt herself fall into them. She wrapped her arms around his neck and stood on her toes to get closer. His lips found hers and she gave in completely. The feel of his hands on her body, his skin against hers, was an undeniable pleasure. She had to give in to it, even if it put her heart even more at risk.

They moved together, still clinging to one another as they slow-danced across the room to the bed. Her bare back hit the silky softness of the duvet a moment later. Liam wasted no time covering her body with his own.

As his lips and hands caressed her, Francesca noted a difference in his touch. The frenzied fire of their first encounters was gone, replaced with a leisurely, slow-burning passion. He seemed to be savoring every inch of her. At first, she wondered if maybe she'd had too much champagne tonight. That perhaps she was reading more into his pensive movements.

But when he filled her, every inch of his body was in contact with hers. He moved slowly over her, burying his face in her neck. She could feel his hot breath on her skin, the tension of each muscle in his body as it flexed against hers. When he groaned her name into her ear, it sent a shiver through her whole body.

Francesca wrapped her arms around his back and pulled him closer. She liked having him so near to her like this. It was a far cry from their wild, passionate encounter in her kitchen. Nothing like the times they'd come together over the past week. Something had changed, but she didn't know what it was. It felt like...

It felt like they were making love for the first time.

The thought made Francesca's heart stop for a hundredth of a second, but she couldn't dwell on it. Liam's lips found the sensitive flesh of her neck just as the movement of his hips against hers started building a delicious heat through her whole body. She clung to him, cradling his hips between her thighs as they rocked closer and closer to the edge.

When she reached her breaking point, she didn't cry out. There was only a gasp and a desperate, panting whisper of his name as her cheek pressed against his. His release was a growl against her throat, the intense thrashing of his body held to almost stillness by their tight grip on one another.

Instead of rolling away, he stayed just as he was. His body relaxed and his head came to rest at her breast. She brushed a damp strand of hair away from his forehead and pressed a kiss to his flushed skin.

As they drifted to sleep together, one of Francesca's last thoughts was that she was totally and completely lost in this man.

Nine

"Aunt Beatrice," Liam said, trying to sound upbeat.

After the maître d' had led Francesca and him to the table where the older woman was seated, she looked up at him and frowned. "Liam, do you ever wear a tie?"

He smiled, pleased he'd finally pushed her far enough to mention it. And now he got the joy of ignoring her question. He turned to his left and smiled. "This is my fiancée, Francesca Orr. Francesca, this is my great aunt, Beatrice Crowe."

Francesca let go of his hand long enough to reach out and gently shake hands with the Queen Bee. "It's lovely to meet you," she said.

Aunt Beatrice just nodded, looking over his fiancée with her critical eye. Liam was about to interrupt the inspection when she turned to him with as close to a smile on her face as she could manage. "She's more lovely in person than she is in her pictures, Liam."

He breathed a sigh of relief and pulled out Francesca's chair for her to sit. He hadn't been looking forward to this dinner. In fact, he'd deliberately not told Francesca about it until after the gala was wrapped up. She would just worry, and there wasn't any sense in it. His aunt would think and do as she pleased.

"I can't agree more," he said.

The first few courses of the meal were filled with polite, stiff pleasantries. His aunt delicately grilled Francesca about her family and where she came from. She was subtle, but Liam knew she was on a fishing expedition.

Francesca must've realized it also. "So what brings you to D.C.?" she asked, deflecting the conversation away from herself.

Liam swallowed his answer—that she was here to check up on him and their agreement.

"I'm speaking before a congressional committee tomorrow," Aunt Beatrice said, allowing the waiter to take away her plate.

She had mentioned that before, but Liam thought it had just been an excuse she'd made up. "What for?" he asked.

His aunt's lips twisted for a minute as she seemed to consider her words. "I'm speaking to a panel on federal funding for cancer treatment research."

Liam couldn't hide his frown. He also wasn't quite sure how to respond.

"Have you lost someone to cancer?" Francesca asked. Better that she ask the question because she had no real knowledge of her family history, as Liam should.

"Not yet," Beatrice said. "But the doctors give me

about three to six months. Just enough time to get my affairs in order before I take to my bed permanently."

Liam's glass of wine was suspended midair for a few moments before he set it back down. "What?" He couldn't have heard her correctly.

"I'm dying, Liam. I have stage four brain cancer and there's nothing they can do. Some of the treatments have shrunk the tumor and bought me a little more time, but a little more is all I'm going to get."

Unable to meet her eyes, his gaze strayed to her perfectly curled gray hair and he realized, for the first time, that it was a wig. How long had this been going on? "When did this happen? Why haven't you told anyone?"

At that, his aunt laughed. "Please, Liam. The sharks have been circling me for years. Do you really think I'm going to let them know it's close to feeding time?"

That was a true enough statement. The vultures had been lurking outside her mansion his whole life. This must be why she was so insistent on Liam marrying and taking over as head of the family. She knew the shoes needed to be filled quickly. She'd given him a year knowing she'd never live to see it come to fruition.

She'd been silently dealing with this for who knew how long. Worrying about her estate planning and altering her will even as she went for treatments and reeled from the aftereffects. "How can you go through this on your own? You need someone with you."

"I have someone with me. Henry has been by my side for more than forty years. He's held my hand through every treatment. Sat by me as I cried."

Henry. He'd never understood why her butler stayed around, even at his advanced age. Now perhaps he comprehended the truth. Neither of them had ever married.

They'd grown up in a time where they could never be together due to the wide social chasm between them, yet they were in love. Secretly, quietly making their lives together without anyone ever knowing it.

And now Henry was going to lose her. It made Liam's chest ache for the silent, patient man he'd known all his life.

"I don't know what to say, Aunt Beatrice. I'm so sorry."

"Is there anything we can do?" Francesca asked. Her hand sought out his under the table and squeezed gently for reassurance. He appreciated the support. Like her mere presence at his speech, knowing she was there made him feel stronger. As if he could handle anything.

"Actually, yes. I'd like the two of you to get married this weekend while I'm in town."

Anything but that.

"What?" Liam said, his tone sharper than he would've liked after everything they'd just discussed.

"I know our original agreement gave you a year, but I've taken a turn for the worse and I'm forced to move up the deadline. I want to ensure that you go through with it so I have enough time to have all the appropriate paperwork drawn up. I also want to see you married before I'm too much of an invalid to enjoy myself at the reception."

Francesca's hand tightened on his. It was never meant to go this far. He never expected something like this. "This weekend? It's Monday night. That's impossible."

"Nothing is impossible when you have enough money to make things happen. I'm staying at the Four Seasons while I'm here. I spoke to the manager this morning and he said they could accommodate a wedding and reception there this Friday evening. They have a lovely terrace for the ceremony and the Corcoran Ballroom is available for the reception."

Liam felt a lump in his throat form that no amount of water or swallowing would budge. He turned to look at Francesca. Her gaze was focused on her plate, her expression unreadable. She looked a little paler than usual, despite her olive complexion. Obviously, she was as pleased with this development as he was.

"I see no reason for you to wait any longer than necessary," his aunt continued, filling the silence at the table. "After all, you've found a lovely woman. By all accounts you two seem to be very much in love."

Her pointed tone left no doubt. His aunt had nailed them. He thought they had put on a good show. That it would be enough to pacify her until he could find the funding to buy her out. But he'd already heard from his accountant. The amount of money he needed was nearly impossible to secure, especially with the network in such a vulnerable place. They were looking at some other alternatives, but it would take time. Certainly longer that the few days they'd been given with her new deadline. That would take a miracle.

The Queen Bee was calling their bluff and he had too much riding on this hand to fold.

The waiter arrived then, setting their dessert selections in front of them. His aunt had never been much for sweets, but he noted a glimmer of pleasure in her eye as she looked down at the confection before her. He supposed that once you know you're going to die, there was no sense holding back on the things doctors told you were bad for you. What was the point?

Aunt Beatrice lifted a spoon of creamy chocolate

mousse and cheesecake to her mouth and closed her eyes from pleasure. Liam couldn't find the desire to touch his dessert. He'd lost his appetite.

"Don't make my mistakes, Liam. Life is too short to wait when you've found the person you want to spend your life with, I assure you."

At that, Francesca pulled her hand from his. He suddenly felt very alone in the moment without her touch to steady him. "We'll have to discuss it, Aunt Beatrice. Francesca's family is from California. There's a lot more to pull together than just booking a reception hall. But we'll be in touch."

Liam pushed away from the table to stand and Francesca followed suit.

"Aren't you going to finish your dessert?" his aunt asked, watching them get up.

"We've got a lot to sort out. I'm sorry, but we have to go."

His aunt took another bite, not terribly concerned by their hasty exit. "That's fine. I'll take it back to the hotel with me. Henry will enjoy it."

Liam's car pulled up outside Francesca's town house, but neither of them got out. It had been a silent drive from the restaurant. They must've both been in some kind of shock, although Francesca was certain they had different reasons for being struck mute.

When his aunt first started this, Liam had asked Francesca to be his fake fiancée. There was never even a mention that they would actually get married. He assured her it would never go that far. It seemed safe enough, even as she could feel herself slowly falling for him. Nothing would come of it, no matter how she felt. She wanted the kind of marriage Liam couldn't offer, but they only had an engagement.

Marrying Liam was a completely different matter.

Not just because it would never work out between them. But because a part of her wanted to marry him. She loved him. She wanted to be his bride. But not like this. She wanted to marry a man who loved her. Not because he had a metaphorical shotgun pointed at him.

When Liam killed the engine, she finally found the courage to speak. "What are we going to do?"

When he turned to her, Francesca could see the pain etched into his face. He was facing the loss of everything he'd worked for, and he wasn't the only one. She might not agree with Aunt Beatrice's methods, but she understood where the woman was coming from. Desperation made people do crazy things. This was an ugly situation for everyone involved.

"She called my bluff. I'm just going to have to call hers. Tomorrow I'm going to tell her that the engagement was a setup and that we're not getting married. I don't think she'll sell her stock to Wheeler. It's not what she wants. She's a woman accustomed to getting her way, but she's not vindictive." He ran his hand through his hair. "At least I don't think she is."

Francesca frowned. She didn't like the sound of that plan. She didn't exactly get a warm maternal feeling from the Crowe family matriarch. His aunt had nothing to lose. If she was willing to go so far as to force him into marriage, she had no doubt she'd follow through with her threat. "You can't risk it, Liam."

"What choice do I have? I can't ask you to really marry me. That wasn't a part of the deal. I never intended for it to go this far."

Neither did she, but life didn't always turn out the way you planned. "When would you get the balance of the stock?"

Liam sighed. "It doesn't matter. I'm not doing it. She's taken this way too far."

"Come on, Liam. Tell me."

"I have to be married for a year. The ANS stock would be an anniversary gift, she said."

A year. In the scheme of things it wasn't that long. But she'd managed to fall in love with Liam in only a few weeks. A year from now, how bad off would she be? That said, the damage was done. Maybe a year of matrimony would cure her of her romantic affliction. It might give her time to uncover all his flaws. It was possible she wouldn't be able to stand the sight of him by May of next year.

And even if she loved him even more...what choice did they have? Their network would be destroyed. They were both too invested in the company and the employees to let that happen. Her heart would heal eventually. It was a high price to pay but for a great reward.

"We have to get married," she said.

Liam's eyes widened. "No. Absolutely not."

She couldn't help the pout of her lower lip when he spoke so forcefully. She knew what he meant, but a part of her was instantly offended by his adamancy. "Is being married to me so terrible that you'd rather risk losing the network?"

Liam leaned in and took her face in both his hands. He tenderly kissed her before he spoke. "Not at all. I would be a very lucky man to marry you. For a year or twenty. But I'm not going to do that to you."

"*To* me?"

"Yes. I know you're a true believer. You want a marriage like your parents. I've seen your face light up when you talk about them and their relationship. I know that's not what I'm offering, so I won't ask you to compromise what you want, even for a year."

She couldn't tell him that *he* was what she wanted. If he thought for a moment that their arrangement had turned into anything more than a business deal, he would never agree to the marriage. He'd chosen her because he thought she could keep all of this in perspective. Knowing the truth would cost ANS everything.

Francesca clasped Liam's hands and drew them down into her lap. "I'm a big girl, Liam. I know what I'm doing."

"I can't ask you to." His brow furrowed with stress as he visibly fought to find another answer. They both knew there wasn't one.

"You are the right person to run ANS. No one else can get the network back on top the way you can. Ron Wheeler might as well carve up the company if you're not running it because the doors will be closed in a few months' time." She looked into his weary blue eyes so he would know how sincere she was. "It's just a year. Once you get your stock, we can go our separate ways."

"But what about your friends and family? It's one thing to lie about an engagement that gets broken off. But to actually get married? Can you look your father in the eye and tell him you love me before he walks you down the aisle?"

Francesca swallowed the lump in her throat. She was very close to both her parents. They could read her like a book, and even as a teenager she couldn't lie to them without getting caught. This would be hard, but she could do it because it was true. Just as long as they didn't ask if *he* loved *her*…

"Yes, I can."

"What about your town house? You'll have to move in with me."

That would sting. Francesca loved her town house. She could hardly imagine living anywhere else. But she saw the potential in Liam's place. She could make that place her own for a while. "I'll rent out my town house."

"You don't have to do that. It's only fair I cover your expenses to keep it up even while you're not living there."

"Don't you think your aunt would find it odd if the place was left vacant?"

"This is going to sound a little harsh, but if what she says is true, she won't be around long enough to know what we're doing. She will probably write the marriage stipulation into the stock agreement, but she can't dictate what you do with your real estate holdings."

Francesca wouldn't put it past her. She didn't seem like the kind of woman who missed anything. "I suppose we can worry about the details later." She waited a moment as she tried to process everything they'd talked about. "So…is it decided then? We're getting married this weekend?"

Liam sat back in his seat. He was silent for several long, awkward minutes. Francesca could only sit there and wait to see what he said. "I guess so."

"You're going to have to work on your enthusiasm pretty quickly," she noted. "We'll have to tell our families tonight so they have enough time to make travel arrangements."

He nodded, his hands gripping the steering wheel as

though someone might rip it away from him. "I'll have Jessica call Neiman's again and get you a bridal appointment. Can you call Ariella and Scarlet tomorrow? They did a good job on the engagement party. Maybe they can pull off a miracle of a wedding in three days."

"I can. They'll think we've lost our minds."

Liam chuckled bitterly. "We have. Let's go inside," he said.

They went into her town house, and Francesca went straight into the kitchen. She needed something to take the edge off and she had a nice merlot that would do the trick. "Wine?" she asked.

"Yes, thank you."

Liam followed her into the kitchen as she poured two large goblets of wine. When she handed him his glass, he looked curiously at her hand for a moment before he accepted it. "Can I see your ring for a minute?"

Francesca frowned, looking at it before slipping it off. "Is something wrong with it?" She hadn't noticed any missing stones or scratches. She'd tried really hard to take good care of the ring so she could return it to him in good shape when it was over.

"Not exactly." Liam looked at it for a moment before getting down on one knee on the tile floor.

Francesca's eyes widened as she watched him drop down. "What are you doing?"

"I asked you to be my fake fiancée. I never asked you to marry me. I thought I should."

"Liam, that isn't neces—"

"Francesca," he interrupted, reaching out to take her hand in his own. "You are a beautiful, caring and passionate woman. I know this isn't how either of us expected things to turn out. I also know this isn't what you've dreamed about since you were a little girl. But if you will be my bride for the next year, I promise to be the best husband I know how to be. Francesca Orr, will you marry me?"

She underestimated the impact that Liam's proposal would have on her. It wasn't real. It lacked all those critical promises of love and devotion for her whole life, but she couldn't help the rush of tears that came to her eyes. It felt real. She wanted it to be real.

All the emotions that had been building up inside her bubbled out at that moment. Embarrassed, she brought her hand up to cover her mouth and shook her head dismissively. "I'm sorry," she said. "Just ignore me. It's been a rough couple of weeks and I think it's catching up with me."

"That wasn't the reaction I was hoping for," he said with a reassuring smile.

Francesca took a deep breath and fanned her eyes. "I'm sorry. Yes, I will marry you."

Liam took the ring and slipped it back onto her finger. He rose to his feet, still holding her hand in his. His thumb gently brushed over her fingers as he brought her hand up to his lips and kissed it. "Thank you."

Francesca was surprised to see the faint shimmer of tears in his eyes as he thanked her. It wasn't love, but it was emotion. There was so much riding on this marriage. She had no doubt that he meant what he said. He would be as good a husband as he could be. At least, as good as he could be without actually being in love with his wife.

Liam pulled Francesca into his arms and hugged her fiercely against him. She tucked her head under his chin and gave in to the embrace. It felt good to just be held by the man she loved. As she'd said before, this had been an emotionally exhausting couple of weeks. The next year might prove to be just as big a challenge. But somehow, having Liam hold her made her feel like it just might work out okay.

It felt like he held her forever. When he finally pulled away, they both had their emotions in check and were ready to face whatever the next week might hold for them.

"It's official then," he said with a confident smile. "Let's call your parents."

Ten

Francesca's precious retreat was a mess. Her beautiful townhome was in a state of disarray with moving boxes and bubble wrap all over the place.

Liam was maintaining the payments on her town house, so the bigger pieces of furniture she didn't need could stay, but everything else was going to his place. She'd probably need these things over the next year. This wasn't some overnight trip or long weekend she was packing for. She was getting ready to move in with the man who would be her husband in a few days' time.

Her parents had taken it well. At least they'd seemed to. Who knew how long her father had ranted after they hung up the phone. Either way, they were making arrangements to fly to Washington on Thursday afternoon. Liam's mother was thrilled. She didn't hesitate to say how excited she was to come and meet Francesca. Liam's mother and sister were coming Friday morning.

Their story was that they were so in love they didn't want to wait another minute to be husband and wife. Incredibly romantic or unbelievably stupid, depending on how you looked at it. But no parent wanted their child to elope and miss their big day, no matter what they might think about the situation.

Things were coming together, although it didn't look like it from where she was sitting.

The doorbell rang and Francesca disentangled herself from a pile of her things to answer the door. She'd asked Ariella to come over for lunch, hoping she and Scarlet could pull off the wedding hat trick of the year.

When she pulled open the door, she found her friend on the doorstep, but Ariella didn't have the bright smile Francesca was expecting. Her brow was furrowed with concern, her teeth wearing at her bottom lip. She had faint gray circles under her eyes as though she hadn't slept. And, most uncharacteristic of all, her hair was pulled back into a sloppy ponytail. That wasn't the Ariella she knew at all.

"Are you okay?"

Ariella's weary green gaze met hers as she shook her head almost imperceptibly.

Alarmed, Francesca reached for her friend's hand and pulled her inside. She sat Ariella down on one of the overstuffed living-room chairs that wasn't buried in packing tape and cardboard. "I'll make tea," she said, turning to the kitchen.

"Is it too early for wine?" Ariella called out.

Probably, but if her friend needed wine, she'd serve it with breakfast. "Not at all. Red or white?"

"Yes," she responded with a chuckle.

At least she was able to laugh. That was a step in the

right direction. Francesca quickly poured two glasses of chardonnay, which seemed more of a brunch-appropriate wine, and carried them into the living room with a package of cookies under her arm.

It took several minutes and several sips before Ariella finally opened up. She set the glass on the coffee table and reached into her purse. Pulling out an ivory envelope, she handed it over to Francesca to read the contents.

Francesca quickly scanned over the letter, not quite sure if what she was reading could possibly be true.

"It's from my birth mother, Eleanor Albert," Ariella said after a moment, confirming the unbelievable thoughts Francesca was already having.

The letter didn't give many details. It was short and sweet, basically asking if Ariella would be willing to write her back and possibly meet when she was ready. There was nothing about the circumstances of the adoption, the president or where Eleanor had been the past twenty-five years. Nothing about the letter screamed authenticity aside from a curious address in Ireland where she was to write back.

"When did you get this?"

"It came yesterday afternoon. To my home address, which is private and almost no one knows. Most of my mail goes to the office. I must've read it a million times last night. I couldn't sleep." Despite her weary expression, there was a touch of excitement in Ariella's voice. She'd waited so long to find out about her birth mother. Yet she seemed hesitant about uncovering the truth.

Francesca understood. The truth wasn't always pretty. People didn't always live up to the fantasy you built up in your mind. Right now, Ariella's mother was like

Schrödinger's cat. Until she opened that box, Eleanor would remain both the fantasy mother Ariella had always imagined and the selfish, uncaring woman she'd feared. Was it better to fantasize or to know for certain?

Francesca looked at the envelope and shook her head. After everything that had happened in the past few months, she'd grown very suspicious and protective where Ariella was concerned. It wouldn't surprise her at all if a journalist was posing as her mother to get details for a story. But she hesitated to say it out loud. She didn't want to be the one to burst the small, tentative bubble building inside her friend.

"Go ahead and say it," Ariella urged.

Francesca frowned and handed the letter back over to her. "I'm excited for you. I know that not knowing about your birth parents has been like a missing puzzle piece in your life, even before the news about the president hit. This could be a step in the right direction for you. I hope it is. Just be careful about what you say until you're certain she's really your mother. And even then, you can't be sure she won't go to the press with her story if someone offers her money."

Ariella nodded, tucking the letter back in her purse. "I thought the same thing. I'm going to respond, but I'm definitely going to proceed with caution. I don't want to be the victim of a ruthless journalist."

"I'm sure the letter is real, but it can't hurt to be careful."

Ariella reached for her wineglass and then paused to look around the living room. "What's going on here?"

"I'm packing."

Ariella's nose wrinkled as she eyed the boxes stacked around. Her mind must've been too wrapped up in the letter to notice the mess before. "You're moving in with Liam? So soon?" she added.

"Yes."

"Wow," she said with a shake of her head. "You two certainly don't move slowly. Next thing you'll be telling me you're getting married next weekend."

Francesca bit her lip, not quite sure what to say to that.

Ariella's head snapped toward Francesca, her green eyes wide. "Tell me you're not getting married in a week and a half, Francesca?"

"We're not," she assured her. "We're getting married Friday."

Ariella swallowed a large sip of wine before she could spit it out. "It's Tuesday."

"I know."

"What is the rush with you two? Does one of you have an incurable disease?"

"Liam and I are both perfectly healthy." Francesca wasn't about to mention his aunt's incurable disease. That would lead to more questions than she wanted to answer. "We've just decided there is no sense in waiting. We're in love and we want to get married as soon as possible."

With a sigh, Ariella flopped back into her chair. "Scarlet is going to have a fit. Putting together a wedding in three days will be a nightmare."

"We have a venue," Francesca offered. She loved how she didn't even need to ask her friend if she would do the wedding. It was a foregone conclusion. Francesca wouldn't dare ask someone else. "The Four Seasons. We've reserved the terrace for the ceremony and the ballroom for the reception."

Ariella nodded, but Francesca knew she was deep in planning mode. "Good. That's the hardest part with a quick turnaround. We'll have to use the hotel caterer, so I'll need to get with them soon about the menu for the reception. Did you guys have anything in mind?"

Francesca was ashamed to admit she didn't. As a child, she'd always fantasized more about her marriage than her actual wedding. And even if she had dreamed of a princess dress and ten thousand pink roses for the ceremony, none of that seemed appropriate for this. She wanted to save those ideas for her real marriage. One that would last longer than a year.

"We will be happy with whatever you two can pull together on short notice. We don't have room to be picky."

Ariella reached into her purse and pulled out her planner. She used her phone for most things, but she'd told Francesca that weddings required paper and pen so she could see all the plans laid out. "Color or flower preferences?"

"Not really. Whatever is in season and readily available. I'm not a big fan of orange, but I could live with it."

Her friend looked up from her notebook and frowned. "Live with it? Honey, your wedding isn't supposed to be something you *live with* no matter how short the notice. Tell me what you want and I'll make it happen for you."

She could tell Ariella wasn't going to let her off the hook. She would give her friend her dream wedding no matter how much Francesca resisted. She put aside her reservations and closed her eyes. Fake or no, what did she envision for her wedding day with Liam? "Soft and romantic," she said. "Maybe white or pale-pink roses. Candlelight. Lace. A touch of sparkle."

Ariella wrote frantically in her book. "Do you like

gardenias? They're in season and smell wonderful. They'd go nicely with the roses. And maybe some hydrangeas and peonies."

"Okay," she said, quickly correcting herself when Ariella looked at her with another sharp gaze. "That all sounds beautiful. Thank you."

"What does your dress look like? It helps sometimes with the cake design."

Francesca swallowed hard. "My appointment is tomorrow morning."

"You don't have a dress," she said, her tone flat.

She'd been engaged less than two weeks. Why would she have a dress already? "I don't have anything but a groom and a ballroom, Ariella. That's why I need you. I will make sure that Liam and I show up appropriately attired. The rest of the details are up to you."

"Please give me something to work with here. I know you trust me, but I want you to get what you want, too."

"I've got to buy off the rack with no alterations, so I'm not going in with a certain thing in mind because it might not be possible. I'm hoping to find a strapless white gown with lace details. Maybe a little silver or crystal shimmer. I don't know how that would help with the cake. It doesn't have to be very complicated in design. I prefer white butter cream to fondant. Maybe a couple flowers. I just want it to taste good."

"Any preference in flavor?"

"Maybe a white or chocolate chip cake with pastry cream filling, like a cannoli. My mom would love that."

"I can do that," Ariella said, a smile finally lighting her face.

"And speaking of food, I did invite you over here for lunch. Are you hungry?"

Ariella shoved her notebook into her purse and stood up. "No time to eat, darling. I've got a wedding to put together."

Francesca followed her to the door and gave Ariella a huge hug. "Thank you for all your help with this. I know I haven't made anything easy on you two."

"Do you know how many bridezillas we usually have to work with? You're easy. Anyway, that's what friends do—pull off the impossible when necessary. It's only fair considering you just talked me off the proverbial ledge over this stuff with my birth mother. And taking on a huge job like this will take my mind off everything, especially that upcoming reunion show."

The president had agreed to Liam's show proposal right before the gala. Francesca had jumped from one event to the next, getting everything in place for the televised reunion. "You don't have to do it, you know. You can change your mind."

"No, I can't." Ariella smiled and stepped through the doorway. "I'll email you our preliminary plans and menus to look over tomorrow afternoon."

Francesca nodded and watched her friend walk to her car. It all seemed so surreal. She would be married in three days. Married. To a man she'd known less than a month. To a man she'd grown to love, but who she knew didn't feel the same way about her.

A deep ache of unease settled in her stomach. She'd first felt the sensation when the shock wore off and she realized they were getting married on a Friday. That was considered to be very bad luck. Italians never married on a Friday. Unfortunately, the hotel wasn't available any other day.

Francesca hadn't seen a single good omen since that

ladybug landed on Liam's shoulder. Marrying Liam was looking more and more like a bad idea. But there was nothing she could do about it now.

Liam clutched a thick envelope of paperwork and a sack of Thai takeout as he went up the stairs to Francesca's town house. He'd met with his lawyer today to go over some details for the marriage. Now he planned to help Francesca with some packing.

"Hello," he yelled as he came through the door.

"I'm upstairs," Francesca answered.

He shut the door behind him and surveyed the neat stacks of labeled and sealed boxes in the foyer. "I have dinner."

"I'll be right there."

Francesca came down the stairs a few minutes later. Her hair was in a ponytail. She was wearing a nicely fitted tank top and capris with sneakers. It was a very casual look for her and he liked it. He especially liked the flush that her hard work brought to her cheeks and the faint glisten of sweat across her chest. It reminded him of the day they met.

God, that felt like ages ago. Could it really have been only a few weeks? Now here he was, helping her pack and clutching a draft of their prenuptial agreement in his hands.

"I see you've been hard at work today."

She nodded and self-consciously ran her hands over her hair to smooth it. "I probably look horrible."

"Impossible," he said, leaning in to give her a quick kiss. "I picked up some Thai food on the way from the lawyer's office."

"Lawyer's office?" Francesca started for the kitchen and he followed behind her.

"Yes. I got a draft of the prenup ready for you to look over."

Francesca stopped dead in her tracks, plates from the cabinet in each hand. Her skin paled beneath her olive complexion. There was a sudden and unexpected hurt in her eyes, as though he'd slapped her without warning. She set down the plates and quickly turned to the refrigerator.

"Are you okay?" Liam frowned. Certainly she knew that with the size of both their estates they needed to put in some protective measures now that they were making their relationship legally binding.

"Yes, I'm fine," she said, but she didn't look at him. Instead, she opened the refrigerator door and searched for something. "What do you want to drink?"

"I don't care," he said. Liam put the food and paperwork on the counter and walked over to her. "You're upset about this. Why?"

"I'm not," she insisted with a dismissive shake of her head, but he could tell she was lying. "It just surprised me. We hadn't talked about it. But, of course, it makes sense. This is a business arrangement, not a love match."

The sharpness in her tone when she said "love match" sent up a red flag in Liam's mind. He wished he could have seen her expression when she said it, but she was digging through the refrigerator. Then again, maybe he didn't want to see it. He might find more than he planned for.

He'd chosen Francesca for this partly because he thought she could detach emotionally from things. After she walked away from the elevator, he thought she could handle this like a champ. Maybe he was wrong. They'd spent a lot of time together recently. They'd had dinner, talked for hours, made love.... It had felt very much like a real relationship. Perhaps she was having real feelings.

Francesca thrust a soda can at him and he took it from her. She spun on her heel and started digging in the take-out bag. "So what are the high points?" she asked, popping open a carton of noodles.

She would barely look at him. She was avoiding something. Maybe the truth of the situation was in her eyes, so she was shielding him from it. If she was feeling something for him, she didn't want him to know about it. So he decided not to press her on the subject right now and opted just to answer her question. "Everything that is yours stays yours. Everything that is mine stays mine."

She nodded, dumping some chicken onto her plate. "That sounds fairly sensible. Anything else?"

"My lawyer insisted on an elevator clause for you. I couldn't tell him it wasn't necessary since we only plan to be married for a year. He said he likes to put them in all his prenups, so I figured it was better for it to be more authentic anyway."

"What is an elevator clause?"

"In our case, it entitles you to a lump sum of money on our first anniversary and an additional sum every year of our marriage after that. The money goes in trust to you in lieu of an alimony agreement. The longer we stay married, the more you're given."

Francesca turned to him, her brow furrowed. "I don't want your money, Liam. That wasn't part of our agreement."

"I know, but I want you to have it. You've gone far

beyond what we originally discussed and you deserve it. I'm totally uprooting your life."

"How much?"

"Five million for the first year. Another million every year after that. Milestone anniversaries—tenth, twentieth, etc., earn another five million."

"Five million dollars for one year of marriage? That's ridiculous. I don't want anything to do with that."

"If we pull this off, I'm inheriting my aunt's entire estate and all her ANS stock. That's somewhere in the ballpark of two billion dollars. I'd gladly give you ten million if you wanted it. Why not take it?"

"Because it makes me look like a gold digger, Liam. It's bad enough that we're getting married knowing it's just for show to make your aunt happy. If people find out I walked away after a year with five million bucks in my pocket...I just..." She picked up her plate and dumped rice onto it with an angry thump of the spoon. "It makes me feel like some kind of a call girl."

"Whoa," Liam said, putting his hands up defensively. "Now back up here. If we were getting married because we were in love, we'd probably have the same prenuptial agreement. Why would that be any different?"

Francesca shook her head. "I don't know. It just feels wrong."

Liam took the plate from her hand and set it on the counter. He wrapped his arms around Francesca's waist and tugged her against him. When she continued to avoid his gaze, he hooked her chin with his finger and forced her face to turn up to him. He wanted her to hear every word he had to say. "No one is going to think you're a gold digger. You will have earned every penny of that money over the next year. And not," he clarified, "on your back. As my wife, you're like an on-call employee twenty-four hours a day for a year."

He could tell his explanation both helped and hurt his cause. It justified the money but reduced her to staff as opposed to a wife. And that wasn't true. She was more than that to him. But if she was having confusing feelings about their relationship, would telling her make it worse?

"This isn't just some business arrangement anymore, Francesca. We're getting married. It may not be for the reasons that other people get married, but the end result is the same. You didn't have to agree to do this for me or for the network, but you chose to anyway. You're... *important* to me. So I'm choosing to share some of the benefits with you. Not just because you've earned them or because you deserve them. And you do. But because I want to give the money to you. You can donate every dime to charity, if you'd like. But I want you to have it regardless."

That got through. Francesca's expression softened and she nodded in acceptance before burying her face in his chest. Liam clutched her tightly and pressed a kiss into the dark strands of her hair.

It wasn't until that moment that he realized what a large price they were both paying to save the network and protect his dream. The reward would be huge, but the emotional toll would be high.

Five million didn't seem like nearly enough to cover it.

Eleven

Liam stood at the entrance to the terrace where the ceremony would take place. As instructed, he was wearing a black tuxedo with a white dress shirt and white silk tie and vest. A few minutes earlier, Ariella had pinned a white gardenia to his lapel. He looked every bit the proper groom, even if he didn't feel quite like one.

Beyond the doors was possibly the greatest wedding ever assembled on such short notice. Rows of white chairs lined an aisle strewn with swirls of white and pink rose petals. Clusters of flowers and light pink tulle draping connected the rows. A small platform was constructed at the front to allow everyone a better view of the ceremony. A large archway of white roses and hydrangeas served as a backdrop and were the only thing blocking the view of the city and the sunset that would be lighting the sky precisely as they said their vows.

About an hour ago, Ariella had given him a sneak

peek of the ballroom where the reception would be. It seemed as if an army of people was working in there, getting everything set up. The walls were draped in white fabric with up-lighting that changed the colors of the room from white, to pink, to gray. Tables were covered with white and delicate pink linens with embroidered overlays. Centerpieces alternated between tall, silver candelabras dripping with flowers and strings of crystals and low, tightly packed clusters of flowers and thick, white candles in hurricane vases. In the corner was a six-tiered wedding cake. Each round tier was wrapped at the base with a band of Swarovski crystals. The cake was topped with a white and pink crystal-studded *C*.

It was beautiful. Elegant. And completely wasted on their wedding, he thought with a pang of guilt.

Nervous, and without a herd of groomsmen to buy him shots in the hotel bar, he'd opted to greet guests as they came through the door. The wedding party itself was small with no attendants, but there were nearly a hundred guests. It had been a lightning-quick turnaround with electronic RSVPs, but nearly everyone invited had said yes, even if just out of morbid curiosity. So far, no one had asked any tacky questions at the door, like when the baby was due, but he was certain talk was swirling around the crowd inside.

"Ten minutes," Scarlet reminded him as she brushed by him in her headset, a clipboard clutched to her chest.

Ten minutes. Liam swallowed hard and pasted the wedding-day smile back on his face. In less than a half hour, he would be legally bonded to Francesca with all his friends and family as witnesses. A month ago, he'd been celebrating his purchase of ANS and looking forward to the excitement of fulfilling his dream of running a major network. Now he was about to marry a virtual stranger to keep the dream from crumbling into a nightmare.

"Liam," a proper female voice called to him.

He looked up to see Aunt Beatrice rolling toward him in a wheelchair pushed by Henry. He knew she was sick, but seeing her in a wheelchair was startling. Surely she could still walk? He thought back to every time he'd seen her in the past month. She had already been seated whenever he arrived. On their last few visits, she hadn't so much as stood up or walked over to get something from her bag. Now he realized it was because she couldn't. She'd done well hiding it until now.

"Aunt Beatrice," he said with a smile, leaning down to plant a kiss on her cheek. "And Henry," he added, shaking the butler's hand. He had a new appreciation for the quiet, older man who had served and loved his aunt all these years. "Seats have been reserved for you both in the first row on the right."

Aunt Beatrice nodded, and Henry rolled them into the room. There wasn't a "congratulations" or a "last chance to back out" from her. She hadn't even bothered to question him about his and Francesca's relationship any longer. He supposed that even if they were faking it, as long as it was legally binding, she was getting her way. She probably figured that within a year, they'd fall for each other for real. Or she'd be dead and wouldn't care any longer.

"Liam," Ariella said, approaching him quietly from the side. "We have a problem."

He wasn't surprised. As quickly as this had come together, things were bound to go awry. "What is it?"

"Security has spotted an uninvited guest in the lobby heading this way."

Liam frowned. "Who? A reporter?"

"Sort of. Angelica Pierce. How would you like us to handle this?"

Oh. That was certainly cause for a bit of excitement, especially where Ariella was concerned because Angelica had been suspended for her possible involvement in the hacking scandal that had revealed Ariella as the president's secret daughter. "Don't do anything. She's liable to make a scene if we have her escorted out. Better just to let her come and act like it's not a big deal."

Ariella nodded. "Agreed." She turned away and muttered into her headset. "Five minutes," she added, before disappearing toward the room serving as a bridal suite.

Liam busied himself greeting other guests and tried not to worry about Angelica. He'd only met the woman in person once, and he got the distinct impression that she was a suck-up who would do anything to keep her job. Right now, she was suspended pending the results of Hayden Black's investigation, so he wasn't surprised she'd shown up today. She was here to make an appearance and kiss up to her boss and his new bride.

He hoped that was all she was up to. He knew for a fact that Hayden and his fiancée, Lucy Royall, were already inside. Lucy was Graham Boyle's stepdaughter and there was some bad blood between her and Angelica. With any luck, they would sit far apart and not cross paths the whole evening. But he wasn't feeling very lucky today.

That's when he saw her. "Angelica," he said with a smile, accepting the hug she offered. "So good to see you." He wanted to keep this evening together, so he wasn't about to let on that she was an unwelcome party crasher.

Angelica seemed very pleased by the warm welcome. She'd certainly dressed up for the occasion, looking radiant even, if not a touch heavier than she had been a few weeks ago. Her face was rounder and her purple dress was a bit snug. The stress of Hayden's investigation must have been catching up with her.

"I wouldn't miss this for the world. I just love weddings. And my boss's wedding is an especially important event. I wish you both great happiness together."

Liam smiled and thanked her, turning to the next guests approaching. It was his rival network's former star, Max Gray and his new bride, Cara. They'd been married in March and had just come back from their extended honeymoon in Australia. The two of them were practically beaming with love for each other, and Cara's dress showed the gentle swell of her pregnancy. She had started doing public relations for D.C. Affairs since leaving the White House, but he could tell that motherhood was her true calling. She was just glowing.

As they approached the door, they both stopped to watch Angelica go inside. Max's jaw dropped, his eyes widening. His field research had helped uncover the hacking scandal back in January. "What is she doing here?" he asked.

Liam shrugged. "Trying to make friends, I suppose. Did you two have a nice trip?"

"Amazing," Cara said. "We slept in late, ate great food, did some sightseeing. It was wonderful. Where are you and Francesca going on your honeymoon?"

That was a good question. "We don't have anything planned yet. Things moved so fast and work has been so busy, we haven't had a chance. We're hoping things will slow down soon and we'll have the opportunity to get away. Sounds like a trip to Australia is a great choice. I'll have to talk to you two about it more later."

Max and Cara went to their seats and the last few arriving guests followed them. Liam straightened his tie and took a deep breath as he saw Scarlet and another man in a suit heading toward him with determination and purpose.

"Okay, showtime. This is your officiant, Reverend Templeton. He will go down the aisle first, then you. We'll seat the parents, and then the bride will come down the aisle with her father. Are you ready, Liam?"

That was another good question. He was ready as he was ever going to be for a corporate, shotgun marriage of convenience. The only thing that made him feel better was that he'd get to spend the next year with a sexy spitfire who made his blood boil with passion and excitement.

"I am."

Francesca sat still as stone at her dressing table, letting her mother pin the large, white gardenia in her hair. Looking at herself in the mirror, she was the perfect image of a beautiful bride on her big day. Her shiny, black hair was twisted up into an intricate updo, the gardenia pinned just to the side. Her makeup was airbrushed and flawless. She'd found the perfect gown in her size without much trouble. Even with such a time crunch, everything had worked out just as it should. It was as though this wedding was meant to be.

Only it wasn't.

Her persistent stomachache had kept her from eating

too much at breakfast or lunch. She had a plate of fruit and crackers beside her that she would pick at from time to time, but it just made the feeling worse.

Not even a saltine cracker could cure the ache of impending doom. This wedding was a mistake. She knew it. But the part of her that loved Liam and cared for ANS and its employees was overpowering her common sense.

She took one last look at herself in the mirror and inhaled a deep breath to pull herself together. Now was not the time to fall apart. Not while her parents' concerned eyes were watching her.

Since her father had come in, he'd been sitting in the corner, scowling in his tuxedo. Honestly, he'd had the same look on his face since she had met them at the hotel the day before. There had been a moment when he first saw her in her gown that his expression had softened and tears came to his eyes, but it hadn't lasted long.

Francesca was pretty sure her own wary appearance hadn't helped. But there was nothing she could do about it. She had to save her smiles and energy for the wedding and reception.

"Are you okay, *bella?*" her mother asked. She was a tinier version of Francesca, with the same dark eyes and warm brown skin. Her thick, brown hair was pulled back into a bun, with elegant streaks of gray running through it like professionally added highlights. She was wearing a shimmering gray dress with a jacket. Ariella had pinned a pink and white rose corsage to her lapel earlier. Her father had one very similar on his tuxedo.

Francesca nodded and stood, straightening her gown. She'd hoped for and found a white, strapless gown; there had been many to choose from because that style was in fashion. This one had a lace overlay that went to the floor and was delicately embroidered in a pattern with silver beads, crystals and pearls down to the chapel train. What she liked best about it was the silver sash around her waist with a crystal embellishment in the center. It accented her hourglass figure and gave the dress a little something special.

"Why do you ask?" Francesca asked innocently.

"You just don't look as happy as I was expecting. Where is my beautiful, blushing bride?" Her mother reached up to gently caress her face.

She stopped fidgeting with the dress and smiled, gripping her mother's hand reassuringly. "Yes, Mama, I am fine. I'm just a little nervous."

"You should be, marrying a man you hardly know," her father snarled from the corner.

"Victor!" her mother scolded over her shoulder. "We discussed this. We did the same thing, didn't we? And aren't you happy thirty years later?"

He shrugged and slumped into his chair. This was one argument he would lose, and he knew it. But he didn't have to like it. Francesca could easily see where she got her own stubborn streak and fiery temper.

"Mama, could you give me that small hand mirror so I can see the back?"

Donatella handed her the silver mirror and Francesca held it so she could make sure everything looked okay. Satisfied, she laid it on the edge of the dresser, but it tipped with the heavy weight of the handle and fell to the floor with a crash.

"Oh, no," Francesca lamented, crouching down to pick up the shattered hand mirror. There were only a few slivers of the reflective surface left, the rest scattered on the floor. Slumping into her chair, she looked at the broken glass and shook her head. "Seven years bad luck," she said. "As though I needed another sign."

"Nonsense," her mother chided. "Your *nonna* filled your head with silliness when you were a child. This means nothing aside from having to sweep up and buy a new mirror. Your marriage will be whatever you make it. And if you believe in your heart that it is doomed before it starts, you'll be right. You must fill your heart and soul with joy, not fear, as you walk down that aisle, *bella*."

Francesca hoped her mother was right. She should ignore the signs and try to make the most of her year with Liam. It was all she was going to get so she shouldn't spend the precious time she had moping about losing him.

A gentle rap sounded at the door and Ariella stuck her head in. "Mrs. Orr, it's time for you to be seated. I'll be back for the bride and her father in just a moment." She gave Francesca a quick wink of encouragement as they slipped out of the room.

Now was the moment Francesca was dreading the most. Five minutes alone with her father without her mother to be the buffer. Hopefully she could distract him with idle conversation until Ariella returned.

"How do I look, Daddy?"

The large Irishman crossed his arms over his chest and admired her for a moment before he spoke. "Like the saddest, most beautiful bride I have ever seen."

Francesca frowned at him. How could he see into her so well? "I'm smiling. Why do you think I'm sad?"

"There's something in your eyes. Something isn't quite right about all this—I can tell."

"Don't be silly, Daddy."

Victor stood up and walked over to her. He helped

Francesca up from her seat and held her hand tightly. "Look me in the eye and tell me that you love him."

Francesca fixed her gaze on her father. If she really wanted to back out of this wedding, this was her chance. All she had to do was say the word and he would have her on a plane to California before Aunt Beatrice knew what hit her. But she couldn't do that. Wouldn't.

She had to answer him honestly, or he would know. He sensed a problem, but he was barking up the wrong tree. If he wanted the truth of the matter, he should be asking Liam these questions. Without blinking, she spoke sincere words to him. "Yes, I love Liam. Very much."

"And you want to marry him?"

She did. It was fast, but she had fallen hard for her fiancé. Her trepidation was in knowing that no matter how she felt about him, their marriage would be over this time next year. How could she walk down the aisle knowing their wedding was a pointless exercise? Yes, it would save ANS and make a dying woman happy, but Francesca herself would be crushed in the process.

"Yes, Daddy. I want to marry Liam."

His gaze moved over her face, looking for a thread to pull at to unravel the truth, but there was nothing to find.

Another knock at the door came and Ariella stepped in holding Francesca's bouquet.

"It's beautiful," Francesca said as she took the flowers and admired them. There were pink and white roses, white hydrangeas and tiny white stephanotis. She'd given Ariella very little direction on this wedding, but with the bouquet, at least, she'd hit the nail on the head. Everything else would likely be just as perfect.

"Did you expect anything less?" she said with a smile. "It's time."

Francesca's father took her by the arm and led them down the hallway to the terrace. When she got the cue, Ariella opened the doors. They stepped onto the balcony to the sound of music from a string quartet. A hundred people stood up from their seats and turned to look Francesca's way as they kicked through rose petals down the aisle.

She was almost halfway down the aisle when she finally got the nerve to look at Liam.

Francesca had avoided it because she didn't want to see the truth in his eyes. He would likely look nervous. Maybe even fearful for what he'd gotten himself into. There would be no tears of love and joy. He would not be beaming with pride after seeing the woman he adored looking more beautiful than ever before. She knew she would be disappointed. But she looked anyway.

When her gaze met his, she felt her stomach do a flip. He looked so incredibly handsome. She'd seen him in a tuxedo before, but there was something different about the way he looked tonight. It was the expression on his face. There wasn't love there, but she did see admiration. Unmasked attraction. Deep respect. He knew how big a sacrifice she was making for him and he appreciated it. He just didn't love her for it. Not the way she loved him.

Francesca had to remind herself to smile and not get lost in her thoughts as they took the last few steps to the ceremony platform.

The minister began the ceremony, and her father leaned in to kiss her before handing her over to Liam for good. She couldn't meet his eyes then. If he saw the panic and fear there, he'd drag her down the aisle while everyone watched in horror. Instead, she closed her eyes and leaned in to his kiss.

"I love you, Daddy."

"I love you, too."

At that, he put her hand in Liam's and they stepped up together to be married.

Francesca thought she would be okay until she had to take that first step and her knees turned soft. It was only Liam's firm, reassuring grasp that kept her upright. He guided her to the minister, her hand clasped tightly in his.

"I won't let you fall. We can do this," he whispered with a smile and a wink.

She nodded and squeezed his hand.

The ceremony began, but it was a blur to her. The minister spoke, she repeated her vows, they exchanged rings and the next thing she knew, she was kissing her husband in front of a hundred people.

The roar of applause and the cheers were like a slap in the face, snapping her back into reality. The minister presented them as Mr. and Mrs. Liam Crowe as they turned to the audience. She clung to Liam's arm as they walked back down the aisle together as husband and wife.

When they rounded the corner to exit the terrace, Ariella was waiting for them. She escorted them back to the bridal room to wait for pictures while the guests made their way to the ballroom for cocktails.

Francesca rested her bouquet on the dressing table beside the broken mirror and slumped into her chair.

It was done. They were married.

They still had to sign the official paperwork for the license, but that would arrive any second now.

She almost couldn't believe it. She felt numb, like she was walking through a dream wedding instead of one in real life. It had been a beautiful ceremony, but it wasn't how she imagined her wedding day would be. No matter how many different ways she had pictured her big day, there was always a common element.

She looked over at Liam. He eyed the champagne glasses for a moment before crossing the room to pick them up. He handed one to her and held out his own for a toast.

"One day of marriage done. Three hundred and sixty-four to go."

With a sigh, she took a deep draw from her champagne flute and closed her eyes before the tears threatened to spill over.

One critical thing was missing from her fantasy wedding: a man who loved and adored her more than anything else on earth. And that was the one thing Scarlet and Ariella hadn't been able to provide.

Twelve

Liam was worried about Francesca. As she'd walked down the aisle toward him, she was literally the most beautiful bride he'd ever seen. The white gown was quite flattering against the warm color of her skin and it fit her curves like a glove.

For a moment, it had all become a little too real. His breath had caught in his throat. His mouth had gone bone-dry. His heart had raced a thousand miles an hour in his chest. Francesca was about to be his wife. And in that instant, he'd wanted her to be in every sense of the word.

It was a strange feeling. One he hadn't experienced before. He'd been fond of a lot of women over the years. He genuinely liked and respected Francesca. That was probably as close to "love" as he'd ever gotten. Marriage hadn't crossed his mind yet. He assumed he would get to that point in his life eventually. The Queen Bee had just accelerated his schedule.

Liam wasn't sure if it was the flowers or the music. The way she looked in that dress or the happy tears of his mother. But he was committed to the moment. He was excited to marry Francesca. Maybe this year wouldn't be so bad. Maybe…maybe there could be more than just a business arrangement between them. A real relationship.

He was snapped back to reality by the stony expression on Francesca's face. There was no happy, bridal glow. No tears of joy. No smile of excitement. She didn't look outright unhappy; she was covering it well, but Liam knew she was on the edge. The reality of lying to all their friends and family must be weighing heavily on her. He understood. That was why he'd given her the option not to go through with the marriage. But she'd insisted. She wasn't the type of woman to go back on her word. She would choke it down and do what had to be done.

Since they'd left the bridal suite, she'd become like a robot. She smiled, she went through the motions, but her dark eyes were dead. He wasn't sure what would happen when she couldn't hold in her emotions any longer. But he knew it wouldn't be pretty.

Fortunately, they were able to lose themselves in the smiles, handshakes and hugs of the receiving line. After that, the reception should be fairly short. With little notice, Scarlet and Ariella had only been able to arrange a catered hors d'oeuvres and cocktail reception. No band or dancing, no five-course sit-down dinner. Just an hour or so of mingling and cake, and then everyone would be on their way. It should be fairly simple to get through it without drama.

The last few guests came through the line and Liam and Francesca were able to leave their stations. He put his arm around her waist and leaned into her. "Are you okay?" he whispered.

Her wary eyes looked to him and she nodded. "I'm just a little overwhelmed."

"Do you want me to get you a drink?"

"Yes," she said with emphasis. "Please."

Liam left her side to get them both something from the bar. He was returning with a glass in both hands when he caught an unwelcome sight out of the corner of his eye. Hayden Black and Angelica Pierce were chatting. No, that wasn't the right word. They were having a discussion that verged on heated, if Angelica's stiff posture and tight mouth were any indication. What was she thinking, having a conversation with the investigator out to prove she was guilty? This couldn't be good.

As far as Liam knew, Angelica hadn't been called to testify before the congressional committee about the hacking scandal. He assumed it was because Hayden hadn't been able to piece together the details of her involvement. Or at least, to prove it. The suspicion of her guilt was nothing Liam could act on. He needed hard evidence to fire her, and if Angelica was involved, she had been very, very careful. She wasn't stupid. She was a ruthless, cunning reporter willing to do nearly anything to get the big story. He appreciated her ambition. But not her moral code.

Secretly, he hoped Hayden would find what he needed. Liam was nervous running ANS with Angelica still in his employ. He needed a reason to cut her loose permanently.

Their discussion was getting a little more animated. Liam searched the room for Ariella and Scarlet, but he didn't see them or the security they'd hired. He might have to intervene on this situation himself. Francesca's drink would have to wait.

As Liam got closer to them, he could hear what they were saying a little better. They were trying to speak quietly, but their passions were getting the best of them. At least, Angelica's were. Hayden was always very calm and collected.

"I find it laughable that people seem to think you were behind this whole thing," Hayden said. "As though the peroxide-bleached brain cells you have left could plan something more intricate than what kind of shoes to wear with what outfit."

A flush of anger rose to Angelica's cheeks. Her eyes narrowed at Hayden. She didn't notice Liam approaching them because she was so focused on their argument. "You think you're so smart, Hayden, but I'm not going to fall for your tricks. Is calling me a dumb blonde the best you've got? I expected better of you. All men see is what women want them to see. The hair and the makeup and the clothes blind you to the truth. But don't let appearances fool you. We may have the same hair color, but I'm not sweet and pliable like your precious Lucy. I earned my place at the company. It wasn't because my stepfather owned the network."

Liam expected Hayden to take offense at the insults Angelica was levying at his fiancée, but it didn't seem to faze him. "Yes," he agreed, "but Lucy has something you'll never have no matter how hard you work or how many people you trample."

Angelica nearly snorted with contempt. "And what's that? The love of a man like you?"

"Nope. Her daddy's undying affection. She's the beautiful little girl he always wanted. The one he raised as his own. He bought her ponies and went to her ballet recitals. He got her a convertible on her sixteenth birthday. I bet it breaks his heart that he'll be in jail and can't walk Lucy down the aisle when we get married."

Angelica stiffened beside him, but she brushed off his words with a shrug of indifference. "So what? Her stepfather spoiled her. Am I supposed to be jealous of her for that?"

"No. But you might be jealous because he didn't have to bribe people to keep *Lucy* a secret. He wasn't embarrassed of her."

"I don't know what you're insinuating," she said slowly, although the tone of her voice said otherwise. It was cold and flat, issuing a silent warning to Hayden.

It made Liam wonder what they were really talking about. He'd heard that Lucy and Angelica hadn't gotten along, but Lucy had left ANS to work with Hayden before he took over. He certainly didn't know anything about Angelica's past or her family. Why did Lucy's relationship with Graham make Angelica so angry?

Hayden really seemed to know how to push her buttons. Was he rattling her cage for amusement or was he trying to get her to make a mistake? Liam turned to his left and spied the wedding videographer, a field cameraman from ANS. Perfect. He waived the man over.

"I want you to very quietly, subtly, record their conversation. She can't know you're taping them."

The camera man worked on ANS investigations and undercover stings, so he was likely more comfortable doing this than taping greetings for the bride and groom. He eased into the crowd, coming up from behind Angelica, partially hidden by the towering wedding cake beside them.

Liam watched Hayden's gaze fall on the video camera for an instant, then back to Angelica. They both knew this was their chance to catch her at something when she didn't expect it.

"Admit it, Angelica. All this hacking business had nothing to do with presidential scandals or career-launching headlines. It was just a high-profile distraction to get what you were really after. The truth is that you were trying to ruin him. Getting your revenge, at last."

Liam held his breath, waiting to see where this conversation might go when she thought no one else was watching.

"That's a ridiculous, unfounded accusation. Graham was a lousy boss with questionable ethics, but he was hardly a blip on my radar. I've got better things to do with my time than try to ruin someone like him. In time, they always ruin themselves."

"It's interesting you would say that. But I've got a stack of pictures that say otherwise. Pictures of you modified to remove your fancy hairdo and contact lenses. It made me think of something Rowena Tate told me. She mentioned that you reminded her of a troubled, unstable girl at her private school. The girl had always gloated about her rich father, but he never showed up for parent weekends. He just mailed a check."

"I didn't go to private school," Angelica said, her jaw clenched tighter with every word he said.

"I did a little research and found old school records showing her tuition was paid for by Graham Boyle. Isn't that odd? He's always told people he didn't have any children of his own. It must've been hard growing up knowing your father didn't want anything to do with you. That you were just a mistake that could be fixed with enough money. If it were me, I'd want revenge, too."

"Shut up, Hayden."

"He didn't even recognize you when you came to work at ANS, did he? Sure, you looked different, but a father should be able to recognize his own daughter, right? Then you had to sit back and watch him fawn over Lucy, a child that wasn't even his."

"I don't have to listen to your wild stories. You're obviously grasping at straws." She shook her head, turning to walk away from their discussion.

"The sad thing is that you went to all this trouble, ruined so many lives, and in the end, you failed."

Angelica stopped dead in her tracks. She swung back to him, her eyes wide and furious. "Oh, really? What makes you think this isn't exactly the way I planned it? Those fools they arrested, Brandon and Troy, will take the fall for the wiretaps. All the evidence shows that Marnie Salloway orchestrated it. Graham Boyle is going to rot in prison and his precious network will be destroyed before too long. It sounds pretty perfect to me. My only regret is that in the end, I couldn't find a way to get Lucy's hands dirty enough to send her to jail with dear old dad."

"But he didn't go to jail because he loved you and wanted to protect you. It was pure guilt."

"I don't need his love," she snapped. "I've gotten this far in life without it. What I did need was to see that bastard brought to his knees. And I got that."

Hayden smiled wide and turned toward the cameraman. "You get that, Tom?"

The videographer pulled away from his lens and nodded. "Every single word."

Angelica's jaw dropped open, her skin flushing crimson in anger. "You bastard!" she shrieked. "You deliberately set me up. If you think I'm going to let you ruin my career with no physical proof of my involvement with the hacking, you've got another think coming. Even with that tape, no one will believe you."

Hayden just shook his head. "I didn't have to ruin your career. Like you said, in time, people always ruin themselves. I just happened to get that moment on film. I'm pretty sure ANS will terminate you when I show them that tape. And the FBI and congressional committee will find it very interesting. Soon, people will start rolling on you to cut a better deal for themselves. There's no loyalty among criminals. You'll be wearing matching orange jumpsuits with your daddy in no time."

Graham Boyle was Angelica's father? Liam frowned in confusion but was jerked away from his thoughts when Angelica reared back and slapped Hayden. He barely reacted to the assault, simply shaking his head and looking at her with pity in his eyes. "It's a shame you wasted your whole life on this. I feel sorry for you."

By now, a large crowd of the wedding guests had gathered around the argument. More witnesses. The more people that gathered, the higher Angelica's blood pressure seemed to climb. "I don't want your pity," she spat.

Liam watched her fingertips curl and uncurl as she tried to keep control, but she was unraveling quickly. At last, she reached out, and before anyone could stop her, she grabbed a large fistful of wedding cake. Less than a second later, she flung it at Hayden, silencing him with a wet slap.

"What are you looking at?" she screamed at the crowd. She grabbed more cake in each hand and started launching it at the crowd. Buttercream icing flew through the air, pelting the wedding guests. They screamed and scattered. Liam checked to ensure Francesca, Aunt Beatrice and his mother were out of the line of fire, but Henry wasn't so lucky. He took a large piece of cake to the front of his suit. But he only laughed, scraping it off his shirt and taking it in stride. After forty years with Beatrice, flying cake was probably nothing.

Before Liam could turn to get help, two burly security officers rushed past him. Angelica's eyes went wild when she saw them. She started kicking and screaming when they tried to restrain her.

"Don't you touch me!" she howled. "Let me go!"

Liam could only watch in amazement as she wrenched herself from the men's grasp, only to stumble backward into the cake table. It turned over, taking Angelica and the cake with it. Angelica landed smackdab in the middle of the towering confection, coating her from hair to rear in buttercream. She roared in anger, flailing as she tried to get up and couldn't. When she did stand again, it was only with the help of the guards gripping her upper arms.

On her feet, she was a dripping mess. Her perfectly curled blond hair was flat and greasy with white clumps of frosting. Icing was smeared across her face and all over her purple dress. She huffed and struggled in her captors' arms, but there was no use. They had her this time. At last, Angelica had gotten herself into a situation she couldn't weasel out of.

"You know," Hayden said, "looking like that, I'm surprised people didn't see the resemblance before."

Angelica immediately stilled and her face went as pale as the frosting. "I don't look anything like *her*."

"Oh, come on, *Madeline*. There's no sense lying anymore about who you really are."

The calm in her immediately vanished. "Never call me that name. Do you hear me? Never! Madeline Burch is dead. *Dead*. I am Angelica Pierce, you understand? Angelica Pierce!" she repeated, as though that might make it true.

Several people gasped in the crowd. Cara stood stock-still a few feet away with Max protectively at her side. "Rowena and I went to Woodlawn Academy with Madeline," she said before turning to Angelica. "We were right. It *is* you."

"You shut up," Angelica spat. "You don't know anything about me."

"You're right. I don't," Cara answered.

The guards then escorted a wildly thrashing Angelica—or *Madeline*—out of the ballroom. By now, the local police were likely on their way to take her into custody. First, for disorderly conduct and assault. Then, maybe, for her involvement in the hacking scandal. Either way, a scene like that was enough cause for Liam to terminate her from ANS for good.

"I'm sorry about the mess," Hayden said, wiping some cake from his face. "I never expected her to come talk to me. She was so confident that she had me beaten. I couldn't pass up the chance to put a crack in her facade, but I didn't realize she'd go nuclear. It ruined your reception. Just look at the cake."

Liam shrugged. Somehow knowing it wasn't his real

wedding made it easier to stomach. "Nailing Angelica is important. You have to take every opportunity you can get."

He walked with Hayden out of the ballroom to where a few police officers were waiting outside. They answered their questions and gave out their contact information. Hayden opted to go with them to the station, but Liam knew he needed to get back inside and salvage what was left of his wedding reception.

When Liam returned, people seemed to be milling around, at a loss for what to do with themselves. "Sorry about that, folks," he said, raising his hands to get everyone's attention. "Please stick around and enjoy the reception. I'm sad to say there won't be any cake, though." A few people chuckled and most awkwardly returned to nibbling and drinking as they had before the fight broke out.

Liam noticed the drinks he'd fetched from the bar still untouched on the table. He'd gotten wrapped up in the scene and had forgotten to take Francesca her champagne. He picked them back up and turned, looking for her. After all that, they'd need another round pretty quickly.

But she was nowhere to be found.

Frowning, he searched the ballroom, finally turning to a frazzled Ariella for help. "Have you seen the bride?" he asked.

"Not since I put her in a cab."

"A cab?" Liam frowned. "You mean she's left her own reception? Without me?"

Ariella bit her lip and nodded. "About ten minutes ago. Right about the time Angelica started bathing in wedding cake. She needed to get out of here."

Liam glanced around the mess of a ballroom. Scarlet was frantically informing staff of their cleanup duties. The guests were still standing around, but despite his assurances, they seemed unsure of whether they should stay. It was a wedding disaster.

He didn't blame Francesca one bit for leaving.

Francesca couldn't get out of her wedding dress fast enough. The corset-tight bodice made her feel like she couldn't breathe. It was all just too much.

Initially, she'd been relieved when Hayden and Angelica started making a scene. For the first time that day, every eye in the room wasn't on her. It was a blessed break. It was the first moment since she started down the aisle that she thought she might be able to let the facade of bridal bliss drop and regather herself.

And then the cake started flying.

Her *nonna* had never specifically mentioned that having her wedding cake flung across the room was bad luck, but Francesca was ready to make her own deduction about that. Their reception was a disaster. Their sham of a marriage would no doubt be a mess, too. It was just one more thing, one more blazing neon sign trying to point her in the right direction. She'd ignored all the other portents of bad luck. The fates had ensured this last one would be undeniable.

When she'd asked Ariella to get her a cab, her friend probably thought she was upset about having her reception ruined. The truth was that she just couldn't pretend anymore. If she'd had to be in that ballroom one more minute, she would have blown everything for Liam and ANS.

Now that she was back at Liam's place, in a pair of

jeans and a light sweater, she felt better and worse all at once. Boxes of her things still sat around the ground floor of his town house ready to be incorporated into her new life with him. But they might as well go back onto the moving truck.

She poured herself a glass of wine to calm her nerves and went upstairs to the master bedroom to repack. The only things of hers that had been put away were her clothes and personal effects for the bed and bath. Those could easily be rounded back up, and she intended to do it right now.

If she hurried, she would be sleeping in her own bed tonight. Not quite the wedding night everyone was expecting her to have.

She had one suitcase filled and zipped closed when she heard the front door open.

"Francesca?" Liam called.

"I'm upstairs," she answered and pulled another bag onto the bed. She was stuffing it with lingerie and pajamas when he came through the doorway of his bedroom.

Francesca tried not to think about how handsome he looked in his rumpled tuxedo. His tie was undone, his collar unbuttoned. She liked him tousled. Despite everything, she felt her body react to his presence. Her pulse started racing, and her skin tightened in anticipation of his touch. But thinking about how much she wanted Liam wouldn't help. It would make her want to stay. And she needed to go.

"What are you doing?" he asked. His voice wasn't raised. It was quiet and tired. They'd both had a long day and didn't need any more drama. But this had to happen tonight.

"I'm packing my things and moving back into my

place." Francesca shoved another few items into her bag and looked up. "Don't worry, I'll lie low until Aunt Beatrice leaves town on Monday, but then I'm calling the moving company to come get my stuff."

Liam took a few steps toward her. She could feel the magnetic pull of him grow stronger as he came closer. She wanted to bury her face in his lapel and forget about everything that was going wrong. But she couldn't.

"Why?"

Francesca put the last of her clothes into the bag and zipped it closed. She looked at the bag as she spoke to ensure she could get all the words out. "I'm sorry, Liam. I thought I could do this. But I just can't."

There was a pause before he answered, his voice a touch strained. "Do you want an annulment?"

She looked up at him and shook her head. "No. I'll remain legally married to you for the sake of the network. Hopefully that will be enough because I can't play house with you. It's too hard on…" Her voice started to falter as tears rushed to her eyes. She immediately turned from him before she gave away how she really felt. "It's too hard on my heart, Liam."

He took another step forward, but stopped short of reaching out to her. "What do you mean?"

Francesca took a deep breath. "I want more."

"More than the five million?"

At that, Francesca jerked her head up to meet his gaze. "You just don't get it, do you? I don't want your money. I never did. I have plenty of my own. I want the things that you can't give me. I want love. A real family. A marriage like my parents have. I want a man who cares for me more than anyone or anything."

She shook her head and hoisted the strap of the bag

over her shoulder. "This isn't your fault. You were right when you said I was a true believer. I am. But I've been lying to myself. First, I told myself that I could be with you and it would be fine. That I could spend the next year pretending. But I can't because I was stupid enough to fall for you. Then I kept hoping that maybe, just maybe, you would fall for me and this could become more than just a business arrangement. Silly, right?"

Liam reached out to her, but Francesca sidestepped him. "Don't," she said. "Just don't. I know you don't have feelings for me. Anything you say right now will make it worse."

She extended the handle of her suitcase and rolled it to the bedroom door.

"Francesca, wait."

She stopped and turned to him. This was the moment everything hinged on. If she was wrong and he did care for her, this was the time for him to say it. She looked into his dark blue eyes, hoping to see there the love she wanted so desperately. Etched into his pained expression was desperation and confusion. He didn't want her to go, but he didn't know how to ask her to stay.

"Liam, would you have ever considered marrying me if your aunt hadn't forced us into this situation? I mean, would you even have asked me on a date after what happened between us in the elevator? Honestly."

Liam frowned and shoved his hands into his pockets. "No, I probably wouldn't have."

At least they were both telling the truth now. Nodding, she turned away and hauled her luggage down the stairs. It was time for her to go home and pick up the pieces of her life.

Thirteen

Liam signed Angelica's termination paperwork and pushed the pages across his desk. He thought he would be happy to see this issue put to bed, but he wasn't. He was the most miserable newlywed in history.

For one thing, he hadn't seen the bride since their wedding night. It had been a long, lonely weekend without her there. He'd quickly grown accustomed to having her around. Now his town house felt cold and empty.

The office wasn't much better. Francesca didn't greet him first thing with coffee and a kiss. He wasn't even sure if she was at work today. He wanted to call her. Email her. But he knew he shouldn't. It would make it easier on her if he took a step back and let her have the space she needed. She deserved that much.

But he missed his wife.

How quickly she had become that in his mind. She was no longer his employee. She was his wife. There was no differentiation in his mind about the terms of their marriage. Their engagement may have been a ruse, but the wedding and the marriage felt real to him. Frighteningly real.

Liam had never given much thought to a wife and family, but the minute Francesca walked out the door, a hole formed in his chest. It was as though she'd ripped out his heart and taken it with her. All he was left with was the dull ache of longing for her.

That didn't feel fake to him.

Yes, he'd been pushed into the marriage to please his aunt. He had to admit that much to Francesca because it was true. But now that he was married to her, it felt right. It felt natural. He no longer cared about Aunt Beatrice's opinion on the matter. He…was in love with Francesca.

"I love my wife," he said out loud to his empty office. There was no one to hear him, but saying it had lifted a huge weight from his shoulders. Unfortunately, admitting the truth was just the first step.

How could he prove to Francesca that he really did love her? That this wasn't about the network or stock deals? There was no way for her to know for sure that he wasn't just playing nice for appearances.

The only way to convince her, the only sure path, would be to take the stock deal and the network woes off the table. If his aunt had no negotiating power over him, then he stayed married to Francesca because he wanted to, not just because he had to.

But to do that without risking the company would mean that he needed enough stock to control ANS without his aunt's shares. That seemed virtually impossible. Unless…

Liam grabbed his phone and leaped out from behind

his desk. He had to find Victor Orr before they returned to California. Francesca had mentioned they were staying on a few days to tour the Smithsonian, so if he had any luck, they were still in D.C.

It took two phone calls and a drive to their hotel in bumper-to-bumper traffic, but Liam was finally able to track down Francesca's parents. He was standing at the door, waiting for them to answer the buzzer, when he realized he didn't know exactly what he was going to say to them. He would have to admit the truth. And that would mean that a very large, angry Irishman might be beating him senseless within minutes for hurting his daughter.

Victor answered the door with a frown. Without speaking a word, he seemed to realize something was wrong. Why else would his new son-in-law show up alone just days after the wedding? He led Liam into their suite and gestured for him to sit down in one of the chairs in the living room.

He watched Liam through narrowed eyes for a few minutes before Liam gathered the nerve to speak.

"There are some things I need to tell you," Liam said.

"I'm sure there are." Victor leaned back in his chair, ready to listen.

Without knowing the best way to tell the story, Liam chose to start at the beginning. He began with the stock arrangement with his aunt, delicately skipping over the elevator debacle, and followed with Beatrice's later demand that he marry to keep control of the network.

"And my daughter agreed to go along with this phony engagement?"

"Yes, sir. She seemed hesitant at first, but apparently she saw a sign that she should do it. A ladybug."

Victor shook his head. "Her and those damned signs. She gets into more trouble that way. Married to a man she hardly knows because of a ladybug!"

"We never intended to go through with the marriage, but my aunt was adamant we do it now. She's ill and wanted to make sure we followed through. I told Francesca she didn't have to do it, but she insisted."

"She's stubborn like I am."

Liam chose not to touch that statement. "What neither of us realized was that we might actually fall for one another. On our wedding night, Francesca told me she had feelings for me that she knew weren't mutual and she couldn't go on that way."

"You just let her walk out like that?"

Liam frowned and looked down at his hands. "I didn't know what to tell her. I wasn't sure how I felt about everything. What was real between us and what was a fantasy? I didn't know."

"And now?"

"Now I know. I love your daughter, and I want to ask your permission to marry her."

"Son, you're already married."

"I know, but things are different now. I want to be married to her for real. I want to go to her and tell her how I feel, but I need your help. Francesca will never believe our marriage is anything more than a business deal as long as my aunt is holding the stock over my head. I can't afford to buy her out. But if I could get enough minority stockholder support, I might be able to get majority control without her shares."

Victor nodded. "I don't think I have enough, but I've got a good bit. So does my friend Jimmy Lang. Together, that might tip the scales. Let me make a call."

As Victor got up and headed into the bedroom, a simmer of hope started bubbling in Liam's gut. He really hoped that he could pull this off. He didn't want to go to Francesca and tell her he loved her if there were any suspicions about his motives. This was the only way.

"Good news," Victor said as he returned a few minutes later. "I spoke with Jimmy and did the math. Combined with yours, we have fifty-two percent of the company stock. Close, but we made it. Jimmy and I are both really excited about the direction you're taking the network, so we have no qualms about delegating our voting authority to you. So," he said, extending his hand to Liam, "congratulations. You're still running this network."

Liam leaped from his seat and excitedly shook his father-in-law's hand. "Thank you so much, sir."

Victor shrugged. "I didn't do it for you. I did it for my little girl. You have my consent to marry her, so get out of here and make it right between you two."

Liam's eyes widened as he nodded. There was no arguing with Victor Orr, even if he wanted to. "Thank you again," he said as he turned and bolted from their hotel suite.

As badly as he wanted to rush to find Francesca, he had one other stop to make. Fortunately, that stop was located in the same hotel.

Liam rang the doorbell at the penthouse suite and waited for Henry to answer the door. The older man arrived a few minutes later, welcoming Liam with the same smile and nod he'd always received.

"Come in, Liam. I don't believe she's expecting you this morning. We're packing to return to New York."

"I'm sorry to pop in unannounced, Henry, but I need to talk to my aunt. It's important."

Henry held out his hand to gesture toward the bedroom. Liam didn't wait for him, moving quickly across the carpet and around the corner.

Aunt Beatrice looked up as he charged in. She was sitting in her wheelchair folding her clothes. "Liam," she said. "I expected you to be off somewhere basking in wedded bliss."

"No, you didn't," he said, sitting on the edge of the bed beside her. "You and I have been playing a dangerous game that could end up doing nothing but hurting people."

She didn't bother acting offended by his insinuation. "I did what I thought was best for the family. And for you, despite what you might think."

"I know," Liam agreed. "And I came here to thank you."

That, at last, got a rise out of the Queen Bee. She sat up straight in her chair, her eyes narrowing at him in confusion. "Thank me?"

"Yes. If you hadn't forced me to get married, I might've let Francesca walk right out of my life. I love her. And I hope she stays married to me for forty years—not for the network, or because of your demands, but because I want us to grow old together. That said, I'm not going to let you control me any longer. I don't need your ANS stock or you holding it over my head. I now have enough backing to maintain control of ANS without your shares or your billions. I don't care about any inheritance."

Aunt Beatrice sat silently for a few minutes, absorbing his words. After a while, he began to wonder if she was mentally going over the new changes to her will. He didn't care. Cut him out. Cut him *loose.*

"Those," she said at last, "are the words of a man who can take charge of this family." Beatrice smiled softly to herself and placed a blouse in her suitcase. "It's what I've been waiting for. I never intended to sell my stock to Ron Wheeler. I just wanted to see you settled down, in control and happy with your place in life. Francesca is the right woman for you. I knew that just as certainly as I knew you two were pretending. In time, I figured things would work out between you. Once you both stopped fighting it. It's a shame I'll be dead before I can see you two genuinely happy together."

"You knew we were faking the relationship?"

"It takes a smart, observant person to head this family. Very little gets past me, even now. But it's okay. I'm sorry for meddling in your private life. Blackmail really isn't my forte, but I did what I thought I needed to for the good of you and the family. I'll call my stockbroker this afternoon and have the shares of ANS transferred to you."

"What? Now?" He had years and millions to pay off before he owned those shares outright.

"It's your wedding present. Most people don't give networks as gifts, but you're not the typical bride and groom."

Liam reached out and took his aunt's hand. It was something he rarely did; she wasn't very affectionate, but he was seeing the dents in her armor. Her illness was revealing the person inside that she kept hidden. "Thank you, Aunt Beatrice."

She turned her head, dismissing his sentiment with a wave of her hand, but he could see a moist shimmer in her eyes. "It will be thanks enough when you save that company and take over handling our motley crew of relatives when I'm gone."

"Do I really have to be executor of the estate?"

"Absolutely. And don't worry. Eventually, you will grow accustomed to the constant ass-kissing."

Francesca left ANS early. She'd been a self-imposed prisoner in her office all morning, afraid she'd run into Liam in the hallway. She had had a few days to sit at home alone, licking her wounds, but she wasn't ready to see him again. Especially knowing that everyone still expected them to be a happy, newly married couple.

After overhearing Jessica tell someone on the phone that Liam was out of the office, she figured this was her opportunity to escape.

She made it back to her town house without incident. Relieved, she dropped her purse on the coffee table, kicked off her shoes and went into the kitchen for a drink.

When Francesca rounded the corner and found Liam sitting at her kitchen table, she nearly leaped out of her skin. *"Oh, dio mio!"* She jumped, pressing her back against the counter and clutching her rapidly beating heart. "What the hell are you doing here, Liam? You scared me to death."

He looked a little sheepish as he stood up and came over to her. "I'm sorry. I didn't mean to scare you. I thought you'd notice my car out front. You gave me a key, so I figured I would wait around until you got home. When I called Jessica she told me you'd left."

"I gave you that key when we were going to be a happily married couple. Using it after everything that happened is a little creepy. Why are you here, anyway? We don't have anything to talk about."

Liam shook his head and came closer. She was able to catch of whiff of his cologne and her body immediately began responding to him. Apparently, it hadn't gotten the message about the breakup of their nonrelationship.

"We have a lot to talk about. Starting with how much I love you and how miserable I've been since you left."

Francesca started to argue with him and then stopped. *Did he just...* She couldn't have heard him right. "What did you say?"

Liam smiled, sending her heart fluttering at the sight. He was wearing a navy collared shirt that brought out the dark blue of his eyes as he closed in on her. She noticed a few weary lines around them. He looked a little tired and tense, but she had attributed that to the stress of running the network and the fiasco of their wedding.

Could it be that he was losing sleep over her?

He stopped just short of touching her, forcing her to look up at him. His hands closed over her upper arms, their warmth sinking deep into her bones. "I love you, Francesca. I'm in love with you."

As much as she wanted to melt into him, she couldn't let herself fall prey to him. She ignored the excited flutter of butterflies in her stomach and pulled back out of his grasp, watching him with wary eyes. "You didn't love me Friday night. You could've told me then and you didn't. You let me leave. And now you show up singing a different tune. What happened? Did your aunt find out? Trying a different tactic to keep the network?"

Liam swallowed hard, a flash of resignation in his eyes. "I thought you would say something like that.

Which is why it took me so long to come see you today. I had some important business to take care of."

Francesca crossed her arms defensively over her chest, but she didn't think it would do much good. Her armor where Liam was concerned had been permanently breached. "It's always business first with you."

"You're right. First, I had to go confess to your father."

Francesca's eyes grew wide with unexpected panic. "You told my father? Why? He's going to kill me. How could you do that without asking me?"

"Because I needed his help. And his blessing to marry you."

"It's a little late for that."

"It's never too late where an overprotective father is concerned. Not only did he give his permission, but he and his associate have pledged their stock to support me at ANS, giving me a majority share without my aunt."

Francesca tried to process what he was saying, but she kept getting hung up on what kind of conversation he'd had with her father when she wasn't there. "You don't need your aunt's stock anymore?"

"No."

That meant they didn't have to be married. "But you don't want an annulment?"

"Absolutely not." Liam crowded back into her space, closing the gap she'd put between them. "I have no intention of letting you out of my sight, or my bed, for the next forty years."

The butterflies in her gut went berserk. She brought her hand to her belly to calm them. "Wait. You love me. You want to stay married to me. And it has nothing to do with the network?"

Liam nodded. "Not a thing. I told my aunt this morning that I wasn't going to play along anymore. I didn't want you to think for a moment that I wasn't one hundred percent sincere in my love for you. This isn't about my aunt or the network or appearances. It's about you and me and the rest of our lives."

His arms snaked around her waist and this time, she didn't pull away. She molded herself against him and let out a small sigh of contentment at the feel of being in his arms again.

"I am in love with you, Francesca Crowe. I want to stay married to you until the day I die."

Her heart skipped a beat at the use of her married name. She hadn't heard anyone use it since the wedding. "I love you, too."

Liam dipped his head down to capture her lips with his own. This kiss—their first as two people in love—blew away all the others they'd shared before. Every nerve in her body lit up at his touch. She wrapped her arms around his neck to try and get closer to him, but it could never be close enough. She lost herself in the embrace, letting his strong arms keep her upright when her knees threatened to give way beneath her.

Pulling away after what felt like an eternity, he said breathlessly, "I want us to get married."

Francesca wrinkled her nose and put her palm gently against the stubble of his jaw. "*Mio caro,* we're already married."

"I know," he said with a devious smile. "But I want a do-over. With a tropical honeymoon. And this time, it will just be the two of us. No family, no pressure and especially no cake throwing."

Epilogue

Francesca had no idea a vacation could be so perfect. With Ariella's televised reunion show coming up, they didn't have the luxury of taking a long honeymoon, but they did manage to sneak away for a long weekend in the Caribbean.

So far, they had sunbathed, swum in the ocean, dined on the best seafood she'd ever tasted and renewed their vows in a private white gazebo hovering over the water.

Their previous ceremony had been legally binding but tainted by his aunt's machinations and Angelica's tantrum. Their vow renewal had been just for them. A chance to say the words again and wholeheartedly mean it. Afterward, they drank champagne in their private bungalow and shared a tiny cake for two that no one could ruin.

Today they had planned a snorkeling trip in the morning, followed by marathon lovemaking and lots of luxurious naps. The snorkeling trip had been excellent. The water was crystal clear and a rainbow of fish was in abundance. They were on their way back to the bungalow when Francesca stopped and tugged at Liam's arm.

"Liam, stop. Look," Francesca said, pointing out the television mounted above the cantina bar.

It was the live coverage of Madeline Burch's arraignment. Before they left, the video of her confession had played repeatedly at every news outlet, with ANS breaking the story. The media had jumped on the tale about her involvement in the hacking scandal after both Brandon Ames and Troy Hall agreed to testify against her. The news of her double life was just the icing on the ratings cake.

For a moment, Francesca almost felt badly for Madeline. She looked awful. Orange was not her color. Going without her expensive hair coloring and extensions, she had mousy brown roots at the crown of her stringy, thin hair. Her last dose of Botox had faded away, as had her spray tan. Her colored contacts had been replaced with thick, prison-issued glasses. Several more pounds also had been added to her frame since their reception. There was no doubt that Angelica was Madeline Burch now.

"The news is out," Liam said as the news banner at the bottom changed. They couldn't hear what was being said on the television, but the words scrolling at the bottom announced the breaking news that investigator Hayden Black had testified that Madeline was Graham Boyle's secret, illegitimate daughter. Liam had told Francesca what he'd overheard during the argument at the reception, but her motivation for taking down Graham had been withheld from the press so far.

"Wow," Francesca said, shaking her head. "It's just so sad. And senseless. How many lives were ruined just so she could get back at Graham for the way he treated her?"

When she turned, Liam was pulling his phone out of his pocket. He had done well to unplug from the news world while they were on their honeymoon, but now that the news was out, all his journalistic buttons were being pushed.

He unlocked his screen and started typing something, and then he stopped. He pressed the power button and slipped the phone back into his pocket.

Francesca arched an eyebrow at him in surprise. "Really?" she asked.

"I am sure the network and my employees have this story well in hand. And even if they didn't, I am on my honeymoon. I couldn't care less about Graham Boyle's secret daughter."

He turned to face Francesca, snaked his arms around her waist and pulled her tightly against him. She melted into him, surprised to feel the firm heat of his desire pressed into her belly.

"Right now," he said with a wicked grin, "I'm more interested in making love to my wife."

* * * * *

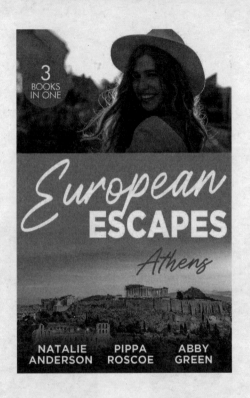

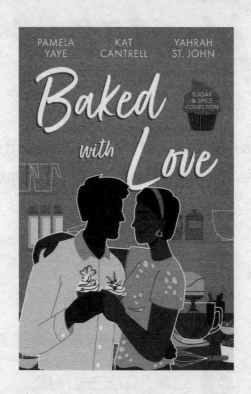

LET'S TALK
Romance

For exclusive extracts, competitions
and special offers, find us online:

- **f** MillsandBoon
- **X** @MillsandBoon
- **⊙** @MillsandBoonUK
- **♪** @MillsandBoonUK

Get in touch on 01413 063 232

For all the latest titles coming soon, visit
millsandboon.co.uk/nextmonth

MILLS & BOON

THE HEART OF ROMANCE

A ROMANCE FOR EVERY READER

MODERN

Prepare to be swept off your feet by sophisticated, sexy and seductive heroes, in some of the world's most glamourous and romantic locations, where power and passion collide.

HISTORICAL

Escape with historical heroes from time gone by. Whether your passion is for wicked Regency Rakes, muscled Vikings or rugged Highlanders, awaken the romance of the past.

MEDICAL

Set your pulse racing with dedicated, delectable doctors in the high-pressure world of medicine, where emotions run high and passion, comfort and love are the best medicine.

True Love

Celebrate true love with tender stories of heartfelt romance, from the rush of falling in love to the joy a new baby can bring, and a focus on the emotional heart of a relationship.

HEROES

The excitement of a gripping thriller, with intense romance at its heart. Resourceful, true-to-life women and strong, fearless men face danger and desire - a killer combination!

 **afterglow BOOKS**

From showing up to glowing up, these characters are on the path to leading their best lives and finding romance along the way – with plenty of sizzling spice!

To see which titles are coming soon, please visit

millsandboon.co.uk/nextmonth

MILLS & BOON
True Love
Romance from the Heart

Celebrate true love with tender stories of heartfelt romance, from the rush of falling in love to the joy a new baby can bring, and a focus on the emotional heart of a relationship.

Four True Love stories published every month, find them all at:

millsandboon.co.uk/TrueLove